RAKSHASA

RAKSHASA

Max Overton

RAKSHASA

DOUBLE DRAGON

ISBN 978-1-78695-589-0

Double Dragon
is an imprint of
Fiction4All

Published 2021
Fiction4All
www.fiction4all.com

Cover Art by Julie Napier

Prologue

I am Rakshasa.

Men will tell you I am a child of Nirriti and Nirrita, or born from the sage Pulastya or that I am a descendant of Kasyapa and Khasa, a daughter of Daksha, through their son Rakshas. More fantastically, it is said that when Brahma created the waters he made us from his foot, to guard them. Others say we are the descendants of the old stone-wielding races that lived in this land before the coming of the ones called Aryans. Men are liars however, telling tales around the hearth fires at night as they seek to control the unknown by talking about it. Men fear what they do not know. They do not know me and rightly, they fear me.

I cannot remember that I ever had a mother and a father, nor brother and sister, just being, coming from nonexistence to existence between one breath and the next, between one heartbeat and the one following. Not that I have either, but I seek to put my existence in terms that mortal beings can comprehend. I have no physical body, save when I desire one, and then it can take the form of whatever my mind desires. I have been man and woman, beast and fowl, serpent and fish. I have even been a tree when occasion warranted but I do not like to take on the form of a plant for their minds are slow and uninteresting, being concerned solely with water and soil, wind and sun.

Where did I come from if I had no mother to bear me, no father to quicken his seed in his woman's belly? In truth, I do not know. My first memory is of a low and dusty plain, the grass cut up and furrowed, the red soil stained darker by fluids that leaked from ragged lumps of meat strewn about this dark and silent place. Men lay in heaps and mounds, glassy eyes staring sightlessly, limbs hacked and loose, bodies rent with gaping wounds that disgorged glistening coils and liquids. Over everything swarmed the eaters of the dead, from jackals and vultures to dark clouds of flies and the pulsating white mass of their grubs. Instruments of this destruction lay scattered too, thin feathered wands and thicker staves tipped with stone, curved pieces of metal, all stained with the fluids that leaked from the bodies. Beasts larger than men were lying here also, four-legged with limbs that ended in a single horned toe. They were attached to strange things of wood and beaten metal, with two round things like large river stones on edge. I did not understand these things then, seeing them for the first time, but now I know them for the aftermath of a thing called 'battle' when men's minds become red and violent, acid and sweet, delicious to one such as myself.

I think I was born of battle, engendered by the rich and violent thoughts of men on the brink of death, when terror and ecstasy vie for control, when the heart beats faster, the breath of life gushes and the limbs tremble in expectation. I can give no better explanation for my becoming, for I enjoy all these things, take pleasure in the instant of death. When I feast, I do so on the hot sweet flesh of men, drinking in their energy and life, crunching their bones and sucking on the delicate brains as their last fleeting, terrified thoughts scurry across my consciousness. So, men call me Rakshasa, or demon. For long ages I thought this was my name as men died with it

6

on their lips, yet now I know that it is the name men give to ones like me. I have never wanted a name though and am content to be known by this generic term.

Why Rakshasa then and not Rakshasi if I have no body, no gender? Why do I choose to be predominantly male rather than female? For no other reason that I can be whatever I want and in my experience, men are destroyers and women creators. Men have power in this world and women do not. Why would I give up power unless I benefited? I like to think of myself as a balancer between the two extremes of man and woman, destruction and creation, enjoying both, though I admit, my natural inclinations favor destruction. I feed on humankind and, like any good farmer; I seek the health of my meat animals. I seek to preserve them. In this I, and humankind, men and women, are bound together like the three-fold god Trimurti – Brahma the Creator, Vishnu the Preserver and Siva the Destroyer.

Do the gods exist? Of course – can any doubt it? But they are seldom as men imagine them to be. A man sees their power and clothes them with a body not unlike his but stronger, more beautiful, more majestic. He imagines they wield power much as he would, capriciously and selfishly. Driven by the urges of his own organs of procreation, he endows these genderless beings with the weaknesses and foibles of his own life. The gods and demons both are seen as man wants to see them – gods as what he aspires to and demons as what he fears he will become. But his aspirations and fears avail him little; the spark of his life burns too low for him to become either. I have been present at the deaths of many and feasted upon the flickering embers of life. I know that once the body

7

dies, the life within rapidly dissipates and disappears. That is why I must be there at the moment when one leaves the other, in order for me to feed.

To be honest though, I have met men whose life force is a raging furnace rather than smoldering coals. These men, I could believe, will survive the separation of death, but what they will become, or where they go, I do not know. I have never been privileged to attend upon such a one at the moment of death. Not for want of trying, I assure you, but they have the ability to prevent me feeding. These ones I have learnt to enjoy for other reasons. The minds of such ones often have insights beyond those of common men and knowledge of the ways of the gods.

Have I met the gods? Some of them – but it is not healthy for one such as me to be close to the gods. Even the ones who are most concerned with living things, with the preservation of creation, show a disturbing inclination to destroy Rakshasas, Nagas, Yakshas, Anusaras, Asaras and all the other beings who are called demons by these self-righteous beings. I try not to stay close to gods – they are not trustworthy and far too powerful. Hardly better are the men who are called heroes by mankind. They too will destroy demons but heroes at least have weaknesses and with a little thought and cunning, can be survived.

I once met a hero and a god together and lived to learn from the experience.

I cannot tell you what battle it was that gave me life, or even when, for I did not learn to count the years until many seasons had passed. In those early days I wandered the hot and dusty plains, clothing myself in whatever form I chose, sometimes letting the flame of my being re-animate a dead man or woman on a whim, or traveling as a breath of wind or pale, dancing flame under the pale glow of the stars. I roamed the streets of towns and cities, watching, learning, and feeding, mingling with prince and peasant, merchant and farmer, child and courtesan. When I felt the need for solitude I wandered the dark forests or rested among the tombs and graves in the lonely places, knowing that few people would venture there.

After a while I came to a place where two great rivers meet, the Yamuna that flows south from the White Mountains, and the Chambal, coursing from setting to rising sun. Mighty floods of water they are, with many people living along the banks but I felt myself drawn to the north and presently, on the banks of the Yamuna River I found the forest known as Khandava. Entering it, I felt at peace – a strange feeling for I had never been one to stray far from violence. I walked through its leafy glades, along sun-dappled paths and into bright open pastures of lush grass where elephant and gaur grazed alongside red and spotted deer. Swarms of brightly colored butterflies danced around blossoms high in the trees or gorged on rotting fruit among the leaf litter; birds called and monkeys screamed. At night, the darkness pulsated with the sounds of insects and frogs, constellations of fireflies lighting up the meadows. Tigers dwelt here too, but these predators are intelligent and could see past the disguise I had assumed to my inner flame. They melted silently from my path and all I glimpsed was a hint of red pelt or soft white underbelly.

Men lived in the Khandava, though to hear the stories in later times one would think they were a race of demons. They called themselves Nagas and worshiped snakes, in particular the great hooded cobra. Their priests handled the huge serpents fearlessly and were seldom bitten. The Nagas were as one with their forest and tended it, keeping out the woodchoppers and the charcoal makers, preventing hunters from pillaging the thickets. Being eaters of fruit and grain, the Nagas were not feared by the animals of the forest and carried no weapons to defend themselves. The only animal that occasionally did them harm was the leopard and against this night killer they had no defense save to barricade themselves inside their huts at night.

I stayed in the Khandava forest and preyed on the Nagas as I needed, taking the guise of a leopard. This did them little harm, for I took only as I needed and my presence repelled real leopards which would otherwise have killed many more. I never entered their villages, being content to find a lone traveler on the less-frequented paths and appear to him or her. My guise was perfect and as the traveler's terror reached a crescendo, my teeth and claws extracting their life, I fed on the delicious storm of emotion that raged within their dying minds.

I could have lived like this for years, but unknown to me, the Nagas had bitterly offended five kings who lived in the city called Indra-Prastha on the borders of the forest. One of these kings, Arjuna, and his cousin the god Krishna, sought revenge and brought raging destruction down on this peaceful place.

Here is how it happened …

Chapter One

The Khandava forest lay clean and sparkling in the early morning light. Mists rolled and swirled above the deep waters of the Yamuna River as it meandered through dense thickets, grassy meadows that swept down to the dark rush-clothed water's edge and between rock-strewn shores where the surface of the flood roiled and danced above the dimly heard clatter of boulders in its green depths. Dew hung in myriad tiny droplets from grass and leaf, bending the light of the rising sun back in a sparkling array of jewels that flashed like the gems in a king's treasury. The air hung heavy and cool, moist still, but already the touch of the sun promised the burning heat of summer.

Down by the water's edge a small herd of chital deer drank, the does and half-grown young with heads down while the buck stood with head raised, snuffing the air for the least scent of danger. Nothing stirred and the faintest of breezes blew from across the river, bringing with it nothing more ominous than the whiff of fresh elephant. The buck snorted and stamped a forefoot, bringing two of the does to alert. After a few moments they relaxed again and the buck turned to slowly scan the meadow behind him once more. The wind, such as it was, blew from him toward the meadow and his questing nostrils could not tell him anything. Instead, his eyes sought for any sign of danger, his ears for the sounds of bird and beast that might warn of the presence of a predator. A pair of jays chattered in a tree top nearby, seeing nothing that might disturb them.

A fallen tree lay angled across the meadow, the gnarled and splayed-out roots closest to the herd. The buck swept his eyes over the trunk and as the wind bent the grass stems a hint of red caught his attention. He froze, staring at the place, looking for the flash of color to come again. The wind died away and the green of the grass was once more unbroken against the peeling brown bark of the fallen tree. After long moments, the buck stamped his foot again and dipped his head, lowering his lyre-shaped antlers for an instant before turning away.

As he turned, the chattering of the jays in the nearby tree stilled. At the same instant, the grass by the fallen tree parted and a half-grown tigress erupted from cover, the rippling muscles of her hind legs and flanks propelling her in a burst of reddish death toward the small herd. The bark of alarm from the buck as he pivoted, launching himself away from the predator, startled the does into panicked motion. They scattered. The tigress raced by the buck, so close they almost touched, but she disregarded him, her attention fixed on the doe she had spent the last hour stalking. She closed on her even as the doe bunched her legs beneath her, her mouth gaping, eyes wide in terror. Predator and prey collided at the water's edge, the force of the impact carrying them both into the shallow water. The doe bleated once before her spinal cord was severed, and her legs kicked spasmodically for a few seconds.

The tigress stood over her prey, straddling the body of the chital doe, her eyes scanning the now deserted meadow and the faint sounds of the scattered herd fading into the forest. Slowly, the bird song started up again. Lowering her head to nuzzle the doe, the tigress gripped the deer by the base of the neck and walked stiff-legged from the water, head held high. She carried the body to the fallen tree and deposited it near the tangle of roots. After licking the blood from the wounds around the neck she lay down, ripped the thin skin around the doe's anus and started to feed.

The sun climbed higher, driving the mist from the river and banishing the dew. The tigress finished her meal and walked sedately down to the water's edge to drink heavily before seeking the shade of the forest. A monkey screamed an alarm from the tree tops and followed the tigress as she walked slowly along a game trail toward her lair at the base of a tall sandstone outcrop near the top of a small hill. As she climbed beyond the trees, the monkey fell silent, staring in the direction of the hill and grumbling to itself. The tigress slumped to the ground in the shade of the rock and stared out over the tops of the forest trees toward the edge of the woodlands where small figures could be seen. Neither scent nor sound carried that far and the tigress disregarded them, settling down to sleep her meal off. Her eyes closed though her other senses remained alert for several minutes. At length, she was lulled by the serenity of the sun-bathed forest beneath her, and she slept.

Far below, on the edge of Khandava forest, a light chariot stood facing the dense vegetation, the two white horses in the yoked traces stamping and blowing with the effort of staying still when their senses told them they should be moving. In the light wooden framework of the chariot itself stood two men, one tall and fair, the other shorter and stockier, dark-haired and dark-skinned. Both carried themselves with a regal bearing, the fair one with

13

the consciousness of being a king in his own lands, the darker one with the unassuming arrogance of one who knows himself above all others.

The tall, fair man raised his eyes to the flag fluttering at the tip of a supple bamboo pole fixed to the rear of the chariot. The figure of a gray and blue ape squatting on a yellow background was a well-known standard even beyond the realms of Indra-Prastha and gave the king one of the names by which he was known – 'Kapi-dhwaja' or 'ape-standard'.

"The wind has changed," the king known sometimes as Kapi-dhwaja commented matter-of-factly.

The darker one nodded and smiled, white teeth gleaming in his dark face. "You will have good hunting, cousin."

"You will not join me? The more I practice, the better I get." The fair man held up his strung bow and pointed toward the forest with it. "Besides, Gandiva is hungry."

"I do not need to practice," the dark one said softly. "None are more skilled with the discus than I."

The fair one laughed. "Sometimes I forget you are a god, Krishna. You take on the ways of men so well; I could almost believe you to be one."

Krishna inclined his head graciously. "And you cousin, are so skilled with the bow, one could almost believe you to be a god."

The fair one grinned. "So you will not hunt today?"

"No, but I will drive your chariot if you will let me."

"Gladly. There is no-one I trust more."

"Then see, Lord Arjuna," Krishna pointed to where the path leading into the forest had been cleared to allow

14

the free passage of the king's chariot. "The master of the hunt approaches."

From the forest a man came hurrying. He wore a white cotton churidar and tunic like his lords in the chariot and his lustrous black hair was swept back and tied behind with a scarlet ribbon. Across his chest from left shoulder to waist he wore a sash of bright red as befitted his rank. He slowed to a walk as he neared the chariot and dropped to his knees, staring up at the tall figure of his king, third son of Pandu and one of the five rulers of Indra-Prastha. Beside his monarch a pearly nimbus, hardly visible in the bright sunshine, surrounded the features of the dark one.

"My lords," the master of the hunt said. "All is prepared. At your signal we shall beat the forest and drive the game."

Krishna frowned and it seemed for a moment as if the sunshine lost its strength. "You are having the game driven toward us? Where lies the sport in that?"

Arjuna laughed and handed the reins of the chariot to his friend. "Nothing so tame. I have had the path widened to take a chariot but the game will be driven across our path. We shall drive through it, never knowing what will appear before us." He looked quizzically at the god. "Of course, if you have not the courage ..."

For an instant the air around the chariot crackled as faint blue sparks jumped from the metal fastenings. The horses reared and screamed in sudden panic, calming only as Krishna held out his hand. "We shall see who lacks courage today, cousin," he said softly. Cracking the reins, the god urged the horses forward, forcing Arjuna to grip the sides to prevent himself falling back. Bouncing and

15

jolting, Krishna drove the chariot across the field toward the gash in the forest wall. Behind them, the master of the hunt leapt to his feet and waved his hands frantically to his servants waiting by the forest edge. Horns blew urgently and within minutes a great cacophony of sound rent the air as a thousand men sounded horns, clashed bronze swords on shields, beat on drums or just used their voices, ululating wildly into the still air, shattering the peace of the forest. Other men armed with long staves beat the bushes and grass, driving out the animals.

The chariot charged down the forest track, the horses in full gallop with the light wooden carriage bucking and heaving, sometimes leaving the ground entirely only to return with a teeth-jarring thump. Krishna stood flatfooted on the wicker flooring, his only grip being on the reins with which he guided the straining horses. He moved with the swaying chariot, effortlessly, a smile on his dark face, as if he stood on solid ground. Arjuna shook back his long tawny locks and grinned fiercely as he hooked one strong leg around an upright and reached for the first arrow from the three quivers attached to the front of the chariot.

A herd of chital burst from the undergrowth fifty paces in front. Arjuna slipped an arrow into place and in one fluid movement raised the bow Gandiva and loosed the arrow. The buck took the shaft behind the left front leg and cart-wheeled, dead before it slammed into the ground. Two does followed their leader into death before the chariot flashed by, Arjuna yelling in triumph. A brief pause, during which the only sounds were the drumming of hooves and the rumble of the wheels then a wild pig appeared. The beast stopped in the trail, facing the onrushing chariot and Arjuna sent an arrow into its eye. The horses trampled the fallen animal and the chariot wheel bounced high, forcing Arjuna to grab the frame. A peacock flew overhead, its streaming tail of blue and green a brief beacon in a patch of sunlight before it fell dead in an explosion of feathers. A flock of pigeons, a darting hare in an open glade, more chital deer, gaur, and an old water buffalo, crossed the path of god and king and died, each one pierced by Arjuna's shafts. After several miles through the dense forest, the winding track re-emerged into bright sunlight where gaily-colored pavilions of cotton and silk fluttered in the breeze of the open meadows. The ape standard flew prominently and men hurried to catch the bridles of the sweating horses, to rub them down with toweled cloths, to hand gold goblets of chilled fruit juices to man and god.

"You have not lost your eye," Krishna said calmly, offering a blessing to a servant proffering a tray of fruit. "Seventeen arrows and every one of them a hit."

Arjuna wiped the sweat from his face and grinned. "I cannot miss with Gandiva in my hand. But neither have you lost your touch with horses, Lord Krishna. I thought we were going to come apart there once or twice."

"The horses love me. They merely do what I ask of them." The dark one handed his goblet to a servant and looked back at the forest. "Shall we return?"

The king nodded. "I have not yet killed a tiger. No hunt is complete without one." Arjuna accepted a bundle of arrows and refilled the quivers in front of him. "The cowardly animals will have passed by now. The courageous ones will delay until the beaters drive them

17

out. We should go." The fair one set his jaw grimly and gestured back toward the forest.

The chariot leapt forward again, re-entering Khandava along the packed earth and scythed grass of the trail. Almost at once a leopard bounded across the track, turning as it reached cover to defy the pounding horses. Its ears flattened and it spat angrily, a snarling whine of rage as its muscles bunched beneath the glossy spotted pelt. Arjuna smiled and loosed an arrow that sprang across the rapidly closing gap, piercing the creature's right eye. The leopard reared, clawing vainly before falling shuddering to the leafy floor of the forest as the chariot swept onward.

The game of the forest was now in full flight as the beaters advanced, the cacophony of sound making the air itself shudder. Animals and birds poured across the trail, sometimes right under the flying hooves of the horses and the blurred wheels of the chariot. Krishna's iron control held the horses on their course and Arjuna was in constant motion, sending arrow after arrow into the fleeing animals. He emptied two quivers and was starting on the last when a great trumpeting cry sounded, the leaves on the trees shaking as the blast passed over them.

"Hathi," Krishna said with a smile, drawing the chariot to a halt. He lifted his face and sniffed. "A bull in musth. Do you wish to flee, cousin?"

Arjuna snorted derisively. "There is no man or beast I will not face."

"He is cunning," Krishna said. "He will not leave the forest."

"So take us into the forest."

18

Krishna smiled again and urged the horses forward into a gap between the tall trees. The wheels slammed against exposed roots, hurling the chariot into the air and forcing Arjuna to hold on grimly. Krishna stood his ground, seemingly unaffected by the careening vehicle. They plunged deeper into the forest, passing between the tall columnar trunks of teak and the more twisted ones of neem and pipal. They crushed the spindly young seedlings worshiping the sun with up-stretched arms and bruised the briars and the young bamboo. The dhaak trees blazed with orange blossoms that shivered and fell as they passed, and they plunged through thickets heavy with the scent of honeysuckle. The ground dipped toward tall grass meadows taller than a man and became softer underfoot, the horses having a harder time of it as the mud clung to the chariot wheels and their hooves. The squeals and trumpeting of the unseen Hathi led them on to an area of shorter grass before suddenly stopping. Krishna reined in the horses and they listened.

"He comes," Krishna said softly. "Over there." He pointed to a thick stand of Acacia a hundred paces away to their right.

A gray shadow moved beneath the trees, silently, the only sign of his passing the whipping of the branches. The elephant burst out of the thicket and came straight for the chariot, trunk outstretched between two stained tusks. The tarry deposits of musth dripped from the inner corners of the beast's eyes, staining his cheeks. A bellow of rage whipped the ape standard about, flicking the cloth out with a snap.

Arjuna calmly fitted an arrow to Gandiva and let fly, but the shaft bounced harmlessly from the bony dome of

19

Hathi's skull, merely drawing blood from a shallow wound.

"You'll have to do better than that, cousin," Krishna observed, and turned the horses away from the onrushing beast, urging them into flight.

Arjuna did not answer but picked another arrow from the quiver and deliberately took the time to examine the shaft. He fitted it in his bow and looked up at the charging elephant that filled his sight. Soundless now except for the rushing of air, Hathi stretched out his trunk until it was but a hand's breadth from the man with the bow. Calmly and without seeming to hurry, Arjuna measured the rise and fall of the chariot as it careered over the soft ground, then lifted his bow. At the instant the finger of the elephant's trunk touched him, he released the bowstring, Gandiva flexed convulsively and the arrow leapt down the animal's pink gullet. Hathi squealed in agony and dropped back, shaking his great head.

Arjuna touched Krishna's shoulder. "Turn us. I will finish him."

Krishna nodded and swung the chariot in a wide circle, leading them back to where the elephant stood trumpeting his rage and pain. Blood gushed from his mouth and his trunk sought out his enemies, though he ran no more, but lurched and staggered.

"Take me past on his left side."

The horses responded to a finger touch and changed course. As they neared the elephant swung round in an effort to face them but could not turn fast enough. Arjuna fitted an arrow and placed another between his teeth and, as they passed Hathi's great head, the fair one leapt from the chariot and landed running. He stumbled and almost fell before stepping forward into the shadow of the elephant. Arjuna drew back the string and pressed the arrow tip to the great chest beneath whose gray hide he could hear the muffled drum of the beast's life. He released and the arrow disappeared, sucked deep into Hathi's chest.

The elephant's head went up and he screamed loudly, spraying blood in a pink mist, rounding on his tormentor. Arjuna danced back, snatching the second arrow from his teeth and fitting it to his bow. Hathi lurched forward, trunk questing, but his life fled as he moved and he fell like an avalanche in front and around Arjuna.

For several seconds the man stood still, looking wide-eyed at the outstretched trunk to his left and a great tusk that ripped a furrow in the grass right up to his right foot. A smile grew to a grin then by leaps and bounds to a roar of delighted victory. He raised Gandiva suddenly and fired it directly upward, without looking, piercing the burning humid air.

Krishna leapt down from the chariot and ran lightly across the grass and up the elephant's trunk to its domed head, the swelling curve of its belly, and to where Hathi's backbone stood out as great knuckled fists beneath the wrinkled hide.

"A noble animal, cousin, and bravely fought. I withdraw my earlier accusation."

Arjuna bowed smiling. "Accepted, my Lord Krishna." A muffled thump on the grass behind him swung Arjuna round, his hand drawing uselessly on his empty bow. A dozen paces away lay a transfixed crow, a few feathers drifting in the still air, his last arrow firmly

21

wedged in its body. He laughed delightedly and the dark one joined in from the back of the dead elephant.

"Today I cannot miss, even when I do not aim."

"Who is it that hunts in the sacred forests of Khandava?" The voice hung in the still air, seemingly directionless. Arjuna pivoted, scanning the edge of the forest and the long grass.

"There." Krishna pointed a dark finger toward the Acacia trees from whence the elephant had charged only minutes earlier. A short, stocky man in a plain brown robe stood in the shadows. The hair on his head hung to his shoulders in a silvery mane, merging with his beard to form a gleaming halo around his head. Despite the man standing motionless the robes writhed about him ceaselessly.

"What is it to you, stranger?" Arjuna asked. "Who are you?"

"I am Naga Mura. These are my forests. I allow none to hunt here."

Arjuna laughed. "Has no one told you these are the forests of Khandava, gifted to the sons of Pandu as their inheritance from King Dhrita-Rashtra? I am Arjuna, one of the five Pandava."

Naga Mura gave no sign he was awed by the presence of the king. He nodded toward the body of the elephant. "And who is that who so arrogantly bestrides the body of fallen Hathi?"

"I am Krishna," the dark one said, leaping down to the ground. He walked over to Arjuna's side and looked intently at the man in the brown robe. "You are of the sons of Kasyapa and Kadru, Nagas created to rule below the earth. Why are you so far from your domain?"

"I am Naga Mura and I answer to no-one save the god Indra, under whose protection these forests lie."

"Then you will know that I am his son," Arjuna said. "And that I and my brothers rule from the city of Indra-Prastha."

"I care nothing for those that call themselves sons of Indra. I honor his holy name and keep his sacred forest clean of wood cutters, charcoal makers and hunters. In his name I bid you leave at once and never return."

"And if I will not?"

Naga Mura shook the sleeves of his robe out. "Then my servants will kill you," he said calmly. Two long cobras slithered out of his sleeves and moved rapidly toward Arjuna. "Their bite is certain death, arrogant king."

Krishna bowed his head and made a subtle gesture with his right hand. The snakes stopped and coiled, rearing up with hoods expanded.

A look of fury came over Naga Mura's face and he hissed loudly between his teeth, stamping the ground in a complex rhythm. Within minutes, the grass of the meadow started swaying and rustling as other snakes converged on the spot, from long black cobras to small but deadly krait, and even giant pythons from the forest depths.

Krishna gestured again but not all of the serpents stopped. "I would suggest a tactical withdrawal," he commented.

Arjuna bared his teeth. "Call them off, Naga, or suffer the consequences."

"Go. Leave my forest and never return."

Arjuna sidestepped the coiled cobras and ran to the chariot. He snatched an arrow from the almost empty quiver and whirled to face the Naga, his bow drawn. "Are you willing to die, Naga?"

"You cannot kill me."

"You think not?" Arjuna released the bowstring and the arrow sped across the clearing, transfixing the Naga, slamming him back against a tree and holding him upright. The man slumped down and his eyes clouded in death.

"A pity," Krishna commented. "I was hoping his arrogance was founded in power. It would have been an interesting experience."

"Leave this forest."

"What?" Arjuna and Krishna stared at the lifeless corpse pinned to the tree. "Who speaks?"

"I, Naga Mura." A man in brown robes stepped out from behind the tree, his silver hair and beard glowing like a halo under the sun-dappled trees.

"What are you?" Arjuna asked, frowning. "Are you that one's brother?" He pointed at the dead man.

"I am Naga Mura. I rule in this forest in Indra's name. Leave, vile hunter and never return."

Arjuna turned and snatched another arrow from the quiver on the chariot. "If you are Naga Mura, then you must die. I am happy to oblige."

"Wait," Krishna said, holding up one dusky gray-blue hand. "He is a Naga priest. You cannot kill him this way."

"I recognize you, Lord Krishna," Naga Mura said. "Do not interfere. This fight is between me and this man."

Krishna brought his hands together in front of his face and he bowed slightly. "He is my friend."

"Then I regret you will die with him." Naga Mura gestured and the snakes broke free of the god's restraints and resumed their approach.

"My friend, we must leave. Come, before my beautiful horses are killed." Krishna leapt up onto the chariot platform and held out a hand to Arjuna. With a show of reluctance, the fair king stepped up beside the god and Krishna urged the horses into flight.

Arjuna never took his eyes off the Naga priest as they rode back into the cover of the forest. "I make a vow," he said softly. "And I call on the gods to witness it. I will kill every Naga within this forest."

"And how will you accomplish that? You saw the effect of your arrows."

"I will find a way. There must be a way."

Krishna kept silent until they were out of the Khandava forest. Around them, the king's men hurried to collect up the dead animals, marveling at the precision of Arjuna's bowmanship. "There is a way," he said at last.

"Tell me."

"Fire. Even the Naga priests cannot withstand the flames."

Arjuna snorted. "Nothing simpler. I will send my thousand beaters back with torch brands. I will lay waste to Khandava."

"Even at the cost of destroying your property? Would it not be wiser to seek another solution? Take the problem to your brother Yudhi-shthira."

"I have made a vow. I cannot take it back."

"Fire alone will not suffice."

25

"What do you mean?"

"The forest is wet. Lord Indra is generous and brings heavy rains to soak the trees, the shrubs and the grass. An ordinary fire will not consume the forest."

Arjuna scowled, his eyes flashing with anger. "Then what will?"

"Agni."

"The god of fire? Why should he help?"

"Lord Agni has long coveted Khandava. Only Indra has kept him out."

"Then let us invite him to a feast." Arjuna smiled. "I can offer him a meal that will satisfy even the appetite of a god."

Arjuna and Krishna returned to the great palace at Indra-Prastha. Dismissing the servants and making excuses to Arjuna's brothers, the other four kings, they made their way up onto a great flat roof that overlooked the palace gardens and many miles of rich farmland in front of the distant blue-green swathe of the Khandava.

"How do we invite the Fire god?"

"I know a mantra that will invoke him," Krishna replied. "It is not to be used lightly for a man invokes the gods at his peril. However, in this case, your purpose matches his." The dusky god sat cross-legged, facing the sun and started a low droning murmur. Arjuna strained to hear but could not make sense of the words. After a long time, Krishna fell silent.

"Is he coming?"

Krishna nodded. "Watch the sun."

The ball of white flame darkened as Arjuna shaded his eyes, squinting up into the blinding glare. The disc of the sun lengthened and a great pillar of orange flame descended through the dusty air toward the palace roof, as terror-stricken cries echoed up from the streets of the city. The flame washed across the roof, scorching and crumbling the brick. Plants in pots, citrus trees in flower and fruit, burst into flame and crisped to charcoal in seconds, and the great stone roof groaned and cracked in the immense heat. Then between one moment and the next, the heat and light disappeared and a Brahman stood before them in flowing white robes, his skin glowing yellow, his hair and beard tawny red and waving as if in a breeze. His eyes flashed brilliantly and focused on Arjuna and the king staggered. A wave of heat passed through him as if his bones were melting and the distant roaring of flames sounded in his ears.

"Who calls Agni?" the fire god asked. "Tell me why I should not burn you to ashes for your presumption."

"I called you, Agni, not he."

The Brahman turned his attention to the dark one seated to one side. "Lord Krishna? You called me? Why?"

"My cousin, King Arjuna, has a proposition for you. He wishes to give you a gift."

"What can a man, even a king, give that a god would desire?"

"Khandava forest," Arjuna said.

Agni's gaze swept over the king, the light pouring from his eyes casting a deep shadow behind the man. "You interest me. Go on."

"I offer you a feast, Lord Agni. Khandava forest is mine and I offer it freely to you."

"I thought it Lord Indra's, for every time I seek to devour it, he sends the rain. Are you more powerful than Indra?"

"Alone, he is not," Krishna interposed. "But together we are unbeatable."

"And you would fight Indra that I might feast?"

"Yes."

The Brahman who was Agni smiled, his countenance growing still brighter. "Before I accept your gift, tell me why you offer it."

"I have made a vow."

Agni frowned and the roar of the flames grew louder. "You made a vow to do what?"

"To kill the Nagas of the Khandava. They have insulted me by ..."

Agni flicked one hand dismissively, sending a buffet of heat crashing over Arjuna. "I do not need to know the reason," he interrupted. "I accept your gift."

"Then let us begin."

Arjuna, Krishna and Agni rode in the king's carriage of state back to the forest. Larger than the hunting chariot and four-wheeled, the state carriage had seating and shade from the heat of the sun. Agni tamped down his thermal discharges to prevent the fabric of the carriage from conflagrating, but even so the ride was discomforting for Arjuna and the driver. Krishna did not appear bothered at all as he lounged in one of the seats and stared out at the fields, humming to himself.

The carriage halted a hundred paces from the forest's edge and the three dismounted. Arjuna told the driver to retire another hundred paces and to wait for them. When man and horses were at a safe distance, Arjuna led Agni to the forest's edge.

"Behold, Lord Agni, your feast awaits you."

Agni faced the forest and raised his arms high. His clothing burst into flames and as he walked forward he lost his human shape and became a raging pillar of fire reaching into the azure sky. The leaves shriveled and crisped, puffs of steam exhaling from tortured vegetation, and the sound the trees made as they burned was a scream that reverberated through the heavens.

Far away, in the White Mountains to the north, Indra heard the cry of his forest and hastened south along the Yamuna River, on the backs of the storm clouds Pushkala and Avartaka. Great was his anger at seeing his forest in flames and leaving the storm to deluge the forest, he swept down from the sky to face his foes.

Krishna saw him coming and the great discus Sudarsana-Chakra appeared in his hand. He held it high and it started to revolve, ever faster. "I will face Indra, cousin," he said. "You must disrupt the storm clouds and prevent them putting the flames out."

Arjuna laughed wryly. "Not even Gandiva can accomplish that. I have a single quiver of arrows. Once they are gone, I am helpless."

Krishna moved his free hand over the quiver, calling down a blessing of return on the shafts. "Release your arrows, Lord Arjuna, they will return to you as often as you send them." He turned and lightly ran toward Indra, his discus revolving like a golden wheel, growing in size, the sound of its turning rising to a scream.

Agni marched through Khandava like a triumphant army, the flame of his being incinerating everything he touched. Every flame begat other flames and soon the forest blazed on a front many thousands of paces wide.

Above the as yet untouched parts of the forest, the storm clouds darkened and grew in size, blotting out the sun. The first raindrops fell, spattering the vegetation and sizzling into steam where the hungry flames licked them. The downpour became heavier, the drops merging and fighting back the fire, soaking the forest.

The roaring of the flames faltered and from the smoke a great voice cried out. "King of Indra-Prastha, remember your promise."

Arjuna raised the great bow Gandiva and in quick succession, sent six arrows hurtling up into the lowering and roiling storm clouds. The deluge slackened momentarily before resuming its intensity. The arrows plummeted back down to earth, landing at Arjuna's feet.

"Again," roared the divine fire.

Arjuna applied himself and kept a constant barrage of arrows winging into the clouds. The wind of their passage hurled the vapor aside, disrupting the pattern and slackening the rain. As each arrow returned to his feet, he snatched it up again and hurled it back into the heavens. As he sweated and strove he became aware of a scream that vibrated through to his bones, the scream of Krishna's discus as he leapt to do battle.

Indra stood in the plains before Khandava, his eyes flashing with a righteous anger. He raised two of his arms, each holding a spear, and brandished them at the dark god. "You presume to burn my forest, Krishna? I will destroy you all, man and god, unless you surrender to me now."

"My cousin, Lord Arjuna of the Pandava, has made a vow, a sacred vow witnessed by the gods. I am sworn to help him," Krishna replied. He released the golden disc and it spun in an arc toward the four-armed, red-skinned god of war and weather.

Contemptuously, Indra gestured and a lightning bolt blasted the discus aside, but it wheeled and returned to Krishna's hand. Again he flung it and Indra gestured again, raising up a wall of whirlwinds in front of him. Obscured by the swirling dust and grass, the discus missed, sweeping back through the wall of wind to its owner's hand.

Krishna's face became harder and he spun Sudarsana-Chakra faster, the screaming of its passing rising in pitch and intensity. Again he threw and again his weapon was blocked. Then out of the swirling winds strode Indra and each of his four long arms bore a thunderbolt. He hurled them in quick succession and Krishna blocked two with the discus, leapt aside from another, but the last struck his chest in an explosion of light. He was thrown back several paces across the churned up field, his clothing smoking. Indra turned toward Arjuna, hurling the whirling wind at him.

The winds caught at the son of Pandu and prevented him from sending more arrows aloft. The ones that were in flight returned and the tattered remnants of the storm clouds, Pushkala and Avartaka, started to reform.

In the furnace of the Khandava, Agni laughed out loud. "I have eaten!" The pillar of heat and flames and smoke poured upward, stretching far above the storm clouds. Winds poured in from every direction, fanning the fires into ever fiercer rages. The clouds themselves

31

were sucked into the inferno, their bodies vaporized instantly and their beings fled north with thin cries of anguish.

Indra watched in horror as his sacred groves disappeared and at last, covering his face with his cloak, he too rose into the air and fled from the heat toward the cold white mountains of the north.

Krishna limped across to his cousin Arjuna and helped anchor him as the cyclonic winds threatened to uproot him and fling him to his death. He pointed to the north where the remnants of the forest still stood green along the river's edge.

"Do you see, Lord Arjuna?"

The king shaded his face from the bright flames and squinted into the heat-hazed air. "I cannot see that far. My eyes are but a man's."

"The Nagas of the forest are escaping."

Arjuna bellowed with rage and, snatching up his arrows, ran as fast as he could against the raging winds toward his carriage. The driver had withdrawn several hundred paces and then more as the conflagration spread, but seeing his king fighting his way toward him, turned the carriage and urged the terrified horses toward the fire. Minutes later, Arjuna and Krishna were being driven northward along the wall of flames to intercept the escaping people of the forest.

"There are women and children among them," observed Krishna.

"I do not war on the weak and the helpless," Arjuna growled. "It is the priests who must die."

"And what of the animals?"

"They are part of Agni's feast, but I am reluctant to kill unnecessarily. The Naga priests will suffice – and maybe a tiger or two."

Man and god raced into position in the space between the main forest of Khandava where Agni gorged and a narrow strip of riparian forest along the Yamuna River. Already, the air was teeming with birds fleeing the disaster and the grasslands speckled with running beasts. Arjuna set his arrows into the ground in front of him and strung one in Gandiva, waiting for his prey to appear. So crowded was the air that the teeming birds almost blocked the already smoke-hazed sun. Beside him, Krishna spun the discus and the golden wheel screamed and flew through the herds, not killing this time but parting the stampeding animals so they thundered on either side, leaving them in an island of peace.

A different motion, creatures walking upright, at the edge of the sere forest caught Arjuna's eye and he swung his bow, releasing, fitting another arrow and releasing again. Two Naga priests fell sprawling on the grass and a number of women and other men of the Naga scattered with cries of terror.

Krishna stilled his whirling discus and raised a hand. "Men and women of the Naga," he cried, his voice rising easily above the stampede of animals and the crackling roar of Agni's divine fire. "Your lives are spared. I, Krishna, stand guarantee for your lives. Only the lives of your priests are forfeit."

The men hesitated in the forest for a little longer, unsure whether they could trust the dusky god, then as the smoke thickened and the heat grew, they ran, their women and children with them. Scores passed across the open

33

land and disappeared into the woods along the Yamuna, but among them were priests, bent low, attempting to hide from Arjuna's wrath. His arrows sped, slipping between man and woman, woman and her child, leaving them untouched but the priests dead on the trampled ground. One priest took advantage of a group of women, holding two children himself as a shield. Gandiva tracked the group across the open ground and at the last moment a hint of brown robe showed through colorful shawls and an arrow sped. The priest threw up his arms with a cry of agony, the children tumbling with wails of anguish to be scooped up by the women as they ran for the cover of the woods. The stricken priest clutched at the arrow in his leg and stared angrily at Arjuna.

"I curse you, evil man. May the gods ..." An arrow took him in the throat and his curse died with him.

The flood of birds and animals died down and the sun shone again, though red, obscured by a heavy pall of smoke. Nothing stirred in the open grass save for late-comers and injured animals. Arjuna released many from their agony, and as his stocks of arrows ran low, Krishna renewed them. A little later and the open grass lay silent except for the roaring of the flames and a steady drizzle of sparks and ashes.

"Did we get them all?" Arjuna asked.

Krishna scanned the fields. "I count eleven priests. One you killed in the forest. Traditionally the Naga have twelve priests. I think you got them all."

"Are they truly dead? The one in the forest took on a new body."

Krishna shrugged. "I doubt any man has that ability. I think that was another priest."

34

Arjuna nodded and leant on his bow. His face and clothing was soot-streaked and sweat-stained, though Krishna looked as fresh as he had that morning, save for the charred area on his chest where Indra's thunderbolt had taken him. He surveyed the roaring wall of fire advancing on them, and the thin skirt of lifeless forest between.

"I think we should be leaving. Agni draws close."

"Agni has left," Krishna replied. "This is ordinary fire. Still, there is nothing to be gained here."

"Except that." Arjuna pointed toward the far edge of the open grass where a promontory of the forest almost joined the riparian woods. Slipping through the long grass was a huge tiger. With a grin, Arjuna fitted an arrow to Gandiva again. "As I said before, no hunt is complete without a tiger."

Krishna smiled and measured the distance to the great beast with a practiced eye. "Can you kill it from this distance?"

"Watch me. A hundred maid-servants skilled in dancing and singing say I can place an arrow in its heart."

"A wager? Very well, I accept."

Arjuna drew back the bow and lifted it high, judging the direction and force of the wind. The string thrummed its song of death and the arrow flashed in an arc across the sky, descending toward the tiger. At the moment before the strike, the flick of darkness against a glimmer of clear sky, gave warning and the tiger reared up, the arrow creasing a path across its chest. A few pale hairs floated free in the breeze.

"A miss," Arjuna cried. "I do not believe it ..." His voice died away as he saw that the tiger still stood upright

35

on its hind legs. The limbs lengthened and the body shortened as they watched, until the body of a man appeared, though with the snarling face and ruffed head of a tiger still.

"Rakshasa," Krishna hissed. "There was a Rakshasa in the forest and I did not see it."

Arjuna cursed and launched another two arrows quickly. The demon dodged them easily and it roared full-throatedly, its guttural cries turning into a great laugh as the tiger head dissolved into that of a Naga priest for a moment. The body shimmered and broke up into a swirl of dust that fell apart on the breeze.

"Where is he?" Arjuna said, his great bow tracking back and forth across the grass. "He is another priest. I must kill him."

"He is no priest," Krishna replied. "I can see his flame, dimly now, but enough to be sure. He is Rakshasa and he flees north."

"Good. I do not want demons in my kingdom."

"I will follow and kill him, for I have no love of his kind." Krishna kissed his cousin Arjuna lightly on the cheek and signed a benediction over him, before turning and running lightly toward the Yamuna and the north.

Within seconds he passed from sight and Arjuna unstrung his bow and trudged back to where his carriage awaited, tired and sore, but happy with the day's events.

Chapter Two

I fled from the dark one; cursing the day I had grown lazy and so sure of myself that I thought it amusing to pretend I was the second priest Naga Mura in the forest of Khandava. I had grown to enjoy the presence of the Naga people and not just because they provided me with sustenance. I was fascinated with the power their priests had over serpents and followed Mura that day. I saw him challenge the white one whom I found out later was a hero called Arjuna, and the dusky gray-skinned one wholly unlike any other human I had seen. His inner flame burned blindingly bright and I quickly found this was not a man, but a god called Krishna. I saw another god that day – Agni – and there was a being I have no desire to get close to. He does not have an inner flame so much as an all-encompassing fury that singed me though I was miles away.

When the forests caught fire I had thought to disguise myself as a Naga priest but after I saw the destruction wrought on these men I quickly changed my form to a magnificent tiger. I should have realized that a hunter like Arjuna would at once be attracted to this form, but I was deluded by my love of power and savagery. I do not know whether his arrow would have hurt me, after all I had an illusory body, but when I saw it coming I reacted without thinking, forgetting for a few moments whether I was disguised as man or tiger. Krishna saw my inner flame and I knew then that no disguise would protect me. I shed my physicality and fled north, seeking to distance myself from both man and god.

I do not know that I can adequately describe my method of movement to one restricted by flesh and exhaustion – after all, I have no limbs. In later years a wise man described it as travel by the power of thought and it is, inasmuch as I can visualize a place and be there, though it takes a lot longer than the thinking. Back in the valley of the Yamuna I was handicapped by one other factor – I had never been this way before and could not visualize my destination. The most I could do was look ahead and imagine myself somewhere along my line of sight and travel there. So my flight was, perforce, slow and disjointed and Krishna had little trouble keeping up.

The northern plains and the foothills of the White Mountains were not heavily populated in those days but even so, villages and towns lay scattered along the rich floodplains. I would have liked to stop and eat for I was growing hungry, but I dared not, knowing the dusky god was so close behind. After several days of travel I realized that perhaps he followed so close behind because I was doing something as elementary as following the course of the river. At once I struck out due east but presently came across another even larger river also flowing from the north.

You may laugh at this, for I have learned that men are quick to make fun of those more ignorant than themselves, but it was not obvious to me that all the rivers in this region would be flowing in the same direction. Remember, I had no schooling, no-one to teach me, and what knowledge I have is gleaned from the minds of dying men, and their minds are usually occupied with more urgent concerns than geography. Later I found out about slope and watersheds and water cycles, but at the time I shrugged mentally and set off up this new river, the Ganga or Devanagari.

My change of course did throw off my pursuing god for a time, which told me that my flame was not acting like a beacon after all, and that maybe I had a chance of losing him altogether.

The river valley narrowed and the water flowed faster as the land rose, and by the time I entered the foothills of those great mountains, I found myself moving faster in the thin air. I reveled in the crisp, bright mornings, the hot sun of midday burning through the rarified atmosphere and the shadowed afternoons as the high peaks threw a cool umbra over the forested slopes. I found I could leap from peak to peak, not only speeding up my rate of travel, but also introducing a random factor. It was here, as I reached Nanda Devi, that I lost Krishna.

Men say that the gods live on mountain tops and as I rested on the summit of this colossus I could appreciate that thought. If I was a god concerned with nothing but my own desires, I would want to live there. The world lay beneath me and around me, rank after rank of snow-covered giants spreading east and west and north. To the south I could barely make out the vast plain from whence I had so recently fled. Nearer at hand was the crumpled cloth of Nanda Devi's skirts, clothed in forest and teeming with life. I felt, even then, a desire to know it, but I still felt the presence of the dark one nearby and resolved to journey on. I cast about me for a sanctuary and felt a pull far to the northeast, to a mountain not much smaller than the one I sat upon.

I took on the body of a great bird, larger than any I had seen and launched myself into the thin air, swooping down to a level where I felt the tug of frigid winds grip my outstretched wings. I soared, and found that unlike lesser birds, I did not need to seek the upwelling columns of warmer air to glide – I could employ my thought travel even when encompassed by a body. I passed rapidly through the craggy valleys, their upper reaches barren wastes of loose rock, ice and snow, across chilling mountain passes and on, until I came at last to the mountain called Kailasa Parvat.

Rising from a high plateau, the mountain itself does not look as impressive as others in the great chain of peaks supporting the thin skies, but I could tell that I was at an extreme elevation from the chill in the air even in strong sunlight. Two lakes stand at the foot of Kailasa, one with curved shores, almost oval, pleasing to the eye; the other drawn out and irregular with islands poking out of the southern end. When first I saw it from aloft I thought it looked like a puddle into which someone had thrown a handful of pebbles. This led to the disturbing realization that the only ones capable of such a feat are the gods. I hoped I was wrong as I had had enough of gods.

In case I was right about the presence of gods I decided against visiting the peak, and instead landed by the shores of the rounder lake, Mansarovar. The area is barren, being far too high for trees, and bitterly cold. However, temperature does not affect me so I clothed myself in the body of an ordinary looking man and set off around the lake. There is very little to see, unless you like flat plains of tussock grass, dirt and loose rock. The wind lifts dust and sand and obscures the view, which, unless you are facing the mountain, is little loss. The lake itself is a clear blue near the shores, reflecting the sky above but emerald green farther out, deep and cold. I traveled maybe half way round it before I found humans, a man with his two wives and a small herd of shaggy-coated cattle. I greeted them and accepted their meager hospitality in their tent and though it ill repaid their kindness, I was truly ravenous, so I ate them. A little later I left the campsite and the small herd, already starting to wander off, and headed toward the mountain.

Kailasa rose black and forbidding, capped with snow, and I knew now, from the fleeting thoughts of my meal that the mountain was thought to be the abode of the god Shiva. The last thing I wanted to meet was another god, but one of the women had told me that nobody ventured onto the mountain and that there were many caves. One of these would provide a suitable home until I could work out why I was here, and the absence of visitors would prevent the sparse population from finding out about me.

One thing that disturbed me was a thought the herder had had as he died. He assumed I was a Naga because the Mansarovar is called the Lake of the Great Nagas. These serpent-demons are supposed to dwell deep beneath the earth and to kill any human that disturbs them. I had just come from the Khandava where I lived with Nagas, yet these were ordinary men and women. The priests had powers, but they were not demons. In fact, the sole similarity was their kinship with serpents. In those early days I was unaware that legends everywhere are based on the same hopes and fears. The serpent is a common enough thread and I was to meet it many times over the years.

41

I found my cave after some searching, a blind gullet that looked out on both lakes. Facing south, the winter sun warmed the rock around me and encouraged plants to grow. A trickle of water when the snows melted in the brief summer, together with the sun and tiny pockets of soil in the black rock, fostered stunted grasses and low herbs. I do not need warmth or plants to survive but the presence of their slow life pulse was strangely pleasing.

Animals came too, though cautiously at first until they saw I meant them no harm. I learnt early that the only suitable prey for one such as me is human. I have tried animals but their thoughts are too fleeting, too basic, and they rarely have a proper self-identity, an essential ingredient in that piquant moment when the victim realizes personal extinction is but a heartbeat away.

I cannot say how long I lived in my cave on Mount Kailasa overlooking Lake Mansarovar but it must have been many years. I felt no great desire for the company of others of my kind, or for the company of men save for my occasional forays to sustain my existence. I found that I got hungrier when I put on a body, whether illusory or physical, so I stayed as my almost invisible flame, burning blue and gold, most of the time. I was content to sit in the mouth of my cave or wander the slopes of Kailasa, watching the pulse of life, the passing of the seasons and the incredible beauty of the high mountains at sunrise, sunset and by moonlight. Often I was accompanied by one of the solitary snow leopards. I enjoy the single-minded blood-thirstiness of their minds and when I descended to the plains to kill, I often took on their shape. In hindsight I suppose I did them no favors by my imitation as in later years the area got a reputation for the fearsome beasts and they were hunted almost to extinction. So life passed for me and gradually men increased in numbers. The Mountain, which had always been considered sacred, became a place of pilgrimage, people coming from both north and south to walk around the mountain and bathe in the pure waters of Mansarovar. A few came to stay, holy men or those seeking enlightenment through meditation and mortification, seeking ways to liberate their being from worldly bodies. I helped several to liberate themselves as I quickly found that a dead pilgrim attracted attention whereas a dead hermit did not. However, not every hermit was an easy kill.

Chapter Three

Bhatta Padhyay came to the city of Karnapur in the autumn of his twenty-sixth year. Born in a little village outside of the town of Pataliputra, on the northern bank of the sacred river Ganga, Bhatta Padhyay was the third son of shopkeeper Bhatta Vasha, who ran a thriving business in the town. As long as his father was alive, Padhyay was content to while away his days helping him in the store, bartering with the local farmers and helping to teach his younger siblings. It was this latter task that earned him the respect of the Brahmin community and led to his birth name of Sarda being changed to Padhyay, which means 'teacher'.

In Padhyay's twenty-fourth year, his father died, leaving the family house to his wife and family, and the business to his two eldest sons. They immediately set about enjoying the profits carefully built up by their father over many years. Padhyay continued to work in the store as his father had desired but his heart was no longer in it. One day in the summer of his twenty-sixth year, while he was in one of the outlying villages, negotiating for a share in the rice harvest, a wandering guru happened by and after watching the workers in the fields for a while, sat beneath a pipal tree on the edge of the village. The gaunt, bearded man settled himself into a cross-legged position with his hands upturned on his thighs, and stared into nothingness. Dressed in a faded loincloth, his only other decoration was wood ash smeared liberally over his upper body and head and a broad blazon of red pigment covering his forehead and tingeing his matted and stringy hair. Over the next few hours, several of the more well-

44

to-do villagers visited the holy man, putting their hands together in front of their faces and bowing in silence. Most left an offering of food or flowers, bhiksha from the wealthiest of the villagers to the poverty-stricken holy man. Soon his battered wooden bowl on the ground beside him was filled with rice and cooked vegetables, and a half full cup of thin milk sat beside it. Garlands of flowers now lay on either side of him but throughout the afternoon the holy man ignored his visitors, staring straight ahead. His presence on the outskirts of the village brought the blessings of the gods and by the giving of alms the villagers could demonstrate their piety and in some small way, touch the divine.

Padhyay watched the holy man for a long time as he sat unmoving in the heavy shade of the pipal tree. He came and sat down opposite him in the dappled light at the margins of the umbra cast by the tree. Gradually the sun moved westward, sinking in redness toward the horizon. The workers in the fields packed up their tools and started back toward their homes in the dusk, the tang of the evening cooking fires sharp in the clean air, the smells of spiced rice and chapattis reaching out to Padhyay and making his mouth water. He was tempted to go and look for his evening meal but he thought instead of the reason he had sat all afternoon in the shade of the pipal tree and stayed where he was. At last, as the day faded into night, the holy man stirred and looked at Padhyay, his eyes gleaming faintly in the last glimmerings reflected from the pale, dusty fields. He beckoned and Padhyay got up stiffly and walked deeper into the shadow, sitting down opposite the man.

"What is it you seek?" asked the holy man.

45

"I ... I don't know," Padhyay stammered. "I saw you come and sit beneath the tree, so still I thought you had died."

"I was meditating."

"On what, guru?"

"On the infinite."

Padhyay said nothing for a while but frowned, trying to think of the infinite but the concept eluded him. After a while he asked, "How?"

"By contemplation."

Padhyay's frown deepened. "Contemplation of what, guru?"

"Of a leaf trembling in the breeze, a wisp of dust, a dead dog by the side of the road, an insect as it feeds on my blood, or nothingness. God is in everything."

"How can you contemplate nothingness?"

"You ask a lot of questions." A smile crept into the holy man's voice.

"How else am I to learn?"

"Ah, you have a love of learning. That is good." The holy man nodded, the movement dimly perceived in the darkness. "All men are born ignorant – they are Shudra. If a man learns to discipline his body through Samskaras, he may become a Dwija, or twice born. Through a study of the scriptures he becomes a Vipra, or scholar. Then for those for whom enlightenment is given, is the realization of Brahmajnana, the Supreme Spirit. Such ones become Brahmin. I am such a one."

Padhyay nodded vigorously. "I, too, am Brahmin."

"Indeed? Then can you discourse on the scriptures? Tell me of the threefold meaning of Sri Rama's banishment from Ayodhya."

46

"I … I do not know this tale."

"It is one of the first stories one learns as a pupil sitting in the shade of a master. No-one who calls themselves a Brahmin should be ignorant of the scriptures." The holy man sat silently for several minutes, then said quietly, "Perhaps an easier question for this young scholar. What color is the skin of Rama?"

"I know this one," Padhyay exclaimed. "I have seen a depiction of Rama in a temple. His skin is blue."

"Why?"

"Why? You mean why it is blue?" Padhyay shook his head, grimacing with shame. "I don't know."

"It is a symbol of his divinity."

The two men sat in silence as the full Bharath night descended on the plains. So quiet was the night that in the distance they could hear the lap and gurgle of the great River Ganga, and farther off in a village across the broad waters, pi-dogs yelped. Padhyay's eyes became accustomed to the starlight and he found he could start to see some detail in his surroundings. He saw the dim scurrying of a mouse as it hip-hopped across the dusty ground, sniffed at the guru's dish of rice, then thought better of it and hurried away again, its footsteps faint against the bare earth. Something in the dead leaves at the base of the tree rustled and an agonized squeak ripped the darkness.

"Will you eat with me?" the holy man asked. He picked up his battered wooden bowl, full of rice and vegetables, and placed it between them.

"I thank you, guru, but I should refuse. That food was given to you by the villagers. I would not want to deprive you of its sustenance."

47

"You say you are a Brahmin, yet you would prevent me from performing one of my duties – being hospitable?"

"I had not thought of it like that."

"Every day, a Brahmin should perform all six duties. I have taught you a little tonight, I have learned much, I have accepted the alms of the village and now I give you of my wealth. At sunrise tomorrow I will perform the ritual of Sandhyavadanam at the river and offer up a sacrifice of this milk. So come now, eat with me."

Padhyay extended his right hand and took up a small portion of the rice, carrying it carefully to his mouth. He swallowed and waited for the holy man to take some of the food. "You do not eat?"

"I do not need much food and I am loath to carry food with me, yet I would not see it wasted. Eat, young man."

Padhyay ate reluctantly at first, conscious of the gaunt man in the darkness opposite, watching him. As the rice and vegetables stimulated his hunger, he ate most of the food, leaving a little in the bowl for the guru. He licked his fingers and wiped them surreptitiously on his tunic.

The two men sat in silence in the glowing night as the stars wheeled above the pipal tree. After a long time, long after the last fires had died down in the village and even after the dogs fell silent, the holy man spoke once more, repeating his first question.

"What is it you seek?"

"I don't know," Padhyay admitted. My father has died and my mother is looking after their young children. My brothers own our store in Pataliputra but I want

48

nothing to do with it. I want … I want …" His voice trailed off. "I don't know what I want," he whispered.

"Do you seek knowledge?"

"Yes."

"Do you seek to learn the discipline of mind and body?"

"Er … yes."

"Do you seek to teach others?"

"Yes."

"Do you seek the inestimable richness of being one with the creator?"

Padhyay could not speak as the tears welled in his eyes and he drew a racking sob. He nodded instead and stifled his cries in his sleeve.

The holy man said nothing, neither comforting nor complaining, just waiting patiently for the young man's emotion to run its course.

"I am sorry," Padhyay said at last, wiping his nose on his sleeve. "What must I do?"

"What do you want to do?"

"Find god."

"Look about you. God is everywhere."

"That is not quite what I meant," Padhyay said. "How can I know god? How can I get enlightenment?"

The holy man stared at Padhyay, the bright starlight glinting off his eyes, the ash smeared over his head and torso making his body seem ethereal, insubstantial. "What prevents you from contemplating god now? Why do you not seek enlightenment in your everyday life?"

Padhyay frowned. "You think I could?"

"Tell me what you do every day?"

49

"Well, I rise at dawn and pray, and then I greet my mother and my brothers and sisters. I eat, then I go to my father's store – my brothers' now – and work at tallying the goods, buying and selling, while my lazy brothers sit around and gossip, eyeing the women of the town. At sunset I return home, eat, offer up prayers again and sleep. If I have time I try to teach my brothers and sisters."

The holy man nodded. "So when will you contemplate god? When will you seek enlightenment in your busy day?"

"I … I could stop teaching the children, or maybe I could ask my brothers for an hour each day to meditate."

"Yes, you could," said the holy man. "And in a hundred lifetimes you might be one step on the path to enlightenment."

"So what do I do?"

"That is not for me to say. You have your own life, your own karma."

"You will not help me then?" Padhyay sat and stared down at the ground in front of him, tears of frustration starting in his eyes again. "There must be something," he muttered. "What about you? How did you become a sadhu?"

"I died."

"Eh?" Padhyay's head snapped up and he stared at the holy man's ghostly image, the hairs on his forearms lifting. "H … how do you mean?"

"I too had a mother and a father, brothers and sisters. I even had a wife and children of my own. Then one day I realized I could continue living on the slowly turning wheel of life, death and rebirth or I could choose to die?"

50

"How did you die?" Padhyay whispered.

"I renounced everything I had, I gave away my belongings, swore never to touch a woman again. I died to my former life and after a time in the womb, where I was nourished by my guru, I was reborn wonderfully as a sadhu."

"Then that is what I must do?"

The sadhu said nothing.

"Then that is what I must do," Padhyay stated, conviction growing in his voice. "I shall find myself a guru and start on the path to enlightenment."

The sadhu still said nothing. Instead he sat up straight, putting his upturned hands on his thighs, with thumb and forefinger touching. Closing his eyes, he started humming, deep and constant, the sound resonating in his chest.

The stars wheeled and faded, and as the eastern sky paled, the holy man ceased his mantra and opened his eyes. "It is nearly dawn. I must prepare for Sandhyavadanam." Uncurling his feet, he rocked forward and stood up.

Padhyay scrambled to his feet and watched as the sadhu picked up his empty bowl and the half full cup of thin soured milk and started walking toward the river. "How do I find a guru, sadhu?" he called after him.

The holy man did not stop but pointed a bony hand toward the west. "The temple of Shiva at Karnapur."

Padhyay returned home and immediately informed his mother and older brothers that he was leaving for Karnapur. A week of arguments followed, for his brothers did not want to lose a fine worker and did not relish the idea of having to perform his duties themselves.

51

His mother, reluctant to lose one of her offspring so totally, also sought arguments against his leaving but had at last given way to Padhyay's pleas and allowed him to seek the way of enlightenment. Enquiries of the village and town priests revealed that the guru at Karnapur was one of the greatest gurus of the time, Sarada Sivaya. Padhyay, never having traveled further from his village than the next one, quailed at the thought of the long journey over the narrow dusty roads of northern Bharat, with such a famous personage at the other end. Surely he would not accept a storekeeper's son as an acolyte, even if he was a Brahmin. Then he remembered the night with the sadhu under the pipal tree and strengthened his resolve. Packing a small cloth with some food and spare clothes, Padhyay set off on the path of enlightenment. Two months later he arrived, footsore, covered in dust and very hungry, at the temple of Shiva in Jajmau, outside of the city of Karnapur.

The temple of Shiva was an imposing structure of stone and mud brick, set about by tall trees and luxuriant gardens tended by robed monks. The main road from the east passed directly by the massive wall and wide gate, the wooden doors flung wide to allow people to throng inside the temple courtyards and outer galleries. Situated only a few thousand paces from ancient Karnapur, the road was packed with travelers, both to the temple and other parts. Padhyay stopped outside the open gates and looked in at the temple proper, staring at the ornate stone carvings that covered the walls, and at the great seated figure of the god. The jostling crowd put up with him standing in the entrance for a while, amused by the fact that his staring showed him to be a stranger, but in the end they moved him aside and into the shade of the temple wall and a small grove of glossy-leaved fig trees.

Padhyay dropped his bundle beside an old, cracked watering trough in the shade of the dusty grove and dipped his hands into the tepid water. Offering up a prayer of thanks to Shiva and his priests he washed the dust of two months travel from his head and body, disregarding the stares and half-heard comments of passers-by. Slipping on the cleaner of his two tunics, he smoothed down his hair and beard as best he could, picked up his meager belongings and pushed his way gently but firmly through the crowds and into the temple courtyard where he presented himself to one of the priests of Shiva.

"Excuse me," Padhyay said, bowing low with his hands together. "Can you direct me to the ashram of guru Sarada Sivaya?"

"Who?"

"Guru Sarada Sivaya, honored sir. I was told he had an ashram here."

"Then you were told wrong," the priest snapped. "Now unless you have an offering to make, move along. I cannot waste the whole day talking to you." The priest turned and walked away.

Padhyay bowed to the priest's back and went in search of someone more polite. He found him, in the form of an old gardener. The old man, naked but for a stained dhoti, looked up from his slow but painstaking removal of caterpillars from a beautifully blooming shrub. A smile lit up his face and he carefully put the caterpillar he had just removed, into a finely woven wicker basket before bowing and putting his hands together.

"Yes, young sir, I know of the ashram, but you are in the wrong temple."

"Are you sure? I was told the temple of Shiva outside of the city of Karnapur."

"Indeed, young sir, this is a temple of Shiva but there is another temple on the banks of the Ganga." He looked around to see whether anyone else was in earshot. "The other one is holier. You can feel the presence of the god there."

"And the guru? Is he as good as they say?"

The old man shrugged and smiled again, stroking his long gray beard. "I think he has much yet to learn but he enjoys the presence of both young and old."

Padhyay smiled. "Then why do you not work there?"

"There is more gardening work for me here. You will see when you get there, young sir. It is a poorer temple but holier."

"I will leave you to your work then and seek out this temple with its ashram and holy man. I thank you, old man. May the blessings of Shiva be upon thee."

The old man bowed again. "And upon you, young sir." He turned back to his shrub and its caterpillars.

Padhyay turned to go but hesitated. "Why do you pick them off one by one and put them in your basket?" he asked. "Would it not be faster to destroy them?"

The old man nodded. "I believe killing should be avoided."

"Even of caterpillars?"

"Only the gods give life, only they should take it."

"I see," Padhyay said doubtfully. "An interesting concept." He stood looking down at the ground for a few moments, frowning. "Well, I suppose I should be going.

54

Thank you again old man." He turned away and walked off.

The other temple of Shiva by the sacred river Ganga was old. No walls surrounded this small, ruined building consecrated to the Destroyer. Long ago, a banyan tree had sprouted nearby and over the years had grown into a forest. The branches sent down long snake-like roots that touched the rich river soil and anchored themselves, sending up more shoots and providing support for the lengthening branches. Slowly, the growing grove enveloped the temple, broke down the walls and surrounded the holy place in a deep gloom.

Padhyay felt a frisson of fear cascade down his neck and back, raising the hair on his arms as he looked at the deserted ruins, then, as he took a step forward, a warm feeling of security and welcome flowed over him.

"Peace be with you stranger."

Padhyay gave a start and stared into the shadows near one of the tumbled walls. A man sat with his back to the stone, his hands folded in his lap. Lustrous blue-black hair cascaded around his head and his beard covered his chest. Dark eyes twinkled and white teeth showed in smile of greeting.

"Are you guru Sarada Sivaya? I have come a long way to find you."

"We all travel on the journey of life. You have not come far yet." The seated man lapsed back into silence for several minutes before sighing and, unfolding long thin legs, standing up. "I am Vasu, a seeker at the feet of Sarada Sivaya. Come with me and I will provide you with food and drink."

55

Padhyay bowed and clapped his hands together softly. "Please do not trouble yourself, honored sir. I came only to see your master."

"He will not be here until nightfall," Vasu said. "But I would be failing in my duty if I did not offer you the hospitality of the ashram."

"In that case, I accept with thanks." Padhyay bowed again.

After a frugal meal of rice and fresh water from a small well in the temple courtyard, Vasu led Padhyay into the cool recesses of the temple and sat him down in a small side room where the roots of the great tree had split the roof allowing a thin shaft of filtered sunlight to illuminate the cracked floor tiles.

"Please wait here," Vasu said. "Compose your mind and contemplate the words you will use with the master. I will return for you when he is ready to see you."

"A moment before you go, honored sir. I have seen no-one but you since I arrived. How many people are in this ashram?"

"Six. Seven if the master accepts you, but three are on a pilgrimage to Kailasa." Vasu bowed and left the room.

Padhyay remained seated for a few minutes before he got up and walked around the room, examining the inscriptions on the walls, running his fingers over a stain on one wall where the rain had leached the dead leaves caught in the roof and spilled the brown stain downward. He sat down again and tried to concentrate on a mark on the far wall but was distracted by a faint humming from a tangle of roots in one corner. Investigating, he found a small wasp nest. He watched it for a while, and poked at it with a stick to see what would happen. The wasps erupted into the air angrily and though Padhyay retreated quickly, he was stung on the knuckle of his right hand. Sucking the red pimple, he sat down again and attempted to concentrate. The pain in his hand nagged at him and he found his attention wandering. The pain lessened after a little and he closed his eyes, leaning back against the cool stone.

He awoke in the fading heat of late afternoon to find that the light had almost fled the room. Looking up at the gaping roof he caught a glimpse of sky deepening to dusk and he heard the thin piping cries of bats as they flittered and danced in the upper air. A movement in the doorway swung Padhyay around quickly and his eyes opened wide in surprise as the old gardener he had seen at the other temple, walked in.

Padhyay greeted the old man with a smile and namaste, bringing his hands together in front of his heart. "What are you doing here? I thought there was no work at this temple."

"Namaste, young man. Gardening is not my only task."

"Oh, you do other things? I think the guru here could use you to clean up a bit."

"The Lord Shiva will look after his own," the old man said. "Did you spend the afternoon in meditation, young sir? Or have you instead wandered around disturbing the wasps and sleeping?"

"Of course I … how do you know these things? Are you a magician or … are you guru Sivaya?"

"I can see your footprints in the dust on the floor, a wasp sting on the knuckle of your right hand and I could hear your snores throughout the temple courtyard. And yes, I am Sarada Sivaya."

Padhyay scrambled to his feet then dropped onto his knees in front of the old man. "Forgive me, guru. I did not know it was you."

Sivaya smiled. "How could you? Sit, sit. I am uncomfortable when men kneel to me; I am really only a gardener who has been blessed by the god."

Padhyay sat and tried to marshal his thoughts, unsure now as to how he should proceed. "I want ... I er, have come to ... that is, I desire to ... to become enlightened."

"And you think that I can enlighten you?"

"Yes, master."

Sivaya shook his head sadly. "Enlightenment comes from within, my son. No man can teach it or bestow it on another."

"Then can you show me the path that I might set my foot on it?"

"Good, good." Sivaya nodded. "A guru can teach and he can show, but it is by your own efforts that you progress. Are you prepared to spend your life in contemplation of the infinite?"

"It will take that long?"

"Most seekers never attain that goal, young man, not in this life or the next or the hundred after that. Only those who turn their whole being toward the infinite can hope to achieve nothingness. Are you prepared to die?"

Padhyay gulped. "Die? I ... I know all men must die, master, but I had hoped to ... to ..." His voice trailed off as he remembered the sadhu under the pipal tree outside far-off Pataliputra. "To die in what sense, master?"

"Good, you can think. If you study with me you will be dead to your previous life. You will be born anew. You will own nothing, not even your name. You will refrain from any contaminating practice, anything that concentrates your mind on this world."

"Wh ... what if I fail?"

"No man fails, my son. It is merely a matter of 'when' rather than 'if'. If you do not succeed in this lifetime then your study will stand you in good stead for the next."

"Then will you take me as a student, Master Sivaya?"

"What is your name?"

"Bhatta Padhyay."

Sivaya shook his head. "You are not a teacher yet so you cannot hold this name. Rather, you are a child, so 'Balaka' you will be called."

So started Balaka's new life, one in which he grew old.

Lessons were like nothing Balaka had ever imagined. Used to the regime within village schools he thought he would be in classes with other young men, reciting facts or listening to learned discourses by the guru. Instead, he, sometimes with Vasu and the other seeker, Ankur the sapling, would accompany the guru on his daily excursions from the ruined temple. Balaka found himself plucking caterpillars from shrubs or sweeping the leaves from paths or clearing the dung from the stables and elephant lines of the various small rulers in the vicinity of Karnapur.

"Master," Balaka would ask, "Why is it we carry dung for this prince when he has many men to do his bidding?"

"Pity the rich man, Balaka. He has wealth and scores of men and women to answer his every need. How can he ever be persuaded to leave this world behind and seek the infinite?"

"But why do we work for him? Do we not help him remain tied to this world?"

"No-one can make that decision for him. If he desires the infinite, he will seek it. We who do seek it learn humility by toiling for others without recompense."

On other occasions, Balaka, Ankur and Vasu sat at the feet of their guru while he expounded on some topic, but rarely in the same place twice. There was no classroom. Instead, they sat in the leafy shade of the banyan or by the river side. Sometimes they went into the city and sat in the marketplace, the noise and stink and bustle of the teeming population a counterpoint to the quiet, unhurried pace of the holy man. A favorite place was in the lea of the old temple walls where the cobra hid in the crevices, waiting until dusk to come out and lap the milk that the solitary priest left out. The subjects talked about were numerous, but they all turned back to Shiva as their tutelary deity and to the infinite that they sought.

Seasons passed and years followed obediently and Balaka's hair turned gray and his beard hung low on his chest. Students came to join the temple's small ashram, others left. Vasu went his own way into the world and presently word came back that he had formed his own ashram. Balaka found himself greeting and interviewing new seekers. He sat with his back to the crumbling walls and watched them as they walked down the dusty road from the city toward the cool shade of the spreading banyan. He fed them and showed them into the room with the split roof and the wasps' nest, leaving them to decide their own futures.

One day Sivaya led Balaka to an old soot-stained ivory carving of four-armed Shiva in the inner recesses of the ruined temple. The image of the god was seated, two hands in his cross-legged lap, and two raised. The raised hands clutched a trident and a drum.

"Observe the god Shiva, the Pure One. He is regarded as Ishvara or one of the aspects of Trimurti. Who is Trimurti, Balaka?"

"The three-fold god, master. Brahma the creator, Vishnu the preserver, and Shiva the destroyer."

"Who is greatest of these?"

Balaka looked troubled. "None is greater, master. They are all aspects of one god, equally powerful."

"Not so. Shiva is most powerful, though many would dispute this. We who worship Shiva as paramount are called Shaivist. In the beginning Shiva produced Vishnu, who in turn produced Brahma, and thus the universe came into being. All other gods came later and are subordinate to the Pure One. He performs five functions, which together encompass all aspects of our universe and our lives – creation, preservation and destruction you know about. To these we add release from evil, and blessing. Quick, Balaka, name an evil."

"The Rakshasa, master. The demons of air, water and forest."

"And a blessing? Quickly."

"Namaste."

"Very good, Balaka. When is the namaste blessing used?"

Balaka thought a while. "One uses it regularly but does not stop to consider its origins and meaning. When greeting or saying farewell, it is proper to say namaste, to put one's hands together in the mudra and to bow. The namaste is a recognition that the divine dwells in all of us so when we greet or farewell, we do so as if to ourselves. The mudra combines the two hands which represent the worldly self and the spiritual self. By this gesture I show my connection to the person I meet."

"And the bow? What does that symbolize?"

Balaka smiled. "No symbolism, master, save that of love and respect."

Guru Sivaya nodded, allowing himself a small smile. "You have been paying attention, Balaka. Now attend to this statue of Shiva that I may explain his form."

Sivaya bowed low to the image before picking it up and bringing it to where Balaka sat. Placing it on the cracked stone floor between them, he pointed at the head. "The bindi or third eye. For this Shiva is known as the Lord with Three Eyes or Trinetrishwara. It is a symbol of his wisdom."

"The priests say that a holy person has a third eye, master. Is this a literal one or symbolic?"

"Have you seen a holy man with more than two eyes, Balaka?"

"I have not seen any holy men, master, save the old man in my village – and you."

Sivaya smiled. "And do I have a third eye?"

Balaka examined his guru carefully then bowed his head in prayer. "You are renowned for your wisdom, master. In this respect you possess the eye of wisdom."

"Observe his matted hair. This tells us he is Vayu or Lord of the Wind, the breath that fills the lungs of every living thing. Here is an exercise for you, Balaka. When you are next sitting quietly, concentrate on your breathing and consider that Shiva pervades your very being. As you breathe in, think 'Vayu'; as you breathe out, whisper the name of 'Pashupatinath'."

"And the crescent moon in his hair?" Balaka pointed.

"Wait, there is more. The Ganga, the holiest river of Bharath, flows from the matted hair of Shiva, bringing purifying water to men. The crescent moon is near the third eye of wisdom and represents Soma, the drink of the gods. Through it, Shiva possesses the twin powers of procreation and destruction. See how he wears the tiger skin? It symbolizes his victory over force. He also sits on tiger skin. Here it represents lust and he has conquered it. Sometimes, Shiva is represented with elephant skin and the hide of a deer. Can you tell me why, Balaka?"

"No master, unless the thick elephant hide is armor against his foes."

"Who could possibly battle Shiva?" Sivaya laughed. "No, think of why kings own elephants."

Balaka frowned. "To show their wealth and importance?"

"Excellent. They are a symbol of pride, and by wearing it, Shiva shows he has conquered pride."

"And the deer skin?"

"Deer are skittish, always nervously moving. So too is the mind of untrained. Shiva wears deer skin to show his perfect mind control."

"What of the trident in his hand, master?"

63

"The trident is threefold and the interpretation is also threefold. Creation, sustenance and destruction are in his hand, controlled by him. So too, the trident is an instrument to punish the evil doer on the three planes of existence ..."

"The spiritual, the physical and the subtle," Balaka murmured.

"And it may be that the trident is past, present and future. Shiva holds eternity in his hand."

"And the drum?"

Sivaya smiled and got to his feet. He placed the statue back in its niche and bowed solemnly to it before rejoining his pupil on the stone floor. "The drum of Shiva is called Damru. When he sounded it, the note it gave off was 'Aum' – have you heard that before, Balaka?"

"Yes, master," Balaka said in surprise. "It is what the priests chant and holy men murmur beneath their breath. It is a holy mantra. "

"Many priests chant it without knowing its true power. It is the primordial sound, the first word, and the most ancient of the mantras. Aum is Brahman." Sivaya traced the form of the syllable in the dust on the floor. "Three curves that represent the waking state, deep sleep and dreaming; the semicircle is Maya, the illusion which grips most of mankind, the illusion that all this we see around us is reality. Lastly, the dot within the semicircle is the Absolute, toward which all men should strive. The Absolute is not enclosed by Maya but is infinite. Learn how to say the divine syllable, Balaka, learn to understand its parts and learn how it controls you. Say it with me now – Aum."

"Aum."

"Do not just pronounce it, feel it, make it resonate within your chest."

"Aum."

"Better. Go now to the grove, Balaka. Study this mantra tonight. Learn how to say it with meaning. I will examine you at dawn tomorrow."

Balaka rose and bowed, with mudra and namaste, before leaving his guru in the temple. He walked into the banyan grove in the afternoon heat and sat down against a great knotted trunk in the padmasanam position, composing his mind. He intoned the mantra, over and over, feeling its meaning, savoring the taste of each part, seeing in his mind's eye how each part joined with the others, encompassing him and leading him toward the infinite. The lessons of the past months aided him and as the hours passed, his concentration grew. Balaka did not notice the light fading for he dwelt on the curve of deep sleep; he did not notice the biting mosquitoes as they landed on face and arms for they were within the curve of dreams. Phantasms haunted him; visions conjured up to distract him. Balaka consigned these dreams to the curve of waking and they fled, gibbering. With the dawn, Maya assailed him in full force but the holy word thrummed within him, raising his consciousness until the trees shimmered around him, becoming as wisps of vapor and for an instant, Balaka glimpsed the Absolute.

He gave a cry of joy and the world returned crashing around him. His heart faltered and his head spun and he staggered to his feet and stumbled out of the grove.

Sivaya saw Balaka lurch from the trees and stand swaying in the open courtyard, his face upturned toward the bright morning sun. Overwhelming joy chased deadly

65

sorrow over his face as tears cascaded over his gaunt cheeks, staining his gray beard dark once more. A pale nimbus flickered around his pupil's head.

"You have seen the Oneness," Sivaya stated. "Do not sorrow, Balaka. You will see it again. This is but the first step on the path to true enlightenment."

"I saw it, master. For an instant I saw the infinite."

"Describe it."

"It is ... it is ..." Balaka collapsed to the ground, shaking with sorrow. "I cannot describe it. I see it before me in my mind's eye yet I do not have the words to tell you." He pulled at his hair with both hands as if trying to extract his vision from inside his head. "I saw ..."He stopped and a horrified look came over him. "I cannot remember," he wailed. "I saw it so clearly a moment ago yet the memory flees from me like a dream."

"Rather it is reality that flees from you now that you are immersed once more in Maya, the world of illusion." Sivaya knelt beside the sobbing man and put his hand on Balaka's gray locks. "You are ready for the next step, my son. Do not despair, you will see reality again."

Sivaya took Balaka apart from the other students and for days instructed him in the form of mantras and their meaning.

"When Brahma created the universe he spoke a word – Aum – and it came into being. We do not have the power or the will or the inner goodness to create a universe by using this mantra, but we can sometimes glimpse the truth of the creation behind the illusion that is the world. Aum is the simplest yet the most powerful of the mantras for through it we taste the divine being that is Brahman. Other gods give power too, and the repetition

66

of their names will deliver insights into the true reality. The Maha mantra, or Great Mantra, uses the names of Hare, Krishna and Rama to form a powerful magical mantra if intoned correctly. Pronounced incorrectly, the words and sounds are meaningless and ineffective." Sivaya struck his breast lightly with his right hand and declaimed in a measured monotone, "Ha-re Krishna Ha-re Krishna Krishna Krishna Ha-re Ha-re Ha-re Rama Ha-re Rama Rama Rama Ha-re Ha-re. These sixteen names will remove the ill effects of Kali. Use them judiciously."

Balaka listened intently, rehearsed the sounds in his mind and repeated them back several times until Sivaya declared himself satisfied.

"You have heard me speak of the mantras to counter demons. They are many and varied and I will not repeat them here, but they are moderately efficacious against demons. Few can stand against them if you are pure of mind. Commit them to your mind and heart."

Taking a string of beads from around his neck Sivaya passed it to Balaka. "Use this to perform Japa, the repetition of the mantra in cycles of auspicious numbers. This mala or necklace has one hundred and eight beads and the meru or head bead. Take it and use it, one bead for every repetition of the mantra, Balaka."

"How many mantras are there, master?"

"An infinite number. It is enough just to take the name of a god and link it to the universal 'Aum' – thus – Aum namah Shivaya – Aum I bow to Lord Shiva. The Gayatri mantra you have heard me intone before. It invokes universal Brahman as the source of all light and knowledge."

"Which one is best?"

"There is no such thing as 'best', Balaka. Practice as many as you can, become familiar with them, recite them with meaning and a strong desire for truth. Invoke the gods by the 'Aum namah', devise your own mantras, decide for yourself which one you will make your own."

Balaka smiled ruefully. "That will take a long time."

"There is a hill a day's journey to the north and two rocks that lean together to form a shelter. Go there, Balaka, and find your word of power. Do not return until you find it."

Balaka got up immediately and bowed to his master, then, without a backward glance, set off for the hill though he had never been there nor knew the way. He slept in the open that night and found the hill and the leaning rocks at noon the next day. Settling himself down into Padmasanam, he adjusted his breathing and settled his vision into a contemplation of the distant silver ribbon of the Ganga River.

For eleven days he fought against Mara, the illusion of the world, feeling hunger and thirst, the discomfort of the ground, the scorching heat of day and the chill of night, the biting flies and mosquitoes, the wild animals and the intrusive curiosity of humans. Eleven days, in which he fought back, immersing himself in illusion to fight illusion. On the twelfth day he decided to give up and return to his master at the ruined temple. His head pounded, his senses reeled and his body ached. A thought intruded, creeping on insect legs across his parched mind.

I cannot return. I must succeed here or die. Balaka closed his eyes and turned his attention inward, ignoring the screaming demands of his body. He imagined the form of Aum and recited it silently, over and over, his mouth and throat too dry and cracked to utter the sacred syllable.

The sun went down and the stars came out, far over the plains of Bharath, yet Balaka remained awake and alert, repeating his mantras again and again. Presently, he opened his eyes again and rejoiced in the creation. The east paled and burst into glory, the sun arcing overhead visibly. Night came again, and day and his body moved automatically to take sustenance from the small bowl of rice and flask of water that appeared beside him. He saw no-one, but footprints formed in the dusty ground and he knew in some distant part of his mind that a nearby village had taken over the care of a new holy man. The cycle of days moved faster, sun burning him, dust enveloping him and rain drenching him, the cold of winter's nights chilling him deep in his bones. Balaka was aware of the passing seasons yet they were a part of a reality that was becoming less important, less real.

Fifteen years later, as one of many days drew to a close, a sound split the still air and Balaka's eyes flickered and focused. He looked about him with all the curiosity of a new-born kitten, but none of the fear. Around him, the ground was cleared; the weeds and grass pulled and tidied, and a few woven garlands of flowers lay in the dust in front of him. Reaching out, he touched a red blossom lightly with the tip of a finger, marveling at its texture, color and scent. A tiny aphid sat at the base of one petal and Balaka made the mudra toward it, a gentle smile cracking his gaunt and parched face.

I heard a sound, he thought. *What was it that drew me back from the infinite?*

The sound came again as if in answer to his thought, a shocking sound, full of terror and pain. "Sadhuuu!"

At the base of the hill, near where the long grass merged into the first sprinkling of trees that heralded open woodland, a tiger strode along a narrow game path. Locked in its open jaws hung the body of a woman, her torn sari dragging in the dirt. With the last of her strength she beat at the tiger's head with one hand and her head turned up toward the hill with a final quivering shriek for help. "Sadhuuu!"

Without conscious decision or knowing he moved, Balaka found himself running swiftly down the hill and over the clumps of grass and small thorn bushes, on a course to intercept the predator. His dhoti slipped and fell from his skeletal hips but he ignored it, racing on naked. Reaching the game trail, he stopped and faced the approaching tiger.

The beast did not see the man standing on the trail until it was almost on him. It jumped back a pace and flattened its ears, its lips curling back from white teeth. A whine of surprise rapidly escalated into a snarl of anger and the tiger dropped its victim, settling back on its haunches, gathering its powerful muscles.

Balaka snatched a mantra out of the air. "Aum namah Pashupati – Aum, I bow to the Lord of Beasts." He took a step forward, repeating the mantra, then another, and again. The tiger backed slowly, spitting with rage before suddenly turning and bounding off into the trees, leaving Balaka standing over the bloody body of a young woman.

He knelt and ran his hands and eyes over the almost naked body of the young woman, adjusting the folds of

70

the torn sari to cover her. She breathed still and a pulse fluttered in her neck but the wounds to her upper body revealed white strips of bone showing through the meager meat of her chest. The blood covering her breasts bubbled brightly as air hissed from ripped lungs.

"Aum namah Dhanvantari." Balaka bowed his head and concentrated his will on the god of healing, invoking his presence and his power. Closing his eyes, he felt the power flowing through him, surging up from the ground and from the surrounding air, into him and gushing out through his hands. He touched the woman's head and felt her shudder. His hands moved, smoothing and running lightly over her throat and chest. Minutes passed and Balaka's hands fell to his sides though he remained bowed over the woman.

"Sadhu?"

Balaka opened his eyes, feeling the power leave him like water from a burst pot. The woman stared up at him, her eyes fearful and her limbs trembling as she held her ripped clothing together. "Sadhu, the tiger, it ..."

"It has gone, and the gods have been kind to you."

The woman felt her body, her throat and her head gingerly at first, then more confidently. "I ... I felt the beast's teeth and claws. I saw the blood and felt it pierce me ... yet I am unharmed. How can this be, sadhu?"

"Give thanks to Dhanvantari."

"You invoked him, sadhu?"

"Yes, I felt this version of reality was better than the other one, though neither are real, merely illusions that we conjure up to strengthen our ignorance." Balaka smiled, seeing the woman did not understand him. He rose to his feet and helped the woman up.

71

She paid no attention to his nakedness, as was proper, for this man was obviously a great sadhu, a holy man, and had no need of clothes. She bowed and offered a mudra before pointing off down the game trail.

"My family lives down here. Will you bless our village by your presence, holy one?"

"I will accompany you to be sure that no further ill befalls you, child, but my presence is required elsewhere."

The path divided soon after and down one, Balaka could see huts and children playing, could smell the wood smoke, and hear the sizzle of chapattis on the cooking stones. The young woman knelt at his feet and Balaka blessed her, then watched as she ran lightly down the path, clutching her torn sari around her.

Balaka spent that night in contemplation in a small grove of trees, needing neither food nor sleep which was false desire fostered by Mara. The following morning he reached the ruined temple and the banyan tree.

A new seeker kept vigil by the wall, whiling away the hours in self-study, and holding himself in readiness to help any traveler whose destination was the temple. The man scrambled to his feet and bowed low before the ancient, naked man who walked slowly toward him.

"Namaste, holy one. May I offer you food or shelter?"

Balaka blessed him. "Thank you, I have need of neither, but I would talk with Guru Sivaya."

A worried look came over the man's face. "Alas, holy one, the master prepares to move into the darkness ..."

"So he may once more return to the light."

72

"Indeed, holy one, but I regret that he can see no-one."

"Take me to him."

"Holy one, I cannot."

"Take me to him."

The man looked into Balaka's eyes and bowed. He led the way past the ruined temple where Balaka saw the room with the cracked roof had at last succumbed to the burgeoning banyan and had collapsed into rubble. At the rear of the temple was a small lean-to where a youth sat watching a motionless man on a straw pallet. The youth got up and bowed as the two men approached.

"Leave us, Riki," the man said, waiting as the youth bowed again and walked off.

Balaka sat cross-legged on the ground beside his guru's head and studied the ravaged features intently. Nearly forty years had passed since Balaka, Padhyay then, had arrived at the ruined temple on the banks of the Ganga. Sivaya was old then but now he looked ancient, the flesh melted from his bones and his skin gray and tight. Balaka closed his eyes and saw the threads of life pulled taut and thin, ready to snap.

"Master," he whispered. "I have returned."

"Holy one, are you a healer?" the man asked. "Can you save him?"

"Have you learned nothing in your time here?" Balaka rebuked. "Guru Sarada Sivaya stands upon the brink of waking from his dreams to reality. Would you have me cast him back into illusion?" He leaned forward over his master again. "I have returned."

The ancient man's eyelids flickered and opened. The dry lips formed syllables though the words themselves

73

were no more than vague movements of air that reached no further than Balaka's ears. "I ... waited ... knew ... come." Sivaya's eyes moved and his lips smiled faintly at the sight of the gaunt, naked man sitting beside him, a faint but definite pearly corona surrounding the long matted hair that cascaded from his head. "You ... found ... Moksha? Transcendence?"

Balaka smiled and made a mudra with his hands.

Sivaya caught his breath and struggled weakly for a few moments before relaxing once more, his breath coming in rattling gasps. "T ... take ... my robe." His hand scrabbled at the thin yellow fabric of the robe that draped his body. "You ... are Balaka ... the child ... no longer."

Sivaya's breath died away and the man looked on anxiously. "Is the master dead?"

"No." Balaka shook his head. "One more thing remains."

Minutes passed and Sivaya drew a shuddering breath. He opened his eyes and raised one hand to touch Balaka. Drawing on his remaining strength, he said in a thin but clear voice, "You are a child no longer, but strong. No longer Balaka, but Bala." The light left his eyes and the breath his lungs.

Bala folded his master's arms and closed his dead eyes. Together with the young man, whose name was Nara, he ritually washed and anointed the body. As dusk approached he carried his master to the pyre by the banks of the sacred river and laid him on it, unwinding the long yellow robe and wrapping it around himself. The few students remaining in the ashram chanted the prayers to Yama, invoking his aid.

74

Nara kindled twists of kusha grass and Bala touched them to the dry tinder, stepping back as the flames roared upward, consuming the body. When the fire burned low and little remained of the calcined and blackened bones, Bala took a stout bamboo pole and cracked the skull, ceremonially releasing the spirit from the entrapment of the body. The ashes were cast into the sacred river Ganga and the small group of men and boys turned and left the funeral site, never looking back.

Bala did not stop with the others in the ruined temple that night, but set out on the road, the ashes of his master still caking his hands and robe.

"Will you not stay and lead us, holy one?" Nara asked. Then, as Bala kept walking, he called out, "Where will you go?"

Bala walked a few more paces then stopped in the middle of the dirt road. Without turning, he answered, "Kailasa."

Chapter Four

The mountain and lakes gained a fearsome reputation as the years passed. I thought myself moderate in my harvesting of men but as the numbers of hermits living in the warren of caves in the lower slopes of Kailasa became decimated, would-be holy men thought twice before braving its black rocks. Further down, on the grass and sand plains around the lakes, men died too, but here the blame was laid for the most part on the depredations of the snow leopards. I took on the form of other beasts too, whatever a man most feared, for terror lent a rich piquancy to the taste of a dying mind. Eventually, the pall of death that surrounded the mountain was such that few people ventured near.

Being sacred to Shiva, the pilgrims were still drawn to the vicinity of Kailasa, but rather than braving the terrors of the mountain, they started on a long and arduous circuit of the mountain, passing completely around it within the space of three or four days. No longer did a pilgrim have to actually touch the mountain, the sight of it from every angle proved sufficient to accomplish their religious duty. After a time, I grew hungry and came down the mountain to join the pilgrims and select my victims.

You may ask why, as I am so powerful and have this need to feed on human death, I do not just ravage the countryside, killing as often as I please, and openly. The reason is simple; I do not wish to attract undue attention. I was still, after these many years, conscious of the gods Krishna and Agni. I believed, rightly or wrongly, that if they or other deities knew of my presence, I would be

76

hunted down mercilessly. So I was as circumspect as my nature and my appetite allowed.

I joined the pilgrims easily enough, being able to tailor my appearance so as not to cause alarm. Sitting cross-legged, facing Kailasa as if deep in my devotions, I waited beside the rough path that wound through the lonely terrain for travelers, as patient as any spider. Most often, pilgrims journeyed in groups, having come from a distant village or town together, and these I left alone. Occasionally, and I needed no more than one or two a month to eat well, a man came alone. Seeing me, in my guise as a holy man, they would as often as not come and sit beside me, hoping that some of my seeming holiness would rub off on them.

"Namaste, sadhu," they would say. "May Lord Shiva bless you."

"Thank you, traveler. I feel that he has. And you? Have you found what you seek?"

"Not yet, sadhu, but I mean to journey right around Kailasa and wash myself in the sacred lake."

I would extend my hand in a benediction, always accepted gratefully. "Why do you travel alone, my son? Do you not fear this wild country?" As I asked my questions, I would brush the surface of his mind, finding that which he feared most – bandits, snakes, wolves or tigers. Sometimes the fear would be 'demons' as the reputation of this lonely mountain has suffered since I took up residence – so much so that they have named the other lake that lies at the southern foot of Kailasa, Rakshas Tal. When a man fears demons I laugh and manifest as a tiger-headed man or a ravening monster with tusks or whatever their imagination comes up with.

77

Whatever a man's secret fear, whether demon or man or beast, he found it in me, and died in terror. I would drag his corpse off the trail and rend his body, seeking the last vestiges of life that scurried and hid in the cooling body. Men believe that when the heart stops and the lungs cease their panting, that the brain expires and all awareness flees. That is not so. I have found that life remains in a body for many minutes, hiding within the viscera or cowering in the chest cavity. It is my delight to search for the last vestiges, savoring each delectable morsel, appreciating each quivering memory before the inner spirit vanishes. Where it goes when it leaves the body that housed it, I have no idea. What is that to me?

I leave the fragments of the body where it lies for the scavenger beasts of the high plateau and the birds of the air and move on, further round the path that encompasses Kailasa, there to wait for my next victim.

I cannot remember how many times I encircled the holy mountain, nor how many men met their end on my long journey but gradually I began to get hints of a new holy man in residence on the black crags. I took the time to examine my next meal more carefully and he told me with a sense of breathless wonder, before the screaming began, of a gaunt holy man by the name of Bala who now lived on Kailasa, higher up on the flanks of the mountain than any before him.

"He will need a name like 'strong' to live there," I said. "It is summer now but what will he do when the snows arrive and nobody can bring him food?" I accentuated my comparison by drawing my woolen cloak about me as if to ward of the chilling wind that blew over the high passes.

78

"It is said he is very holy and does not suffer from the cold or hunger."

"Most holy men I have met are neither holy, nor do they suffer, having gullible people to bring them warm cloaks and food."

The man frowned at my impious words. "Go and see for yourself if you doubt his holiness."

"Perhaps I will," I said. "After I have eaten."

Later, as I sat under a silver moon, amusing myself by throwing small pieces of meat to a family of silver foxes, I thought of his words again and resolved to confront this holy man, this Bala the Strong, and reveal to him just how useless was his faith. I dissolved my body back into smoke and dust and, conjuring up a vision of the high crags of Kailasa, sped across the intervening miles. He would not be too difficult to find as, being flame myself, I can easily detect the dimly flickering pulse that is man's life.

This Bala stood out like a watch beacon on a hilltop, the fire of his being blazing like a miniature sun as he sat in the entrance to a small cave, close to the one I used to inhabit, overlooking the two lakes Mansarovar and Rakshas Tal. I approached him at night, donning the form of a fellow holy man, exact in every detail down to the threadbare yellow robe and wooden begging bowl. I left my feet bare and actually unformed as I did not wish to create a sound, even the slight crunch of a footfall on firm-packed snow.

Bala sat unmoving, his hands upturned on his thighs and his eyes open and unblinking stared over the snow-clad heights down to where the distant star fields of pilgrim fires burned on the shores of Mansarovar. I sat down on the snow near to him but to one side, out of his direct-line vision and awaited his attention. The moon rose, scudded swiftly across the sky and faded as dawn unfolded over the high peaks of Himalaya. An icy wind picked up and flapped the end of his robe, though seated within the cave mouth he must have been somewhat protected from its bone-chilling effects. The yellow robe he wore, though stained, appeared of good quality and was undoubtedly well-woven. I smiled to myself, being careful not to let my sense of triumph show on my face. He too, like the other hermits of Kailasa, resorted to trickery to appear holy. The robe flapped again and intelligence returned to his staring, vacant eyes. He blinked and turned his head in my direction.

"Namaste." His quick, intelligent eyes passed quickly over and seemingly through me. I checked my disguise but it was flawless. "I have little to offer," Bala went on, but what I have is yours."

I greeted him in turn, bowing. "I ask only that I may sit here for a time, for I have heard much of your holiness."

"Exaggerations, I am sure. I am but a seeker after enlightenment. I have been a child most of my life."

He used the word 'balaka' to describe himself and I frowned, for he was an old man. I said as much.

"I speak not of years but of a state of mind. For most of my life I was as a child, believing what I saw around me to be reality. I now know it to be but a dream – Mara, the illusion of the World."

I nodded sagely, as if I understood what he was saying. "Why did you come here?"

Bala smiled faintly. "I am still a child in many ways. I find myself still locked within this illusion. Caught as I am, I cannot fully realize that one place is like any other, for truly I know there is no such thing as 'place'. However, until I achieve enlightenment I will frequent the holy places. My master was a follower of Lord Shiva and Kailasa is his abode."

"And have you found this place to be holy?"

Bala looked at me with a tiny frown creasing his forehead, the response making the three parallel lines of ash which marked his faith bend and twist. "Can you not feel the presence of the god?"

I met his gaze firmly, resisting the urge to look up at the mist-shrouded peak. "People talk of demons on these slopes."

The sadhu looked at me for a few moments longer before turning back to stare out over the two lakes lit by the morning sun. "People talk about many things – including demons."

I opened my mouth to reply then caught the double meaning of his words. Had he seen through my disguise? But how could he, for he was a man, not a god? I smiled and decided to push him further. "Are you not afraid of meeting a demon on these slopes?"

"Why should I be afraid?"

"Demons have a fearful reputation." I went on to describe some of the more dreadful things that had been done – that I had done – to the victims, all the while reaching out to probe the surface of his mind. I wanted to play on his greatest fear before I revealed my nature. To my amazement, I felt only a hard, adamantine texture.

"The nature of a demon intrigues me," Bala said. "They, along with a myriad of other spirit creatures were formed by Brahma when he created the world and man. The gods are good by nature, as is proper. Man displays both good and evil. He is born good, for how can a child know anything of evil, yet he often takes the lower course to self-degradation. An asura or a Rakshasa is commonly thought of as wholly evil, yet how can that be? They were created by Brahma for a purpose, as is all his creation, yet unlike man, a Rakshasa has no choice. It is his nature to prey on men."

Bala paused and adjusted the folds of his stained yellow robe. "The tiger was created to prey on the animals of the forest. Some would call him evil, yet can any animal, being without choice, obeying the dictates of its heart set in it by the creator, be truly evil? An animal can be true only to its god-given nature. In the same way, a demon was created to prey on man. Can his actions be considered evil? A Rakshasa has no choice; he must act as he does."

His words disturbed me. I preyed on men because I chose to, didn't I? What right had he to deny me a choice?

The sadhu continued, searing me with his words. "Men, having choice, can aspire to goodness. They can set their minds and hearts on the path that leads to truth and justice; and ultimately, to enlightenment. An animal lacks choice. We are told that through the operation of karmic laws the spirit of a man may reside in a beast for a time but this is not to allow the man in beast an opportunity to correct his evil deeds but to allow him time to reflect on past actions. When he then is born as man again, he can advance spiritually. A demon, like the

82

beast, has no choice. He is neither born nor dies. Not dying, he cannot be reborn. Karma does not apply to a demon and so his actions, dreadful though they may appear, are karmically neutral – neither good nor evil. A Rakshasa can only do as he is meant to, he has no choice." Bala looked at me again, that enigmatic smile playing around his gaunt face. "Do you not find that to be the case, stranger?"

"I? How would I know? You are the holy man."

"Then why do you appear before me dressed in the yellow robe of a sadhu? Did you not mean to deceive me?"

"You know who I am?"

"I know what you are."

I smiled and my outline shimmered as my hunger grew. "It does not frighten you that death has come for you?"

"You are not death, though death may come at your hands, Rakshasa. Why should I fear you? If my body dies I will be born again into this dream."

"What of pain then?" My mouth opened in a sharp-toothed grin, larger than a man's, and horns sprouted from my forehead. "I can make your death extremely unpleasant."

Bala smiled but said nothing. I was non-plussed. Every man I had ever met, hermits included, would be in terror by now, their thoughts delicious and feeding my appetite. This one though, regarded me with cool interest, dispassionately, as if I were a strange animal or plant rather than a horror.

I shrugged and morphed, appearing as a ravening beast. "Well, it does not matter, though I enjoy the flavor of fear. I will still feed on your thoughts, holy man." I started toward him.

"I am not without defense, Rakshasa."

I stopped. "Against me? I think not."

"Then why do you stop?"

I thought about it, flexing my talons. "Why indeed?" I resumed my advance.

Bala gestured with his right hand and muttered under his breath. I felt a cool wall of crystal slide between us and I could go no further.

"What is that you do, holy man?"

"A gesture dismissing the impure and a mantra upholding righteousness. I have found it to be efficacious in the past."

I applied my mind to the invisible wall and found that it was not as impervious as I first thought. My flame could penetrate it, but not my assumed body. I dissolved my fearsome appearance and an instant later reformed it inside the invisible wall. "Your efforts come to nothing, holy man," I laughed.

"I would prefer not to fight actively against you, Rakshasa, but I will if you force me to."

"If you could defeat me, you would have done so already. Your crystal wall is all you have and I have overcome that. Your flesh is mine, Bala the holy man." I had been creeping forward as I spoke and as I finished, I leapt, jaws agape and talons bared.

Bala gestured and I slowed as if the air about me thickened into honey. A deep, repetitive hum rose from his chest and throat, forming into syllables I did not recognize and the first cold threads of fear crept through me. The intensity of the chant increased and I was thrown back, even as my illusory body shivered and disintegrated. The force flung me out over the snow-spattered slopes and down the mountain, the chanting of the mantra making the very flame of me vibrate.

The holy man's voice pursued me as I tumbled through the thin air. "You are banished, Rakshasa. Be gone from Kailasa, Lord Shiva's holy mountain. Never again shall you defile its sacred slopes."

I caught myself and hovered, an invisible flame in the morning sky above Lake Mansarovar. Even at this distance I could feel the thrum of the mantra and knew that Bala could hear me. "I shall return, holy man. Even you cannot live forever."

"Go Rakshasa." Bala's voice held overtones of kindness. "My mantra can kill you but I refrain because you do not have a choice in your way of life. But do not return. I will teach the mantra to my disciples and Kailasa will be free of your kind down the ages."

I fled then, southwest again through the crisp clean air, until I found myself above the softly-clothed mountains around that snow-covered peak I had rested on many years before. Nanda Devi stood clean and pristine; the rivers ran swift and crystal clear; and the forests around her teemed with life, animal and human. I could live here. In fact it felt like I was coming home.

Chapter Five

A temperate broadleaf forest covered the slopes of the middle Himalayas, a mountain chain rising to five thousand metres that stretched across the north of Bharat. Great snow covered peaks reared up through the forest, so high that trees gave way to first scrub, then alpine meadow and at last to the bleak and windswept rock with its thin clothing of ice and snow. Far below these icy peaks, cold torrents cascaded off the mountain sides, leaping from rock precipices and drizzling through a wet lace of moss and fern to gather together in the warmer valley floors, moving as ribbons of silver toward the plains and the mighty rivers they would become.

The land is steep here, densely forested ravines climbing to open-wooded ridges and down again, a profusion of thickets, forest and grasslands. Oak, alder, rhododendron and pine dominate, with a sprinkling of magnolia, maple, birch, cinnamon, and walnut. In the cooler areas, great bamboo thickets burgeon in the shaded light of the forest floors, their smooth, hollow stalks rising like cathedral columns, their broad grass-like leaves fluttering in every stray gasp of wind. Mosses, ferns and a plethora of herbaceous plants fill in the gaps and epiphytes hang in festoons from the branches high up in the canopy.

Animals are found in abundance but are seldom seen except as flashes of color winging across open areas, the dance of insects around blossoms, or the quiet and cautious approach to the water's edge at dawn and dusk. The forest is seldom quiet though, the chatter and hum of its occupants a surer indication of its burgeoning life.

Deer bark the alarm as a predator passes, monkeys scream and chatter and a chorus of birds is almost always present.

Paths exist through this crumpled land, both game trails worn by the passing of hooves and pads, and the wider trails made by men. Along one of these latter, moved a man and a boy. The man, short and lean with a wiry strength revealed in the tight muscles that rippled under his dark skin was in his late twenties, though the hardness of his life showed in the worn lines of his face and the limp he was at pains to hide from the boy. The youngster, a lad of seven summers, trotted and scrambled along behind his father, his face eager and interested in everything they passed. A brightly colored flower, a beetle, a piece of fresh scat humming with black and red flies and a broken twig commanded his attention at every other step – the flight of a bird, the alarm call of a langur, the rush and spray of a mountain streamlet.

The man stopped on the steep grassy slope of the ridge they had just ascended and swung his tools to the ground. "We will stop here for a few minutes, Harish," he said. He looked up at the sky and noticed the position of the sun and the behavior of the few wisps of cloud around the dazzling peaks, nodding cautiously as he made his decision about the forecast.

The boy nodded and looked around, back down to the distant ribbon of the Alaknanda River then up at the distant peaks. "Are we nearly there yet, father?"

"Very near." He pointed up the ridge to a rocky outcrop, then down to one side where the feathery foliage of a dense bamboo clump broke through the canopy. "That's where we are going."

Isha, the boy's father, led the way up the ridge to a spot above the bamboo clump before angling down through the scrub and suddenly, into the dappled green shade of the forest again as it clung precariously to the steep-sided hill. Helping his son down the steeper drops, he descended to a wet area where the runoff from the ridge had collected in a broad but shallow bowl of rock. From this natural depression grew a thick clump of tall bamboo, rising high into and through the leafy canopy.

Harish stopped and looked upward, his mouth open as he stared up the smooth, shiny stems of the giant bamboo. He ran his hand over the surface of one before trying to wrap his arms about it. "Are you going to chop them down, father?" he asked in awe.

Isha said nothing but took an iron axe with a worn and chipped oak handle out of his bundle of tools. He ran his fingers lightly over the bright blade and nodded in satisfaction. "Move out of the way, Harish. Stand over there."

"Can I chop one down? I'd smash right through them." Harish made a show of swinging an imaginary axe but did as he was told.

"When you're older." Isha took a stance, settling his bare feet into the moist soil. He took a practice swing, measuring the distance, before swinging the axe back and sweeping it forward into the green stem with a satisfying chunk. Cream-colored wood chips flew and after another three blows the tall stem fell sideways off its base and leaned over, its top caught in the other stems. The man put his axe carefully to one side and took hold of the bamboo, wrestling it to the ground. He beckoned to his son.

"Pull all the leaves off, Harish, all the way up to the top."

Leaving the boy to strip the foliage from the downed bamboo stem, Isha set about chopping another one down. He did not stop until eight great poles lay on the ground. Standing back, catching his breath, he watched his son at work. After the first burst of enthusiasm, Harish worked slowly but steadily at his task, distracted only by insects and spiders disturbed by the destruction of their habitat. When three poles lay stripped, he called the boy to him and told him to take a rest, pulling a small packet of chapattis from his bundle. He gave one to Harish and as the boy ate, quickly finished stripping the leaves from the remaining five poles.

"Take the narrow end of this pole, Harish. I want you to climb with it back the way we came, up to the ridge."

Harish looked at the pole, then at the wooded slope. He picked up the end of the pole and took a hesitant step. "I can't do it father, it's too heavy."

"You are not going to do it alone. I'm taking the heavy end and I'll be pushing it up the hill. I just want you to guide it through the trees and hang onto it when I have to find another place to push from."

After a lot of grunting and sweating, after several false starts and near mishaps, the man and boy wrestled the long bamboo pole up onto the ridge and laid it out on the tussock grass.

"Now what?"

"Now we get another one."

Eventually all eight poles lay in the open, next to each other. Harish groaned and sucked the ball of his thumb where a splinter from the bamboo had exacted revenge.

"How do we get them home, father?"

Isha chuckled and ruffled his son's dense black hair. "It is still mid-morning, son. Another twelve before noon and maybe another twelve after that. Then we prepare them and see about getting them home."

Harish worked gamely, stripping the leaves and guiding the long springy poles up the steep hillside and by noon he collapsed into the grass on the ridge, nearly too tired to eat another chapatti spread with a little ghee that was only slightly rancid. A swallow of water from a goatskin water flask and he curled up in the sun in the lee of a bush and fell asleep.

Isha watched his son sleeping and planned the afternoon's activities. After a while he checked the position of the sun and looked long and hard at the clouds gathering over the peaks. He grimaced, not liking all he saw, before leaving his son asleep and clambering back down to the bamboo grove. Presently, the tops of the bamboo started shaking and the muffled thuds of the axe mingled with the natural sound of the forest.

The sun had moved appreciably across the sky before Isha returned to the ridge top, his bundle of tools in his hand. Setting it aside carefully he shook Harish's shoulder. "Come, little Lord of Monkeys," he said, for that is what Harish means. "We have work to do." He led his son back down into the forest and one by one they wrestled the long poles up onto the ridge.

Isha took another axe from his bundle and standing with his bare feet bracing one of the poles, set about chopping it into lengths slightly longer than his height.

When all the poles but one was in lengths, he set Harish to gathering them together while he took a sharp knife and started peeling long thin strips from the outside surface of the last one. These he knotted together to form a tough but flexible twine and began to bind the lengths of bamboo into bundles.

By the middle of the afternoon, as the westering sun slid behind a bank of gray clouds, eight tightly bound bundles of bamboo lay on the grass of the ridge. Each was slightly longer than Isha was tall and reached nearly to his waist when he stood beside them.

"How are we going to move them?" Harish asked, pushing against one experimentally. It rocked slightly and settled down further into the grass. "Are we going to roll them home?"

Isha smiled, wiping the sweat from his eyes. He eased the pain in his back and leg surreptitiously, not wanting his son to see. "If we rolled them, they would come apart. I will carry them."

"All at once?" Harish looked dubious. "And what do I do?"

"You stand guard, with my tools." Isha squatted down beside the boy and looked him in the eyes. "I will have to leave you alone while I move the bundles one at a time. Can you sit here quietly until I return?"

Harish's eyes grew wide. "How long will you be?"

"Not long, and you'll be able to watch me this first time." Isha pointed down the slope of the ridge to the point where they had emerged early that morning. "I'm taking them all down there first."

Isha pushed one of the bundles on end and bent down, angling his bare back against the smooth poles.

91

Gripping the knotted cords with both hands he rose to his feet slowly, hauling the bundle up onto his back. He started down the ridge, concentrating on where he put his feet, dismissing the weight of his burden. Reaching the lower part of the slope, he slid the bundle to the ground and stood a moment, easing the pain in his back before heading up the ridge again to where his son sat, guarding the other seven bundles. Seven times he repeated his labor, and the last time, Harish accompanied him, bounding down the slope with the bundle of tools clutched tightly in his arms.

When Isha reached the other bundles he did not put the last one down but with a muttered, "Wait here," he pushed past and through the thin screen of bushes onto the trail. He was gone longer this time and when he got back he found Harish sitting, hugging his knees, a woeful expression on his face.

"I thought you'd left me," he whispered. "It's getting dark and I was scared."

Isha squatted down and hugged his son tightly. "I won't leave you, I promise." He looked around at the sky and the gathering cloud. "And it is not getting dark yet, but there might be a storm." Flexing his arms, Isha picked up another bundle. "I won't be long."

By the time Isha returned for the last bundle, it really was getting dark. The storm clouds swept in from the west and distant rumbles of thunder could be heard. "The gods are battling the demons again," Isha observed.

Harish looked around nervously. "Will … will they come here?"

92

"No," his father replied seriously. "They are fighting much further down the valley. And the gods will not let any demons come here."

Overcast as it was on the open ridge, the light within the forest was far gloomier. Isha had chosen an open glade a thousand or so paces down the track for his next depot, where the fading light from the sky accentuated the forest shadows. He placed the last bundle across two others, creating a small shelter for his son.

"Stay in here, it may start to rain soon." Thunder grumbled closer, down-river. "I won't take the bundles so far this time."

"I'm scared," Harish whispered. "What if a tiger comes and eats me?"

"Tigers don't eat monkeys. Besides, it is going to rain soon and tigers hate rain. They will be moving as far from here as they can get." Isha ruffled his son's hair. "Be quiet and brave, son. The sooner I leave, the sooner I return."

Traveling down the slope was relatively easy, even when burdened by a cumbersome load, but the journey became very much harder as Isha crossed a tumbling rivulet and started up the next ridge. The thin saplings on the forest floor caught in the bundle and lashed him as they broke loose. His feet slipped and caught off balance by the weight on his back, he nearly fell several times. He dumped the bamboo bundle and started back for the next.

The glade where Harish waited was nearly in darkness by the time Isha returned for the fifth bundle. The sky was completely overcast and the first heavy slugs of rain were ripping through the foliage. Thunder roared and lightning lit the forest opening, revealing a very scared boy.

"Come on, son. You're coming with me this time." Isha shouldered his fresh load and set off again, Harish almost bumping into his legs he followed so close behind his father. When they reached the bundles, Isha rummaged in the bundle his son was clutching and pulled out a small pottery oil lamp wrapped in a dirty cloth. A tightly rolled plug of leaves kept the contents safe, though the cloth was damp where some of the oil had leaked. He dipped a coarse wick in the oil and worked assiduously with a flint and the blunter of his two axes to create a spark. Finally, the wick caught and a smoky yellow flame grew and banished the shadows a few feet.

"You stay here with the lamp, Harish. I'm going to start taking these ones further."

"What about the three back there?" Harish pointed back toward the open glade.

"We'll leave them and get them tomorrow." Isha hesitated. "I did not think there would be a storm, son. It is a lot darker than I thought it would be and we should not be in the forest at night."

Harish opened his mouth to ask, "why not?" then decided he really did not want to know. Instead, he waved to his father before sitting with his back against the bole of a large oak tree and nursing the dull glow of the oil lamp between his legs. He found that if he stared at it and ignored the sounds of the forest and the battling gods and demons high above him in the canopy; it did not seem nearly as frightening sitting here alone in the dark forest. His father returned twice for bundles and when he had been gone for a little while longer, Harish felt a mounting urge to relieve himself. At first he was going to wait until his father came back, but the urgency grew rapidly and he decided he could step around the tree for a very short time. Leaving the lamp flickering on the ground, Harish gingerly took a step into the shadows, then another. Loosening his dhoti, he relaxed and felt considerable relief as his urine arced into the darkness.

As he was finishing, he looked up and frowned. Far off, through the trees, he saw a faint blue light, rather like his little oil lamp but a different color. What's more, this new light did not sputter and flicker like his but shone with a steady glow. Overhead, the thunder still groaned and lightning flashes still lit up the forest but through it all the blue glow shone steadily, closer now. Harish hurriedly fixed his dhoti in place and retreated to the dubious safety of the oil lamp. He cast an anxious look down the trail but his father was nowhere to be seen.

The blue glow approached, drifting between the trees, growing stronger as the lightning flashes slackened in intensity and frequency. Soon it was apparent that the light came from flames that danced and weaved, hanging in the air at about chest height on a man. Harish fell to his knees and put his palms together, praying to whatever god of the forest this was to have mercy and pass him by. Then a horrible thought occurred to him. *What if this is a demon?*

The blue flames reached the path and turned toward where Harish knelt by the two remaining bundles of cut bamboo. The boy shivered again and started gabbling his disjointed prayers out loud. "Parvati, daughter of the mountains, protect me. Aranyani, goddess of forests, help me. Kali, killer of demons, come to my aid ..." Harish fell silent as a feeling of dark amusement swept over him. Fingers of smoke tickled his brain and his worst fears flooded to the forefront of his mind. He got to his feet and took a hesitant, stiff-legged step forward.

"Harish, come to me. Obey your father. Now."

The boy jerked his head around and saw Isha standing a few paces behind him, his axe in his hand.

"Come to me, Harish. We are going home. Obey your father." The blue flame pulsed brighter and the boy recoiled, stumbling back until his father's strong hand stopped him. "Pick up the oil lamp, Harish," his father said calmly.

Waiting until the boy started off down the trail, the lamp casting a dim pool of light on the rough path, Isha followed, sliding his feet back slowly, not wanting to take his eyes off the strange light. A hint of laughter coursed through his mind though Isha could not think of anything funny about the situation. When a curve in the track hid the blue flame from his sight, Isha turned and ran, pushing his son ahead of him.

"Run, Harish, run," he urged. "Run until you reach home. I will be behind you and nothing shall pass me."

They scrambled up the ridge and down the other side, slipping and falling several times in their haste and in one of these tumbles the lamp blew out. Harish yelled with fear and Isha dropped his precious axe and gathered his son in his arms, setting off at a run. Though the forest was dark, small glimmers of light filtered through the canopy from the last flickers of lightning as the storm moved eastward. Isha knew the track well, having worked the woods all his life, and his feet were sure on the dimly-perceived path. The three bundles of cut bamboo loomed like squat creatures beside the track and Isha knew they were within a few thousand paces of home. He ran on, ignoring the pain in his back and leg, the gathering exhaustion, focusing solely on getting his son home safely.

After what seemed like half the night, Isha staggered out of the forest into the broad clearing around his hut. A small, thatched dwelling made of sticks caulked with mud; it included a fenced-off lean-to where a single milk cow cropped from the great heap of cut leaves that was its fodder. The last glimmers of daylight still hung in the sky and a blaze of golden light blazed from the open door of his home. From within came the sounds of his family, and Isha lowered Harish to the ground and leaned against a tree, taking large whooping breaths as he willed his heart to slow. Harish started moving toward the hut and his father called him back.

"Do not say anything to your mother, Harish. It will only worry her."

The boy chewed his lip for a moment before nodding. "What about Gopal? Can I tell him?"

"Tell him what?"

"A ... about the demon."

"It was not a demon, Harish, or if it was it was not going to harm us. More likely it was some lost spirit. You prayed to the gods – I heard you – and they heard you too because you were protected."

"I suppose so." Harish thought about this, then his face lit up. "You really think the gods heard me?"

"Yes, I do. Tomorrow we shall make a small offering of milk to Parvati, Aranyani and yes, even Kali."

"Do the gods like milk?"

97

"Of course, why not? They know it is all we have to offer."

"So can I tell Gopal?"

"Tomorrow, but don't scare your brother – or your sister Dipak for that matter."

Isha called out as they crossed the clearing toward the open door of the hut and a woman appeared, framed in the light.

"Where have you been, husband? I was worried about you in the storm." She reached down and gave Harish a quick hug as he squeezed past her into the one-room hut, scurrying over to the straw pallet in one corner where another, older boy sat.

"Hey, monkey," said the older boy. "Enjoy your little trip in the forest? You didn't get eaten by a tiger, then?"

"There was one, Gopal," Harish replied, puffing his chest out and swaggering. "But I frightened it off."

Isha caressed his wife Malati lovingly and looked across at his two sons arguing in the corner, then at little Dipak, his daughter, playing in the dust near the fire. The hearth, cunningly worked into the side wall of the hut, was built of large, rounded river stones hauled up one by one from the Alaknanda. It provided warmth on the cold mountain nights and a comfortable cooking facility. When the wind blew from the west, or the east and north, smoke billowed inward but at least it kept the mosquitoes and biting flies at bay during the rains.

"Where are your tools?" Malati asked sharply. "You have not been robbed, have you?" She peered out into the gathering darkness. "And the bamboo you set off to cut. Where is that?"

98

"Peace, woman," Isha grumbled. "Harish and I have been working hard all day. We want our supper."

"As if I have been idle while you have been wandering the forest to no purpose," Malati shot back. However, she smiled when she said it and lifted the iron pot off the fire and brought it to the heavy wooden table. While she ladled a thin vegetable curry laced with a little meat into wooden bowls, little Dipak placed two large brown chapattis beside each bowl and three beside her father's. They all ate slowly, spinning the frugal meal out to make it seem larger. Malati found an extra spoonful in the iron pot for her husband and two sons and they quickly made it disappear. She poured half a cup of milk for each of the children and brewed a dark, bitter cup of herbal tea for Isha and herself.

While his wife put the children to bed and cleared away the bowls, washing the pots in a tub of water outside the hut door, Isha sat back and sipped his drink, watching her. When she finished she blew out the extra oil lamps, leaving a single one burning. She shut and bolted the door and came and sat near him at the table.

"What happened today, husband?" she asked quietly, glancing toward the pallet where the children slept.

Isha grunted. "What do you mean? I just got caught by a storm that blew in quicker than I thought."

"You left your tools behind, you did not bring any wood back with you and Harish is scared. I can see it in his eyes."

"It's nothing; he got a bit scared of the thunderstorm and the dark. I decided to leave my tools behind with the wood and bring him home. I'll go get them in the morning."

"That's all? There's nothing you're not telling me?"

"Nothing, woman. Now let me drink my tea in peace."

In the morning, Isha left early, alone. He returned at intervals during the morning, carrying his tools first, then, one by one, the eight bundles of bamboo. Early as Isha was to rise and set off, Malati was up earlier, setting about her daily routine in the pre-dawn darkness. She scraped out the ashes of the old fire and set a new one, igniting it from the glowing embers still present. Then she took a goat-skin pail and set off for the nearest stream to fetch water. On the way she took advantage of the privacy to squat and examine herself for signs of pregnancy. She and Isha had been married ten years and in that time had produced seven children, four of whom had died in infancy. She wanted no more, knowing that her already stressed body could take no more. Only twenty-five years old, she had the bent body and gray hair of a woman twice her age. Sighing, she straightened her clothing and set off for the stream again, hoping her missed monthly was due to some other cause.

Malati arrived back at the hut with her thin arms aching from the weight of the water skin just as Isha set off. Nodding a farewell, she roused the children and set them about their chores. Gopal, the eldest, had the responsibility of their sole remaining cow. It was his daily duty to lead the cow out to pasture each day, guarding it vigilantly. He also set out fodder that his mother had cut for it, milked it morning and night, and groomed it, giving the beast as much attention as he would his wife when he married. Harish, the mischievous one, named for the Lord of Monkeys, was harder to

100

control. Likely to forsake his duties by being distracted by anything out of the ordinary, he helped Isha with his work as woodcutter and charcoal burner. Only seven, he could not be of much assistance as yet, but he was learning a valuable trade. Malati set him to work digging out the great pit that would soon be filled with bamboo.

Dipak, her three year old daughter, wandered the fringes of the forest, picking up any dry sticks and twigs she could find, bringing them back to drop in a tiny heap beside the hearth. As dawn broke, Malati called the children in and fed them a light meal of the ubiquitous chapattis and a cup of warm, milky tea.

Gopal then led the cow out on a long rope halter, taking her down the track that led toward the distant river. Along the way he would find meadows and patches of grass and sometimes he would cut fresh fodder from the oak trees along the track. He took with him a bamboo basket and would search for food while the cow grazed. Usually all he could find were fallen fruit and mushrooms, some of which his mother would reject, but occasionally he would find the remains of a fresh kill. He never approached an unattended corpse, knowing that the tiger or leopard would be lying up close by, but would wait until the crows and vultures were eating before dashing in a cutting off a hunk of meat. The meat was often riddled with maggots and smelled, but spices and herbs hid a multitude of ills and the family was always grateful for a bit of meat.

Malati checked on Harish's progress, knowing that she would be too busy to keep an eye on him. She then went back to the hut and banked up the fire carefully, setting her iron pot filled with fresh water to heat slowly.

Picking up a broom of twigs she swept out the dirt floor and tidied her cooking utensils before gathering Dipak and setting off for the forest by any number of tiny trails. Her first task was to gather bamboo; not the huge woody trunks that interested her husband, but the thin springy canes that she could weave into baskets. Clumps of just the right age were not common, for she had found that if the canes were too young they were not strong enough; too old and they were not flexible. When she first started weaving, she had cut out a whole clump when she found one. This destructive technique resulted in waste and she soon had to travel a lot further to find her canes. Now she farmed the bamboo in her forest, finding each clump and cutting out a few canes at just the right stage of growth before moving on. Dipak pulled each cut cane out and gathered them together in a small pile for her mother to tie off.

After an hour or two, Malati started back down toward the hut, picking up the cut bundles as she went. She walked slowly for Dipak's sake as the three year old was tired, but was also grateful for the slight respite that allowed her to ease her aching joints. While on her way down, she kept her eyes open for any of a host of medicinal plants she could prepare that would keep her family healthy. Not all grew in the forests close to her home but she knew that what she did not find here she would be able to find in other places within half a day's travel. Others could be traded for when they made their half-yearly trip down to the village of Karnaprayag on the rushing Alaknanda. Other villages were closer but Malati's sister lived there, wife of a prosperous storekeeper, and everything they needed was available at good prices. Karnaprayag was also a good market for Isha's charcoal.

Arriving home, she set the bamboo down near a small patch of cleared and dug-over soil where she grew a few vegetables for her family. Malati checked on Harish and gently encouraged him back to work, sending him with a wooden scoop to collect the rich, odiferous dung from the lean-to cow shed. She picked up a hoe and started weeding down the long rows of vegetables. Dipak stayed close, turning over the leaves and pulling off caterpillars and other insects that were chewing the leaves and developing pods. When Harish arrived with the dung, she spread it between the rows and sent him off to collect used dish water from the tub outside the door.

By late morning, Isha was back with all his bundles of bamboo to add to the huge piles of cut and drying wood already stacked up near the wide, shallow pit that would become the base of the charcoal kiln. Leaving the women to attend to the necessary chores, Isha commandeered the use of Harish and started him hauling the large mud bricks over from a huge thatch-covered pile behind the hut. He started arranging these in a layer over the floor of the pit, then upward in a large circle about six paces across. Every layer was moved inward slightly so the circle of bricks started to take on the appearance of a cone. At intervals he left gaps in the bricks and slathered a thick coating of mud inside and out so the walls were impervious and airtight. When the wall reached knee height, Isha stopped construction and started hauling the bundles of bamboo across, stacking them carefully in tight-fitting layers. He filled in the cracks between the cylindrical trunks with shavings of wood and dried kindling.

After a meal, Isha continued building the kiln, raising the mud brick walls in ever decreasing circles, pausing every few rows to pack the interior with bamboo. At last the conical structure was finished, except for a small opening in the top and a dozen or so gaps in the bricks. The center of the kiln, below the top opening, was packed with dry kindling, ready for the firing. Isha walked around the kiln, carefully examining it, looking for flaws and patching them with handfuls of mud when he found them. He looked up at the fading light and realized the whole day had passed. The firing would have to wait until morning.

Isha called out to his wife as he washed, squatting and sluicing water over his limbs and body to remove the mud. There was no answer and he knew she was not back yet from the forest. Afternoons were a time for cutting fodder and collecting wild edibles like nettles and mint. He dried himself off and rewrapped his loincloth before sitting in the last rays of sunlight and contemplating the great kiln. Normally, he used oak to make charcoal, but the effort involved in cutting so much wood was considerable and he had heard about the use of bamboo. A month ago he had filled a much smaller kiln with bamboo and fired it, waiting anxiously for the process to finish. The quality of the charcoal was impressive and Isha had determined to try a much larger amount. Bamboo was hollow and therefore much lighter, making it easier to cut and carry, but the finished product was smaller. He contemplated the tradeoff in time against the weight produced and he would wait a while before making the final decision.

Malati arrived home, staggering under a huge bundle of fodder, with a weary Dipak clinging to one hip. Isha would have liked to help her but cutting and carrying fodder was women's work and it would demean both of them if he assisted. Gopal arrived soon after, leading the cow on its long tether. Of all of them, Gopal was the least tired, having spent the day sitting with his back to a tree watching his charge or lying asleep in the hot sun. Isha did not begrudge his son his easy day; he knew the responsibility the boy carried was enormous. The cow represented wealth and when it could be bred again, would ensure the family's survival. If anything happened to it, the future of the family would be bleak.

Isha fired up the kiln next morning, after Malati had left for the river valley seeking medicinal herbs and the long-leaved stringy *bhabhar* grass that could be made into ropes. He transferred a glowing coal from the fire to a clay pot and nurtured it, fanning the glow into fierce flames. Climbing carefully to the cone of mud, he tipped the crackling contents into the dry tinder, waiting until heat and smoke started pouring out. Taking the bricks and mud Harish passed up to him, Isha quickly sealed the chimney and slathered more mud over the top, where wisps of smoke were curling through fine cracks. Satisfied, he clambered down from the already warm structure and circled the kiln, dabbing mud here and there. Black smoke poured out of the upper spaces where the bricks had been left out as he built it, but apart from these the mud cone seemed airtight.

The smoke became thicker and curls started issuing from the lower apertures. Isha kept moving round sealing up any cracks with Harish eagerly calling out if he found any. Over the course of the morning, the color of the smoke paled until it was pure white.

Isha nodded. "Bring the bricks, Harish, and fresh mud." He started at the top, slipping a brick into the gaps in the kiln wall and dumping a load of wet mud over it, smoothing it and pressing more into the cracks. Working around the structure, he gradually filled in every hole, turning the kiln into a great oven where no air could reach the burning wood.

"What do we do now, father?" Harish asked, looking at the brick cone. Already, the dried mud and heated bricks rippled the air above them and he could feel the heat of the enclosed fire on his face.

"Now we wait."

"How long?"

"I think about five to seven days. Oak takes longer as it burns slower, so I'd leave that ten or twelve days." Isha pursed his lips and nodded. "Yes, I think about seven days."

Isha and Harish disappeared into the forest again over the next few days and brought home many more loads of bamboo for the next firing. While they were gone, Malati and Dipak did the household chores in the early dawn and collected fodder, then set about weaving the thin bamboo canes into large baskets, ready to take the charcoal when it was ready. As she soaked and bent the canes, twisting them into a framework then bending them into shape, Malati oversaw her daughter as the young girl stripped the *bhabhar* grass into long fibrous threads. The easiest way

106

of doing this was to draw a bunch of the grass repeatedly through an acacia branch and let the long wicked thorns rip through the dried blades, leaving only the long strands of fiber. These would later be plaited into rope. The task focused Dipak's mind wonderfully as a moment's inattention brought pain from the sharp thorns.

Late on the fifth day, after Isha had cleaned up and enjoyed a refreshing cup of herbal tea, he walked over to the charcoal furnace and felt the dried mud of the kiln. For the first time found he could touch the sides without hurting himself. He called Harish over to experience the sensation.

"Ow, it's hot." Harish snatched his hand back.

"Don't be foolish, boy. If the fire was still burning you'd blister your hand. The fire is out and tomorrow, or the next day, we can open it up."

Isha judged it to be still too hot on the evening of the sixth day so he waited until the morning of the seventh to swing his mattock and batter his way through the crumbling heat-weakened walls, releasing a cascade of shiny black tongues of charcoal. He picked up one of the still hot chunks and sniffed it, tasted it and felt its brittle texture, nodding with satisfaction at the blackness left on his hands. Taking one inside the hut he squatted by the hearth and placed it on a hot ember, grinning as it burst into flame, liberating a burst of heat but almost no smoke. Going back out, Isha set about demolishing the rest of the kiln, saving what bricks he could and shoveling the crumbled remains aside to be reused. Then everyone, with the exception of Gopal who was off with the cow as usual, packed the charcoal into the bamboo baskets,

107

stacking them behind the hut and covering them with a thick layer of thatch.

"This is good charcoal, Malati," Isha said. "We must take it down to the markets at Karnaprayag."

"It is a month before we were to go, husband. Should you not make more charcoal first? After all, you have cut the bamboo, ready for burning."

"We will have difficulty enough transporting what we have. What is the point of making more? No, we leave day after tomorrow."

Malati spent the next day fashioning harnesses for the cow and for each of them so they could carry the baskets of charcoal without undue effort. Normally, Isha would not have taken the whole family, often leaving Gopal behind alone to take care of their cow, or Malati when little Dipak was a baby. This time, however, there was too much quality charcoal and everyone would be needed to carry it, even Gopal. As they could not leave the cow behind, it must perforce go with them, and if it was going, it could carry its share of the burden.

They were up before dawn as usual, feeding the children and packing food for the journey, as well as organizing the panniers and baskets. Just after sunrise, while the morning mists still curled through the forest and the *kaleej* pheasants were giving vent to loud whistling chuckles in the undergrowth, they set off on a journey that would take them nearly a week. First, the long winding trail down to the stream meadows where Gopal often grazed the cow, then over the stream and following its leaping course, along the wider road down to the river. Two days later they would leave the road and take a short cut over a low ridge, arriving by dusk on the fourth day, if

108

all went well, at the rope bridge across the Alaknanda. Here, they would join other travelers journeying between the cities and towns of Garhwal and Kumaon. They would likely make their first sales here as charcoal was a useful, light fuel for travelers. The money would pay the toll on the rope bridge, and they would cross the swaying structure, trying not to look down through the sticks and bhabhar rope to the rushing river far below. Another three days along the left bank of the Alaknanda would bring them to Karnaprayag, one of the busiest and richest cities in this part of the hills. Malati's sister Jyoti lived in Karnaprayag, the wife of a wealthy merchant and mother to a horde of children. She would welcome them warmly enough but would also make it plain that she thought her sister could have done better for herself than to marry a poor charcoal burner from the hills.

This year, however, Isha would not have to bear the humiliation of his sister-in-law's barbs for on that last lonely ridge before the rope bridge, where the trail wound through a stunted Chir pine forest near the deserted cemetery; they met three strangers on the road.

The first they knew of them was when a man stepped out in front of Gopal. The tall, lean man with a cast in one eye and sores covering one side of his face, grasped the cow's halter rope and put a hand on the boy's chest. Gopal stopped in confusion and turned to his father for direction. Another man, solidly built with a scar running from his eye across his face and down to one shoulder, moved out of the scrub and stood in front of Isha. He kept his right hand by his side, grasping a rusty looking blade. The third man, short and tending to fat, moved behind the family to prevent any retreat. Dipak ran immediately to her mother and hid her face in Malati's skirts.

"Namaste," Isha said, eyeing the men cautiously. "We are taking our charcoal to the Karnaprayag market. Are you traveling in our direction?"

Scar looked Isha up and down, then leered at Malati. "You got food?"

"We have a little," Isha replied. "You are welcome to travel with us and share our meal tonight. We hope to …"

"Now," Scar interrupted. "We are hungry now."

Isha looked at the man in front of him carefully, before turning slowly to face his wife. "Give them the food, Malati."

"Jasmine?" jeered the short one. "A pretty name for an old hag, though she still has something that interests me."

"You've been too long on the road," Scar growled. "Now where's that food?"

Malati slipped the sack off Dipak's shoulders, the supplies being her daughter's only burden, and threw it on the ground.

Short grunted and pushed past Malati, his hand brushing her thigh as he passed. Opening the bag he rummaged inside. "Chapattis and cooked vegetables," he said with a tinge of disgust. "No meat? Is this all you have to eat, little Jasmine?" He approached Malati again, anger and lust in his eyes.

"What else you got?" Scar asked. "You got any … any weapons or tools? Anything we can sell?"

"Nothing I can afford to give away," Isha said. "I'm a wood cutter and a charcoal burner. All I have is a lot of

110

charcoal we hope to sell." He hesitated and glanced at the other men before lowering his voice. "Look, I have a family to take care of, and nothing valuable. I suggest you go and look for somebody else to rob."

"You calling us thieves?" Scar pushed Isha hard in the chest and he staggered.

Isha slipped the ropes from his shoulders and forehead and let the baskets of charcoal fall to the ground. He grabbed his knife from his belt and swept it in a clumsy blow at Scar. The man jumped back with a startled look and raised his own blade.

"Put it down, wood cutter," Scar snarled. "I don't want to cut you but I will. All we wants is a bit of food and we'll be on our way."

"That's right," nodded Short. "Though as yous haven't any meat, maybe we could ... you know." He made an obscene gesture toward Malati, who responded with an outraged gasp and backed away, hugging her daughter close.

"You leave my wife alone, you thief," yelled Isha, swinging round toward Short, his knife raised. Scar leapt forward and brought the rusty iron blade down hard on Isha's arm. The blade was as dull as it was rusty and cut nothing. The weight of the blow snapped Isha's forearm, the crack clearly audible. He screamed, dropping the knife and clutching his broken arm with his left hand.

Malati's attention was dragged by the scream from the swaggering advance of Short as her husband doubled over. She saw Scar drop the blade, then bend and pick up Isha's knife from the dusty road. As the man straightened he slashed upward, ripping through the wood cutter's stomach and up into the chest, the knife clattering against

111

ribs. Her scream of despair and loss mingled with her husband's grunt of agony, and the burbling cry that broke from his lips.

Raising his unbroken arm toward his wife, Isha stared at her with a puzzled expression and took a step forward. "Run," he whispered. His feet slipped in the blood that poured down his legs and he could not control his limbs. He collapsed, the light leaving his eyes before his skull cracked on the hard earth of the road.

Malati stared down at her dead husband for a heartbeat, then up to meet the eyes of her horrified sons. "Run," she screamed. "Run Gopal, Harish. Go to the bridge ..." Short made a grab at her and she hit him in the mouth with her fist, grabbing at Dipak with her other hand. "Run," she screamed again.

Gopal dropped his panniers and ducked past Tall, racing down the road toward the bridge. Harish scrambled under the cow, shedding his own baskets and dived into the long grass by the side of the road with Scar hard on his heels. He weaved and ran, quickly outdistancing the man.

Scar returned to the road where the body of the wood cutter lay, a great stained patch of bloody mud around him. He swore and kicked the body. "We only wanted food, you fool."

Tall returned, shaking his head. "Got away. Where's the woman."

Scar swore again as he realized Short and the woman were missing. He cupped his hands and called.

"Up here," came a yell from beyond the stand of Chir pines on the crest of the ridge. "I've found her ... and something else."

Scar and Tall hurried up an overgrown path through the pines to an open area where the rocks of the hillside showed through the thin soil like broken bones. The woman stood at bay between two tall rocks, her crying daughter behind her, and she held out a dead branch, swinging it at Short if he got close enough.

Tall looked around at the rocks, which appeared to be too regularly spaced to be natural. Beneath some, nestled in the earth at the base of the tall stones, were pottery jars. Reddish pottery with black figures sketched on the sides. Around the jars lay dried and scattered flowers, small empty dishes and small heaps of henna and ochre.

"This is a cemetery," Tall said, backing away. "We shoulds not be here."

"He's right," Scar agreed. "Leave the woman and come away."

"No," Short snarled. "There's nothing else. I wants her."

A breeze stirred the still air, the dried grass around the pottery urns rustling. Scar saw one of them was broken, the charred bones spilling out onto the ground. He backed away, glancing at Tall for support.

The wind lifted a handful of the ashes from the broken urn, flinging them up into the air and swirling them between the men for a moment before passing down through the Chir pines in the direction of the road. The air became still again, hot and oppressive. Scar wiped the wood cutter's knife on the grass and tucked it into his waistband.

"Go on then. If you're going to have her, make it quick. I don'ts like this place."

113

Short nodded and leapt forward only to be met by Malati's branch. He fell back with an oath, and rubbed his ribs.

Tall laughed. "What's the matter? Can't handle a woman?" He stopped and turned toward the pine grove. "Did you hear something?"

Scar stared down the path, his ears straining. "One of the boys?" he asked. "Perhaps he's come back to help his mother." He frowned. "Don't sound right though. He's not trying to be quiet." The wood cutter's knife reappeared in his hand.

"There." Tall pointed down the path. "I can see someone, it's ..." The man's mouth fell open. He gulped and shut it again, his eyes staring. "It's ... it's the wood cutter. I thought you killed him?"

"I did," Scar snarled. He pushed Tall aside and stared at the approaching figure, a frown creasing his forehead.

The wood cutter advanced slowly up the path through the pine grove, his limbs moving in a jerky fashion like a string puppet. The front of the man's body was covered in dried and sticky blood to which copious amounts of road dust adhered, and the great rent in his abdomen gaped, red and purple coils of intestine glistening within the cavity.

Malati caught sight of her husband's body swaying toward the cemetery and moaned, turning away and hiding her face. The figure stopped as she did so and stood in the path a few paces from the bandit leader, swaying slightly. The man's eyes were open but unfocused and the bloody lips twitched as if trying to form words.

114

Short and Tall crept up behind Scar and nudged him. "You didn't kill him," Tall whispered. "Finish him off."

"How can any man live with those wounds?" Scar said. "There's something not right here."

"What's not right is you not killing him," Short grumbled. "Look at him though, he's dead on his feet. Knock him down now and he'll stay down." The fat man pushed past Scar and stepped in front of the wood cutter. He looked the man up and down with a sneer on his face before reaching out one hand to the man's chest. "Farewell, wood cutter."

Scar's view of the man was blocked by Short's bulk and he did not see what happened but suddenly his companion was reeling to one side with a wet ripping sound. He followed Short with his eyes as the man careened into one of the upright rocks and collapsed in the long grass. Short's tunic and churidar were soaked with blood and the man was screaming, a thin wailing screech as he held out one arm toward the wood cutter, the other one ending at the shoulder in a ragged mess of torn flesh and white bone. Scar stared, stupefied, his mind refusing to comprehend the sudden events. Another wet sound dragged his attention back to the wood cutter and his eyes widened further at the sight.

Life had appeared in the wood cutter's expression, but Scar found himself wishing for the vacant stare again as the eyes fastened on him. Fresh blood streamed from the wood cutter's mouth as the jaws moved. An arm lifted, carrying a hunk of raw meat to the figure's lips where the gore-stained teeth ripped off another piece. Scar's stomach churned when he saw that the meat was

Short's arm, torn off from his companion's shoulder by a horrific force.

Behind him, Tall moaned and bolted, running wide around the figure on the path, crashing through long grass and scrub as he raced for the cover of the Chir pines and the safety of the road beyond.

The wood cutter dropped the arm and whirled, his movements no longer disjointed and awkward but fluid and powerful. He surged forward, legs pounding through the long grass and arms outstretched, overtaking Tall as if he was standing still. Leaping onto the back of the fleeing figure, he bore Tall to the ground and Scar heard the crackling snap of neck bones, even above the weakening cries of the blood drenched Short. It occurred to Scar that he should flee now, while the creature's attention was diverted. This was obviously no man. This was not the wood cutter, no matter the form it took, but a Rakshasa. What else could do this? He took a step back, cautiously.

The creature's head lifted above the grass by the pines, strips of meat dripping blood hanging from its mouth. It looked at him and Scar felt hot urine cascade down his legs. He backed away faster, his voice rising into a shrill scream as the creature rose from its bloody feast and loped back up the path.

"No, no, go away, Leave me. O Vishnu, Brahma, Shiva, help me. Gods of hill and forest, have pity on a poor man. I have been a g ... good man but I will ... I will become better. O gods, protect me and I ... I will become a monk ..." Scar backed into one of the rocks and lost control of his legs, falling in a heap among the pottery bone urns.

The creature looked down on Scar and swallowed what was in its mouth. It wiped the back of one hand across wet lips, smearing blood across its cheeks. The lips moved violently and the tongue lolled as the creature forced air from dead lungs through a dead throat. "Derh cor ohn goth ..." It stopped and stood still, its attention turned inward, then tried again. "Don' call on gods. They won't hep."

Scar was not listening. He gabbled away in a low voice, appealing to every god he could remember, dredging up childhood memories and seeking to expunge what was happening to him from his mind.

"Stop," the creature said. "Where was your pity t'day?"

The words shocked Scar out of his fugue. "Eh? Who are you?" He stared around at the cemetery and the body of Short lying a few paces away – and at the blood. Scar started to scream again but with an effort got himself under control. "Y ... you're a demon, aren't you? A Rakshasa? Who are you to talk of pity? You show no pity. You mean to k ... kill me."

"Yes, I am Rakshasa," mouthed the corpse of the wood cutter. "I do wha' I do because I am wha' I am, but you are human. You had a choice."

Scar stared without comprehension. "You're going to kill me."

The corpse shrugged awkwardly. "As you wish." Reaching down it lifted the large man easily; drawing Scar's terrified face close then swiftly bent its head and ripped out the bandit's throat with bloody teeth, dropping the flapping, gurgling body back into the dust. The demon spat, clearing its mouth of blood and flesh, then turned and walked over to where Malati huddled, shielding her daughter's face in her skirts.

The woman raised a pale, tear-ravaged face as the body of her husband approached. "Are … are you Isha?"

"No. Your husband is dead."

"You have brought him to life."

"This body is dead, woman. My own life powers it, fills it and drives it to exact revenge on these men for their deeds."

"Are you going to kill me too? My child?"

The demon in the corpse said nothing but its head turned and it appeared to be listening. "Men are coming up the road. They will be here soon." The body jerked and collapsed, raising a swirl of dust from the dry ground. The swirl clung together, coalescing into the faint outline of a man. A voice thrummed in the air. "Your husband came after you and killed the bandits before succumbing to his wounds. Wild beasts scavenged the bodies. They will not believe anything else."

Malati watched the dust dissipate in the still air. She could hear the approach of the men down on the road and the excited calls of her sons as they discovered their father's body had gone. She spoke to the empty air. "Why did you do this? Take revenge for my dead husband? You did not need to."

For the space of ten heartbeats, the only sound was the whispering of a faint breeze through the pine needles and the humming of the first flies. Then, softly, came the sound of laughter, fading into stillness.

Chapter Six

I surprised myself, that day in the cemetery on the ridge.

When I fled Kailasa and the strength of the sadhu Bala, his words burned me. Not his mantra, for that ceased to have an effect once I passed beyond the range of his words, beyond the range of his thoughts. No, what scalded me were his words on the choice that men and gods are born to but that is denied to one such as myself. It enraged me that I, who am so powerful, should be counted less than the meanest street-sweeper, the lowest handler of corpses, or even a woman. I sat on Nanda Devi and brooded on this a while, feeling my anger grow. I railed against the gods, my unknown parents, the whole smug population of gods and men that consigned me to my fate, my position, and shouted aloud my curses and profanities. At last I swept down from the heights of the mountain, as I felt the presence of a god walking the frigid ice wastes of the great peak, and did not care to encounter him. Instead, I wandered the ridges, the river valleys of a land that men called Garhwal and Kumaon, killing any whom I chanced upon, unleashing my anger on men and women.

By degrees my anger left me, to be replaced by deep resentment and I exacted great revenge on mankind. I no longer killed in anger; now I killed in cold hatred those who had never harmed me. I was powerless to harm the gods and holy men like Bala, of whom I came upon a few. Not many, for the race of man seems peculiarly drawn to evil. That was as well for me because the thoughts and fears of a good man are not as tasty as the imaginings of

119

the wicked. I set out to turn the mountain valleys of Garhwal and Kumaon into a nightmare. I started by plain indiscriminate killing, openly entering villages and taking my victims in plain sight of all. If one, braver than most, sought to turn a weapon against me, he rapidly found that nothing physical can do me harm. After a while I felt something – a something that puzzled me. If you have sat on an open hillside of an evening in a gathering storm and suddenly the clouds have parted for an instant, releasing a golden ray of light from the setting sun that pierces the atmosphere to highlight some part of the hillside, you will know what I mean.

The clear skies above me were murky – I carried out my killings without a care. Then suddenly the murk dispersed and it felt as if rays of sunlight were slashing through the air, traveling the roads and ridges, searching out my presence. I wondered for a day or two, hiding in a small cave on Nanda Ghunti, from where I saw one of these beams sweep out from the snow-covered peak of Nanda Devi. I knew then this was the gaze of a god and they were looking for me. I remained in my cave while the seasons cycled and at last those divine ones lost interest. I ventured out again, ready to continue my depredations, but infinitely more cautious.

I became a tiger. Well, 'became' is not strictly true, but I found out I could enter the body of a living creature and influence its actions. I happened on a young tiger lying up in a thicket of Sal, trying vainly to dislodge a sheaf of porcupine quills from its paws and face. I entered the beast and with a nudge, induced it to abandon its regular prey – which it was having trouble catching anyway – and start hunting humans. I showed the tiger that it need not fear man, I showed it what men did and where they went and its natural killing instincts took over. I slipped out of its body and followed it as the young tiger became a man-eater. I had doubted it at first, but I found that I enjoyed the death of a person beneath the jaws and claws of a tiger almost as much as when I encompassed their demise myself. I was there as the first frissons of fear raced up their spine as they realized they were being stalked; I savored the horror of the tiger's hot breath and the terror of the full knowledge of what was about to happen to them. I reveled too, in the mounting hunger, excitement and lust of the predator. I have watched as my tiger and a female called across the moonlit hills, their cries of want and hunger sending every man, woman and child who heard them, quivering inside their huts, the doors barred and latched. I watched as the great striped cats met, saw the fury and the blood and stroked their fur in the lonely glades as they coupled with violence and passion. Best of all, the gods did not appear to be much interested in the actions of a mere beast and I was left alone to enjoy myself.

Time passed. When at last the tiger died, whether by old age, accident or because a hunter got lucky, it meant little to me. I moved on, finding another predator, tiger or leopard, and started another man-eater. For over three hundred years there was always a man-eater roaming the hills of Kumaon and Garhwal – often more than one – as I was not the only source of these killers. When a tiger or leopard lost the ability to hunt its natural prey, whether from injury, sickness or age, it often turned to that weak, pitiful creature that swarmed over the hills and valleys like monkeys, for its food.

121

Others of my kind haunted those mountain valleys too, but not as many as men would like to believe. Whenever a man or woman died in the forests, whether by predator or accident, a demon was blamed; whenever an accident happened, like a tree falling on a hut or the lightning striking a tree, a demon was held to be responsible. Sometimes they were, but not often. In all those countless miles of river and stream, ridge and plain, terraced hillside and icy peak, over a period of many, many years, I found no more than a handful of Rakshasa. There were not many gods either – or at least I never saw them. Krishna had been the last I actually saw, though I felt their presence from time to time. Men, though, I saw all the time, and in growing numbers.

One day I was following an ageing man-eating tigress up through an oak and rhododendron forest toward the area where bamboos grew in profusion. The tigress had passed this way before, two years before, and found and killed a lone traveler. In the direct, uncomplicated mind of the cat, having found food here previously meant finding food here again. She was pregnant now, probably with her last litter, and getting hungry.

From a valley or two away, the tigress' ears picked up the chopping sounds of a woodcutter at work. She moved steadily through the forest, moving slowly with her swollen belly, and onto the ridge where the man worked. Lying in a dense thicket just off the path that wound down off the ridge, she watched as a man and a boy walked the track in the fading light, bearing some strange things on their backs.

As the storm clouds gathered and the light dimmed, the tigress got up and stretched, then set off slowly down the track after them. The man and boy stopped once more in an open glade, where they constructed a flimsy green cave of the objects they carried before the man walked off carrying one of them. The boy crept inside his shelter and the tigress lay down in the long grass at the edge of the forest and watched, curiosity holding her hunger at bay. The man returned and left again, bearing away part of the green shelter, and still the tigress waited. Again and once more, the man came and went and each time the shelter grew smaller. Hunger grew and the tail of the tigress twitched. Although she could scatter the bamboo bundles without effort, she waited for one more to be removed before she struck.

The storm moved closer and lightning flickered and lit the glade. Then the rain started, a first few fat drops spattering against the foliage, then more, piercing through to the forest floor. The tigress snarled as rain splashed, her complaint drowned out in renewed thunder. Her desire wavered and she gathered herself for the brief violent charge across the open ground, her mind already savoring the hot, salty taste of the boy's blood. The sky ripped apart in a blaze of light and she felt the concussion of the thunderclap. Her ears flattened against the damp fur of her head and she cringed, then her incipient charge turned into flight and she raced for the cover of the ravine.

I watched her go, knowing she would not return that night. The boy could not see me though I stood in the open, near his flimsy shelter. Had he looked in my direction all he could have seen was a pale fitful light drowned by the actinic glare of the storm above me. I was energized, I could feel the power of the storm around me and it exhilarated me. The wood cutter arrived back and left with his son and another of the bamboo bundles. I stayed behind in the open glade awhile, drinking in the energy of the storm before I followed.

I caught up with them deep inside the forest. The man had gone on ahead, leaving the boy with a tiny light to brave the terrors of the darkness. He got up to relieve himself and I drifted closer, revealing my presence. Interestingly, there was no fear in his mind at first, only curiosity and wonder. I stroked his mind and he thought of gods and demons, childish prayers dribbling from his lips. The man though, returning, instantly knew me for what I was and I could feel the prickle of fear that raced across his mind and down his spine, curling like a whipped dog in the base of his belly. I moved forward to harvest his life when I found I had no desire to feast. I was not hungry.

I stayed, watching as the man hurried his child away. I looked in on myself, wondering at my lack of desire. I knew I could not pity or feel mercy; one has to have choice of action for such decisions. The only thing I could think of was the storm. I had reveled in it, feeling joy at the crashing strokes of lightning. Had I somehow fed off the power of the discharge? I could think of nothing else and it amused me. The man heard my laughter for he turned back and stared. I felt then a flicker of … what? It could not be respect, or liking, or any of the weak emotions of men, for I do not feel them. Curiosity, perhaps, a mild interest in a man that put the safety of his child above his inner terror. I followed, at a distance and invisibly.

I watched the wood cutter and his family for several days as he built his charcoal kiln and fired it. I followed his wife and daughter into the forest, observing their interactions, and I shimmered in the open, dusty heat while the man's older son tended their cow. I could not really say why I was so interested in this family of humans, but I found myself looking at men for the first time not as food but as other beings with their own lives and purposes. At length, I grew hungry again but I did not want to feed there so I took the road down toward the rope bridge on the Alaknanda ahead of them.

I found a minor official in the court of one of the petty kings of Kumaon traveling the road alone and relieved him of his worries and cares along with his life. Then, wanting solitude, I searched out an old, neglected cemetery on a ridge overlooking the Alaknanda River, and settled down among the ashes and old bones to think.

I am a demon, Rakshasa. What does that mean? According to what I have heard, to what I have gleaned from men's minds, Brahma created everything. Did he create me too? And the other Rakshasa? If so, why? Am I here merely to play out my role as an opponent of all things good and pure and upright? Is my life to be spent alone, preying on men when I get hungry, hated by all? Do I have a say in this? Legend has it that one Vibhishana, younger brother to Ravana the king of Lanka was a good-hearted Rakshasa, so perhaps it is possible. The question is, if he really existed, "How did he achieve it?"

The sadhu Bala said I have no choice. I was created to be evil and evil I must be. He believed I am incapable of a right action, a merciful course of action. Yet I have already proved him wrong. There are many times over the centuries I have refrained from killing, the last time

125

being with the wood cutter and his family. I felt a warm smug glow of satisfaction as I recounted my many merciful actions, then the glow died away as I realized I had not deliberately refrained. Each time I had been sated with death, glowing with energy. It was not mercy that stayed my 'hand', it was lack of hunger. Even with the wood cutter and his son, I was alive with the energy of the storm, that vitality staying with me for days. It must be as Bala said – I am a creature without a choice. I must resign myself to my fate.

Voices interrupted my thoughts, voices tinged with hatred, anger and lust, filtering up through the Chir pines from the road over the saddle. I flitted down through the trees and saw the death of the old wood cutter, the flight of his sons and the imminent danger to his women. Without thinking, I invaded the body of the woman and guided her willing feet up the trail toward the cemetery. The fat man followed, his bandit companions being engaged in capturing the two runaway boys. So light was my touch on the woman that she did not even know I was there. She thought it her own idea to escape through the pines, to stand at bay among the upright stones and funeral urns, and to arm herself with an old branch.

I left her and watched until the other two men found us. Their minds were truly evil, filled with thoughts and memories of a whole series of crimes. The fat one was a rapist, the tall one a thief even of the poor, and the man with the scar was a murderer, many times over. I would enjoy their deaths and when the edge was off my hunger, I would lap up the sweet grieving of the widow and the innocence of the child. But how to do it? How would I achieve maximum terror?

I flew down past the men, a small whirlwind of ash and dust following my rapid passing. On the road, the ripped body of the wood cutter lay face down in the blood-soaked dust. I entered him and was immediately appalled by how difficult it was to do anything inside a dead man. None of the muscles worked and when, after much effort, I got the man to his feet, my coordination was terrible. I shuffled and stumbled up the path and through the pine grove, slowly working out how to do things, which parts of his nervous system to stroke to get the required movement, and when all else failed, moving the limb by the sheer power of my being.

I confronted the men, wondering how I should proceed, when the fat one acted for me. He thrust his hand at my chest and I grabbed it and ripped his arm from its socket. He fell back in screaming agony and I compounded his shock by ripping flesh from his still-living arm. His thoughts were delicious. The tall one ran and despite my brief stay within this body, I hurled myself after him so efficiently I caught him before he reached the trees. The last man, the scarred one, was truly terrified and tasted best of all. When all were dead, I turned to the woman.

"Are you my husband?" she asked.

I assured her I wasn't, in a voice that improved rapidly as I practiced, and she asked if I was about to kill her to. I reached out to put an image in her mind even more horrible than that of her dead husband, but I hesitated. At that point, voices came from the road and I knew that the boys had found help. Help against bandits though, not help against demons. I have feasted amongst a crowd for no man can stand against me unless armed with strong mantras. I had no fear of being interrupted, yet I felt a strange reluctance to kill the woman and child. Her sons were on the road below, her dead husband's body stood before her ...

I left the body and it slumped to the ground. I told her to downplay the story of a demon and tell the rescuers her husband saved her before dying of his wounds. I drifted away toward the pines.

She spoke to the empty air. "Why did you do this? Take revenge for my dead husband? You did not need to."

I stopped and returned to the woman. Why had I done this? I killed the men to satisfy my hunger but I was still hungry and unafraid of the approaching men. Why did I not complete my meal? I thought back to my days observing the family in the forest and the interactions between parents and young. I had no parents, nor will I ever have young, but for an instant it felt as if I had both. I could not kill this mother. I would not kill this mother.

The shock nearly blew my flame out. I realized I had made a decision, and what is more, a decision to do the right thing by this creature. Bala had been wrong – I did have a choice. I left the ridge laughing, the sound filling the quiet air of the ridge cemetery until it died away in the sighing of the wind in the pines and the babble of the approaching men.

Chapter Seven

He came from the southwest, walking along the left bank of the Alaknanda River from Srinagar. His saffron robe was worn and stained, his head shaved, a staff and begging bowl his only burdens. Sonaka strove for the middle course in all his actions, neither over-zealous nor lazy, for pitfalls lay along either path. He walked briskly but without hurrying; when he met a fellow traveler he would greet him politely but not stay to talk, moving on steadily toward his destination.

The village of Rudraprayag lay at the confluence of the Alaknanda and Mandakini Rivers. Spreading up from the triangle formed by the two rushing rivers, the village was only accessible by rope bridges, one across the gorge of the Mandakini on the other side of the Alaknanda, and a sturdier one joining the path on which Sonaka now stood with the village itself.

The swaying rope and wood structure was a toll bridge and the keeper of the bridge exacted a small fee from any traveler desiring to enter the village. Sonaka had neither money, nor any goods he might barter with save his robe, his staff and his bowl. Seating himself beside the great rope-bound pillar of rock that anchored the bridge, Sonaka set his bowl out and waited. A few travelers came and went, some looking curiously at the shaven-headed man in the saffron robe, others ignoring him. Toward sunset, as a chill wind started to blow up the valley, a man dropped a handful of cold rice into the begging bowl. Sonaka thanked the man and uttered a brief blessing before rising to his feet and approaching the bridge keeper.

The keeper accepted the bowl with the rice and nodded. "It is enough." He hesitated before tipping it into his own bowl and cast his eyes quickly over Sonaka's gaunt frame. "Would you not be better off eating this yourself and waiting for fresh alms in the morning?"

"It was given to me that I might secure passage over your bridge," Sonaka replied.

"Or as a meal. It is late now and there may not be many people willing to give you food."

Sonaka smiled. "Then I will go hungry. It will not be the first time."

The keeper handed the bowl of rice back to the monk. "Then please accept this rice as my offering."

Sonaka bowed and blessed the keeper before treading carefully over the uneven sticks of the swaying bridge. On the other side, he walked through the village, glancing about until he saw a stunted pipal tree on the slope above the scattered wood and brick houses. Sonaka cleared a space beneath the tree and sat cross-legged, looking out and down the valley. He ate his rice slowly, trying not to savor the sensation of food entering his belly once more, thankful it was plain boiled rice and not fried or spiced in any way. 'Sensation is the enemy of Equanimity', he reminded himself. Placing his bowl carefully to one side, Sonaka turned his mind to the rice inside him, the pipal tree above and behind him, the ground beneath him, the village in front of him and the world spreading out around him. All were parts of a whole and in their deeper meaning were interchangeable and indistinguishable. Night fell and Sonaka composed himself for sleep, lying on his right side with his right hand cushioning his head and his left arm following the contours of his body.

The next day he rose with the dawn and found his way down to the rocky gorge of the Mandakini. Stripping off his robe and laying carefully on the shaded rocks, he slipped out of his dhoti and waded into the icy water up to his waist. He dipped himself beneath the surface and scooped a handful of sand from the river floor, scrubbing it over his body vigorously before rinsing off and coming out of the water. Ignoring his shivering body as just another example of the way the world intruded on his consciousness, he dressed and climbed back up to the village streets where the bustle of daily life was starting anew.

The villagers eyed Sonaka warily. Buddhist monks passed that way regularly but most had donned the saffron robe as a way to make a living without having to work, rather than through conviction and a desire to achieve enlightenment. They would wait and see, measuring his commitment before making him welcome. In the meantime, a handful of rice, some cooked vegetables and a chapatti allowed them to perform a good deed. That, at least, was an on-going benefit of having a monk around.

Sonaka thanked the people for their offerings and walked back to the shade of the pipal tree. Putting the bowl of food aside for a noon meal, he assumed the contemplative position and turned his mind inward.

A magpie-robin flew into the branches of the pipal and cocked its head, staring down at the saffron robed visitor. It uttered its sharp 'tschwee tschwee' call and flew away again. A little later, a streaked laughing thrush, out hunting for grubs happened upon the tree and the seated figure and watched for a while from the cover of long grass. Its bright eyes saw the bowl of food nearby

131

and the thrush moved closer, darting from grass to bush, from bush to log. The shadow of a hawk flashed across the ground and the thrush raced for cover, all thoughts of food gone. A little later the magpie-robin returned.

Sonaka returned to the physical world just after noon. He picked up his bowl of rice and vegetables and scattered some for the magpie-robin who, after a cautious search of the surroundings for danger, flew down quickly and snatched the food, flying off to eat it.

The following days saw Sonaka enter a routine. He left the shade of the pipal tree only at dawn, to wash in the river and to beg for food in the streets of the village. Only begging enough for his midday meal, he often went hungry in those early days. Gradually, however, the villagers came to see he was indeed a holy man, spending his days in contemplation, and would visit the pipal tree to refill his bowl just before sunset.

The flowers of the pipal tree fell and its fruits started to mature, falling in turn and providing food for a wide variety of birds and mammals. Flocks of green pigeons descended on the fallen fruit, along with barbets and tree pies, turning the area into a raucous feeding station. With the last of the frugivores came the first of the humans, drawn by the obvious sanctity of the Buddhist monk and the way in which the birds trusted the presence of this man.

First an old man, bent and withered, sat down in silence before Sonaka, followed a day or two later by a youth, a boy and the next day a beautiful young girl. Sonaka said nothing, continuing his contemplative routine as though alone.

132

At length, Sonaka stirred and looked from one to the other of his audience of four. "What is truth?" he asked, closing his eyes again.

For a few minutes, nobody said anything. Then the youth coughed gently and asked, "Do you want us to answer, Master, or do you mean to teach us?"

"I am not your Master," Sonaka replied. "And if you know what truth is, I want you to tell me."

"Truth is not lying," said the youth.

"The gods are truth," said the old man.

"I do not know what truth is," said the boy. "But I think it is the love between a mother and her son."

"I also do not know what the truth is," said the girl. "I only know that the truth of my life is pain and suffering. I am only fifteen years old but I want to find a better way."

Sonaka opened his eyes and smiled at the young girl. "You are right. Life is suffering. Human nature is not perfect, and neither is the world. Name me some of the sufferings that afflict us."

"Pain," the girl whispered. "Fear, terror and despair."

"Frustration," added the youth. "And disappointment."

"Loneliness," the boy added. "Sadness, toothache."

"Old age," the old man said, his voice quivering with bitterness. "Death."

"All of these," Sonaka agreed. "There are good times too in almost every life. We experience love, comfort, a full belly, happiness. Yet the bad outweighs the good for humans are imperfect and the world is imperfect. Nothing lasts, for the world is forever changing. We live our lives in the knowledge that we will suffer and one

133

day, every one of us will die, bringing any happiness we might have had to an end. There are Four Noble Truths; this then is the first of them."

"Then there is no hope?" the youth asked.

"Ask first where suffering originates. If the world is imperfect, where do we look for happiness?"

"That is easy," the boy laughed. "A good meal, a warm bed and the love of my mother."

"Passion," the youth added with a grin. "Love and a good marriage."

"Money," said the old man. "With money you can buy more of anything when the first is used up."

"Knowledge," the girl replied.

Sonaka nodded. "All things change, all things dissolve into nothingness. You are born naked and even the richest king can take nothing out of this world with him when he dies. A rich man desires gold and fears the loss of it so much he loses sight of the impermanence of his life. The beggar on the street lusts after what he does not have and is likewise bound to the things of this life. Because all things are transient, their loss must follow, and hard on the heels of loss is suffering. This is the Second Noble Truth – suffering is caused by our attachment to the things of this world."

"But how can anyone not want the things of this world?" The youth fluttered his hands in agitation, frowning deeply. "If we do not seek food and shelter, the money to buy these things with, then we die, which is itself suffering. You are saying that life is suffering but it is inescapable."

"Why do you want these things?" Sonaka asked. "Food and shelter and money?"

"To avoid hunger, to keep warm ..."

"And dry," the boy added. "Money's good too. It buys sweetmeats." He grinned and rubbed his stomach.

"Therein lies the problem," Sonaka said with a smile. "Let us take food as an example because you enjoy it so much. To live means to suffer and one of the things we strive for each day is food, to satisfy our hunger, to nourish our bodies, to sustain our life. But life is suffering, so by our desire to eat we add to our suffering. Because we desire food, we miss it when we do not have it; we plan for our next meal, think up recipes to delight our senses and work to earn money to buy the food."

"Are you saying we should stop eating?" the girl asked.

"No, only that you should not desire food."

"We should not enjoy our food?"

"The enjoyment of a meal is transitory, the nourishment we take in passes, the life we seek to sustain ends. And for what? Our very 'selves', these bodies sitting here today, are as impermanent," Sonaka held up his begging bowl, "as this bowl of rice." He put the bowl down and looked at each of his students in turn. "What happens at death?" he asked softly.

"We ... we die," the boy said.

"Only your body," the youth jeered. "You are reborn."

Sonaka nodded. "As the person you are now, or as another?"

"As another," interrupted the girl.

"Then that which you regard as your 'self' is transitory, just like the food. This idea of 'self' is but an illusion; you imagine yourself to be as if by doing so you

135

make yourself permanent. This is not true. None of us are real entities; we are all merely the coming to be of creation, of the universe."

The old man got up, shaking his head. "I have lived a long time and I would like to think that when I die, as I will soon no doubt, I will be reborn."

"You must renounce the illusion of your existence," Sonaka said calmly. "Only by total renunciation can we forsake the cycle of rebirth."

"I want to be reborn. I'm an old man and I've been poor all my life, but I've been good. My karmic record is positive. With the blessing of the gods I may be reborn into a wealthy family. I don't need you, holy man." The old man turned and shuffled away, leaving the three young people sitting in front of the saffron-robed monk. They watched him leave before turning back to Sonaka.

"How can we end suffering?" the youth asked.

"Only through 'nirodha', the destruction of cravings and the attachment of the senses. Cravings and the attachment to things of the world are forms of passion. Nirodha means becoming dispassionate. This is the Third Noble Truth."

"You are saying that by our own actions we can defeat suffering?"

"We can remove the cause of suffering and by perfecting dispassion we become free from troubles, worries, lies, ideas."

"That's all?" the girl asked doubtfully. "Become dispassionate and we no longer suffer?"

Sonaka smiled. "Yes, that is all. But realize that 'all' means everything and you can see why this is the task of a lifetime – many lifetimes even."

"I must do this all my life?" the boy asked.

"If you wish to attain 'Nirvana', or perfect dispassion."

"Have you attained it?"

Sonaka spread his arms wide, smiling. "If I had, I would not be seated in front of you. I would be one with the universe, like the Lord Gautama Buddha."

Evening fell on three silent students as they each strove, in their own way, to come to terms with the teachings of the Buddhist monk and the three Noble Truths. A woman called in the village, insistently, and the boy rose to his feet.

"My mother is calling me. I must go." He ran off, disappearing into the darkness.

"And what of you?" Sonaka asked the youth. "Will you leave too?"

The youth shrugged. "I have a father and three brothers. They know where I am if it is important. Otherwise I do what I please. I am of the Vaishya – the merchant class."

"And you?"

The girl shook her head. "I have no-one. I have traveled far from Pihokri to find you. I will stay if you allow it."

"Why would I not allow it, child?"

"I think she is a Shudra, or even worse, a Dalit who will contaminate us by her presence." The youth looked distastefully at the girl. "She is not known in the village and who but a low caste woman would travel alone, without men?"

137

"There is no rank here, no caste. All men, and women too, are equal and can attain to perfection. If you cannot accept that you do not belong here."

The youth squirmed, grateful for the covering darkness. "I can accept it, if you order it, Master."

"I am not your master, nor do I order it," Sonaka said. "You stay or you go. It is your decision."

After a few moments, the youth bowed his head. "I stay," he muttered.

"Good." Sonaka produced the bowl of rice and set it down between them. "As we have not yet achieved Nirvana and must eat to sustain ourselves, let us do so."

"But without enjoyment," the girl said softly.

Sonaka chuckled, and offered the rice to both his students. The girl accepted immediately, the youth after a brief pause. When the rice had disappeared, Sonaka put the wooden bowl aside. He gestured at the night sky, ablaze with stars, their faint light glowing off the eternal snows far above and around them. From below came the rippling roar of the two rivers as they joined, heading downward to the plains to become the mighty Ganga. Nearer at hand came the night sounds of the village – dogs barking, children crying and the bustle of family life as it slowed. Surrounding them was the fresh scent of the forest and river, overlain by wood smoke and cooking food, animal dung and spices.

"All illusion," Sonaka murmured. "Yet so beautiful."

All three sat and looked out over the dark forest and thought their own thoughts until the youth coughed apologetically. "How do we achieve Nirvana?" he asked quietly.

"There is a path, a gradual path, to self-improvement. It is described as the Middle Way or the Eightfold Path."

"Will you teach it to us?" asked the girl.

"Yes, but not tonight." Sonaka rose and found his sleeping space, stretching out on his right side, cushioning his head with his right hand. The youth picked out a place near the monk and lay on his back with his arms behind his head, looking up at the starlight filtering through the leafy canopy of the pipal. The girl moved off a few paces and curled up.

After several minutes, in which Sonaka remained motionless and the youth and girl fidgeted, the girl half sat up and looked toward the youth.

"What is your name?" she whispered.

"Your names are meaningless," Sonaka said, cutting off the youth's reply. "Keeping your own name is an attachment to the things of this world. You must forget your names." A few moments later, he added, "Druki and Chanda are good names."

"I will be Druki," said the girl at once.

The youth snorted with mirth. "Then I will be Chanda."

"Good, that is settled. Now go to sleep."

"Is not sleep also an illusion?" Chanda asked mockingly. Nobody replied so he rolled over and after a few minutes immersed himself in this illusion.

They were all up with the dawn and Sonaka led them down to the Mandakini River and introduced them to his routine, sending Druki off behind some rocks to bathe while he and Chanda stripped off and braved the icy waters in the open.

"Why do you send me apart?" Druki had asked. "Is not my female body as much an illusion as your male ones? Surely the sight of my naked body will not stimulate you – or is it that I am a lowly Dalit and caste really does matter?"

"I do not send you off for my own sake, Druki, but for yours and Chanda's. I have passed beyond temptation but you are just starting on the path to perfection and you are still susceptible."

Afterward, Sonaka led them through the village until he found a wood carver. He greeted the man and blessed him, saying, "My pupils have need of begging bowls, but I have no money."

The carver looked uncomfortable. "I am a poor man, with a wife and children to support."

Sonaka nodded. "Perhaps you have pieces you have rejected?"

The carver thought for a few moments. "I may have. One moment." He disappeared round the back of his hut, returning a few moments later with two new, but obviously flawed, pieces. He held them out to Sonaka. "Will this do?"

The wooden bowls were made of teak, turned and carved, but one had a gouge and was cracked, the other had a hole in one side where a flaw in the wood, a knothole, had fallen out. The monk passed the cracked one to Druki and the one with the hole to Chanda.

Thanking the man for his generosity, Sonaka blessed him again and they wandered up the street toward the higher levels of the village where the wealthier people lived.

"Never ask food from the same person more often than you need to. It is a blessing to give and such blessings should be shared. If a man comes to you and offers food, accept it, for that man is seeking to better himself. Bless him and move on." Sonaka walked up to a door and knocked lightly, bowing when a well-dressed woman wearing considerable jewelry opened it. Sonaka held up his bowl and his students followed suit.

The woman nodded and went back inside, returning with a pot of rice and a bowl of boiled goat meat. She ladled a large spoon of rice into each bowl and started to add a few pieces of meat. Chanda and Druki accepted the meat but Sonaka refused, slipping his hand over the bowl. He blessed the woman and led his students back to the pipal tree.

As they sat down in the shade, putting their bowls to one side, Chanda looked hungrily at the scraps of meat in his own bowl and the lack of meat in Sonaka's. "Why do you not accept meat? Is it forbidden?"

"It is morning," Sonaka replied. "We meditate now and learn later." He refused to be drawn into discussion, folding himself into the lotus position and turning his eyes inward. After a few minutes of temptation, Chanda and Druki put their bowls aside and imitated the monk, though their actions reflected form rather than substance.

At noon, Sonaka stirred, his eyes focusing and his breath coming harder. Chanda got up and stretched, while Druki was more discrete about her actions. They ate, though Chanda hesitated before eating the goat meat, wanting to ask Sonaka but not daring to.

Sonaka put his bowl aside and waited until the others had finished before starting to talk. "You ask whether

141

meat is forbidden to a follower of the Eightfold Path. Some consider that as an animal has to die to provide the meat for your meal, it is a wrong action. These ones consider the animal as being the habitation of men's souls when they are working off their karmic burden, therefore, they feel it to be wrong to deprive these ones of what little life they have, merely to provide a man with food. Others believe that man does not inhabit the bodies of insensate beasts and that there is no wrong action involved in eating animal flesh."

"What do you believe, teacher?" Chanda asked.

"It does not matter what I believe. Your actions are your own choice. It is up to you whether you eat meat or not."

"I like meat," Druki whispered.

"I knew it. She is Dalit."

"It does not matter who she is," Sonaka said. "The Way is open to all who seek it. As for liking meat, that is a desire, an attachment to this world."

"Then we shouldn't eat it if we enjoy it," Chanda said slowly. "But if we do not enjoy it, we will not want to eat it."

Sonaka smiled. "Consider – if a man has killed an animal to eat it and you happen along with your bowl, he gives you some meat. If you accept the meat, have you committed a wrong action? Consider again – a man sees you coming with your bowl in your hand and hurries off to kill an animal that he might give you some. If you accept the meat, have you performed a wrong action? In the first case the animal died through the action and intent of another; in the second, it was as if you killed the animal for it was your presence with the begging bowl that led to its death."

"So in the first instance it was alright to eat meat, but not in the second?" Chanda asked.

"That is for you to decide."

"Teacher," Druki said slowly, a frown creasing the taut skin of her forehead. "The woman today who gave us meat did not know we were coming until we arrived at her door, yet still you refused the meat. Why is that if no wrong was committed?"

"I do not like meat."

"You don't like it?" Chanda gaped. "Then what was all that about wrong actions and intent?"

"A lesson," Sonaka said. "You asked about meat, I told you. Now it is up to you what course you follow."

"Eating meat will not prevent me following the Eightfold Way?" Druki asked.

"No, but never ask for it or intimate to others that you want it. Before you know it you will fall into gluttony and fall from the Way. Here, the action is less important than the intent. Wanting meat, or any form of food, is to cling to the illusion of the world and to accept suffering."

Chanda and Druki sat and thought about their teacher's words. While they thought, Sonaka closed his eyes and contemplated the infinite, feeling the strength that flowed into him from the all-embracing oneness of the universe. A little later, he opened his eyes to find his two students sitting quietly and watching him, not willing to disturb his meditations.

"I must teach you to regard the infinite," Sonaka said with a smile. "Then you will have something productive

143

to do instead of sitting there fidgeting. But first, I will tell you of the Eightfold Path."

"Teacher," Druki broke in quietly, her eyes downcast. "Did you not say that there are Four Noble Truths? You have told us that Life is suffering; that the origin of suffering is the attachment to transient things; and that the end of suffering is possible through Nirodha. Will you not tell us the Fourth Noble Truth first?"

"You have been paying attention, Druki. Very well, the Fourth Noble Truth is that there is a path that brings an end to suffering. It is the Eightfold Path and it is the Middle Way between the extremes of self-indulgence and asceticism. It leads to the end of the cycle of rebirth and may take many lifetimes to achieve. It was laid out by Siddhartha Gautama, the one known as the Buddha, over a thousand years ago. Since then, many have trodden the Eightfold Path and some have achieved Nirvana."

"Will you show us the Path, teacher?" Chanda asked.

"First," said Sonaka, "Do not think of the eight precepts as being a sequence of actions, a series of steps on the road to Nirvana. You do not complete one only to move onto the next. If that were so it would be easy to accomplish. Rather, you must grasp all eight principles and learn to apply them together. They are interdependent and cover the areas of Wisdom, Ethical Conduct and Mental Development.

Right View and Right Intention encompass Wisdom; Right Speech, Right Action and Right Living encompass Ethical Conduct; and Right Effort, Right Mindfulness and Right Concentration encompass Mental Development."

"That will take forever, if we are to understand all that," Chanda said.

144

"Not forever, but it may take you many lifetimes."

"Then we had better start," Druki said. "You say they are interrelated concepts rather than steps in the Path. Will you then deal with them altogether or separately, teacher?"

"Initially, as separate concepts but as understanding grows we shall meld one into another. Let us start with 'Right View' for this is the start and the end of the Path. Simply put, it means to see things as they really are and realize the Four Noble Truths." Sonaka went on to discuss the laws of Karma, karmic conditioning; the differences between Right View and a function of the intellect; between wisdom and intelligence. "Because our view of the universe gives rise to the thoughts we have and the actions we take, the right view produces right thoughts and right actions."

Sonaka went on to explain that the right view gave understanding but Right Intention was one's actual commitment to self-improvement. "Buddha recognized three aspects of Right Intention: an intention of turning away from desire, an intention of resistance to such negative emotions as anger and hate, and an intention to renounce aggression and cruelty. These two concepts encompass Wisdom for by resolving to follow them we recognize the world for what it is and make a commitment in our minds to better ourselves."

"That seems relatively easy," Chanda said. "You have shown us this new view of the world and it seems an obvious step to want to improve one's life." He scratched his side as he spoke. "I think I have the first two concepts in my hand."

Sonaka smiled. "Why do you scratch?"

"Eh? Oh, an insect bit me."

"But Chanda, neither your side nor the insect truly exist. They are both illusions created by your mind. How can one bite and the other hurt?"

Chanda frowned. "Truly?"

Sonaka pointed out at the sun-drenched valley. "Everything is illusion. You cannot say you understand that concept, that you possess the Right View, while you doubt the truth of that statement."

"And you, teacher?" Druki asked. "You have been following the Eightfold Path for years. Do you have the Right View?"

"Sometimes, but the pull of the world is strong, so I must continually work at understanding. Now, wisdom leads to ethical conduct which is threefold. Right Speech means we must abstain from lying, we must not use words to hurt others and we should refrain from idle gossip. In other words, tell the truth always, and speak warmly, kindly and gently – and only when necessary."

The afternoon passed slowly, with Sonaka leading his two students hesitantly down the path which leads to perfection. He had no illusions that his words that day would do anything more than point them in the right direction, give them something to aim for. Evening came and went, and the next day. Once Chanda and Druki had the framework of their life's work, Sonaka started taking them through lessons and examples, showing them meditative techniques whereby the concepts they heard could be turned into actions.

"You will remember the Buddha said Right Mindfulness itself has four foundations – four contemplations?"

Druki nodded. "The body, feeling, mind and phenomena."

"The body, though the least of these, is often the hardest to control as we are closest to it, most intimately connected. We sit in contemplation," Sonaka went on, "bending our minds to the infinite, but the body intrudes. Our muscles stiffen and ache after we have sat in one position for a while, the pressure of our bottom and legs upon the ground numbs us. We itch and feel the need to scratch, we grow tired, we hunger and we thirst, we feel the urge to relieve ourselves or empty our bowels. Our mind leads us down strange paths and our bodies follow, betraying us. You, Chanda ..." Sonaka's sudden words roused the youth from his peaceful state of listening. "You are a young man. Your body will lust, rising and intruding on your thoughts – resist it. Druki, you are a young woman. You carry two burdens. One is like Chanda's, you will long for love. Your heart will ache for a man and your loins will melt. Resist the temptation, Druki, for the ways of love bind you to the world. The other burden is uniquely yours as a woman. You know of what I speak, Druki."

Druki shook her head, a puzzled expression on her face.

Sonaka lifted an eyebrow in surprise before continuing. "Your body will intrude on you every month, tugging your will from the Path. Many will view you as unclean, so you must learn to guard against this when you know it is near."

Druki paused for a moment, her head cocked on one side, studying her teacher. Her puzzlement drained away,

147

to be replaced by a surprised smile. "Ah, I did not realize what you meant. What must I do?"

"Remove yourself from the presence of others at that time so you do not speak rashly, neither looking for faults in others, nor harboring resentments, nor encouraging others to wrong speech through your presence. Let this be part of Right Livelihood where your dealings with living beings are steadfast and righteous."

"Can a woman truly find the Eightfold Path?"

"Yes. Any living being can do so, if they truly desire it."

One day, several months after the coming of his two students, Sonaka left them as they walked down to the Mandakini River in the early dawn.

"Do all things as you have been doing. I will return."

Sonaka set off across the swinging rope bridge and turned left, following the steep-sided Alaknanda River for the town of Karnaprayag. Here he wandered the streets until he found first a purveyor of herbs and spices and next a seller of cloth and after a short period of haggling, secured what he wanted for a very small price. The goods would not be ready for two days so he begged some food from a well-to-do shopkeeper and found a banyan tree on the outskirts of town, settling down for a couple of days peace and solitude.

On the second day he returned to the cloth seller. He paid for his purchase with the alms he had been given in the town and set off down the river again. This time he crossed by another rope bridge not far below Karnaprayag, drawn by the many pilgrims along the roads. He asked a merchant where he was going.

"The temple at Rudranath," the merchant replied, dropping a small coin into Sonaka's bowl. "This road leads to Pokhri and thence over the hills to Rudranath."

"Pokhri? You mean Pihokri. I have heard of it."

The merchant shook his head. "It is Pokhri. I know because I have a cousin who lives there. I have never heard of the other."

"I know of a Pihokri," a passerby chipped in. He bowed to the saffron-robed monk. "It is not a village though. It is a lonely ridge top where a shrine stands to a brave man who once fought off a hundred men to save his family. He fought on though he was cut into pieces." The man coughed, realizing he appeared gullible. "So the story goes, anyway. You can see the shrine for yourself, it is up that road." He pointed.

Sonaka thanked the merchant and the passerby, turned off the main road and began climbing the steep ridge toward the shrine. He found a dense stand of Chir pine and a small stone shrine dedicated to a hero called Isha. Behind the shrine sprawled an overgrown and derelict cemetery of the ancient hill people, numerous upright stones with pottery jars at their bases, many of them shattered and empty. He looked around and though seeing nothing that warranted his further attention, he went and had a talk with the keeper of the shrine. When he departed, he took the road back to Rudraprayag that ran along the right bank of the Alaknanda. He arrived back at the old pipal tree in the afternoon, walking silently up the path. Chanda and Druki sat cross-legged under the tree, eyes closed and meditating, so rather than disturb them, Sonaka seated himself between them, the bundle of cloth on the ground in front of him.

149

"Teacher! You have returned." Druki had her eyes open and was looking with some astonishment at Sonaka.

Chanda too, stared open-mouthed. "How did you get here without us hearing you? Are you a Rakshasa or a ghost?"

Sonaka smiled. "I am as tied to this physical world as you, Chanda. No, I can tread softly when I want and I did not wish to interrupt your meditations."

"How was your journey?" Druki asked, eyeing the bundle with great curiosity. "Was it successful?"

"Open it."

Druki unfolded two lengths of beautifully dyed cloth, the saffron color rich and glowing. "For us?"

Sonaka nodded. "You have both made good progress these last few months. I felt you should both be wearing the robes that will set you apart as a seeker."

"But where is yours?" Chanda asked, lifting the lengths of cloth.

"I already have one."

"Worn and thin, teacher. I would not feel right wearing such glorious color while my teacher sat in faded robes."

"Then I fear you have not advanced as far as I'd hoped, Chanda. If you think the newness and richness of the robe defines you, then the desires of the world are still strong in you."

Chanda flushed and hung his head. "You are right, teacher. I ... I must refuse the robe."

"No, you will take it for by refusing you proclaim your feeling of self-importance. Chanda," Sonaka reached out and patted the youth on one knee. "I would not bring the cloth if I did not think you ready. You and

Druki take it down to the village and find two seamstresses to fashion it for you. Two, mind, it is not right that we put such a burden of toil on one woman."

The youngsters scrambled off with barely concealed haste. Sonaka sat and breathed in the fine fresh air blowing up the Alaknanda Valley and listened to the bird song. A small flock of *Kokila*, the orange and green pigeon, descended on a tall *Morus* tree a hundred or so paces down the slope, swinging from the branches and greedily swallowing the ripe fruit. Sonaka felt himself sinking into a meditative state. He had a problem and he was not sure what he should do about it. Closing his eyes, he looked inward, concentrating on the illusion of his existence. An hour later he returned, satisfied that he had the answer to his problem.

Just before sunset, Druki and Chanda returned from the village, resplendent in their new robes and feeling very pleased with themselves, though they hid it well. They also brought with them a bowl of rice and a freshly baked millet loaf. Chanda said the loaf was a gift from one of the village elders, happy that a new acolyte had been raised up from among the villagers.

After meditation and the noon meal next day, Sonaka started questioning the two new acolytes, probing their understanding of the Four Noble Truths, the Eightfold Path, and many other topics they had discussed over the months. He asked them searching questions, set them debating points of ethics and law, sitting back and listening as they argued each point. Chanda showed a remarkable grasp of the Buddha's teachings for one so young, but Druki still asked more questions than she answered. She obviously had a good knowledge but lacked the confidence of expression the young man displayed. Sonaka thought he knew why.

The questions and debates continued and after a week, Sonaka drew the sessions to a close. "I will continue these talks with you one at a time. Druki, please leave us for an hour. I will speak with Chanda first."

Druki got up and bowed before walking off down the path toward the village. Just before she passed out of sight she turned and stared back at the two seated monks. She stayed away longer than an hour, finding a rock far above the village where she could look out over the whole valley. The village was almost hidden from her vantage point and the pipal tree that was their home showed only its crown. Her eye was caught briefly by a flash of saffron on the path leading down to the rope bridge but it was not repeated. She dismissed it as the plumage of a bird, and turned her mind to her memories, thinking back over the years and comparing her life then with her present situation.

Druki returned to the pipal tree as the light of the setting sun poured up the Alaknanda Valley, turning the high snow-covered peaks to the north a beautiful rosy gold and bathing the seated monk in gold. "Where's Chanda?" she asked, looking around.

"He has gone away. I sent him out to find students of his own. He is ready."

"And I am not?"

"No."

There was a long silence, broken at last by Druki. She held her voice even and calm but there was an edge of anger, hiding deep. "Why?"

"You know why," Sonaka said, his eyes locked on Druki.

"Because I am a woman?" Druki sneered. "You told me my sex did not matter and I believed you. You have lied to me."

"I have not lied to you, Druki. And it has nothing to do with your sex."

"Really? You preach about Right Action and the avoidance of sexual misconduct but all the time you hold women, or at least this woman, in low regard. It would not surprise me if all this time you were lusting after me. Is that it, Sonaka? You lust after my young body?" Druki loosened her robe and it slipped off her shoulders, falling to the ground. She stepped out of it, sinuously moving her naked body closer to the seated monk. "Well, here I am. Satisfy your lust."

"Enough," Sonaka said. "Put your robe back on or assume your natural form. You will not tempt me so cease your games."

Druki stopped and stared at the monk. "You know? How can you?" She squatted and looked closer, staring into his eyes. "You do know!" Abruptly she stood up and laughed, her body rippling and flowing, the features changing until what stood before Sonaka was no longer a fifteen year old girl but a giant man clothed in long brown hair with a tiger's snarling visage atop his shoulders. "How's this?" Incongruously the voice was still Druki's.

"You do not frighten me."

"No? You should be frightened. Do you know what I can do to you? Let me give you a taste." Images flooded through Sonaka's mind and despite himself he shuddered,

153

catching himself almost instantly, instituting a calming train of thought.

"You have a creative if somewhat nasty frame of mind," Sonaka said quietly. "However, pain and death are transitory, like all things. I refuse to be governed by them."

The tiger head growled, baring fangs that dripped smoking blood. "I see in your mind that you truly believe that." The demon looked at the monk in a calculating fashion. "How is it that you saw through my disguise? I believed it to be perfect."

"Put on a more reasonable body and sit down and I will tell you."

The demon's body flowed once more and Druki's young body reappeared, naked as before. "I knew you secretly lusted after me," he said with a grin.

"Put on your robe again."

"Yes, teacher." The demon slipped the robe back on and sat down in front of Sonaka, molding his features into those of an attentive and worshipful girl. "So tell me. What gave me away?"

"Many things. You are a young girl who travels alone. When you are asked for the ills that trouble the world you reply 'pain, fear, terror and despair' – hardly the ills of a young girl. You display a formidable grasp of the intellectual side of the Buddha's words yet no real understanding, no commitment of the heart to see them through."

"That is not enough. What else?"

"You are fifteen years old, Druki, or so you told me. You have the body of a woman, as I have seen. Yet even I, who have never known women, having renounced them

154

in my youth, know more about the workings of a woman's body than you."

"Hmm, I made a mistake not inhabiting a woman first, rather than building my body from the thoughts of men. However, that is not enough. Must I search your mind to find the answer?"

"Those things made me wonder at first, and then made me suspicious, but it was chance that revealed your nature to me. When you arrived, you told me you came from Pihokri. I thought no more of it until I journeyed to Karnaprayag. On my way back I met pilgrims who told me they were on their way to Badrinath by way of Pokhri … not Pihokri."

"A slip of the tongue." Druki extended her tongue at least a hand span from her lips and waggled it.

"No, for I found Pihokri nearby. It is a cemetery with a shrine dedicated to a man with the strength of ten men. I talked with the keeper and he told me the truth of Isha and the demon."

"That was a long time ago."

"Demons are not as men. You are already, what? Hundreds of years old?"

"Thousands more likely. But tell me, monk of Buddha, once you knew me for what I was, why did you confront me? Would it not have been more prudent to send me off to gather recruits like Chanda? For now I will have to kill you."

"I was curious. I still am."

"About what?"

"Why would a demon seek to learn about the Buddha? What interest does one such as you have in the Noble Truths and the Path to Nirvana?"

155

"Do you know what it is to be a demon, a Rakshasa? No, how could you? I was created for one purpose, to sow hatred and fear among men, to kill and to satisfy my ever-present hunger for blood and terror. Not that I mind this, you understand. Death, particularly violent, vicious death, gives me great pleasure. The taste of terror-ridden men is delicious but ... but I have no choice." The face of Druki frowned. "I don't know if you can understand this, monk, for although you say I have a good mind and great knowledge, I can no more turn this knowledge into action than can a rock learn to dance or a tree to sing. A man can learn the Eightfold Path and turn what he learns into actions that will bring him eventually to oneness with the universe. I can learn those same precepts but it is not given to me to change. I am a demon and I am what I am."

"Do you want to change?"

"I want to have a choice about changing," the demon growled.

Sonaka thought about this for a time, looking inward at his own mind, then outward to encompass the world. "We are taught that the gods are good and unchanging, that rakshas are bad and unchanging, and that man is both good and bad but can change. Some of this is self-evident, but are these definitions unbending. The question is whether you really do have a choice."

"A sadhu I once knew far to the northeast – Bala – said I did not."

Sonaka looked up sharply. "Bala of Kailasa? He lived nearly two thousand years ago."

"I told you I was older than I looked." The Druki demon smiled. "Was he right?"

156

"I must think on this." Sonaka looked around at the gathering dusk. "It is late. I will sleep and meditate on your problem tomorrow."

"Forego sleep and meditate tonight, monk. I will have your answer with the dawn or I shall feed," Druki demon's jaws gaped widely, "And search for a wiser man."

"Your argument is quite persuasive," Sonaka commented dryly. He settled himself into a comfortable position, closing his eyes against the stare of the demon. Emptying his mind, he dwelt on the concepts of choice and destiny.

A red jungle fowl cock crowed in the chill pre-dawn darkness of the hillside, setting off the domestic fowl in the village. A little later the sky flushed pink and the first rays of the new sun caressed the high peaks of Himalaya. Sonaka opened his eyes to see the face of Druki staring at him in exactly the same position as the night before.

"Well," rumbled the demon. "Do you have an answer for me?"

"First, let me see you as you truly are, not a form taken on to please or frighten men."

Druki's limbs drifted like smoke, streaming away as if a strong wind blew across the hillside, though the fallen leaves remained undisturbed. Her body followed, the saffron robe collapsing into an untidy pile on the ground. Last of all, her head lingered for a few moments before dissolving into nothingness. All that remained was a blue flame, faint in the bright morning light, burning on the saffron robe but not consuming it.

"Well, monk, was the sadhu right?" The voice sounded thin, no longer warmed and shaped by throat and mouth, but perfectly intelligible.

"Choice is a very human concept," Sonaka said. "The gods are powerful and on the face of it would surely have choice. And so we see if we read the legends and the stories. I have never met a god ..."

"I have," the demon interrupted. "Unpleasant beings."

"Really? In what way are ... well, as I was saying, it has come down to us that gods do have choice in everyday matters for they answer some prayers but not others, are quite partisan in their allegiances, and display many weaknesses common to mankind. But, they must remain true to their nature. A god cannot step down from his position, he cannot abrogate his duties, and he cannot take on new ones. The god of forests cannot just become the god of the sea, for instance. Even a god is bound by his position in the overall scheme of things.

"What is this to do with me? I am not a god. Are you trying to extend your life with meaningless words?"

"Exercise patience, demon. I am getting to you. Humans ... well, humans you know about. Their lives are filled with choices and many rail against this, not wanting to take responsibility for their actions. This same freedom to choose, however distasteful it may seem to some, means that a man or woman can better themselves, rising up through the Eightfold Path, until they achieve Nirvana and become one with the universe."

"What of me, monk? You are trying my patience."

"A demon is somewhere between god and man. A god lives forever and a man for a short time, though he is

158

reborn and effectively lives forever. A demon?" Sonaka shrugged. "A demon can be killed, or so the stories relate, but I have never heard of a demon being reborn. This would give it a life somewhat less than forever."

"That is all you have? I knew that much before I asked." The blue flame rose from the saffron robe and moved closer to Sonaka.

"There is more, but I must ask questions of you first."

"What questions? The flame halted its hungry glide toward the seated monk.

"When you kill, do you always do so in the same way?"

"I induce terror and soak up the emotions like parched soil in the first rains. So yes, I suppose I always kill in the same way."

"Do you induce terror in the same way with all men?"

"No, their minds create the image of the terror and I give the image substance."

"No help there then." Sonaka frowned. "You obviously do not eat all the time. What makes you stop eating?"

"I lose the urge to kill."

"But you are hungry now. When was your last kill?"

"Six months ago. I killed a traveler on my way here."

"Why none while you have been here?"

"It might have looked somewhat suspicious." The voice, though not formed from flesh, still managed to sound amused.

"So you made a choice?"

The demon was silent for a time. "I suppose I did," he said at last.

"Good. Now, have you ever refrained from killing even though the opportunity was there? Think back to Pihokri."

"You mean the wood cutter's wife? Yes, I could have taken her too. I was still hungry and the approaching villagers would not have inhibited me. I know that was a choice, but was it a free choice? Could not my action have been tainted by the mind of her husband? I was in his body at the time."

"The wood cutter's mind was still alive when you possessed him?"

"No. He died at the hand of bandits. I gave him but a semblance of life."

"Then you have your answer, demon. It was a choice made freely, by you, not to kill the wife and child. You are capable of choice. The sadhu was wrong."

"Truly?"

"You can prove it right here and now, demon."

"How?"

"Leave without killing me. Make that choice."

Cruel laughter reverberated across the hillside. The villagers heard it and looked fearfully toward the pipal tree, but none ventured closer to investigate. "Is this what your argument leads to? A feeble attempt to save your own life? I thought more of you, monk." The flame danced before the seated man. "Well, maybe I will leave you alive to ponder your weakness and your lack of courage. I will seek out a strong man or three elsewhere to satisfy my hunger."

160

"I had not thought of that," Sonaka responded. "My concern was for your immediate decision. I cannot send you off to kill others less prepared for death than I. You must kill me, demon, and no-one else."

"What? A last meal, then never to eat again? That is no choice."

"Can you not eat anything but man?"

"You mean animals? No, for that would be to kill for the express purpose of feeding myself and you would never counsel that." The voice fell silent for a time, then, "I can exist for a time on the energies of the thunderstorm."

"Then you have a choice, demon. Your first choice is like a drop of rain that falls in the high Himalaya. It moves downward, joins with others, and becomes a trickle, a cascade, a torrent – until your course becomes a mighty river sweeping your being to a new destination. It all starts with that first choice.'

"And what is my first choice, monk of Buddha?"

"Do you seek to be more than a demon?"

161

Chapter Eight

I left Sonaka alive. I had been hungry for six months, a few hours longer was no great burden. Besides, I owed him a debt for the insights he gave me into the workings of men's minds and for proving to me that I was not a mindless beast after all, but a sentient being capable of altering my future. The question that remained uppermost in my mind was what did I want to become?

The future would have to wait, though, for my hunger could not be denied. I kept my natural shape when I left, the blue flame of my being almost invisible in the bright morning sunlight as I sped down the course of the Alaknanda River until it intersected with the main road leading south and west toward the plains. Within an hour I had found a group of travelers and fed, swiftly and without refinement, being content to extract their lives without the piquancy that terror lends. In human terms I suppose it was like eating a bowl of plain rice without the enjoyment of a spicy sauce and roasted vegetables. It filled me, but still left me feeling unsatisfied. Three men and a woman died but I took a small first step toward my new being by leaving a child untouched. I drifted on down the valley leaving the little girl crying by her mother's body. Someone would find her soon and take care of her. I did not even consider the effect the death of her parents may have had on her young mind. I have never, in thousands of years of existence, been close to anyone or suffered a loss, so how could I tell the effect my depredations had on the infrequent survivors.

I continued my westward course down the Alaknanda, not really knowing where I was going or what

I sought. I had come to Rudraprayag from the east, so, not wanting to return to the hill shrine and its ancient cemetery, I decided – no, decided is too strong a word, it implies a course of action; gave into, perhaps – the tug westward.

I passed through Srinagar, unseen, and soon came to Devaprayag, at the confluence of another rushing river, the Bhagirathi. I stayed my course, hovering above the roiling currents where the whiter waters of the Bhagirathi joined the blue current of the Alaknanda. Below me, though still many miles distant, were the great plains of northern Bharat. This river, I knew, flowed through those plains as the mighty Ganga, but I felt no urge to follow its course. The high mountains were my home, so I turned north, following the twisting Bhagirathi. Past Tehri, a bustling town that hummed with the activity of traders and farmers from the surrounding terraced river valleys, and up along the shrinking river into its headwaters. At Dharasu I stopped again, uncertain as to why I was there. The land around me was poor and rocky, inhabited by few people, whereas the lower valley was rich and teeming with my food. I should by rights return there, yet I felt I was up here for a reason. I looked to the west and saw an imposing hill, a mere mound compared to my Nanda Devi, but still the most imposing place around. Maybe the view from this hill – Nag Tibba was the name sliding across a man's brain as I fed once more – would reveal my destination.

You might ask why, when I was no more substantial than a flame, did I not simply rise up through the cold clear air and spy out my destination at any time. Why use a mountain? I don't know. Simply put, it did not occur to

163

me. Perhaps it is because I have never felt sufficiently godlike to be divorced from the physical things of this world. I like to be in the forests, on the rivers and mountains, feeling life all around me.

The summit of Nag Tibba is densely forested and rather uninteresting. I scanned the horizon, seeing great distances in the crystal air. The snow-clad peaks of the high Himalaya embraced the north and the crumpled tapestry of mountains, hills and valleys spread out like skirts below them. To the south, a brown and seared hill caught my eye, differed from the lush blue-greens of the forest that covered the hills like a wave. As I stared toward it I caught the flicker of lightning playing about its summit and I knew, suddenly, why I was here. The only other food source I had ever come across, aside from men, was the energies of the thunderstorm. Rather than wander and chance on these storms, I had sought them out, unconsciously following that rich band of iron ore that spears through these mountains, rising to the surface on occasion. One such place was this dry and withered hill to the south, judging by the number of lightning strokes it suffered. Here I could find food in plenty while I tried to work out what I wanted to do with my new-found choice. You may ask again why I do not just feed on the energies of the storm instead of preying on mankind. Well, if I may use the rice analogy again, the lightning has no taste; it is as if I ate a bowl of rice that had all the interest of tepid water. I can survive on it, but I do not enjoy it.

I lifted into the air, transforming into a great Argul, a lammergeier, and soared southward far faster than those birds can fly, the thin air beating at me and riffling my pinions. Within minutes, I crossed the intervening space and plummeted through the storm clouds toward the bare mound of Pari Tibba. I saw then that the burnt and brown look was not because of dryness or from fires caused by the lightning strokes but resulted from the rusted iron ores that poked through the thin vegetation like the bones of a well-chewed corpse. A bolt blasted an outcrop of rock as I landed and I let my bird form shimmer and vanish as I soaked up a morsel of the energy. This place would suit me nicely while I worked out exactly what I wanted to do.

I found an overhang of rust-streaked rock a little below the summit and settled into the rear of it, looking north toward Nag Tibba and the icy peaks of the high Himalaya. I turned my mind back to a consideration of the Buddhist Way and whether it held out any clues to my future. What am I? I thought.

I am a Rakshasa, a demon, a being created ... but wait, was I actually created? My earliest recollection was drifting across a battlefield lost in the mists of antiquity, awash in the blood and terror of so much violent death. Did I exist before the battle? Had I just lost my memory of previous existence, or had the mental agonies of hundreds of dying men engendered me somehow? I shrugged mentally. How could I ever know? Did it really matter? I knew what I was now. The dying thoughts of the countless humans that have been my prey confirmed my identity. I am a demon.

Let me approach this subject another way. What is a demon? I am privy to the thoughts and emotions of men and though there is some disagreement, most define me as a spirit, having no body, the naked flame of my being the only existence I have. I am malefic, in other words evil; I exist solely to torment and strike terror into the hearts of

165

mankind. I have no redeeming features. I am essentially immortal, though my kind can die. Stories exist of gods and heroes killing demons, and the glimpses I have had of gods like Agni and Krishna confirm this ability. I can shift shape, assuming the guise of anything that exists and a great many things that do not. I can move through the air at great speed, through water and rock and fire unharmed. I can possess the bodies of man and beast, bending their will to mine. That is what I am.

What then, is my future? I seem to be without purpose, without aim, without ambition. I am good at one thing only, ripping the life force from men. That is not much to build a future on. Yet I feel within me a desire, almost a yearning, for something else, something to give my existence purpose. If I was a man I could strive for the Eightfold Path but whoever heard of a saintly demon? What would be the purpose of trying to end suffering? I do not suffer, I am above all that. And what is Nirvana to me? I do not need it.

Or do I? What would it be like to be one with the universe, having no identity of my own but feeling the pervading oneness of the All, being at total peace? Yet I have that already or at least a reasonable simulacrum. I haunt the valleys and ridges of this wrinkled land that men call Kedarkhand and Manaskand and, wandering alone in the high places, feeling the pulses of life around me – the long, slow rolling swell of the rocks themselves as they strain upward to heaven, the varied thrum of the trees answering the call of the seasons and the urgent, hurried staccato of animals busy with their short lives. It brings me something akin to the joy men feel, but a

166

lasting one that spans centuries. Do I need anything more than this?

After I had been on Pari Tibba for a time, I noticed the activities of men even in this remote place. Men shun Pari Tibba itself, confusing the lightning bolts with demons, but as the years passed, bolder souls started venturing upward, drawn by the deposits of iron. A small mine was carved into the hillside and baskets of ore removed. At the base of the hill, a village grew up, based on iron ore smelting and farming. Called Kashi in those days, it rapidly grew and attracted others.

By this time I was bored with my solitary life on the Hill of Storms and decided to come down into the world of men. I would once more sample the varied lives of humankind.

Chapter Nine

The pre-monsoon winds were always welcome in the town of Kashi. Built on a crescent-shaped ridge, the buildings sprawled along its length and down the slopes toward the swift flowing upper reaches of the Yamuna River. Once an ordinary farming village, the advent of metal workers following the outcrops of iron ore across Kedarkhand had wrought changes to the village, increasing its size and introducing clouds of noxious gases into the local atmosphere. The forests were felled and for a time a good living could be made producing charcoal to smelt the ore. However, a pall of smoke and fumes hung over the whole area, affecting crops and livestock, until the monsoonal winds arrived. The rains would follow soon, bringing an end to the iron smelting, but in the meantime, the spring breezes cleared the air and improved tempers.

Mandeep ran a small but efficient smelter at the base of the hill called Pari Tibbi. Two of his workers, Kapil and Jayavant, doubled as miners, extracting the ore from the little open-cast mine halfway up the hillside and transporting it to the smelter in large wicker baskets. Here, Ajit crushed the ore into smaller chunks and a young lad, Gauri, fed the ore mixed with charcoal into two shaft furnaces, readying them for the firing. Mandeep's wife, Damayanti, completed the crew, busying herself all day with washing and cooking, fetching water and gathering wood for the cook fires. She often asked her husband for some of the charcoal for her fires, but he always refused.

"You are lazy and charcoal costs too much," he would say. "You must fetch firewood from the forest."

So Damayanti would rise at dawn and cook a meal before gathering together the clothes and take them down to a nearby stream where she would soak them and pound them on the large smooth stones to dislodge the dirt. Then she would spread them out in the sun to dry, and while this was happening, cut feed for the milk goat. When the clothes were dry, Damayanti shouldered the big bundle of cut grass, gathered the folded garments under her other arm and trudged back to camp. Picking up a bucket, she would walk back to the stream, fill it, and return to camp, tipping the water into a large wooden tub, repeating this arduous task until the tub was full. Shopping followed, a long walk into the town where she bartered for the food and other supplies the smelting crew needed.

The noon meal came next and preparation for the evening meal would begin. In the afternoon, she set out for the forests with a bundle of rope and gathered dried sticks for firewood. With luck, she would find her firewood close at hand and Damayanti would have an hour's rest before returning to her hut to prepare the evening meal. Following dinner, she cleaned the small two-room house before washing and applying cosmetics and ointments to make her skin shine. Mandeep often felt amorous in the evenings and her last duty of the day was to satisfy her husband.

Mandeep's day was, in his view, just as arduous. He rose not long after his wife, and ate the meal she prepared, before touring the site to make sure his workers had all the supplies they needed. The morning was taken up

169

supervising his miners, following them up the hill and watching as they dug out the ore with mattocks. In the afternoon he rested while the sun beat down. Sometimes he almost envied his wife strolling in the shady, cool forest, picking up her sticks. Later on, as the day cooled, he bought supplies of charcoal from one of the burners and supervised the crushing of the ore, its mixing with the charcoal, and its loading into the shaft furnaces in just the correct amounts.

After dinner, he sat with the other men outside the hut on wooden benches, swapping stories and drinking milky tea while his wife cleaned the house and readied herself for her pleasurable duty. He would rise from the bench and hitch at his churidar, often making a small joke, before entering his hut and shutting the door. The other men wandered off to their hut across the clearing and lay down with their own thoughts.

Mandeep surveyed the clearing one morning after Damayanti had set off for the stream. He examined the two shaft furnaces, nodding in satisfaction at one of them, frowning when he saw the other was only half loaded. Clapping his hands loudly to attract the attention of his men who still stood near the hut finishing off the last of the chapattis and hot tea, he pointed at the half-filled furnace.

"Come along then, we have work to do, we cannot be standing around all day."

"We can't but you certainly will," Kapil muttered, though he was careful to keep his voice low. He turned and picked up his mattock and a battered wicker basket and followed Jayavant toward the path that led up the hillside.

170

"Gauri," Mandeep ordered, "Bring a brand from the hearth; it is time to fire the first furnace. Ajit, fetch one of the bellows."

Ajit strolled off to the little storage lean-to behind Mandeep's hut where the charcoal and implements were stored. He picked up one of the goat skin bellows and checked it over quickly, making sure all the stitching was in good repair. The nozzle was burnt and crumbling so he pulled it off and substituted a fresh one – a short length of hollowed-out bamboo. When he got back to the furnace, Mandeep was on his hands and knees, coaxing the firewood at the base into flame.

The furnace itself stood about chest high, a round column that tapered slightly as it rose and with an arched entrance at the base. The bottom of the arch was blocked by a smooth slab of granite with a hole drilled sideways into it and a long wooden handle affixed. The lower part of the shaft was packed with dry firewood and tinder and the space above it a solid mass of crushed iron ore and charcoal. Mandeep fed more kindling into the glowing embers, and blew on them gently. The flames caught at last and started eating upward into the charcoal, trickles of white smoke finding their way through the packed shaft and out of the chimney.

"Where have you been, Ajit?" Mandeep queried as his crusher returned with the bellows. "Get the nozzle fitted. Quickly now, before the fire goes out."

"There is plenty of time," Ajit replied. "I have done this before."

Mandeep harrumphed and sent the lad off to fetch him a cup of water, watching as Ajit expertly fitted the bamboo nozzle of the bellows into a small hole at the side

171

of the furnace. A few gentle squeezes of the goat skin sack to ensure the leather valves were directing a flow of air through the system and Ajit started a steady rhythm with the bellows, supplying fresh air directly into the heart of the furnace where the charcoal was starting to glow.

"Keep the rhythm steady now," Mandeep snapped. "Not too fast, not too slow. We want the ore to heat up smoothly."

Ajit ignored his employer, knowing what to do, setting his mind and muscles to the task ahead. Already, the sides of the brick furnace were giving off heat and Ajit knew that the combination of furnace and sun would be debilitating by noon. "Gauri," he called. "Bring . . . water." The boy hurried over with a bucket and dipper.

The morning wore on and Ajit kept up a steady rhythm on the bellows, streams of air raising the burning charcoal to a white heat. The smoke had disappeared now, the air above the chimney rippling violently in the savage heat, but the invisible fumes that came off caught at the throat and inflamed the eyes of anyone caught downwind of the furnace. Mandeep and Gauri wrestled a stone slab onto the vent; almost closing it and reflecting a good measure of the heat back down into the furnace. Mandeep moved around to the front and peered through the archway into the heart of the fire. It pulsed like a living beast, cycling from fiery red to a fierce yellow-orange and back down again.

"Keep it going, Ajit," Mandeep encouraged. "If you stop it will take a long time to come back up to heat."

"Then . . . find . . . me a . . . replace . . . placement," Ajit panted. Sweat poured over his face and

172

body and Gauri ladled water over his head and shoulders as well as holding it to his parched lips.

Jayavant and Kapil returned with a load of fresh ore and dumped it beside the crushing stand before Kapil took over the bellows from Ajit, scarcely missing a beat. Ajit rested and presently Jayavant had a turn pumping air into the seething furnace. Mandeep had to crouch back several paces to peer into the glowing mass as the heat beat him back, singeing his eyebrows.

Damayanti returned to prepare the midday meal and the men fed in turns, the bellows never ceasing their monotonous panting. Mandeep took a long wooden paddle and dug out an oblong cavity in the sand in front of the furnace with a channel leading back to the granite dam across the entrance.

"It is nearly ready," Mandeep exclaimed. "I can see the glowing lake within the fire's heart. Do not falter now. Keep those bellows working." He stared into the furnace, his face shining redly in the glow and the sweat pouring down. "Get ready. Ajit, take your grip on the handle." Watching his crusher carefully to be certain he was ready, Mandeep ordered the others to stand back and retreated a few paces himself.

"Pull, Ajit, pull the handle. Let the Loha flow."

Ajit tugged the handle and the granite slab slid back, grating against the brick walls of the archway. A glowing, brilliant orange-red liquid poured out of the center of the furnace, splashing down the channel and into the cavity in the sand. The sand spat and crackled where the liquid metal touched and impurities in the sand burst into flame, releasing billows of smoke. The heat was intense and everyone moved back, staring in fascination

173

as the iron cooled, turning from a fiery red to a dull red, crusted with blackened slag until eventually it lay as an inert lump of black material, still steaming and hissing where moisture burst instantly to steam. Ripples of heat still danced above the sand and Mandeep grinned broadly, turning to his workers.

"Very well, that was quite satisfactory. Now we must prepare the second furnace while this block is cooling down."

Coaxing and chivvying, Mandeep got his workers back to their tasks, fetching more Loha-churna, the rich iron ore from the hills; crushing the rocks to powdery gravel and packing the second furnace with this crushed rock and fresh charcoal. By evening, the second furnace was packed and the first lump of smelted iron, the Loha-pindaha, ready to be moved. Gauri tipped the bucket of water over the iron but it did not hiss or splutter, so he gingerly touched it, ready to snatch his hand back if need be. It was warm but no longer hot, so he and Kapil picked it up and staggered toward the lean-to shed to add the block to the others already stacked there.

The next day, the second furnace was fired, and by day's end, a second block of raw iron joined the slowly growing stack in the lean-to. Afterward, when everything had cooled down, Mandeep set his workers to cleaning out the brick furnaces, replacing any cracked or crumbled parts of the walls and chipping out fragments of iron that had cooled within the kilns instead of flowing out into the sandy cavity. When all was cleaned and ready, everyone went back to their old tasks, filling the furnaces for the next round of smelting.

When the stack of iron, now rusting as it sat surrounded by humid air, reached a certain size, Mandeep called an end to iron production. Under his supervision, his workers started to excavate a pit, two paces across. Four channels led up from the pit and bamboo tubes connected the base of the pit to the nozzles for bellows. The channels were then back-filled. Within the pit he packed charcoal before settling into it a large shallow dish of smoothed granite. Into the granite crucible went several ingots of raw iron and the chips of iron removed from the furnaces. Between them they packed fragments of broken glass bought from the glass makers.

"What are we making?" Gauri asked.

"That's right," Ajit replied. "You weren't here last time we did this. We are making ukku steel – what they call wootz in barbarian lands." He looked round to make sure Mandeep was not in earshot. "Ukku steel is the best in the world and commands a high price. This little lot will make Mandeep a moderately rich man and, who knows, we may get to see some small part of it."

Mandeep lit the charcoal fire, thrusting brands of dry wood soaked in oil deep into the dry and crumbling blackness. The heat rose like the midday sun and the blackness reddened by degrees, waves of heat blistering the skin of any who got too close. The three men and the lad applied themselves to the bellows, though slower this time. Air was important as before, to keep the fire burning, but for some reason the process worked better if the combustion was incomplete. Mandeep walked around the edge of the pit nervously, adding more charcoal and exhorting each man to be careful. The iron ingots heated up and the glass fragments softened and flowed around

175

them. The morning passed and the iron turned a dull red. Mandeep took a turn on the bellows, letting Gauri run to get water for the others.

The dull red iron brightened and flowed, the molten glass mixing in with it. Flecks of yellow and even white shone through the crusted melt before Mandeep gave the word and each man leaned back, exhausted from the long hours on the bellows. Ajit took a long wooden pole that had soaked in water all day and dipped it into the molten metal in its granite dish, stirring quickly as the water flashed into steam and the wood flared into flame. The metal and glass roiled and mixed before settling back into a sullen mix of dull colors.

"Why did we put glass in with the iron?" Gauri asked, wiping the sweat from his eyes as he stared at the granite dish.

Ajit shrugged. "I am no metallurgist to explain it properly but I think it brings out the impurities in the iron. See how there is a foamy crust on the surface of the molten metal?" Gauri nodded. "Well, in a few minutes we shall scoop that off and let the metal cool. What's left is ukku steel."

Mandeep signaled once more and he and Ajit took up long-handled wooden paddles that had likewise been soaked in water. Pushing them forward into the smoky haze above the fire pit, they scooped them quickly across the surface, pulling at the stiffening mass of slag on the top of the metal, even as the wooden paddles ignited. Some of the slag they removed, but the rest clung to the cooling surface.

"You couldn't get it all off," Gauri commented. "Will that matter?"

176

"No. The rest will cool in place and we can chip it off later. The important thing is that the glass has floated the impurities to the surface."

As the crucible and metal cooled, the fire continued to burn, so, rather than waste fuel, Mandeep directed Kapil and Jayavant to tip water into the pit, extinguishing the smoldering fire. Much later, when the ukku had cooled enough to handle, they wrestled the granite crucible out of the pit, getting covered in sooty ash, and Ajit carefully chipped the remaining slag away. The ukku steel gleamed in the sunlight, blue on gray, and Mandeep nodded in satisfaction.

Twice more they repeated the whole procedure, until most of the pile of iron bars had been reduced to blue-gray lenses of ukku steel.

"Excellent," Mandeep crowed, rubbing his hands with delight. "I shall take you all out for a feast in the town."

Mandeep was, naturally, not the only iron and steel manufacturer in the area and several other teams had similarly sullied the air with noxious fumes and produced their own lenses of steel. Not all had finished their production but there were still many men celebrating when Mandeep led his workers into Kashi's finest eating place.

"Bring out a whole goat and roast it well," he declared. "Rice and bondas, fried fish and peppered mangoes, for tonight we celebrate."

Ajit noted young Gauri's excitement and took him by the arm, whispering quietly to him. "Eat and drink as much as can, lad, for this is Mandeep's payment for your hard work. You'll not get much else."

While the goat was being prepared and the rice boiled, vegetables cleaned and prepared, and the oil heated for the bondas, the owner of the eatery brought out, at Mandeep's behest, pottery jars of strong drink. He served rice wine, rich and potent, and ragi, the sweet barley brew. Palm liquor was poured into half coconut shells and passed round, the heady liquid rapidly having its effect.

Musicians started up to entertain the patrons as more men packed into the room – on bansuri and veena with one man keeping an insistent rhythm on a small drum. Conversation grew loud as the wine and liquor flowed and when the meat appeared with a dozen side dishes of curries with piquant sauces; rice, plain and flavored with coconut or saffron, fish and deep-fried onions and other vegetables, eggs, and grains heated over the open fire until they burst; Mandeep and his men fell to with a will.

When the food was cleared away, more drink appeared and women joined the men, not wives and sisters, but women trained to entertain men for a fee. They swirled and swayed in time with the music, revealing by degrees a hand or a finely turned ankle, a pair of smoldering eyes from behind brightly colored cottons and gauzes.

One willowy girl caught Ajit's eye, the sway of her hips entrancing him as he stared at her gyrations. He found himself smoothing his mustache and smiling at her when she turned in his direction. Surreptitiously, he looked in his purse and frowned, the frown becoming a scowl as he saw another man across the room beckon to her suggestively. Ajit turned to Mandeep and grabbed his arm.

"Lend me my wages due on the sale of the steel."

"Eh?" Mandeep looked up blearily from his contemplation of his empty cup of ragi. "What for? Oh, the girl." He grinned appreciatively. "She's quite a beauty isn't she? I bet she knows some tricks."

"I must have her. Will you lend me her price?"

Mandeep hiccupped. "Ajit, my friend, for you I will do anything." He flung his arms wide and almost fell off his cushion. "In fact, I will buy you an evening with her. Prakash!" Mandeep yelled across the room to the owner of the inn. "I will buy that woman there for tonight, the beautiful one."

Prakash hurried across to his good customers, an ingratiating smile plastered across his face. "A very good decision, good Mandeep, and well picked, for her name is Manju which as you know means 'beautiful'." He hesitated a moment and lowered his voice so only Mandeep and those closest to him could hear. "But what will your wife say?"

"She's not for me, Prakash, though I could make her cry out with astonishment at my prowess." Mandeep draped an arm around Ajit's shoulders and looked blearily up at the innkeeper. "Where was I? Ah, yes, I want her for my good friend here. Ajit is a worker in a hundred, Prakash, a thousand even, and he deserves to have a good time. Show him and the girl to a room and add the cost to my bill." He belched and pushed Ajit away.

Ajit got to his feet and bowed, putting his hands together in the mudra. He followed Prakash across the room and through into a dim passageway that led to a dozen doors. Opening one, the innkeeper showed Ajit into a room with a large straw-filled mattress on the floor and several cushions. A large empty bowl and a pitcher of water stood in one corner, but there was no other furniture. Prakash lit an oil lamp and handed it to Ajit.

"I will fetch Manju, please make yourself comfortable."

"Bring some wine and two cups also . . . on Mandeep's bill, of course."

Prakash smiled and bowed, leaving Ajit to his mounting excitement. He lay back on the mattress, plumping the cushions about him and a few minutes later the door opened. Manju entered, her veil discarded and her long black hair hanging free. Her scarlet sari and yellow petticoat and choli hung cunningly, revealing nothing but hinting at everything. In her hands she held a pitcher of wine and two cups. She closed and latched the door before crossing to the bed and setting the pitcher and cups to the floor.

"May I offer you wine, sir?" Manju asked, her voice deep and silky. She did not wait for Ajit to answer but poured and handed a cup to him.

"Thank you, Manju." Ajit patted the mattress. "Come sit beside me."

Manju sat gracefully, folding her long legs under her. She sipped at her wine, all the time staring into Ajit's eyes. After a few moments she took his cup from him and set them both down on the floor. Pushing him down onto the mattress, she knelt beside him and started caressing his arms and upper body gently, her fingernails scratching his skin without hurting. Ajit's tunic lay open and her hands wandered over his chest. After a few moments, she slipped the tunic back from his shoulders and Ajit struggled to sit up, shrugging out of his upper clothing. Manju coaxed him back down again and once more ran her hands over his skin. Now, her lips followed as she licked, nibbled and kissed his chest and arms.

Ajit lay back with his eyes half-closed, grinning with pleasure and feeling his lust mount. Manju's sari brushed his arm as she leaned over him and he reached up and slipped it off her shoulder. She smiled and loosened the cloth from around her waist, letting it fall to the floor. Hitching up her cotton petticoat she leaned over him again. He reached for her, plucking at the choli that covered her breasts but she pushed his hands back down with a laugh.

"Patience, sir. All good things will come but we should not rush."

Another round of kissing and caressing followed and just when Ajit started fidgeting, his hands becoming restless again, she changed her focus, loosening his sash and unraveling his dhoti cloth, tugging it loose until he lay naked on the straw mattress. Ajit tensed himself but Manju ignored his erection, running her hands over his legs, tracing the contours of each muscle, lightly tickling his skin with her long brightly painted nails. Her lips followed, nibbling and kissing and her long hair, as it brushed against his upright penis, drew a moan of frustrated pleasure from him.

"Touch it," Ajit commanded. He thrust himself upward to meet her.

Manju smiled and ignored his demand. Raising her hands she pulled her choli over her head, releasing her breasts. Round and firm, teak with dusky coral nipples, they drew another moan of pleasure from Ajit who raised up his hands toward them. Manju laughed and caught his

181

hands, kissing them and pushed his arms behind his head. At first, Ajit resisted, wanting to squeeze those lovely orbs, but as he saw them approaching his face, he desisted and stared upward in wet-lipped anticipation.

She teased him, lightly brushing her erect nipples against his beard. He lunged and caught a nipple awkwardly in his lips, pulling at it, sucking briefly before releasing. Manju moved lower, lightly rubbing her breasts over his chest, downward to his legs. Ajit moved his hands down when she released them and stroked the smooth skin of her back, holding her slim waist, running his fingers over the swell of her buttocks beneath the thin cotton petticoat to the hem where her thighs revealed themselves. Just as he started upward, stroking her silky thighs, she distracted him again, this time with something that made his hands grip the mattress. Her lips opened and enveloped the tip of his penis and she set about 'sucking the mango'.

Ajit groaned long and loud and thrust upward to meet Manju's mouth. He felt his excitement mounting rapidly and he drew away again, writhing in agony and pleasure. Manju raised her head and turned to face Ajit, her pink tongue tracing the contours of her lips.

"Too much?" she asked softly.

"Yes. No. O gods, no. Again?"

Manju laughed once more and in a swift movement straddled Ajit's thighs. She leaned forward, lying on top of him, pressing her breasts against his chest and kissed him, her tongue flickering against his open lips. Then, as he started to return the kiss, trying to hold her in his arms, she broke free and sat upright again. Lifting her petticoat a fraction, just enough to allow Ajit a glimpse of thatched

182

black curls, she edged forward, dropping the petticoat again to hide them both. She raised herself up and gently lowered herself onto his straining erection, and his hot length slipped inside her.

"Yes!" Ajit cried, bucking upward.

Manju sat quietly until he stopped, then started raising and lowering herself, gyrating her hips, her vaginal muscles tensing and relaxing, drawing him along. Whenever she sensed his excitement she slowed the pace until he eased, panting and flushed. Over and over she repeated her dance until suddenly she tensed and arched backward, crying out loudly. She slipped off Ajit and, lifting her petticoats, pulled him over her, opening to him.

Ajit thrust urgently, his pent-up desires breaking over him and he shuddered, crying out with the glorious release. His motions slowed and he lay on her, feeling his heart gradually ease its staccato rhythm, their sweat-slicked bodies slippery. Easing himself off her, he lay back panting and grinning and looked at her, his fingers gently tracing her curves, tugging gently at her matted curls where a drop of semen still clung like a tiny pearl.

They poured fresh wine and drank, lying back, each thinking their own thoughts. After a while, the presence of such female beauty stirred Ajit's interest once more and, with some expert assistance from Manju, he found himself rising again. Their coupling was slower, more inventive, and Manju showed him positions and techniques he had not dreamt of. Ajit was half afraid to ask, knowing she must have learned these things from other men, not wanting to believe she enjoyed herself thus with others.

"No," she replied to his tentative question. "There is a book devoted to Kama, the god of love. I was fortunate to glimpse it once and I learned many things about what a man and a woman can do together."

"There is a book?" Ajit ceased his languorous thrusting for a few moments and looked at her in astonishment. "You can read?"

"A few words only, but there were many pictures of strange positions."

"Show me one."

Manju demonstrated and they tried it, but Ajit collapsed backward with a laugh. "You would have to be a contortionist."

"Or practiced," Manju said. "The man who showed me the book said he had spent years trying every position. Here, try this one." Manju held a pose and guided Ajit. "No, raise your leg a little more … yes, that's it … now, if I … ahh."

A little later she slept, but woke when Ajit roused her in the middle of the night. She protested mildly but opened herself to him as he took his pleasure again.

"You are a tiger," she murmured. She was less civil when he importuned her a fourth time but she rolled on her front and fell asleep as he languidly thrust at her from behind.

When Ajit woke, the first pink glow of dawn showed through the cracks in the walls. Manju had left in the night for her own bed. Ajit rose, washed himself with the water in the bowl and dressed, slipping out through the inn with its scenes of devastation and drinking. Several men lay snoring on the dirt floor and a youth was walking around the room picking up discarded cups and plates.

184

He saw Ajit and grinned broadly, making an obscene gesture. Ajit grinned and raised a hand, slipping out of the door into the chill of the morning.

He had to put up with a lot of ribald remarks back at the huts. Damayanti sniffed loudly and walked off with her nose in the air but Mandeep grinned enviously and Kapil and Jayavanti called out loudly, miming the actions of love. Gauri sidled up to Ajit as he went into their hut to change, asking shyly what it was like.

"Four times," Ajit boasted. "I cannot believe I had such strength in me. It was worth every bit of Mandeep's money." He clapped the youth on the shoulder. "You'll come to it soon enough, lad."

"Was she as beautiful as her name Manju?"

"Better. And as for her Manjusha, her box of jewels ..." Ajit grinned. "You'll find out one day. Now, leave me, I must change and get to work. Yesterday was yesterday, but today Mandeep will have my aching back and empty balls if I don't work hard."

"What about the soldiers?"

"What soldiers?"

"The Katyuri ones."

"Well, of course they are Katyuri. Who else has soldiers in Kedarkhand? You are telling me there are soldiers in Kashi? What do they want? What have you heard, lad?"

"Nothing. I thought you might know."

When Ajit had changed and come outside, Kapil and Jayavant had already disappeared up Pari Tibbi to fetch ore and Gauri was busy scraping out the furnaces and mixing mortar with which to line the bricks. Ajit sauntered over to Mandeep and made a mudra, bowing

185

low and murmuring his thanks for the night. Mandeep regretted his generosity now that he was sober, so merely muttered in his beard.

"Gauri said there were soldiers in Kashi. Do you know anything about it?"

"Gauri talks too much," Mandeep replied sourly. He shrugged. "No doubt they are here to collect taxes or find recruits or some such. It is no concern of mine; I have paid my taxes already."

Mandeep was wrong for just after noon, a squad of soldiers marched into the clearing and rounded up everyone, pushing them into a group by the furnaces.

"What is the meaning of this?" Mandeep sputtered. "Who is in charge here? You have no right to do this. I am a law-abiding and honest citizen who pays his taxes and ..."

"I am Rajiv, commander of King Viradeva's army in these parts." A fat, spectacularly mustached man pushed his way out from behind the other soldiers. He wore a black tunic stitched with gold over a churidar of the same color. A red sash at his waist held a shining saber and jeweled rings sparkled on the fingers of his left hand which clutched a scroll of paper. "You recognize my authority over you?"

"If you are who you say, but why are you here and why are you molesting me?"

The commander consulted the scroll. "Just answer my questions. You are Mandeep? You are in my records as an iron maker."

Mandeep nodded.

"And steel?"

"Ukku steel, yes."

"Who else here knows how to smelt ore and produce steel?"

Mandeep frowned and bit at his fingernail as he stared back at the commander. "Ajit." He nodded in his direction. "The others have been here while it was made, but I would only trust him to do it well."

"Then you are to be honored, ironsmith. King Viradeva is looking for skilled iron workers in his capital city of Kartikeyapura. I will take this Ajit with me."

"But this will cripple me," Mandeep protested. "It is only by his skill and hard work that I have produced ingots of steel already and ..." He shut his mouth quickly as he saw a gleam of avarice in Rajiv's eyes.

"You have steel here? Now? How much?"

Mandeep said nothing, just stared down at his feet.

"I can have my men search but then I would have to mark you down as uncooperative."

"Three ingots."

"Show me."

Mandeep led the commander over to the lean-to and showed him the three gleaming lenses of steel alongside a few of the rusting iron ingots.

"Very good," Rajiv said. "We will take them. My adjutant here will write you out a receipt and you may take it from next year's taxes."

"But my taxes would only be one of them at most. How am I to live if you rob ... take all my metal?"

"Then you will have paid more than a year's tax." Rajiv waved a hand negligently and started walking away. "Besides, taxes are going up."

Gauri sidled up beside Ajit. "Take me with you."

Ajit raised his eyebrows. "Why? You would be a lot better off staying here."

"I want to see Kartikeyapura and the King."

"Kings are dangerous, particularly Viradeva." Ajit lowered his voice and glanced around to make sure they were not overheard. "I have heard he is a tyrant and cruel to those around him. You would be safer here."

"I don't care; I want to see more of the world than just this hill and town. Take me with you, please."

"It's not up to me, Gauri. I'm being taken against my will."

Gauri spun on his heel and started across the open ground toward Mandeep and the commander. Two soldiers ran forward and thrust their spears in front of the youth, bringing him to a halt. He called out, "Commander, I want to go with you too. I am Ajit's assistant. I know how to make steel too."

"Don't listen to him," Mandeep squeaked. "He knows nothing, he is just my fetch and carry boy."

Rajiv considered the youth standing behind the crossed spears of his soldiers. "You do not look old enough to have mastered steel making."

"Not mastered, sir, but learning under a real master." He gestured toward Ajit. "Besides, I'm young and strong. I can carry things and fight."

Rajiv smiled. "Indeed? Well, I have no objections. You can carry one of the lenses of steel."

Gauri bowed and backed away, grinning. "I'm going with you, Ajit."

"Then you are an idiot."

A short time later the squad of soldiers marched out, their spears over their shoulders. Rajiv marched in front

188

and Ajit and Gauri, each burdened with one of the steel lenses, walked stolidly along in the middle of the file. They marched first to Kashi where other squads with other ironsmiths met them. Donkeys awaited them at the town and the confiscated steel was packed onto the beasts as, a hundred strong, the soldiers marched south.

Ajit and Gauri found themselves with a number of other men of the district, all skilled in the art of extracting iron from the basic ore of the hills and turning it into ukku steel. They talked among themselves, each with his theory of why King Viradeva wanted so many ironsmiths when surely he had his own in far-off Manaskand.

"He is making war on the tribes farther east," said one. "And needs arms quickly."

"I heard he is being attacked by them and we will be helping to defend our lands."

"An iron fortress. He is building an impregnable palace."

"Plenty of work for us, then," someone laughed.

"And wages! We could all become rich."

One man stopped the gossip with a gloomy thought. "Perhaps he just wants to prevent us working for anyone else. We may find ourselves imprisoned or killed."

"If he wanted us dead, his men would have killed us already," Ajit said calmly. "I don't know why he wants us but I daresay we shall find out eventually. I am not going to worry about it."

They reached Sahastradhara the next day, a small town where a thousand streams burst from springs in the caves that riddled the mountainside. The air was filled with the sound of falling and gushing water, clouds of mist hung over the forests, so thick at times that the sun hid from sight. Some were hot springs, stinking of sulphur and rotten eggs and it was to these springs in particular that people flocked as the waters were believed to have curative properties. Rajiv led his soldiers through the mists and they camped several miles further downriver.

From there they moved in easy stages to Narendranagar and down to the upper reaches of the Ganga River. Turning upstream, men and donkeys moved slowly up the great river valley road that connected the plains with the high Himalayas. If they journeyed far enough they would arrive at Joshimath, named as their capital Kartikeyapura by the early Katyuri kings. A hundred years or so before, the Katyuri had decided to move their capital south into the less remote hills and valleys of Manaskhand and chose the town of Baijnath for their new administrative center. They named in Kartikeyapura also, and it was to the palace here that Rajiv and his captives were bound.

The valley road followed the course of the Ganga until it became the Alaknanda at Devaprayag, then onward to Srinagar and Rudraprayag. They stayed for short periods in each of these towns as Rajiv spoke with the commanders of the garrisons there and collected more taxes and conscripts. At Srinagar, one of the conscripts from Devaprayag attempted to escape but was easily recaptured. Rajiv paraded all the men to watch the execution.

"This man is a traitor," Rajiv explained. "He accepted, as did you all, King Viradeva's bounty and promised, again like you all, to serve him faithfully for as long as he wants you. Alas," the commander shook his head sorrowfully. "He has broken his promise by attempting to leave without permission. The sentence for this is death." Rajiv stood aside and let his men hack the prisoner to death.

"You see what you have got yourself into?" Ajit murmured to Gauri.

"Yes, but I don't want to leave. This is an adventure."

From Rudraprayag, with the Buddhist monastery on the hill overlooking the town, to Karnaprayag, took another week, but here they left the Alaknanda Valley and turned southeast along the Pindar River to Tharali.

The clouds had been gathering while the troop moved upriver, the pre-monsoon winds freshening and building great cloud banks that hammered the high mountains. For days on end, the peaks were lost in swirling cloud and Rajiv hurried his men onward, worried now that the rains would come and close the roads as the rivers rose. Heavy falls had already turned the roads to mud and the Alaknanda roared, swollen between its banks. He breathed easier when they started up the Pindar, but did not ease the pace and were a few miles from Tharali when the deluge started.

Two days they sheltered in Tharali, commandeering the headman's house. When the rain eased to showers, Rajiv hastened his men onward up the Pindar, slogging through mud and landslips, where the steep-sided valleys had collapsed under the weight of the water-logged soil. A few miles from Tharali the road left the river and switch-backed up the ridge. The mud made even the sure-footed donkeys slip and slide and soldiers and conscripts alike floundered in their wake. At Gwaldam, the rain came down again but the village was too small to offer shelter so Rajiv pressed on for the high ridge.

The cloud cleared briefly as they crossed into the Baijnath valley and Rajiv triumphantly pointed to the fortified city and palace of Kartikeyapura. They arrived at the gates in drumming rain and were quartered in barracks close to the palace. Ajit and Gauri, like the other ironsmiths, never saw the king during the rainy season as he locked himself away with his feasting and drinking, his courtesans and musicians, content to let his kingdom run itself as long as it produced the luxuries he wanted. The ironsmiths could not ply their trade in the wet – nobody had mined any ore, no supplies of charcoal were available, and all the wood was soaked. Rajiv and the other commanders set them to work on menial tasks around the palace and the city.

"Are you still glad you came?" Ajit asked Gauri one miserable day as they scraped rust from piles of old weapons.

Gauri grimaced. "I thought we'd be properly fed," he grumbled. "And housed, but I expect it'll get better when the rains stop."

"It won't," Ajit said morosely. "Don't you listen to the tales the locals tell?"

"About the king, you mean?"

Ajit glanced around. "Just be careful we are not overheard. They say the king is bleeding his subjects dry. Taxes have tripled in the last few years and were already high. Farmers have to hand over all their rice and buy back some at inflated prices just so they have some to plant next season. He plunders the villages for grain and livestock, and forces any man's daughter he likes. He takes the sons too, though they become just ordinary slaves."

Gauri frowned. "That is the action of a king in a conquered land, not in his own country. If these tales aren't lies they must be exaggerations. No king could be that shortsighted."

The rains ended at last, and half a month after the sun broke through, scattering the shreds of clouds, the roads had dried enough for travel. At once, the ironsmiths, Ajit and Gauri included, were set to work collecting the raw materials for smelting ore. The road south led to Almora and Champawat but much nearer at hand were sources of clay for the furnace bricks, timber for charcoal, and the precious iron ore. Every smith was expected to venture out with an armed escort daily to find these necessities and transport them back to the city where other workers started the construction of rows of furnaces.

One such foray found Ajit and Gauri heading eastward toward a hill whence sprung a tiny stream of pure water. Though twelve miles from the palace, they noticed a string of slaves positioned along the road a few paces apart. At first, the sight was just curious, then mystifying. At intervals, great jars appeared and were passed down the line, heavy ones toward the palace, lighter ones returning. Ajit, his pick over his shoulder, approached the officer in charge of their guard.

"What's going on, Sib?" he asked, indicating the line of slaves.

"The king likes the water from the springs at Pahali. The slaves are passing full water jars back to the palace."

"He has that many slaves?"

193

Sib laughed. "When he needs more he sends his army to strip more young men from the villages."

"That is not right."

"No, but be very careful who you say it to, my friend. At best, you would join them. At worst, the king would have one less ironworker."

Another day, they assisted the palace workers bring grain to a village. The people of the village had little in the way of land to grow grain or other commodities but possessed instead a fine mill. They made a living grinding the grain for other villages and on this occasion, King Viradeva also. The king's officer arrived with his company of soldiers, the palace workers and donkeys laden with panniers of grain. First, the officer negotiated with the village elders the quality and amount.

"Seven mat quality, as usual. I have brought five maund of grain. I shall expect to take back five maund of high quality flour."

"Esteemed sir," groveled the headman. "You know that is not possible. Even if our mill grinds exceedingly fine, it will only produce a single maund of the finest flour."

"I see," the officer said coldly, fingering the hilt of his sword. "Perhaps I should take you back to Kartikeyapura where you can explain your failing to King Viradeva himself."

The headman paled. "That ... that will not be necessary, esteemed sir. We will find the flour somehow."

"Good. See that it is ready for me by evening." The officer walked off, leaving a group of very anxious elders.

"How are we going to find five maund of fine flour?" one of the elders groaned.

"We will have to grind all the grain we have. With luck we will have enough."

"But what we have comes from other villages. We cannot just rob them of it."

"Perhaps you wish to tell the king yourself. No? Then I suggest we start bringing the grain up to the mill immediately. We have a lot of work to do."

The grain was milled by just after sunset and the last of the sacks of flour was brought down to the storehouse in the village center. The officer agreed that the decision could not be made until morning and accepted free food and lodging for himself and his men. He demanded the headman's young daughter to entertain him for the night and consequently was in a good mood at sunrise.

The sacks of flour were brought out into the courtyard of the headman's hut the next morning, where the officer supervised the setting up of a stand and seven mats of finely woven cloth were laid out downwind of the stand. As the sun rose in the sky, a breeze picked up and presently the officer pronounced himself satisfied. A sack was lifted up onto the stand and two soldiers shook the contents out over the mats. The wind carried the flour away in white billows, the coarsest fractions falling close to the stand and the finest particles being carried further out. When the first sack was empty, another was lifted up and slowly, as the morning passed, the store of flour was sorted by the wind. At intervals, the officer called a halt and had the fine flour that gathered on the seventh mat carefully collected into fresh sacks. By noon, the winnowing was complete and the officer supervised the

195

loading of five and a half maund of 'seven mat' flour back onto his donkeys.

"Very good," the officer said. "The king will be most pleased with you."

"Er, esteemed sir," the headman said. "Might I broach the subject of payment?"

"Payment?" The officer's eyes narrowed. "For what? I brought five maund of grain to be milled and I'm taking five maund of flour back with me. Are you saying I should pay for my own flour?"

"No, no, of course not, esteemed sir. It is just that, well, we have worked hard all day and ..."

"And your work is valued by your king," the officer interposed. "Consider it a gift."

The headman swallowed. "Of ... of course, esteemed sir. And ..." he wiped a hand over his sweating face. "And the extra half maund of ... of flour?"

"What extra half maund?" The officer stepped closer to the cringing man and gripped his shirt in one fist, turning the man's face up to his. "I see no extra flour."

"N ... no, sir. I must ... must have been mistaken."

The officer released the headman and turned on his heel, ordering his convoy out of the village. Behind them, the villagers scrambled to collect up the rest of the flour and return it to the sacks. The wind spread the flour even as they labored and much was lost as it soaked up moisture from the damp ground and blew away on the breezes.

Gauri led one of the laden donkeys and though the trail was narrow for most of the way, it widened out as they neared the palace. He guided his donkey alongside Ajit and spoke to him in a low voice.

196

"I don't like it here, Ajit. This king is a very bad man."

"You think so? Yes, I think you might be right. What do you intend to do about it, lad?"

"What can I do? Run away, I suppose."

"Think carefully before you do. Remember what happens to deserters."

"You could come with me. Together we'd make it. We could go back to Mandeep."

Ajit shook his head. "I have no wish to go back there. No, this bad king intrigues me. I will stay awhile and see what happens."

As the weather improved and the roads dried out, the king once more traveled around his lands, looking for new opportunities to increase his wealth at the expense of his subjects. He was always accompanied by soldiers, commanded by Katyuri relatives, as he knew that no disgruntled peasant or despairing father could get at him through the armed cordon. At first, Ajit and Gauri remained in the city, working with the other ironsmiths, preparing and firing the iron smelters, but before long they were accompanying the king's entourage on their excursions from the palace.

Gauri was puzzled by their inclusion as they performed no useful function that he could see. The most they were ever called upon to do was to fetch and carry items stolen from the villages, loading them onto pack animals. Ajit had no explanation, though he just smiled and said if the commanders wanted them there, who were they to argue? Still, Gauri thought it odd that every time the guard commander came across them, he stopped and stared for a few moments before shaking his head and

197

wandering off. At these times, Ajit would sit down on the ground and ignore the officer.

Near the palace, King Viradeva rode a horse as the roads were broad and even, and he believed himself to be an imposing and noble rider. Further out the trails became rougher and steeper and he abandoned his horse for the comfort of his cushioned litter. Once, as his litter wound its way along a road that clung to a cliff face, one of the litter bearers stumbled and the litter lurched. Viradeva halted the procession immediately and had the bearers put to death. He confided to the commander of the escort that he suspected the men of plotting to throw him off the cliff and at the next village had iron chains and rings fashioned for the bearers and the litter. Each man was now locked into place so that an attempt on their sovereign's life would automatically mean their own deaths.

The king's actions became more extreme. He saw dangers everywhere and went so far as to have his own commanders disarmed whenever they approached him. No man could get close to him with any weapon. At the same time, Viradeva believed the villagers were plotting against him and his hand lay heavy on the peasantry. He left blood and grief in his wake throughout the countryside.

"I can't take any more of this," Gauri confided to his friend as they left the village of Mansi. "I feel as if I am as guilty as the king because I just stand there and let it happen."

"What will you do?"

"Kill him if I can, desert if I cannot."

Ajit pursed his lips in thought. "How will you kill him? Nobody is allowed near him with a weapon."

"With my bare hands then."

"Also, nobody is allowed near him alone. He always has bodyguards so you would not have time to strangle him."

Gauri remained silent as the procession wound up into the mountains again, heading for the Ramganga Gorge. "I shall desert then," he muttered at last. "I don't care if they kill me for it but I cannot stay here." Ajit shook his head and left the lad behind, striding out to overtake the litter.

The guard commander saw him coming and frowned, moving to intercept him. "Who are you? What are you …?" He stumbled even as Ajit reeled on the road as if drunk. The commander looked around and marched off to the head of the column, bowing to the litter as he passed.

Ajit recovered his balance and moved closer to the litter, watching the bodyguards surreptitiously and noting the progress they made toward the gorge.

The road steepened and narrowed as the cliffs on either side drew together, the thundering of the Ramganga River far below drowning out all other sound. The road wound around a rocky outcrop and everyone moved in single file.

Ajit watched the litter bearers, noting how the one at the rear could see nothing but the litter. He followed blindly in the footsteps of the one in front. Ajit smiled and sat down suddenly. A moment later and the litter lurched forward, moving faster. The man at the rear called out in fear and the king's hand appeared, pushing

199

the curtains aside as he peered out. The front bearer gave a great cry and leapt forward, the rock at the lip of the precipice crumbling under his feet as he launched himself into space. The litter crashed to the ground and hung for a moment on the edge, the rear bearer screaming and trying to scramble backward. A roar of rage erupted from the litter and the king half emerged, scrabbling at the sides as the whole structure swayed. His movements put it off balance and it fell slowly over the side of the cliff, picking up speed as it turned over and over. Both bearers screamed now as, limbs flailing, they dropped to their deaths. King Viradeva plummeted from the litter, smashing on the water-tumbled rocks at the base of the cliffs before washing into the turbulent Ramganga.

Screams and cries erupted from the soldiers and servants, some trying to flee the scene, others rushing to look. In the confusion, Ajit got to his feet and wandered back to where Gauri stood open-mouthed.

"Now you don't have to risk your life, lad."

"What … what happened? Did the bearers just jump off the cliff?"

"The front bearer lost a daughter to the king's depravity last year," Ajit said. "He did not need much persuasion."

Gauri gaped. "Persuasion? By whom? When?"

"It does not matter." Ajit smiled and clapped Gauri on the shoulder. "I think you can desert safely now. Things will be a bit confused for a while. Take Ajit and go back to Kashi. Look after him, he is a good man."

"Take Ajit? But you're Ajit. What are you talking about?"

200

Ajit fell and only his arm around Gauri's shoulder saved him from falling headlong. The lad helped him to the side of the road and sat him down, offering him a flask of water.

"Are you alright? You were talking strangely there."

Ajit peered around at the hills and the gorge, at the milling confusion on the narrow track and the men starting to stream back toward Mansi. "Where are we?" He frowned deeply and stared into Gauri's face. "Where is Mandeep? I ... I went up to Pari Tibbi to collect ore and ... and that is all I can remember." He got to his feet and started back down the track. "Have I been asleep? I dreamed ... strange dreams ..."

Chapter Ten

Ajit was my first serious attempt at possession. I wanted the human experience again but I did not deem it worthwhile just taking on the form of a human as I had with Druki when I sat at the feet of the Buddhist monk. This time I wanted the full experience, to know what it was like to live in such a cramped space, to feel pain and sorrow, joy and lust. I cannot say I was entirely successful in this. Let me use an analogy that relates to the night spent with Manju. Living in a human body, controlling the muscles, directing the thoughts, feeling the emotions, was like touching something through several layers of cloth. In other words, the difference between the bare breast and the breast with the choli and sari intervening. The shape is there but muted.

I might add that the man Ajit did not suffer during his involuntary subjugation. In fact, he seemed inordinately proud of his accomplishments with the woman Manju. I relaxed my hold on his body that night, just lending him my inner strength as I stood back and observed. He was aware of my presence throughout though I got the impression he thought he was dreaming. Sometimes we spoke, talking about events and his uniquely human perspective on them. I thought King Viradeva an extraordinarily interesting human, with many of his desires and actions similar to my own. Ajit, though, showed me what a human would think, and in the end I could see that the people of the kingdoms, Kedarkhand and Manaskhand, would be better off for the king's demise. I left Ajit sitting by the side of the road in the gorge near Mansi and entered the lead bearer,

202

precipitating his suicide. I suppose you will say that I had no right to do this but I was the one in his mind, the one privy to his desires and secrets. The year before, King Viradeva had visited the man's village, seen his twelve year old daughter and had her taken back to the palace where he brutally raped her. She died of her injuries and the man was quite overcome with anger and grief. He wanted to kill the king, had even decided the only way to do it was hurl himself off a cliff when he was next called on to carry the king, but he lacked the courage to end his own life. I merely stiffened his resolve. So for the price of two men's lives, countless others were saved. Incidentally, Viradeva suffered as so many had suffered at his hands, for I fed off the king's last terrified thoughts as he fell through the air – an added bonus.

Of course, it did not really alter things. After Viradeva died, various members of his family made a bid for the throne. The kingdoms were thrown into anarchy and all the little sub-kingdoms, clans and chiefs rebelled. For years afterward, the roads and rivers of Himalaya were not safe places for law-abiding people. I suppose you will blame me for this state of affairs, but this was one of my first conscious decisions and I think I made a right choice.

I do not know what became of Ajit and Gauri for I did not return to Kashi with them. My days of existing on the lightning bolt were over. I had tasted the sweet fruits of possession and I saw my future clearly. I have told you of my ways of feasting and the relative merits of each, but now I must add one more. When I possess a man my flame burns within him and I inhabit every part of his physical body, holding his mind in thrall. He can hide nothing from me, I am privy to every little secret of his, including memories that lie deep within the fabric of his brain. I can see his thoughts and I reach out and strain them through my being as they pass. They are untouched by my presence but in some way I do not understand, they sustain me. It is not dissimilar to feeding on a man's life as I kill him, for then too; I pass his thoughts and emotions through my flame, extracting what I need. With the living man, my feeding is subtler, more refined. If I might be allowed another human food analogy, feeding from a possessed man is like dining with a fork or spoon; from a dying one like using my bare hands. Strong thoughts and emotions are better – terror, hatred, anger and lust – but the weaker ones like love and contentment will suffice. In fact, my year or so in the ironsmith's body have suggested a goal for my endeavors. I will possess others that I may learn more of the human condition but I will try to do no-one any lasting harm – unless they deserve it.

Ah, you say, that is such a mutable word – deserve. What standard shall I apply in my judgments of men? What actions, words or thoughts are deserving of death? Particularly the death that a demon will bring. What if I make a mistake and execute the innocent? If I was a man I could claim fallible humanity as my excuse, but as I am a Rakshasa I will just have to fall back on 'I am what I am'. I find the teachings of Sonaka, the Buddhist monk, have contaminated my thoughts so I will apply his standards as far as I am able. If a man follows the Eightfold Path I will not harm him. That means, of course, that almost everyone falls under my hand as few can aspire to the Buddha's Way. So I make allowances based, as often as not, on my whims. Besides, do not forget that if I choose, I am privy to a man's innermost thoughts and desires. Little escapes me when I chase his skittering thoughts around his brain, feel his fear and trepidation course through his gut and loosen his limbs.

Not long after the death of Viradeva I became aware that other gods existed in Bharat besides the ancient ones worshipped by the country folk. I suppose I should have noticed sooner but I try not to get involved with gods in the hope that they will not get involved with me. I have enough difficulty trying to sort out my own destiny without getting caught up in the machinations of the immortals.

Several hundred years ago, traders arrived from the west with a new faith, a new god, and carried this faith and god with them as they spread over the plains. Eventually, they arrived in the hills and mountains of Himalaya and disseminated their message, sometimes with the sword, more often by the example they showed to others. It is a strange religion, to my thinking, one full of prohibitions and rituals, laws for every aspect of a man's life, and little in the way of mercy for anyone who transgresses. The name of this religion is 'Islam', which in the language of the invader means 'to submit'; and the believers call themselves 'Muslim' or 'one who submits'. The one to whom they submit, of course, is their god whom they name Allah.

I have always thought names interesting. The Hindu gods are named for their attributes. Thus Krishna means 'black' or 'dark one' and I can vouch for his dark-hued looks when I saw him in the Khandava forest so long ago. Similarly, Agni means 'fire' and Shiva means 'good'.

Allah, on the other hand, simply means 'God'. I suppose this is all it needs to mean as Muslims only have one god, their Allah, to whom they offer fanatical devotion. I know this for I have possessed a Muslim and dwelt within him as horror-struck he repeated over and over his creed which defined him as a believer – ''ashadu 'al-la ilaha illa-llahu wa 'ashadu 'anna muhammadan rasalu-llah' – 'I testify that there is none worthy of worship except God and I testify that Muhammad is the Messenger of God'. He thought I was a 'Jinn' which is their word for a demon and prayed that his twin testimony might drive me off. It did not, but whether that was because of the inefficacy of his deity or insufficient faith, I cannot say. I will have to investigate this further.

Anyway, Muslims came to Bharat, or India as it is now called, and they stayed. Years later they dominated and conquered and their kings, called Khans or Sultans ruled over India's cities. One of these, Ghiyath al-Din Tughluq, became Sultan of Delhi, not far from where the Khandava forest once lay, and his son, Muhammad bin Tughluq had a direct impact on my beloved Himalaya.

I could not allow this. It may seem strange that one such as myself feels any ties to a particular tract of land but when, hundreds of years ago, I first caught sight of the pristine snows of Nanda Devi, standing like a queen with the foothills bowed down before her in shades of blue and green and brown, I knew this land called to me. If I have a home, it is not some lonely graveyard or ruined temple deep in the forest, but rather the crumpled skirts and silver rivers of high Himalaya.

And not just the land, but the living things within it. The people are mine. I will decide what will happen to them, not some foreign invader who thinks only of his dynasty and his pleasures. If necessary I will descend like a ravening tiger on the armies of Islam or anyone else that threatens my home. With these thoughts coursing through my mind, I left my cool hills and descended into the stifling heat and dust of the plains. I would seek to know my enemy before I encompassed his destruction.

Chapter Eleven

Fakhr-ud-din Muhammad Junna Khan, Sultan of Delhi, known popularly to his loyal subjects as Muhammad bin Tughluq, sat on the Great Throne in his palace, striving to appear interested and keep his mind on the subject as his generals laid out the details for the coming campaign.

"Exalted One," General Jamaal Khalid said, bowing once more. "You must understand that the river valleys are the principal avenues of access into this region, though once inside Qarachal, there are numerous smaller roads and trails that may be used. An invasion will take time, however, as the roads will not carry large armies."

"I disagree, Exalted One," General Maahir Barachim interrupted, earning him a glare from the older general. "We have the numbers, we can fashion our own roads and drive straight for the heart of Qarachal."

"Foolishness," Khalid spat. "You will spend ten years creating roads and for what? You do not even know where the rebel strongholds are. We need a planned penetration of the hill country, a comprehensive destruction of the rebels, and if we act promptly we will still be able to withdraw again before the rains start."

"You are the fool, Khalid. I am not advocating we build great new roads to move our armies, just that we employ our engineers to upgrade the existing ones as we need them. I know that there are armies at Tehri, Almora and Champawat. That will do for a start. I say we should strike straight through the hills and catch them unawares. Forget about the slow way along the river valleys." Barachim tried on a supercilious sneer that brought the older general to his feet in a purple-faced fury. "I think you are afraid to get to grips with the enemy, Khalid. You hope a slow approach along the rivers will allow them time to retreat."

"How dare you?" Khalid shouted. "You misbegotten son of ..."

"Gentlemen," Muhammed bin Tughluq said quietly. "You will refrain from displays of ill-temper and name-calling. If you cannot conduct yourselves with proper decorum, I will find myself some new generals."

Both generals bowed deeply before their Sultan, containing their anger and anxiously masking their fear.

Muhammed bin Tughluq signaled for them to return to their places. "You will both submit your detailed proposals in writing to my secretary by the time of Maghrib, together with the numbers of men you will need, the objectives you will achieve, and an estimate of the costs involved. I will examine them over the next few days and decide. The one whom I select will lead my armies into Qarachal, the other will offer up his life for failing me so miserably. Now, it is nearly noon and the muezzin will be calling the faithful to prayer. I give you leave to prepare yourselves."

A score of slaves hurried into the throne room carrying a golden bowl of pure water for the Sultan and silver bowls for the lesser personages. Normally, wudu, or ritual cleansing would be performed before the prayers of sunrise and would validate a person throughout the day. This morning, however, while listening to a petition, bin Tughluq had sneezed and a speck of phlegm had touched his right hand. He felt soiled and had ordered the water immediately. And of course, when the Sultan felt it necessary to wash, a wise man in his entourage immediately followed suit. The Sultan sat cross-legged in front of the golden bowl on the floor and composed his mind, thinking of the infinite wisdom and holiness of Allah.

"Bismillah, I perform wudu to cleanse myself of impurities." He dipped his right hand into the water and washed it up to the wrist three times, then repeated the action with his left hand. A slave handed him a goblet of water and a smaller bowl. Rinsing his mouth thoroughly, he spat into the small bowl before taking another mouthful. The nostrils came next, his cupped right hand introducing a small amount of water to both openings. Pinching the top of his nose with his left hand, he exhaled. Three times he performed this ritual of cleansing before moving on. Despite his concentration, bin Tughluq could hear the others in the throne room going through the same set of rituals, though some were behind him, others further along. He deliberately shut them out, turning his attention back to presenting himself to Allah in a spiritually and physically clean state.

The face came next, from hairline to his trimmed beard, the water cool and refreshing. The right arm followed, up to the elbow, then the left, each action repeated three times. He wet his hands once more and performed the masah of the head, his hands running over his turban to the back of his neck and forward again. Masah of the ears followed, and the back of the neck, and last of all he washed his feet from toes to ankles. Allowing himself a moment's contemplation of the clean body and mind he presented to Allah, he started into the recitation of the shahadah, the twin testimonies of faith.

As he did so, he noticed a slave at the window that faced the mosque, signaling with a small white flag. Although Dhurh prayers could be offered at any time from true noon to the start of Asr prayers, the muezzin knew his Sultan liked to be among the first to offer up praise. Hence, the caller would delay the adhan, or call to prayers, until bin Tughluq was ready. It was not strictly a proper action, but the Sultan was prepared to forgive this infraction.

Muhammed bin Tughluq rose to his feet as the cry of the muezzin rang out from the tower of the mosque. A slave hurried forward and unrolled an expensive prayer mat facing almost due west. Far in that direction, well beyond the horizon of the world, lay the holy city of Mecca. The Sultan's geographers had determined the direction long ago, when Muslims first came to Delhi. Bin Tughluq faced Mecca and made a silent niyyah, his intention to approach Allah in prayer. Raising his hands he cried out the takbir, "Allahu akbar!" and knelt, his whole court following a heartbeat later.

Swept up in the fervor of his approach to God, bin Tughluq started the first raka'ah, praising the Name of Allah in all the rounded mellifluous phrases of the first chapter of the Qur'an, the Sura al-Fatihah. Bowing, he repeated the takbir and chanted three times "Glory be to my Lord, the Supreme." Standing, he called out for all to hear, "May God hear the one who praises Him. Our Lord, for You is all praise."

A prostration followed, where bin Tughluq placed his forehead, nose, hands, knees and toes on the prayer mat, reciting the takbir again, and "Glory to my Lord the Most High." Sitting up, he repeated the prostration and stood

211

once more to complete the raka'ah. Another one followed and while still in an upright kneeling position, called out the first portion of the tashahhud.

"All glorifications are for God. All acts of good deeds and worship are for Him. Peace and the mercy and blessings of God be upon you, O Prophet. Peace be upon us and all of God's righteous servants. I bear witness that there is no god but God, and I bear witness that Muhammad is His Servant and Messenger."

As four raka'ah are to be completed for the dhuhr prayers, bin Tughluq led his court through the whole recitation again. And then, in the stillness of the penultimate prostration, as the holiness of the action filled the Sultan with exultation, the unthinkable happened. Behind him and to the right, a man broke wind, once but unmistakably. The Sultan froze in horror, the blasphemy of the action almost overcoming him. He imposed a tight control on himself and completed the last raka'ah, followed by the completion of the tashahhud. Facing his right shoulder he addressed the angel that noted his good deeds.

"Peace be on you and the mercy of God."

Turning to his left shoulder, he addressed the angel that noted his evil deeds, repeating the words. Rising to his feet, Sultan Muhammad bin Tughluq faced his still kneeling court, his eyes flashing angrily as he stared first at one man, then at another, concentrating on the men at the right side of the room.

"Who was it? Who has profaned Allah's name by the breaking of wind?"

Nobody met the Sultan's eyes but men started edging away from one of the courtiers – nothing obvious, but trying unobtrusively to remove themselves from the danger. The courtier, a small, thin man in red robes and turban, his sallow face paling as he looked wildly about at his erstwhile colleagues, prostrated himself once more, but this time he uttered a prayer for mercy and deliverance.

"Exalted one, forgive me. My ... my bowels are upset. I could not help it."

"Did you complete the raka'ah?" bin Tughluq asked quietly.

"Y ... yes, exalted one."

"Your emission of gas rendered you unclean. You presumed to approach Allah in such a state. That is blasphemy and cannot be forgiven. Guards!" The Sultan signaled and two armed men ran forward and hauled the shivering courtier to his feet. "Take him outside and thrust a spear into the part that caused offence."

Immediately, the guards hustled the man toward the door though he struggled and shrieked, imploring the Sultan to have mercy. The door closed on his cries and the courtiers all got to their feet, their eyes downcast as they shuffled and milled, none of them wanting to attract the attention of the Sultan.

"You have leave to go," bin Tughluq said, waving his hand dismissively. The courtiers fled, leaving just one old man, one of his counselors. The Sultan frowned. "Why are you still here, Abdul Zahir?"

"Your pardon, exalted one. In accordance with your earlier instructions, a small meal has been prepared for you. Do you wish to partake of it now, or do you wish to gaze upon the corpse of the blasphemer first?"

Bin Tughluq considered. *I am hungry*, he thought, *but hunger should not rule me.* "I will see the blasphemer first."

Counselor Zahir led the way out into the private courtyard behind high walls at the back of the palace. Despite the sultry heat of the day, the air within the courtyard was cool and refreshing, the odor of lemon and orange blossom strong, and the sound of tinkling water pervasive. The Sultan smiled, as he often did when entering his private paradise, and not always because of the beauty to be found there.

"Where is he?"

"At the rear of the garden, exalted one."

Bin Tughluq snorted with amusement. "Fitting. Show me."

A tall yew hedge separated the business end of the courtyard from the pleasures of the rest of it. Bin Tughluq believed that no matter how serious the crime, a man should have a last taste of beauty before death. For the blasphemers, it would likely be the last pleasurable thing they ever experienced as they certainly would not be permitted into Allah's Holy Presence. He had sometimes watched the faces of the condemned as they were dragged through the garden to their gruesome deaths. It was amazing how few seemed to appreciate the honor bestowed upon them.

Behind the hedge lay a square of close-cropped grass, surrounded by beds of multi-hued flowers. On the grass lay a naked man; face down, his lower body and thighs smeared with blood and excrement. The stench had attracted swarms of large blue flies that swirled above him and crawled over his skin.

214

"Is he still alive?" the Sultan asked.

Zahir called a guard over and put the question to him. The soldier bowed low before the Sultan. "Yes, Exalted One. The blasphemer still moves and utters small cries from time to time."

Bin Tughluq stepped around to the front of the victim and squatted down, carefully arranging his rich robes so they would not be soiled by contact with the blasphemer. "Abul Khayr, can you hear me?" There was no response from the wounded man and he ordered the guard to prod him. He asked the question again and this time was rewarded by a whimper and the fingers of the right hand scrabbling at the grass. The Sultan smiled, nodding.

"Abul Khayr, do you repent of your blasphemy and ask the mercy of Allah?"

When, after a few moments there was no further response, bin Tughluq rose to his feet and moved back to join Zahir. He called another two guards over.

"The blasphemer needs another lesson. Hold his legs apart and delve deeper with your spear."

The actions of the guards roused Abul Khayr to agonized cries as his legs were separated, revealing the gaping, bleeding wound in his anal perineum. The spear blade lanced in and Khayr shrieked and bucked, his blood fountaining again. Abruptly he fell silent and collapsed limply.

"Finish him." The spear thrust forward but with no further result. "Grieve with me, Zahir," bin Tughluq said piously. "A sinner has gone unrepentant to the torments of Hell."

"May Allah have mercy on him," Zahir murmured.

215

"No." The Sultan's head came up and he swung round on his counselor. "He did not call on the Name of Allah and thus forfeited His mercy." He eyed Zahir suspiciously. "Are you too tainted by his blasphemy?"

"No ... no, Exalted One. I merely meant that ... that perhaps he thought the Name at the end and thus may be judged mercifully." Zahir dropped to his knees and clasped the Sultan's ankles. "I beg forgiveness for my clumsy words."

Bin Tughluq frowned, then shook himself free of the old man. "You are forgiven ... this time. Now get up, I am hungry."

The Sultan ate alone in a tiled upstairs room, where wide verandahs kept out the seasonal rains and the heat of the sun. The room itself was decorated in complex patterns and designs, though in keeping with the dictates of the Holy Book, none even hinted at a depiction of anything that lived. Bin Tughluq sat at a small table covered with a white cloth, drinking out of a crystal goblet and dining off silver dishes. Many servants hovered round him, one holding an ewer of pure water so he could rinse his hands, another with a pristine cotton towel; others served food or carried away scraps and plates, poured him refreshingly cool citrus sherbet or fanned him with great feathered plumes. Musicians played quietly in a corner of the room, the music of flute and string soft and unobtrusive. The meal was simple – lamb cooked with onions and green ginger; pastries of meat with almonds, walnuts, pistachios and spices; and chicken with rice, cooked in ghee. Sugared sherbets heightened the taste of the spicy food and barley-water cleansed the palette before desert – in this case mango

216

with pickled green ginger and peppers; sweet oranges, and jack-fruit.

The Sultan pushed his chair away from the table at last and belched mightily. He rinsed his hands and dried them before clapping his hands and ordering the remnants of the meal to be cleared away. "Bring me Ibn Battuta," he ordered.

Abu Abdullah Muhammad Ibn Battuta was one of the most learned men in Dar al-Islam, the Muslim World. A Moroccan scholar, he was renowned for his jurisprudential knowledge and his wide experience of the world. He had arrived in Delhi years before, eager to see the Sultan's court and India and had stayed, at least in part because Muhammad bin Tughluq refused to let him go. He was appointed a judge, given a huge salary, and oversaw the bureaucracy of the whole Delhi Sultanate. When the Sultan took his armies to the south to quell a rebellion by one of the governors, Ibn Battuta was trusted with the charge of Delhi and the Qutb al-Din mausoleum. He had learned from the Sultan what was expected of him and all but ruled in his stead for two and a half years, meting out punishments to the wicked only a shade less severe than the Sultan's.

Upon the Sultan's return from his unsuccessful war, trouble broke out closer to Delhi and once more bin Tughluq led his armies out, this time to greater effect. The traitors were executed by elephants and Ibn Battuta dutifully recorded the details in his journal for later generations. In all things, Battuta was a loyal and dutiful subject, yet no man was above suspicion in the mind of the Sultan, so on receiving the summons, Battuta hurried to the dining hall with his heart beating faster and his

217

stomach, still trying to digest his own more frugal noon meal, churning with apprehension. On entering the chamber, he threw himself at the Sultan's feet and showered him with fulsome praise.

"Yes, yes, get up Battuta," bin Tughluq said. "Bring a chair over here; I want to talk to you about a very serious matter."

Battuta brought a chair, making sure it was a low one that would keep him below the Sultan's eye-level. "I am at your command, Exalted One," he murmured, sitting down. He waited patiently for the Sultan to begin.

Tughluq sat and stared across the room, his right hand feeding pistachio nuts into his mouth one at a time. He chewed cursorily and swallowed before shifting his attention to the seated man.

"You have performed your duties well, Ibn Battuta. I am pleased with you."

"Thank you, Exalted One." Battuta bent as far into a bow as he could in the low chair. "It is an honor to serve you."

"Your family is well? Your wife, Lamya? Your daughter, Jameela?"

"All well, thank you, Exalted One."

"I have arrested Haamid Ghasaan, your wife's father." Tughluq's voice was mild and conversational, but his eyes watched Battuta, looking for the least sign of duplicity. "He is implicated in a rebellion against me, one of many such traitors. He is being put to the question as we speak."

Battuta swallowed and bent his head again to hide his shock and alarm. "Thy will be done, Exalted One. May all proven traitors meet their just ends."

218

"Indeed. But Allah, Blessed be He, commands us to balance mercy with justice. Justice alone demands I kill all who transgress by rebelling against their lawful ruler. Yet I would temper this with mercy, as Allah, the Beneficent, commands, by seeking out the reasons for their transgressions. Hence, I question them."

"And … and what have you determined, Great One?"

"That the rot spreads further than I thought, Ibn Battuta. Muhammad Safwan is another conspirator, who has in turn named his two sons, a cousin, his wife and several members of his household, including a male child. They are all being questioned."

"A child, Exalted One? Has he reached the age of tahara?"

"You mean circumcision? I do not know. Why?"

"My lord bin Tughluq, you surely know that according to Law, a male child who has not yet attained the age of passage cannot be held accountable for the actions of his family? He cannot even be questioned but must be handed over to a faithful and upright man to be raised in the fear of Allah, Blessed be He."

Tughluq frowned. "I do not know if he is circumcised but it does not matter. I will not have him growing up and deciding to avenge himself for the death of his family."

"You are set upon their deaths, then?"

"Why do you seek to excuse them, Ibn Battuta? Has the rebellion spread even to you?"

"My lord knows I am loyal."

"Can I be sure of that? Your wife's father is guilty and will be executed. Is it unreasonable to suppose he has approached his daughter and son-in-law?" Tughluq's

219

frown became a scowl. "Or has he approached you and you have kept silent hoping to strike me down unawares?"

"My lord, I have no knowledge of this plot. Would any man, even Haamid Ghasaan, trust such a dangerous enterprise to the ears and mouth of a woman, such as his daughter? Or to a man raised up by you to be a judge? If Haamid Ghasaan is guilty, then the surest sign of my innocence is that he has not tried to convert me to his cause. He knows I am loyal to you, Muhammad bin Tughluq."

The Sultan sat and looked at his judge for several minutes, stroking his beard and mustache contemplatively. "Yes, it may be that you are right," he said at last. "Heaven knows I am too merciful and forgiving of my enemies, but I must also be just. I will signal my trust in you for all to see by increasing your salary to six thousand silver dinar a year."

"My lord, you are too generous." Ibn Battuta hesitated, knowing he was playing with fire but also knowing he had to try. "About my wife's father ..."

"Do not think you can impose on my good nature," Tughluq said tightly. "Perhaps I have been mistaken about your innocence if you would plead for Ghasaan's life."

"Exalted One, no man should ever attempt to change the mind of such a beneficent ruler as yourself. My plea was not to grant him life, my lord, but a swift death."

Tughluq raised an eyebrow. "Go on."

"My wife is a dutiful daughter and the knowledge that her father is being tortured will greatly upset her. When a woman loses her calm outlook on life, the

220

household suffers. When the household is in turmoil, a husband cannot carry out his duties properly." Ibn Battatu smiled gently and spread his hands. "I live to serve you, my lord, but it will be difficult to serve you as well as I should if my house is in turmoil. That is why I ask a swift death for Haamid Ghasaan so that my wife may grieve and resume her normal duties as quickly as possible."

"An interesting way of putting it, Battuta, but I suppose that is your jurisprudential training. I was thinking I would have to execute you and your wife as well, after suitable questioning, but I have decided to grant your request instead. Haamid Ghasaan will be beheaded immediately."

"Thank you, Exalted One. May the Blessings of Allah be upon you for your merciful action."

Tughluq nodded and changed the subject. "I have decided to invade Qarachal."

"Indeed, my lord. I had heard something of this. May I be permitted to ask why?"

"Their chiefs and kings have defied me too long. They either will not pay tribute, or else it is late coming. I wish to impose my righteous will on them."

"A war will be an expensive undertaking, my lord."

"I can recover my costs and more from plunder."

"Of course, my lord, but you will still need much gold to outfit your army. The treasury is almost empty, except for the, er … copper coins."

A few years before, bin Tughluq had devised a bold new idea to strengthen the economy of his empire. He minted hundreds upon thousands of copper coins and let it be known that they represented the silver and gold he held in his treasury. Unfortunately, two things happened

221

which, with a little foresight, could have been seen. First, traders showed a stubborn reluctance to deal in anything but silver and gold; and second, Hindus saw it as a fine opportunity to gain back some of the economic edge they had lost to their Muslim neighbors. They stated minting their own coins out of cheap copper and trading them with the palace for silver and gold. The flood of copper coins bankrupted the empire and ruined the economy, forcing the Sultan to reverse his action.

"If I might make a suggestion," Ibn Battatu went on. "There is a way to pay for this war."

The Sultan said nothing, just nodded for his judge and minister to continue.

"The hills and mountains of Qarachal are filled with Hindus and where there are Hindus, there are temples. Now, as any Muslim man knows, there is but one God, Allah the Just and Beneficent, not many, and our pagan brethren are surely destined for hell unless we can bring the truth of God's Holy Word, the Qur'an to them. The temples must be destroyed and the pagans converted."

"Admirable sentiments, my friend, but just how does this help me? You give me another reason to war, but not the means to do so."

"Ah, but I have, my lord. Your nobles will pay for the war out of their own bulging coffers."

"They have been remarkably reluctant so far," Tughluq said sourly. "Why should they change?"

"Because this will become a Holy War, a Jihad bis saif, and no man who worships Allah, Blessed be He, can refuse to contribute."

Tughluq clapped his hands together and laughed. "Now I know why I always trust you, learned Ibn Battuta, no matter what the circumstances. You display such sagacity and knowledge of the way men's minds work. None of the nobles can withstand such a request and I will milk them of their wealth."

"I caution you to refrain from greed, Exalted One, and hold out the promise of great plunder that they may recoup their expenses and more."

"Yes, yes, of course."

"And remember always that this is done that men's souls may reach Allah, Blessed be He. Never lose sight of that goal."

"It is the most important work a man can do," Tughluq agreed.

"Have you decided on a general to lead your army, my lord?"

"I had thought to do so myself. General Jamaal Khalid and General Maahir Barachim have differing views on the conduct of the war. They will be submitting their plans by sunset."

"You already know which plan you will favor?"

"Yes, that of Khalid. Barachim will suffer death as a penalty for not knowing his Sultan's mind."

"Such foolishness is deserving of death," Battuta agreed. "However, may I make a small suggestion? Barachim is a fine general and it would be a pity to waste his talents. By all means send Khalid up the valley of the Ganga River, but also send Barachim up through Rudrapur to attack Almora, Champawat and Baijnath. You will trap the armies of Qarachal between two pincers and tear them to pieces."

Muhammad bin Tughluq pondered his judge's thoughts for several minutes, finally striding over to a table and selecting a map from the several there. He pored over it for minutes longer, his finger tracing routes and roads. "Yes, it will work. I will give my generals equal armies, at least a hundred thousand men apiece and set them loose on Qarachal. They will compete for honors and riches and souls brought to Allah."

Three months later, when the rains had cleared and the river floods had abated sufficiently to allow the passage of troops, two great armies assembled. The greater of these, numbering almost two hundred thousand men, was led by General Khalid and started from the city of Chandpur in the valley of the Ganga. It marched northward from the plains into the foothills and by degrees into the mountainous valleys and ridges of Kedarkhand. The other army, somewhat smaller at only a hundred and fifty thousand, marched north from Rudrapur toward the lake in the Naini region and from thence to the crescent ridge of Almora. As they went, hundreds of mobile forces detached from the main army and disappeared up side valleys, or scrambled up wooded ridges, hurrying along the steep and narrow trails to find Hindu temples. These they destroyed by fire or by throwing down the brick and rock and timbered structures, carrying away anything of value and putting the priests of the varied gods to the sword.

After a time, the armies of the Sultan came under attack. King Anand Pal led a fierce resistance in defence of Kedarkhand, now often called Garhwal, while King Dharm Chand of Manaskhand or Kumaon made every nali of ground lost worth many Muslim lives. They could not hope to stand against such strength though, and bit by bit, the armies of the Sultan forced their way into the

224

wooded mountains of Qarachal. Huge treasures were captured and transported back to the treasury at Delhi, while the smoke from the burning towns and temples darkened the skies.

The war was not one-sided, despite the numerical superiority of the Muslim armies. The Hindu tribesmen fought bravely for their towns and farms, often throwing back the invaders for a time before being thrust into disarray. Tales filtered back of feats of heroic proportions, and from both Garhwal and Kumaon came stories of ordinary men suddenly assuming the mantle of heroes and fighting to the death against the enemy despite suffering horrific wounds. It was as if, the people said, the gods themselves incarnated and fought for their towns and villages, their farms and orchards, their shrines and temples.

Then came the rains again and the armies bogged down in the mud, the roads became impassable and supplies grew short as the convoys of food and arms from Delhi and the other city plains were forced to turn back. Generals Khalid and Barachim turned their spread-out armies loose on the countryside to forage what food they could from the devastated farms and to seek shelter in the towns and remaining temples. Throughout the monsoon months, the war marked time, but as hard as the time was on the Muslim armies, it was harder for the people of Garhwal and Kumaon. By the time the flooded rivers receded and the first convoys of food made it through from the plains, the people of the hills were at the point of starvation. Khalid and Barachim gathered themselves for one final thrust at the heart of Qarachal. Then came news from Delhi and the court of the Sultan that shattered those plans irrevocably.

One of the foremost scholars of Islam within the Delhi Sultanate was a Sufi holy man, Shaykh Abdullah Qasir. Known as a man of peace and great learning, he had been wandering in the southern lands when the Qarachal war broke out. He arrived back at the court during the rains and was appalled by the reports he heard of the atrocities being committed in the Holy Name of Allah. Never one to hold back when he saw an injustice being done, Shaykh Qasir immediately started talking outspokenly against the war.

The Sultan's response was predictable and his guards arrested the venerable Sufi as he preached in the court of justice. Bin Tughluq stared down at the gaunt bearded figure of the holy man on the ornately tiled throne room floor, whence the guards threw him.

"Why are you preaching against this war, Shaykh Qasir? Do you side with the traitors and rebels of Qarachal against your Sultan?"

"I preach against an unjust war, Sultan bin Tughluq," Shaykh Qasir replied. He struggled to his feet and stood, clad only in a plain loincloth and open tunic in front of the resplendent court of the Sultan. His turban had come undone during his arrest and he smoothed his beard as he stared up at the man on the throne. "You have called this war a jihad bis saif, a struggle against evil by using the sword, Muhammad bin Tughluq, but I tell you it were better for you had you called a jihad bin nafs and struggled to clean your heart."

Tughluq flushed strongly. "You dare to talk to me that way? The war has brought thousands of souls to the knowledge of Allah. You cannot deny that is a great work."

The Sufi seemed to be searching within himself for the right words. He trembled and jerked and opened his mouth two or three times before replying. "Muhammad himself – praise be upon him – cautioned tribesmen when they returned from a war with the infidel that they had been engaged in al-jihad al-asghar, the lesser jihad. He – praise be upon him – reminded them that the greater jihad, al-jihad al-akbar, would be to conquer their lustful inclinations. You too, Muhammad bin Tughluq, are filled with a lusting after power, after wealth, and after pursuits of the flesh. Give up this lesser jihad of the sword and attend to your greater failings lest Allah, Blessed be His Name, reject you." Shaykh Qasir stood in front of the Sultan and folded his arms. His lip trembled slightly and his left eyelid twitched as he waited for the Sultan's response.

It was not long in coming. Tughluq leapt down from his throne dais and strode across to the Sufi, back-handing him across the face. "Guards!" he roared. "Get this … this miserable traitor and blasphemer out of my sight. Lock him in the dungeon." He whirled to stare at the surrounding courtiers, all of whom bent their heads, avoiding his glaring eyes. "How many of you agree with this so-called holy man? How many of you are traitors too? Well, I shall put Qasir to the question and he will name names before he dies. Then we shall have a fine killing here." The Sultan stormed from the throne room and ensconced himself in his private chambers for the rest of the day, refusing to let anyone in who had not been searched to the skin by his guards. "I am surrounded by traitors!" he would scream at intervals.

The next morning, after dawn prayers, Tughluq visited the Sufi in the dungeon. He had the prisoner brought to the Chamber of Questioning and let him wander round the room so that he could see the instruments of persuasion and allow fear to settle in his stomach.

"Shaykh Abdullah Qasir, who are your fellow traitors?"

The Sufi turned a pale face toward the Sultan, the shadows in the room masking the trembling in his limbs but not the tremor in his voice. "Exalted One, why do you show me these instruments of torture? It is not lawful for a follower of the Prophet, peace be upon him, to be tortured."

"Answer my question. Who are your fellow conspirators?"

"I have none, my lord. I am innocent of the charges you lay against me and thus can have no conspirators."

"Do not think to chop logic with me, Sufi. You accused me of having an impure heart and waging an unjust war. That is treason and such thoughts do not exist alone. Who else shares them? I want names."

"My lord, it cannot be treason for a man to want a fellow believer to be upright and pure in the eyes of Allah. That is all that I want for you – that you should turn your hand from the way of the sword and embrace all that is pure and righteous by cleansing your heart and mind."

"You tell me I do not have a pure heart? I? I who know the Qur'an and quote it daily? I who follow every precept and instruction of the Prophet, peace be upon him, every day? I am well known for my piety and my love of Allah, the Most Holy and Beneficent. How can you accuse me of uncleanliness?"

Shaykh Qasir swallowed and glanced about him at the guards in the light of the flickering oil lamps. Suddenly his trembling stopped and his voice firmed. He pointed a finger at the Sultan. "Your hands are steeped in blood, Muhammad bin Tughluq, blood both of Muslim and Hindu. Your heart is unclean and I call on you, in the Name of Allah and his Prophet to turn your back on your unjust ways and embrace Truth once more. I call on Allah to chastise you that you may repent of your deeds. "

"Blasphemy!" Tughluq cried. "You confirm your guilt. Guards, bind him to the table. You will reveal all to me Sufi, or suffer."

The guards leapt forward and grabbed the shaking Qasir, dragging him back to a heavy, blood-stained table to which they manacled him. The resolve drained out of him and he trembled once more as he craned his neck to see the Sultan.

"It …It is unlawful to torture a believer, bin Tughluq. The Prophet, peace be upon him, himself says: 'Prevent punishment in case of doubt. Release the accused if possible, for it is better that the ruler be wrong in forgiving than wrong in punishing.' I am innocent and you would be wrong to punish me unjustly."

"The Prophet, peace be upon him, also says 'For the wrongdoers We have prepared a fire which will encompass them like the walls of a pavilion. When they cry out for help they shall be showered with water as hot

229

as molten brass, which will scald their faces. Evil shall be their drink, dismal their resting-place.'"

"My lord, you know as well as I that He was talking about unbelievers, those who turned their face against Allah. There is no Sura that supports the torture of a believer."

Tughluq frowned, feeling the argument turning against him. "If I can only torture an unbeliever ... then ... then you must become an unbeliever."

Shaykh Qasir smiled triumphantly. "But I am a believer." He immediately recited the shahadah.

"A believer is known by his actions, not just his words."

"But if I am forced to an unrighteous action, it is invalid and the penalty rebounds on the enforcer."

"Then you must be brought into a state that no believer can be in."

"The same rule applies, my lord. If I profess my faith by the twin testimonies, I am a true believer and cannot be put to torture."

Tughluq snarled and turned to one of the guards. "Shave him. A man without a fist-length beard cannot be a Muslim."

"It is haraam, forbidden, for one man to cut off another man's beard, bin Tughluq."

"Then I shall not cut, I will pluck the hairs out one by one, until you confess your sins and reveal the other traitors."

Shaykh Abdullah Qasir was a brave man but the small pain involved in the plucking of a single hair was multiplied a hundredfold, then by a thousand. He bled and writhed in agony but he refused to name any man as an accomplice.

"Before Allah the Beneficent and Merciful," he gasped out. "I am innocent of these charges."

Tughluq looked down at the raw and bleeding face of the Sufi and nodded. "I believe you Shaykh Qasir. You are free to go." He turned to a guard. "Release him."

The guard gaped. "My lord?"

"Release him, you fool, and escort him to his house!" Tughluq called another guard to him as the Sufi was helped out of the dungeon. "Take a few men and follow him, discreetly. I want to know who talks to him. Report to me by sunset."

Tughluq sat in his throne room as the time of sunset approached, biting his nails and jumping at every sudden sound. Around him, keeping quiet and doing their best not to attract attention were several courtiers and guards. As the sun dipped below the horizon, throwing the palm trees into silhouette, and turning the hot and dusty air a deep orange, the guard returned.

"You have the names?"

"Yes, Exalted One." The guard held a piece of paper aloft. "Three names in all."

"Show me." The Sultan held out his hand then drew it back as the wavering call of the muezzin rent the air, calling the faithful to Maghrib prayers. "Prayers first. You have leave to offer them here." Bin Tughluq led the men in the room through the three raka'ah prescribed for sunset prayers and waited for the prayer mats to be rolled up and put away before holding out his hand again for the piece of paper.

The Sultan scanned the list quickly before looking up at the pale guard. "You saw these men talk to the Sufi? Name them not but tell me the circumstance of each."

"Yes, Exalted One. The first happened upon him as he was escorted home. He helped the guard and went inside with him. He left an hour later and returned shortly with the second man. The third arrived later and was admitted. As sunset was approaching, I wrote down the names and came here as instructed."

"You have done well." The Sultan snapped his fingers and a secretary hurried up, bowing deeply as he got close. "Sign an order to the treasury. This man is to receive a gold dinar. Next," he went on, dismissing the guard with a wave of the hand, "Bring me the Captain of the Guard. Who is it tonight?"

"Nasser Udeen, my lord."

Minutes later, even as servants were lighting oil lamps to drive back the darkness, the Captain appeared, tall and well-bearded, resplendent in his red and gold uniform and tall turban. The officer dropped to one knee and saluted the Sultan.

"Captain Udeen, you will take a squad of men and arrest Shaykh Abdullah Qasir. Put him, under guard, in the Chamber of Questioning. Then arrest Muhammad Ibn Battuta, Abdul Azeem and Sulayman Tariq. It may well be that you will find them at the Sufi's house. When they are all safely locked up, you will return to the Sufi's house and search it thoroughly. Take my secretary Wadee' with you. He will write down the name of any person mentioned in letters, or documents. And Udeen," bin Tughluq added as the Captain started to rise, "These

232

men are traitors. Treat them as such but do not kill them. I do not want them to die just yet."

Shaykh Abdullah Qasir suffered abominable tortures in the Sultan's dungeons, being forced to eat excrement before being beheaded. He revealed nothing, naming no names for, as he steadfastly maintained to the end, his only sin was a desire for the Sultan to cleanse his heart before Allah. Two of the men who tended to him after his temporary release – Azeem, a god-fearing passer-by who had never met the Sufi before that day; and Tariq, a physician – likewise suffered for a time before their welcome release into death. The third man, Muhammad Ibn Battuta, was placed under house arrest where he fasted and prayed for nine days, certain that his death was imminent. He rid himself of all his goods and possessions and was granted permission to join a hermit in a cave outside Delhi. Five months later, Ibn Battuta was recalled and appointed as the Sultan's ambassador to the Mongol court in China.

Many names were discovered in the Sufi's house during the search by the Captain's guards. Most of these men were executed on one pretext or another over the ensuing months, but two names caused Sultan bin Tughluq considerable anxiety – General Jamaal Khalid and General Maahir Barachim. Both possessed armies and both, it seemed, were just waiting for the opportunity to overthrow their Sultan.

After much deliberation, and much sifting through the documents found in the Sufi's house, including rough drafts of letters to the generals, bin Tughluq decided on a course of action. A newly elevated general, Muhammad Musaad, arrived in the camps of the fighting generals with letters commending them on their successes and an invitation to the court at Delhi to receive honors and riches at the hands of their grateful Sultan. They went, suspecting nothing, to their deaths. General Musaad brought the armies home and Qarachal began its long road to recovery. The temples were rebuilt and the Hindu way of life returned to the high mountains, but this time a Muslim presence remained, there being enough men of good will in the Faith to worship Allah while maintaining a peaceful relationship with men of other faiths.

Chapter Twelve

My visits to Delhi were successful, and at the risk of sounding immodest, I can claim to have saved my mountains and valleys from the din of warfare for a time and the unnecessary spilling of human blood. Of course, you cannot make goat stew without killing the goat, as the saying goes, but at least the majority of the deaths I caused were those of the invader rather than my hill-men.

I arrived in Delhi while the preparations for war were in their early stages and, being experienced now, slipped into the body of a minor court official without anyone noticing. The only one who looked at me suspiciously was his wife, but only because I once more sampled the delights of fleshly contact, more often and for longer than she was accustomed. As a minor official I had the run of the court but little of the responsibility, giving me more freedom of movement. I was actually given the task of writing out the war plans of General Khalid just before the invasion.

You may ask why I did not just take over someone of elevated rank, like a general or the Sultan himself, if I wanted to know the plans or work mischief, but I found myself prevented. Let me digress for a moment ...

I have been in close contact with Hindu and Buddhist holy men and entered temples many times. I am apprehensive when entering the abode of a god for I know their power and do not wish to try my strength against them. In the same way, a holy man has a certain adamantine quality to the mind that prevents me feeding on it, or possessing it. I am therefore wary when it comes to the god-man relationship.

When I arrived in the Sultan's capital city I approached the holy men and places cautiously, wondering if this new faith rendered them equally hard to access. The temples of Islam, the mosques, are bleak buildings. Architecturally they are often magnificent with vaulting arches and towering pillars, open porticoes opening onto marbled courtyards, yet within them are little except prayer mats and a few books. Certainly there are no images of their god, no chanting priests and offerings of foods and flowers, not even paintings or carvings from their holy book. I wandered as a naked flame mostly but occasionally within a body and it was at these times that I most often felt the presence of something. The chambers were as empty as before yet it seemed as though something moved within the still air. Was it the god of these people, or was it the imagination of the mind I inhabited? Certainly when a man was in the ecstasy of prayer I sometimes found myself unceremoniously tipped out of his mind as he became temporarily impervious to me.

It was this way with some people who I thought I could invade quite easily. I even tried the Sultan himself, Muhammad bin Tughluq, as I thought such a blood-thirsty monster would not be able to resist me. I was successful – sort of – but while I could get in I found I could not influence. His faith was strong and it fought me. In the end, I gave up and sought to influence his actions by playing on his paranoia. The generals were useless for my purpose – if I had interfered with them, bin Tughluq would have appointed others; Ibn Battuta a possibility but while the Sultan admired and respected this scholar, I felt that false advice from him would be suspicious and be disregarded.

I could see no way to stop the war, so I returned to Kedarkhand and Manaskhand to assist in the defense of the land instead. My lack of experience in warfare and total ignorance of tactics and strategy limited my use – I recognized this before I did too much damage. I thought then of the wood-cutter Isha and his posthumous fight against the bandits. It had not mattered to Isha that I used his dead body but my possession of it helped his wife and child enormously. I decided to try a similar thing in the war.

By chance, my first attempt was at Chamoli, not far from Isha's shrine on the Pihokri ridge. A small group of Hindu farmers were attempting to save their crops from a detachment of Khalid's soldiers and were crumbling under the onslaught. A farmer called Deepak fell with a stab through his heart and moments later rose again to challenge his killer. My control of dead bodies was much improved by experience and Deepak fought with skill and bravery, eventually routing the enemy though repeatedly wounded. Only when the soldiers were in full flight did the brave Deepak succumb to his horrifying wounds.

The example of Farmer Deepak had a two-fold effect: it saved his community, and gave strength to a dispirited people everywhere. Soon there were other heroes as more fatally wounded men apparently found a new lease on life and came to the defense of their lands. Many said it was the gods possessing them and I was content to let that be. People know that demons possess dead bodies but only to harm others, never to rescue them.

237

The war ground to a halt with the coming of the rains but I knew that even with my help, the next season would see a renewed effort by the invader and the devastation of my land must occur. I went back to Delhi, determined to find a solution – and this time I found it.

Sufis are holy men and holy men should be immune to my possession, but this one was not. I think the reason is that Sufis are philosophers rather than fanatics. They put great stock in their knowledge of the Qur'an and the commentaries of a host of Imams and philosophers and this blinds them to the power of faith, even blind faith. Muhammad bin Tughluq was an evil and violent man but he had a great faith in his god so I could not touch him. Shaykh Abdullah Qasir was upright and decent but put his reliance on knowledge rather than faith and was vulnerable to my attack.

I did not stay in the Sufi long, just long enough to ensure his death and set in motion the events that would lead to the liberation of my hills and people. I had some regrets about causing his unpleasant death but it was essential that I arouse bin Tughluqs anger and let his paranoia take over. In the end I only possessed him twice, the first time where I, through the Sufi, called the Sultan unclean. He almost got away from me there, jerking and stammering as he realized another spirit was acting in him. Once more I entered him, when bleeding and faint he entered his house. In his weakened state he was no match for me. When the charitable man left to find a doctor, I made Qasir draft letters to the Generals, in the knowledge that his house would eventually be searched. Bin Tughluqs paranoia did the rest. The successful generals were executed and my land was saved from the invader.

Perhaps you will decry my methods, sending innocent men to their deaths, but this is no more than kings and generals do at any time. Even the gods are not above a little mayhem and destruction when it suits their purpose, so I do not think I can be judged too harshly. When all is said and done, I arose in the land of Bharath, the people of Hind are mine, and the country itself calls to me. What should I do but defend it when threatened by foreign invaders?

I went back to my hills and valleys after the war and watched the rebuilding process, even helping to erect new temples. I worked in the fields and the towns, inhabiting a succession of bodies though doing them no harm save a little weariness and the thanks of their neighbors. At other times I fashioned myself a body and revisited some of the places I had been. I even flew unseen over Mount Kailasa but Balaka's disciples still studied there and I felt once more the strength of their repelling mantra. After many years of wandering, I came back to Nanda Devi's pristine slopes and thence south along the Goriganga River and from there into the Sarda River and down to the wooded slopes of the Champawat countryside in Kumaon. Here I found a tiny village, no more than a hamlet really, clinging to a grassy hillside and surrounded by wooded slopes of pine, spruce and larch and deep ravines choked with denser vegetation. The grassy hillside is terraced in a series of narrow fields bordered by a lip of earth to hold moisture and fringed, as often as not, by leafy oaks. The area abounds with animals, from ghoral and serow on the higher slopes to barking deer and

239

wild boar, leopard and tiger, bear and monkey in the
lower forests. Bird life abounds and the streams are full
of fish. I thought myself fortunate to have come across
this place and decided to stay for a while. I found myself
a suitable host and moved in, ready to study once more
the human condition.

Chapter Thirteen

Parvati Sunanda lived with her family in one of the larger houses of the village of Sunadhura on a steep hillside a few miles from the city of Champawat. Despite the proximity to the city, with its thriving markets and the sometime presence of the kings of Kumaon, Parvati's father seldom left the village. Like almost everyone within the tiny community, he had his part to play in village life and saw no need to venture outside it. Everything the villagers needed could either be grown in the fields, harvested from the forests, or made in the small workshops. Almost every man and woman helped in the fields, but most had other occupations. Parvati's father, Rama Sunanda, was a miller. The back room of the house was the largest and the cleanest, its packed earth floor swept and free of dust, large close woven mats surrounding the large, polished grindstones in the middle of the floor. Here, he ruled supreme, allowing nobody else to touch the stones unless under his direct supervision. Outside the back door of the house was an enclosed courtyard where grain was threshed, the husks being rejected and the kernels moving indoors to the mill. Rama was a kind and gentle man, giving the husks to the widow Karishma, an ancient woman of nearly sixty years who eked out a living mixing the husks with such fragments of dung as she could collect, pressing and drying it into fuel cakes. These she sold to the villagers for a pittance, enough barely to keep herself alive.

The rest of the house consisted of a front verandah, a kitchen and family room behind it and to one side, two bedrooms. Rama and his wife Leela occupied one and the three children; Parvati, twelve; her brother Dhaval, six; and her sister Rati, five; occupied the other. There was little in the way of furniture, a bed for the adults and pallets stuffed with dried grass for the children. A table graced the main room, two long benches, a few chairs and three large chests for clothes. These had been made by the village carpenter, Ganesh, though he was not paid in coin for his services. There was very little actual money in the village, though rumor had it that the headman owned a small hoard of copper coins buried beneath his bed. Any transaction that took place in the village was by barter. Rama had traded his services as a miller and Ganesh his skills as a carpenter.

The village produced enough food to be self-sufficient most years, unless there was a flood, or a drought, or unless some affliction affected the crops. What the village did produce, year after year, without fail, were children. There was always at least one woman pregnant, working bent double in the fields with her swollen belly, right up to the moment when she would drop her hoe or scythe and have her child. Often it was enough for a friend or relative to hold her squatting upright in the shade of the oaks lining the terraced fields. She would bear down, cry out, and with little fuss produce another mouth to feed. Within an hour, the woman would be back at work, perhaps on light duties bundling the cut grain or bringing water to the others. That night she would introduce another son or daughter to her family.

Parvati loved the new babies and longed for the day she would be married and have her own to cradle, to show off, and to play with. The life of a child in a hill country village is short. Sometimes disease, accident or starvation carries them off, sometimes not; but if death does not intervene, adulthood does. A child is expected to work for the family from an early age rather than play or get such rudimentary education as was available from Manish the teacher.

Parvati was the oldest child in her family at twelve, but she had had two older brothers and two younger also, all of whom died in infancy. Now she had a single brother and sister and her mother was past the age of child-bearing. Rama never berated his wife Leela over this, though he was still a vigorous man himself. He looked wistfully at his single son Dhaval sometimes, counting the years to when he could reasonably betroth him and join him in the family business. He never counted the years for Parvati and Rati though. When they married, he would have to find a dowry from somewhere and lose his girls to other houses.

On the cusp of womanhood, though her red flowering had not yet come, she was busy all day with tasks that properly were performed by boys, like taking their milk cow out to pasture, or herding the five goats they owned. Rama's son should have been doing this, but any that might have filled that function had died years before. Dhaval was too young to be entrusted with the family wealth, so Parvati was used. Her mother did not neglect her education either, filling any spare moment of her day with cooking and cleaning, helping in the fields, cutting forage or collecting fuel. After days spent in such work, Parvati looked forward to the evenings.

A huge oak tree stood in a clearing in the village center and beneath its leafy canopy, Karna the headman

243

held an unofficial town meeting every evening after dinner. A fire would be lit and in the dancing shadows sat the men and boys, talking and telling stories. Women were not actually forbidden to attend but it was thought not quite proper for a woman to be idle so long. Sometimes a wife or daughter would sit on the outskirts of the gathering and card wool or clean vegetables, but usually they stayed away, gossiping in their own meetings outside the huts as they busied themselves with their endless chores.

Parvati loved the headman's fire and would sit with her brother a few paces behind her father and listen avidly to the conversations. Mostly, they concerned the village and the crops or juicy bits of gossip that Parvati did not really understand, but just occasionally, the talk would turn to far off places and times and stories would be told. One evening, when the talk of crops and droughts had run its course, the headman called for silence.

"I have had enough of our tiresome lives for tonight. Who has a tale to tell?"

Heads turned to the teacher who was the most educated man in the village and had, so he often boasted, once lived in Champawat in the shadow of the Kumaon kings. This night, however, he shook his head, pleading a head cold.

"I have a story," said a voice from the shadows. Heads turned again and those closest to the voice drew back, allowing the man some room. With a shuffling gait, a young man limped into the firelight, leaning heavily on a stout stick. The murmurings of the group of men broke into a gabble.

"It is Arjuna," someone said, surprise in his voice.

"What story can he tell? He is only a goat herder. I do not want to hear a story about a goat."

"He was a soldier, remember. He was wounded in a war."

"So he says ..."

The headman called for quiet. "Arjuna, you have a story for us? Is it one of war?"

"No," Arjuna replied quietly. "I have seen too much of war to talk about it. I have a tale I once heard from a man who lived in the far-off plains near the great city of Delhi."

"Is it a story about kings and jewels?"

"No," Arjuna said. "It is about a farmer ..." He grinned at the chorus of groans. "And a tiger," he finished.

"Well, that could be interesting," said Karna the headman. "Tell it to us, for we can always stop you if it gets boring."

Arjuna folded his legs carefully under him and sat in the dust near the tree where the firelight showed off his handsome face with its neatly trimmed beard.

"What a pity he is crippled," Kavita said. Her red flower had blossomed several months back and she had a ready eye for the young men. "He is a bit old too."

"Shh," Parvati whispered. "I want to hear the story."

Arjuna cleared his throat and looked round at the circle of men. "A farmer went out with his bullock, a thin scrawny beast, to plough his land. No sooner had he started than a tiger walked out of the forest and said to the farmer 'Give me your bullock, for I am very hungry.' The farmer was very frightened but also a little put out at the tiger's demand. 'But if you eat my bullock, I cannot

245

plough my field, and if I don't plough the field I cannot sow the grain and if I don't get a harvest my family will starve. Go and find another bullock to eat. Please,' he added, because he was a polite man."

A ripple of laughter swept through the listeners and a small boy asked, "Can tigers talk?"

"Yes," Arjuna said, keeping a straight face. "But it is wise not to wait and see what he says if you see one. Now, where was I? Oh yes, well, the tiger did not like this suggestion and said that if the farmer did not immediately hand over his bullock to be eaten, he might eat the farmer too. In desperation, the farmer came up with a plan. 'If you will spare my bullock, I will fetch you a nice plump milk cow my wife has tied up at home.' The tiger agreed, and the farmer led his bullock home, worrying about how he would break the news to his wife.

'You must be mad, husband. If the tiger eats my cow we will have no milk for the children.' 'And if he eats my bullock, we will have no bread,' argued the farmer. They talked, then they shouted, and after a bit they cried because either way the tiger would eat one of their fine beasts. The wife dried her tears and said, 'I have an idea. Go back to the tiger and tell him your wife is bringing the cow in a few minutes.' Well, as you can imagine, the farmer did not like to tell the tiger he would have to wait for his dinner, but he did, and the tiger was so angry the farmer thought he was about to be eaten himself. The wife, meanwhile, ran next door to the headman's hut and borrowed his horse ..."

"He must be richer than you, Karna," Ganesh the carpenter chortled. "You don't have a horse."

246

"Why would I want one anyway?" Karna asked sourly. "Go on, Arjuna, but stop making comments about my poverty."

Arjuna inclined his head politely. "The wife borrowed the horse and dressed up in her husband's most colorful clothes and wound a long cloth about her head so it resembled a tall turban. When she rode off, brandishing her shiny scythe, she looked like a prince. She saw the tiger in the field near her husband and called out loudly, 'Where can I find a tiger, for I am very hungry? I haven't eaten one since breakfast yesterday.'

The tiger, seeing the tall prince on his horse, waving his sword and saying such alarming things, took fright and fled for the safety of the forest. A jackal saw the tiger running away and stopped him. In truth, the jackal was hoping to gnaw the bones of the bullock or the milk cow, so had an interest in the whole business. 'Why are you running away from a woman?' the jackal asked. 'I'm not,' the tiger replied. 'It is a fierce prince who eats tigers for breakfast.' 'Nonsense,' said the jackal. 'It is a woman and she is just trying to make you give up your dinner.'

At this the tiger got angry but he was still doubtful. 'What if this is some trick of yours to betray me to this prince? You will run away and leave me to his hunger.' The jackal laughed and said, 'Then tie our tails together so I cannot run away from you. You will see.' So the tiger tied his tail firmly to the jackal's tail and he marched toward the woman on the horse, with the jackal trotting alongside, drooling at the thought of the coming feast.

The farmer saw them coming and cried out in fear. 'They are coming to eat us!' The wife though, called out in a loud voice. 'Thank you, Jackal, for bringing me such

247

a fat tiger for my dinner. As soon as I have finished my meal, you can have his juicy bones.'

The tiger became very frightened and turned and ran, dragging the jackal behind him. The jackal shrieked and howled as he was dragged over rocks, through thorn bushes and into rivers. By the time the tiger reached his lair, exhausted and vowing never to go near that farmer's field again, the jackal was quite dead, so the tiger ate him instead."

The headman nodded his approval and clapped his hands, the rest of the villagers joining in enthusiastically. Karna passed a pot of beer to the young man and Arjuna grinned and took a long swallow before passing it back.

"Tell us another one!" yelled Johar the cattle owner. "I like tales about cows."

"No, one about kings this time."

Arjuna got awkwardly to his feet. "Another time," he said pleasantly. "I am tired and I have to be up with the dawn. Ask me another night and I will tell you a story about a demon, a rakshasa I once met."

"You met a rakshasa?" Karna cried out in wonder. "When? Where?"

"Another time." Arjuna hobbled out of the firelight towards his little hut and the herd of goats he tended, leaving the village men in an uproar of interest.

The next day, Parvati took the family's milk cow out to the grazing above the fields where the men of the village were preparing the ground for the rice planting. She enjoyed the task because it gave her a respite from the jobs her mother set her around the house.

"It is not fair," she told Devika. "Boys don't have to work nearly as hard and they get to go to the school and listen to stories."

Devika did not answer, concentrating instead on cropping the sweet young grass at the edge of the field. She lifted her large brown eyes for a moment, chewing languidly, before dropping her head again.

Parvati did not mind the cow's silence. She had given the cow its name Devika, which means beautiful, because she thought her lashed eyes quite the loveliest thing she had seen. Besides, a cow was a good companion. She never talked back or argued and when Devika lay under the shade of the oak trees on the upper side of the field at noon, chewing her cud, she made a lovely back rest.

Down below her the men cleared away the last of the weeds in the terraced field, turning over the dry earth and breaking up the clods. The raised lip of the field was repaired and Karna inspected it carefully. This field, and the half dozen terraces below it, already dug over, would represent the village's communal rice crop. Soon, the stream on the hillside above would be diverted to tumble along bamboo conduits until it gushed into the top terrace. Gradually the field would fill up with water and spill over into the one below it, until all seven terraces were brimming with water, ready for the tiny rice plants already growing near the village in a separate plot.

Parvati lay on her stomach in the grass at the lip of the upper field and watched Karna, some fifty paces away and a man's height below her, finish his inspection. Inevitably, he found some fault and directed the other men to make repairs. One of the men bustling about at

Karna's behest was Parvati's father. She smiled fondly at his portly figure as he trotted along the far lip of the field with a bucket of water, slopping some onto the earth to make mud for the walls. Every man helped with the rice field preparation. A good harvest meant the survival of the village. Later, when the water had stood for a while and the earth turned to mud, the village women would plant the rice and tend it as it grew. When the rice harvest was in, everyone would turn out to plant the first wheat crop.

Everyone spent time with the rice and wheat crops as the harvests were communal, but each family also owned a small plot of land on which they grew other crops. Here fields of red waving amaranth or ramdana brightened the hillsides, and small fields of mandua, the finger millet jostled with locust bean, barley and buckwheat. Smaller plots held lobiya bean, bhat or soybean, rajma kidney beans and a variety of peas, lentils and pulses. Cucumber and pumpkin vines ran riot, and ginger and turmeric and chili added spice to the staples. Most had a small planting of bhang somewhere too. Even in a bad season, this spiky-leafed plant could be guaranteed to grow and chewing a few leaves or throwing some on the fire at night, eased the hunger pains and brought pleasant dreams.

Parvati left the men to finish off the field preparation. She threw the old, frayed rope around Devika's neck and led her unprotesting back toward the village. They moved slowly, Parvati being burdened by the large bundle of oak leaves she had cut while the cow chewed contentedly earlier. The road wound up the hill for a way and she could see the large bamboo water conduits leading up to

250

the spring. The pipes led through the grass and scrub in more or less a straight line and where the bamboo pipes crossed the road, the men had dug a ditch and buried the pipes, filling it in again after. The sun was hot in the late morning and by the time they neared the place where the road bent away from the spring, crossing the hillside and dipping to the village, Parvati could feel a prickle of perspiration under her sari. She looked up at the shady path that led to the spring and thought about how wonderful it would be to sit under the trees in the soft grass for a few minutes. Devika could use a drink too, she reasoned, and at once set off up the path, her cow in tow.

The spring bubbled out of the rocks in a depression at the lower end of a limestone reef that slipped back under the soil and vegetation of the ridge like a fingernail under the skin of a finger. Shaded by tall trees, the water formed a broad grass-choked pool before finding the low point in the declivity and leaping off down the stream bed toward the village. The bamboo pipes fed into the lower end of the pond when in use, but now lay disconnected, almost covered by the long grass.

Several small splashes as Parvati approached the pool told her of the presence of frogs and she trod carefully, knowing that frogs meant snakes, especially the deadly cobra, Naja. After a careful look around, she dropped her bundle of fodder, unwound a part of her sari and, laying it on the grass under an oak tree, sat down. *A few minutes*, she told herself, *just while Devika has a drink*. She watched as the cow ambled toward the water's edge.

Devika snorted suddenly and shied back, plunging away only to turn at the edge of the grassy glade and look back at the pool, her eyes fixed on a certain spot.

"What is it, beautiful one? Did you see a snake?" Parvati rose to her feet and rewound her sari before picking up a long stick in the grass near her. "I'll get rid of it for you, Devika my love." She advanced cautiously, her stick held out in front of her, looking in the long grass near the water's edge for the sinuous coils of a cobra. "Mind you, I'm not sure what I'll do if it doesn't want to leave. Get ready to run, little Devika."

Instead of shiny coils, Parvati saw a length of dull dusty brown in the tangled grass. *A log*, she thought, with some relief. Then she saw that one end of the log was wrapped in a cloth and she frowned, leaning closer and gingerly prodding the cloth with her stick. It dawned on her that this was not a log but a human body, possibly dead, and she felt fear creeping up her backbone like gecko feet. Despite herself, she inched forward, moving slightly to the side to get a better view. Another leg came in sight, lying alongside its partner but partly obscured by the grass. The hips, clad in a soaked and stained dhoti, led to a back half-submerged in the shallow water at the edge of the pool and a head, cradled in bent arms, lying with the face turned away.

Parvati stared, searching for the courage to move to the other side of the body and look in its face. *What if he's still alive and needs help*? Then, *What if he's a demon and leaps up and eats me*? She cleared her throat. "Man?" she whispered. "Man? Are you alive?" Reaching out with her stick, she prodded the body gently. The only

252

response was a gentle rocking and the muted suck and squelch of the water.

Gathering her skirts in one hand, Parvati grasped her stick in the other and stepped over the body and forward slowly, holding her breath as the man's face came into view. To her intense relief it was not a horror, nor demonic, but just a very ordinary man's face, eyes closed, mouth slightly open but above the water, his head resting on one forearm. Relaxing slightly, she called out again, louder.

"Man? Are you alright? Do you need help?"

There was no response and Parvati looked helplessly at her cow that had lost interest and was cropping the lush grass farther round the pool. She looked back at the man and almost prodded him with the stick again. *That would not be polite*, she thought. *If he is alive he will think I am very rude*. Instead, she reached down and touched the man on his shoulder.

His eyes flew open and with a cry the man scrambled to his feet before falling backward into the water. He stared at the sari-clad girl and his hoarse scream of anguish met and merged with Parvati's shriller one of shock and panic. She stumbled back horrified as the man, his eyes so wide and staring that white showed all around his dark brown irises, lurched into a kneeling position. One hand clawed out toward the young girl and he struggled to speak.

"Dh … dhuna …" The man coughed and suddenly vomited over his chest, bright flecks and strings of blood mingling with the watery contents of his stomach. His eyes rolled back in his head and he pitched forward into the water with a great splash that sent ripples over

253

Parvati's bare feet. The man shuddered and lay still, floating face down in the shallow water. Curls and wisps of blood and vomit spread out into the pool, thinning to invisibility as the water curled over the lip of the pool and into the stream below.

Parvati dropped the stick and backed away hurriedly. *What do I do?* She asked herself. *The men. They're in the field still.* Hurrying over to where Devika grazed contentedly, she tied her to a low hanging branch before running off down the path that led to the road. Once there she had another moment's indecision as the village was actually closer than the field. Then she remembered that there were few men at the village and the man who needed to be told most was the headman Karna, and he was in the fields. She ran back down the winding road to the rice paddies.

Her cries alerted the men to her coming and they boiled up out of the fields like a swarm of flies off a moved carcass. Rama led the group, his face red with effort and a look of concern wrinkling his round face.

"What is it, daughter? Why so much noise?" He looked up the empty road. "Where is our cow? What has happened to it?"

"Nothing father. It is … there is a dead man in the spring."

"What?" Karna pushed her father to one side and gripped Parvati's arm. "Talk sense, girl. You have seen a man?"

Parvati nodded, blushing at the attention of all the men who clustered around, all talking at once, all offering an opinion.

254

"Silence!" Karna roared. "Let the girl speak." Into the sudden quiet, he nodded. "Go on, girl. You saw a man? Who was it and why should he alarm you?"

"Has he harmed you?" Rama growled. "I will kill him."

"No, no. There is a man, a stranger, up at the spring but he is dead."

"You are telling the truth? This is not just a story or a dream? Karna's eyes searched her face for a few moments, then he suddenly nodded. "I will go up to the spring. Rama, Ganesh, Daud ... you will come too. Johar, you will come but go on to the village to fetch Vijay."

"If the man is dead, fetching a doctor won't help," Johar observed.

"Nevertheless, you will fetch him. Now, the rest of you go back to the fields." Karna lifted a hand and stilled the protestations. "There is work still to be done and you can be sure we will return as soon as possible."

Up at the spring, Karna directed the removal of the man's body from the water. They laid him out on the soft grass under the oak trees and stood around staring down at him. Parvati half hid behind her father but resisted his attempts to send her away.

"Well, she's right about one thing," Daud said. "He's a stranger."

"And he's dead," Ganesh added. "Do not forget she said that too."

Karna frowned and beckoned to Parvati. "He was face down in the water. How did you know he was a stranger?"

"He ... he wasn't dead when I found him."

"Tell us what happened, daughter," Rama urged. "Did he touch you?"

"No, father." Parvati recounted her story of finding the man and what happened. She found herself embroidering the tale a bit and smiled to herself. *I'm as good a story teller as Arjuna*, she thought.

"Dhuna?" Karna asked. "What did he mean by saying 'dhuna'?"

"Perhaps it is his name?"

"Or the place he was traveling to ..."

"Or his home town."

"There is a village called Dhunagiri about two days walk from here," Daud said. "Perhaps he could not finish what he was saying."

Vijay the doctor arrived then, along with a very curious Johar. The doctor examined the man carefully before turning him over.

"What did he die of?" Karna asked.

Vijay shrugged. "It is almost impossible to tell. I cannot see any wounds or a mark upon his skin unless they are under his dhoti, and I am not taking that off while the girl is here."

"Snake bite?" Johar asked. "You might not see the marks of the fangs."

"Possible. There is a slight swelling under his arms and in his neck but that might just be his body swelling as it decomposes."

"But he only died a few minutes before we got here, and he was lying in the cool water." Karna went on to relate Parvati's story but without the obvious embellishments.

256

The doctor raised his eyebrows. "He vomited? With blood?" He turned the body over again and scanned the face and chest, looking closely at the mouth but not opening it. "I cannot see any blood now."

"The water has washed it away."

Vijay stood and dusted his hands off against his robe. "Well, it is probably not important, though it could be the action of a poison."

"Snake bite," Johar said again. "There are a lot around here. He was just unlucky."

"So what do we do with him?" Rama asked.

"We take him back to the village," Karna replied firmly. "He died on our land; it is up to us to provide him with a proper cremation."

"What about his family?" Daud asked. "If he is from Dhunagiri, his relatives will want to know."

"Then you can go and tell them. You and your brother Nikhil can take his ashes back to his grieving family, should they exist."

The next day, after the ashes had cooled, they were carefully scraped up and put, together with a few fragments of bone, into a closely woven basket. Daud and Nikhil trotted off down the road, burdened not only with the earthly remains of the stranger, but also provisions for the four-day return trip.

Six days later, Nikhil limped into the village, his eyes drawn and haggard, and his neck and armpits swollen. Smears of blood streaked his face and chest and he coughed continuously. "Plague," he muttered hoarsely. "They have a plague in Dhunagiri. Almost the whole town has died."

257

The villagers stepped back as one, leaving a wide circle around the man. Nobody said anything except Gita, the wife of Daud. "Where is my husband, Nikhil? What have you done to him?"

Nikhil stooped until he knelt on the hard, baked surface of the road. "Dead. Dead these two days. We left as soon ..." Gita's wails broke across his explanations and she dropped in the road beside her brother-in-law, though carefully separate from him. Nikhil looked around at the encircling faces, features drifting in and out of focus. "Where ... where is Karna? And Vijay? They must decide ... what to do."

Madhar the potter spoke up after a short silence. "They are dead, Nikhil. Every man that touched the body is dead of plague, and almost everyone in their households. Anyone who drank water from the stream that first day too."

"Then we are lost," groaned Nikhil. He fell forward onto the dusty road, fresh blood staining his lips. After a few moments he stopped moving, but nobody went to help him. Gita was helped to her feet by Nisha, her sister, who helped her back to their house. The other villagers left the body of Nikhil on the road where he fell and drifted back to their own houses. As night fell, the remnants of every household barricaded themselves in their home, refusing admittance to any caller, attempting to cut off contact with anyone that might have had contact with a sick person.

The rice plants dried up and died, for nobody went to water them. The milk cows bellowed their hunger and took what sustenance they could from around their pens. Of all the animals in the village, the chickens still roamed

258

free and foraged for their food as usual. Arjuna's goat herd still prospered for he took them out to pasture every day. He had been almost shunned by the other villagers before the plague, and his solitary habits kept him safe now, isolated from others. He sat on the hillside above the village most days, keeping an eye on his charges and thinking his own thoughts. The nanny goats still demanded to be milked and Arjuna distributed the milk to the remaining houses that still had children – fewer each day; leaving the pots outside the door each night.

Within a month, the disease apparently ran its course and moved on, leaving nearly two-thirds of the village dead. The first bodies were burned, as was proper, but when the firewood ran out, few people were well enough or willing to go and find more. Corpses lay putrifying until Madhar the potter, acting as headman, made the decision to have the bodies carried to the edge of the village and cast into a ravine. From then on, the villagers had not only grief to deal with, but also the howling of jackals and the crunching of bones to fill their nights as predators and scavengers feasted on their deceased relatives.

Parvati's father had been one of the first to fall ill and die. His body was cremated and the ashes now lay in a covered basket in the corner of the milling room. Leela, her mother, followed her husband into death a week later, but her body was cast into the ravine, as was that of her brother Dhaval a few days later. Her younger sister, Rati, fell ill too, but the disease had eaten well by then and she survived. Parvati herself seemed immune. She tended to all the sick in her family, even to cleaning up the bloody vomit and feces, and washing the bodies after death, yet she remained healthy. As the food ran out, particularly when Rati started to recover, Parvati went out to the fields to gather what she could from the neglected and overgrown fields. On one such trip she came across Arjuna, minding his goats.

Her greeting was guarded as she was wary not only of his health, but also she was cognizant of the impropriety of being seen with a young unmarried man. The latter thought made her grin suddenly, her first lightening of spirit in over a month. Who is going to see us? And if they did, what does it matter? She greeted the young man and sat down on a clump of grass near him.

Arjuna nodded and smiled sympathetically. "I am sorry for your loss, Parvati. Your father was a decent man. He sometimes gave me flour."

Parvati bowed her head. "My mother and brother have also died."

"I heard. At least their suffering is over."

"Yes." A pause. "You are well?"

"Yes. You are the first person I have been in contact with since this started. The goats do not seem to catch the plague."

"Just about everybody else has though. Only my little sister has survived in our house and I think there are very few people left in the village." Parvati started to cry. "I just want my mother and father back. I want things to be as they used to be."

"That will not happen," Arjuna said. "All life is change and one must learn to make the best of it. Do you have relatives in other villages?"

260

Parvati wiped her tears on the hem of her stained sari. "No. I had an uncle in Champawat, my mother's brother, but he died a year or two ago."

"What will you do then? Who will look after you and your sister?"

"I suppose I will have to."

They sat silently on the sunny hillside for a time, watching the goats graze around them. Insects hummed and thrummed in the undergrowth and a beautiful peacock butterfly hovered around a small flowering shrub, its glossy black wings vibrating, revealing patches of iridescent blue.

"You could get married," Arjuna suggested quietly. "A good man who will look after you."

"Who would arrange it now that my … my father is dead?"

"You would have to do that."

"I couldn't. It wouldn't be right."

"Things change, Parvati. You have a house to live in but how will you live? You cannot operate your father's mill and you would have to raise enough food all by yourself."

"I have Rati … and Devika."

"Devika? Ah, your cow." Arjuna smiled and got up. He limped across to where a young goat had fallen into a burrow and could not get out. Lifting it out gently, he released it into the care of its anxious mother. "Devika is a good name for that cow, she has beautiful eyes."

Parvati grinned. "Yes, she does. Anyway, we will be able to manage."

"If you find you cannot, let me help."

"You? Why would you help?"

Arjuna did not answer for a long time. Then he sighed and turned to face the young girl. "I like you, Parvati. If I was not lame and you still had a father, I would ask the headman to intercede for your hand. That cannot be, so I must ask you myself. Will you be my wife?"

Parvati gaped, became aware of how it looked and flushed instead. "I ... I am too young. I have not yet ... I am ... I cannot ..."

"You are twelve, Parvati, are you not? That is too young for marriage but not for betrothal. Agree to marry me, have the headman witness it and I will support you and your sister. In two years time we can marry."

"It is not right," Parvati whispered. "This is not how things are done."

"Things change."

Now Parvati sat silently for a time. "You are lame and cannot work the fields," she said at last. "How would you support us?"

"By herding goats. Nearly all of these animals are mine. I mind a few for other men but I am quite wealthy. It was before your time but my father was a warrior also, I am of that caste. He was moderately wealthy though he died when I was a boy. I inherited a house and land and, since I returned from war unable to work my own land, goats."

"How were you lamed? Was it in the war or was it ... was it the demon?"

"Demon?" Arjuna frowned. "What demon?"

"In the village center, under the tree ... so long ago. You said you once met a demon. I wondered ..."

"It is a long story."

"Tell me. I would like to hear another of your stories."

Arjuna smiled. "If it will keep you here a little longer … I can tell you a story." He led the way across the hillside to keep in the middle of the wandering herd. Finding a suitable clump of grass he sat down again and waited for Parvati to settle herself. "It was three years ago when I left to go to war. Bhishma Chand was king in Champawat and the Pali district rebelled. I joined his little army seeking excitement and plunder and I found both, but I also found something I was not looking for.

I got separated from the main army after a skirmish and I went looking for food. I liberated a chicken from its Pali captors and settled down in some bushes by the side of the road to enjoy my meal. As I ate I heard someone come along the road and I looked out carefully, my weapons near at hand in case it was the enemy. Well, it was a Pali soldier, but before I could do anything an old man appeared behind him and called out. The soldier turned and approached the old man whereupon something happened that froze the blood in my veins."

"What?" Parvati breathed. She hugged her knees and stared up wide-eyed at Arjuna.

"The old man, before these very eyes, turned into a snake and bit the soldier so he fell down dead."

"No!" Parvati exclaimed. "The old man was a rakshasa?"

"Indeed. He changed back into the guise of an old man and set off down the road. I decided to follow for this was the first rakshasa I had seen and I was curious."

"Weren't you afraid?"

263

"Of course not," Arjuna grinned. "I was young and inexperienced and sure I could take care of myself. So I followed the demon at a distance."

"What happened?"

"He met two women on their way to wash their clothes. The demon became younger in an instant and charmed the women, who allowed him close. They did not live long to regret it for the rakshasa became a leopard and ripped them to shreds before resuming his old man body again and continuing on his way. A boy herding cows was next. The demon stampeded the cows and trampled the boy in the guise of a great bull. This sort of thing went on all day. I followed the old man and saw him kill every traveler upon the road until, near dusk; I came around a corner and saw the old man standing in the middle of the road, looking at me.

'You have been following me all day,' said the rakshasa. 'Are you tired of life, young man?' I laughed and said, 'Not so, for I have never seen a rakshasa before, for that is surely what you are. I was following merely to observe you.' 'And now you know me,' replied the rakshasa. 'It is almost a pity you must die for it.'

I laughed again, for I was young and foolish still, despite having seen what the demon could do. 'I am a trained soldier of Bhishma Chand. You will not find me easy prey like that poor Pali fool.' The next moment the demon disappeared, leaving only a tiny swirl of dust in the roadway and I felt my spear plucked from my hand. I swung round and my bowstring snapped. A blow from an unseen hand felled me and when I drew my sword, the blade snapped in front of me. I knew I was dead and I cried out in despair.

264

The demon reappeared as the old man and squatted down beside me. 'It is lucky for you that I have eaten well today.' The old man grinned, showing sharp teeth. 'Instead, I will leave you with a reminder not to interfere with what does not concern you.' The rakshasa reached out and touched my leg – just there." Arjuna pointed to his leg. "I felt my thigh bone snap and I passed out with the pain."

Parvati stared at the young man with tears in her eyes. "Oh, how you must have suffered. Yet you survived."

"Some soldiers from my unit happened by and found me a surgeon. The thigh set crooked though and I have been lame ever since."

"What did they say when you told them of the demon?"

"I did not tell them. I told them two Pali warriors left me for dead but that I was lucky to survive."

"And that is how you were lamed?"

"No, Parvati." Arjuna smiled gently. "It is a story, nothing more. You wanted a story, I have given you one."

Parvati looked crestfallen. "It is not the truth?"

"What is truth? I went to the war whole; I returned lame. Two Pali warriors or a rakshasa? It is something a rakshasa would do and sometimes men do survive the attacks of a demon, else how would the stories begin?" Arjuna looked around at the dying day. "It is time you got back to the village, Parvati. It is not wise to be out after dark."

"Why not? I like the night. It is quiet and the stars come out and ..."

"And so do predators. The tiger and the leopard are often more dangerous after there have been many deaths from disease or starvation. They lose their fear of man and sometimes become maneaters."

Parvati looked around nervously. "Then I shall go back quickly, but what about you?"

Arjuna smiled, helping the young girl to her feet. "I will collect my goats and be along shortly. The goats will give me warning if there is a killer about."

Parvati nodded and started back down the hill. After a few paces she turned and looked back. "I will think about what you said, Arjuna, but it is not something I can rush at." She hurried off without waiting for his reply.

In the ensuing months, village life slowly got back to normal. Single men married widows and some of the fields were worked. Not all, but enough rice and wheat was produced to feed the depleted population. When people started collecting firewood again, a few of the braver men started venturing into the ravine to find the poor uncremated remains of friends and relatives. Many bone fragments were recovered but in all but a few cases a positive identification could not be made. The rituals were carried as best they could be and the widowed and orphans grieved anew.

Parvati found life hard. Despite her bravado and determination to succeed, she was only twelve years old and she had a five year old sister to care for. She could not help the men plant, tend or harvest the main crops but she raised vegetables, Devika produced milk, and every now and then a gift of goat meat appeared on the doorstep. She rose at dawn and cleaned the house, milked the cow and got her sister dressed and fed. Long hours

266

followed in the fields as together they grazed Devika. Rati watched the cow while Parvati cut fodder. In the afternoons she did laundry, hunted for firewood and hoed her vegetables. The evenings were spent in darning clothes and cooking. She kept to herself as much as possible, exchanging only a handful of words with the other women. She would nod politely at Arjuna if she saw him, but tried to avoid running into him when she went out to the fields or grazed Devika.

Her red flowering came. Parvati knew what it was – one does not grow up in a small village, washing clothes at the stream with the other women, or hoeing the vegetable patches, without hearing the gossip. When the other women in the village became aware of Parvati's menarche, they whisked her off into seclusion for four days of prayers, ceremonial bathing and preparation for womanhood. She learned more in those few days than in her previous twelve years of eavesdropping on adult conversations. One result of her maturation into a woman was the interest the new headman Madhar the potter took in her. Though he was married already and had no interest in her sexually, he did not think it right that a young woman should be by herself and resolved to find her a husband.

"You must realize, Parvati Sunanda, that you have little in the way of a dowry apart from your father's millstone, a little furniture and a cow. Also you have a sister who will, I fear, be something of a liability. I will do my best to find you a husband but it will not be easy. There are so few available men now."

"But I don't want a husband. I am happy by myself."

Lakshmi, Madhar's wife, sniffed loudly. "Nonsense, child. You will do as we … as my husband the headman says. We will find you a husband, though he may well be elderly or infirm. The poor cannot choose their fate."

It was at about this time that a tiger made his presence known in the area. Huge pug marks were found in the soft mud beside the stream and her roaring – for it was a tigress – could be heard at night as she prowled the road and tracks near the village. Goats disappeared at dawn or dusk and Johar's son Govind, who inherited his father's herd, lost several bullocks over a space of several months. Men talked about the tigress as a visitor from across the River Sarda, driven hence by the men of Dadeldhura when its depredations became too severe.

"We should organize a beat and drive her back," said one man, but nobody pursued that thought. Arjuna opined that the creature had fed on dead bodies from this and other villages and would, unless something were done, turn to eating men. In this he was proved right.

Mala, wife of the previous headman was out cutting fodder from the pollarded oaks along the rim of the uppermost field, close to where the forest thickets press up against the cultivated ground. A group of the women were engaged in this laborious task in the late afternoon when the tigress appeared, stretched up against the tree trunk and clawed the unfortunate woman from a low branch. Her piercing shrieks alerted the other women who watched as Mala was carried off, still alive and crying for help, before they took to their heels, leaving the cut fodder and knives behind.

A dozen men arrived a little later and tentatively followed the blood trail. They found her blood-soaked sari a little way along the trail and a bit later, the remains of the woman close to a jumble of rocks at the lower end of the ravine. Growls erupted from a thicket nearby as they approached the body and the men fled, refusing to go back as the light was failing. The next morning, three men returned without incident and removed the scraps of bone and flesh for cremation. A village meeting was held the same day to decide what must be done.

"We must hunt the monster down and kill it," Madhar said. "Unless we do this no-one will be safe."

"What with?" Arjuna asked. "Do you have weapons?"

"Drive it away," was Prabhat's idea. "If we strung ourselves out in a long line, beating on pots and shouting, we could drive it away. I have seen it done."

Kapil laughed. "That was a pig we drove away, Prabhat. Besides, if we strung ourselves out we could not even surround a small thicket. There are only fourteen men left. Do you want the women to join us?"

"No, but perhaps we could ask men from other villages to help."

"The nearest is Dhupagani, two days away. Do you want to spend the night out there, at this creature's mercy?"

"Kill it," Madhar repeated.

"And again I say what with?" Arjuna limped to the front of the group and stood facing the headman, leaning on his stick. "I have my spear still, but does any man here have something better than knives or axes?" He looked around at the worried faces. "I would not want to face a maneater alone with just a spear or with an ax."

"So what are you saying? We should do nothing?"

269

"No, I'm saying there is very little we can do, but if nobody goes anywhere alone, even for a few minutes, even to void himself; if we guard the women near the forest and in the fields; if we work with our knives, our axes always ready; then we may prevent another victim being taken. If the tigress cannot feed she may go away of her own accord."

"Makes sense," Govind said. Kapil nodded agreement.

"I still say we should kill it," Madhar grumbled, but we will try this and see if it works."

For fifteen days the plan worked. The village took to doing things together, gathering fodder, hoeing the fields, doing the washing, and in those fifteen days, the tigress was not seen once.

"I think it has worked," Govind grinned. "The beast has gone away."

Inevitably, people relaxed and two days later a young girl, separated from the group on the way back from the stream, disappeared. A search revealed her washing neatly put down beside the trail where she evidently stepped around a rock to squat down. All that remained was a small patch of blood and a fingernail wedged in the crevice of the rock.

Panic ensued and the villagers rushed back to their huts and barricaded themselves in. For a further two days, no-one ventured out. When the water was finished and food running low, the villagers split into two groups, one to fetch water, another to gather food. As the food gatherers returned from the fields, the tigress burst into their midst, scattering the terrified villagers and bounding up a steep bank into the forest with Kapil in her jaws.

Locked within their huts, the shaking men and women of Sunadhura listened to the cries of Kapil getting weaker and weaker as the terrifying beast carried him away. This time, nothing would persuade them to leave the village, neither hunger nor thirst. Fodder ran out and the animals started bellowing and bleating in distress.

"Their noise will bring the tiger," Arjuna said.

"So are you going to take them out to graze?"

"If I must." Arjuna took his old spear instead of his stick and gathering his goats, led them out to pasture. Govind, together with a few of the braver men, took the cattle out to the road and grazed them within sight of the village.

Parvati smiled at Arjuna's bravery and resolved to fetch water from the stream if only a few others would join her. Five others agreed and they hurried off, carrying as many pots as they could. Ten minutes later they ran back, crying that the tigress was approaching up the stream path. They hallooed and called the cattlemen back and managed to attract Arjuna's attention on the hillside. The animals were back in their pens and the people behind locked doors again when the tigress entered the village.

The setting sun turned her coat red as she paced the dusty street; her head hung low and swinging gently from side to side. She growled softly, particularly if anyone made a noise behind the doors and shutters.

"It is not natural for a tiger to come into a village," Madhar moaned. "I have never heard of it happening. This creature must be a rakshasa."

The cows caught the scent of the tigress and started bellowing, kicking at the walls of the pen. The goats set

271

up an awful racket too and the tigress roared and broke the wall down. Goats scattered, screaming, and the tigress leapt and battered with her huge forepaws, roaring with anger and excitement. When the last goat had vanished into the scrub, four lay dead in the street.

The tigress stood panting, looking up and down the street before crossing to one of the dead goats. She smelled it and licked the blood away from the goat's snout. Then abruptly she turned and padded out of the village, disappearing into the gathering dusk.

"We must light fires," Madhar quavered. "Large fires at each end of the street to keep her out."

With a lot of cajoling and a few threats, the headman got the firewood together and the fires lit before it got truly dark. Nobody wanted to be alone, particularly in any of the huts near the village periphery, so they gathered in the headman's hut, much to the annoyance of Lakshmi, his wife.

Few people slept that night as the tigress returned with the rising moon and prowled the outskirts of the village, roaring with frustration and anger. As dawn flushed the clouds along the high ranges, the tigress entered the village again, skirting the embers of the fire and racing directly for the cattle pen. The rickety timbers shook and fell apart and the cattle stampeded. Devika was one of the last out of the collapsing pen and the tigress leapt on her back, claws raking, struggling to hold on as the cow bucked and plunged, bellowing with terror.

Parvati screamed and threw the door of the hut open, running out into the open with a small knife in her hand, just as the tigress lost her grip and fell to the ground. The cow galloped off into the darkness, snorting and crying.

Parvati suddenly found herself face to face with the maneater.

She froze. The knife in her hand seemed inconsequential and the door of the hut far too far away. Slowly, she backed up, the motion drawing the tigress closer. Dimly, she heard screams and a calm voice telling her to stop moving and to stand very still. The tigress's eyes flicked sideways and back again and she growled, deep in her throat, the sound rising to a whine. Her tail flicked and she eased down, closer to the ground, her legs gathered beneath her.

Arjuna's calm, low voice came from just behind Parvati. "She will charge, Parvati. When I say, you must drop to the ground and roll to your right. Get ready."

Muscles quivered beneath the red and black-streaked fur and Parvati saw the huge yellow eyes with death in them slide upward from her face to stare at something behind her. For an instant, she thought her eyes were hurt as the tigress became unfocused, then realized she had started her charge. She dropped even as Arjuna yelled and rolled, the white underbelly passing over her as the cat launched itself forward.

Screams and shouts erupted unseen as Parvati curled in a ball, her limbs shaking with fright. Roars of anger and pain vibrated through her and as the sound died away, she rolled over and looked up. The tigress lay dead, transfixed by the spear. The haft had snapped under the weight and fury of the beast and Arjuna lay a few paces to the side, a great gash staining his chest with blood.

Parvati screamed again and ran to Arjuna's side, cradling his head and stroking his arms, her tears spattering his face. He moaned and opened his eyes, looking up at the young woman.

"Parvati?" he whispered. "Are you alright? Are you hurt?"

"No, brave Arjuna. I am unharmed, but what of you? I cannot live if you are killed."

Arjuna smiled weakly. "I would not want to endanger your life anew."

"You are alright?" Parvati insisted. "Really?"

"Yes, though I have been scratched by a tiger. I must clean my wounds."

"Lie still, I will do it for you." Parvati leaned closer, whispering. "After all, we are betrothed are we not?" She turned and called for soap and water, even ordering Lakshmi who, with a surprised look, ran to fetch a cloth. "He is my betrothed," she told a startled audience.

Arjuna watched Parvati wash his chest and another smaller scratch on an arm. He frowned and tensed as if in sudden pain. "He has gone," he muttered.

"The tiger?" Parvati said, surprised. "It is dead and it is a she, not a he."

"Yes. Yes, I know."

Medhar squatted beside Arjuna and smiled uncertainly at them both. "You are truly betrothed? So that is why Parvati here resisted my attempts to find her a man. Well, my goodness me, we must have the wedding soon and … and we shall skin the tigress to make a rug for your marriage bed."

Chapter Fourteen

I have decided I must have a sense of humor, and that is a good thing for it puts me closer to humans than the gods. I find the immortals a mirthless group of entities on the whole. Certainly they enjoy inflicting interesting situations on men and standing back to see what will happen – as often as not, the situation ends badly for the human, but the god smiles inscrutably and goes away to try something else on unsuspecting mankind. I must admit I used to be more like the gods in my outlook, inflicting terrible things on men. In the old days around Mount Kailasa I would take the guise of something or someone harmless until all suspicions were allayed before revealing my true self. Their terror released storms of laughter and pleasure in me as I fed on their horrified and surprised thoughts.

No more. Perhaps because I have lived intimately with humans, some of their sensibilities have rubbed off on me. A man and a woman may become intimate, surrounding and penetrating, but that is as nothing compared to the incarnation of a demon. I pervade the body and mind, touching every part as thoroughly as water wets a bowl of sand. Every grain of sand, every fiber of muscle, every tendon, every infolding of brain and gut and lung become part of me. That is intimacy. Yet I believe now it is a river that flows in two directions for I find myself changed by the association as surely as is the human, though to a lesser degree. My blood thirst is dulled, my compassion aroused, along with curiosity, and that indefinable something that men call humor is engaged.

I fled once from a man called Arjuna, friend of the god Krishna, so when the opportunity arose, I thought it a jest to possess another of that name. They both were warriors, but there the similarity ended. The ancient Arjuna lived for battle and excelled in his skill with the bow. Modern Arjuna was a sometimes warrior, picking up sword and spear only when called upon by his king. His skill was not great but his bravery obvious, for I found him battling two Pali warriors of greater experience and skill.

When he fell, a club blow snapping his thigh, I slipped into him, meaning only to give the Pali warriors a fright before he died. His agonized mind revealed his name and history and my interest became aroused. To the amazement of his enemies, the crippling blow to his thigh proved not to be a hindrance and the fallen man's skill with weapons suddenly showed dramatic improvement. The Pali warriors counted themselves fortunate to escape with their lives and when they fled, Arjuna sank back down in great pain. There is a great blood-filled vessel within the leg and sharp slivers of bone threatened to sever it. I interposed fat and muscle, shielding the pulsing cord, moving the slivers through torn flesh until the bone lay together again. I could not greatly speed the healing process, but I was able to immobilize the fractured bone until fellow warriors happened along and crudely set the limb, tieing it between two pieces of spear haft. His pain I could help too as there is a place in the brain that heightens pain and another that lessens it. I have often stimulated the former but seldom the latter.

I decided to stay with Arjuna a while, for I was interested in his memories of village life. His leg bone mended straight but I kept the muscles bunched so he walked with a severe limp, needing a stick to get around. This I knew would keep him from battle. I knew the minds of warriors well enough, and the petty squabbles of minor kings did not interest me. Both Bhishma Chand and the Pali rebel chief whose name I have forgotten were moderately decent men by all accounts, so I was happy to leave them to their war and take my young prize back to his village.

He was not unhappy to leave the army and I let him take me into the hills, along narrow roads and across foaming gorges to his village of Sunadhura. I helped him when he came across trouble he could not handle, for war had brought out other evils and bands of men preyed upon travelers, robbing them of wealth and life. Dakaits they are called, which simply means 'bandit', and they are a sorry lot. With my help, Arjuna left a few dead and more of them sorry that they interfered with his passage. We left them behind us when we ventured off the main roads through Kumaon, for such venal men seek riches, of which there is little in the poor villages. There is another group of men that roam all the roads of the north but they did not trouble us for Arjuna, a poor wounded peasant lad was beneath their notice. Sthaga, Arjuna called them, 'the deceivers', and for a time I thought no more of them.

So we came to Sunadhura and though Arjuna was of the warrior caste and had a little property, he was despised as a poor cripple and shunned. I was tempted to release my grip on his leg and let him make his mark on the village, but I thought again of his kingly namesake and decided to keep him down-trodden, just to see how he would handle the situation. To my surprise and delight, he coped very well. His education enabled him to perceive the best course and his brush with the warrior's life gave him a proper regard for life and other people. A small measure of wealth bought him a livelihood in keeping with his physical abilities and he became first a herder of goats and then an owner of goats.

As I have said, Arjuna was an educated man and when called on to tell a tale by the village fire I gave him his mind and body back, watching and enjoying his lively story. It was that story that brought the young man to the attention of the girl Parvati, though she went unnoticed by him. I had no interest in her either for she was a young girl, not even a woman, and no great promise of beauty.

The plague was none of my doing, but seeing as so many men, women and children were dying around me, I cannot be blamed for feeding. Sipping would be a better description for none of them had the slightest inkling of my presence. I had no need to create fear to spice my food as the horror of their situation overwhelmed them. I took no lives in Sunadhura – they were dying anyway. I fed so their energies would not be wasted.

Arjuna I kept safe from the plague though I am not certain how I did it. The secrets of the human body are laid out before me but I have no training, no certain knowledge of what each part does. Some things I can do, like stimulate the muscles to move or delve the depths of memory but I cannot make hair grow, though I have tried, purely out of curiosity. I know that every organ, every tissue is made up of tiny living boxes or compartments, like thousands of tiny huts in the city of the body. When plague enters, it is as if an acid dust blew through the huts of the body, staining them and eating away at the walls of

278

the boxes, breaking them down. With practice, I found I could gather the dust, isolate it and minimize the damage. Arjuna caught the plague and survived, but Parvati, to the best of my knowledge, never caught it.

I knew what would happen with so many dead bodies thrown out onto the hillsides after that great sickness. I have seen it often after war when for a time there is food for every meat-eating animal. I thought about directing Arjuna to offer a warning but really, there was no alternative. Hindus do not bury their dead and there was insufficient firewood to burn all the corpses. Exposing corpses is the preferred method of disposal in some parts, so it was no great leap of faith.

Then came the tigress, weaned onto human flesh and hungering for it. One might almost think her a demon in tiger form, so strong was her lust for the sweet meat, yet she was not. I know, having been one and having possessed them before. She was a plain man-eating tigress, though that is terrifying enough if she is hunting you. I could easily have left Arjuna and gone into the tigress, leading her away from the village. Perhaps you will ask why I did not if I profess to help men. Well, I was gaining respect for the men and women of Sunadhura as I watched them face the harshness and unrelenting work that was their short lives. Besides, I found a strong emotion growing in Arjuna when he looked at the girl Parvati. She was a woman now, to tell the truth. My heightened senses, even working through the gauze swaddling of Arjuna's body, detected the difference at once. And this emotion was one that men call love.

Certainly I have come across love before, but never have I seen it grow from nothing into a raging torrent that

279

threatened to sweep reason and knowledge away in an overwhelming desire to be with another human being. Lust I have experienced and though there was a measure of that, it was mixed in with an urge to protect and nurture. I found it fascinating and watched to see what would happen. Parvati felt it too I could tell; I am getting adept at reading the language that men and women speak when they do not engage lips and tongue. I think her youth made her mistrust her feelings, for she turned away from Arjuna's proposal. 'Was it really his proposal?' you ask, 'Or was I in control?' That was all Arjuna. I read the desire in his mind and slipped back so I no longer intruded, no longer controlled him. He asked but was rejected – or so we both thought.

You are wondering, no doubt, what Arjuna thought of my presence within him. Did he resent me, fight me, and challenge me? Yes, he did all these things but long before we reached his village he saw I meant him no harm. Having risked his life in war, he saw my possession as a smaller risk. He saw himself as an axe that a neighbor might borrow for a time, guarding it carefully and returning it in the same condition or better than he found it. After a time, we talked. At first he spoke out loud his questions and I answered, using his own voice. It confused and frightened him to hear his own voice in reply, so we soon moved onto silent conversation. He thought the question and I read it as the little ripples of energy coursed through his brain. I replied by stimulating other parts and he 'heard' me as plainly as if I stood behind him.

I told Arjuna stories of my experiences and he told me tales of his short life, of his barely remembered parents, and of what it meant to be human. I think I got the better of the deal because I learned much, whereas he thought my stories mostly invention, for his mind could not truly encompass the length of my existence. I read too, in his mind, a love for the many gods of India and I studied his beliefs carefully. I remembered a saying from Ibn Battuta over two hundred years before. 'Know he who would destroy you', he said, and so I do.

When the tigress attacked, I did not expect such bravery from a young woman, particularly in defense of a cow but I read instantly the bursting forth of Arjuna's love and protective instincts. Without thinking, I released my hold on him and he grabbed his spear and raced out after Parvati, not even realizing he had the use of both legs. He faced down the beast alone – he had no use of me. It was a close-run race but he survived. I did my trick with the acid dust that entered on the predator's claws and left his body. None noticed my pale flame in the brightening dawn, for all eyes were on the young couple and the dead tigress. I watched until he rose and everyone marveled at this straight and strong young man, a beautiful woman standing proudly beside him. I left the village to its celebrations and drifted off down the road.

Many days later, many miles from Sunadhura, I happened on a band of those men that Arjuna had called 'sthaga' and curious, I followed them. My path led me to a confrontation with a fierce and powerful goddess and men who behaved like demons.

Chapter Fifteen

Prabhu Ram was a prosperous merchant of Ranikhet in the kingdom of Kumaon. One of the more well-to-do men of the town, he was liked and respected by almost everyone, for he was a modest man and did not let his riches go to his head. He honored the gods and gave generously to all the temples in the area, his bounty extending even to the less fortunate ones suffering from afflictions of the body, mind and soul. A few spiteful people remarked on his features, plain and distinctly weighty with small eyes almost lost in the folds of his cheeks, but envious comments like this were shouted down by all who knew him. A prosperous merchant was expected to display the signs of good living, and it was obvious that the gods loved him. Prabhu had moved to Ranikhet ten years before with nothing but a single donkey-load of spices and had parlayed his minor asset into a vast and thriving business. Now he owned a fine house with a wife and three sons, a store and a warehouse and several caravans that were upon the road continually, adding to his riches. If his rise seemed faster than could be warranted by his trade, it was surely an indication that whatever was spent on the gods and their temples was repaid a hundred-fold.

Many rich men, even those who give generously, are less generous with their spirit, looking with sour aspect on the world. Striving to gain riches they lose sight of happiness. Not so with Prabhu Ram. He was blessed with a wife who adored him, a dark beauty, Madhu the sweet, who remained slim as Prabhu fattened, and who tended to his every need. She presented him with three children, the first a son, Rajnish, just before they came to Ranikhet, the others, girls, a few years later. The eldest, Rajnish, earned much praise as a quiet, studious, pious lad who honored and respected his parents and was unfailingly polite to every adult in the town. He was his father's pride and happiness and Prabhu often took him out in the evenings to introduce him to friends and acquaintances, showing him off.

One particular night, which Rajnish was to remember the rest of his life, his father came home, as usual, just on sunset. He sat with his family, enjoying a good meal and talked and laughed, asking his son many questions about his day and what he had learned. When the young girls had kissed their father and gone with their mother to their beds, Prabhu signaled to twelve year old Rajnish to stay behind.

"We are going out tonight."

"Yes, father." Rajnish waited patiently for his father to elaborate, curbing his curiosity as to their destination. If his beloved father had one foible, it was a requirement for unquestioning obedience from his son. Obedience came not from beatings, as with many lads his age, but from unstinting love. Rajnish loved his father and would do anything for him.

Instead of turning toward the lights and smoky fires of the town, Prabhu led his son into the darkness of the road that led north to Dwarahat. Many feared the dark and the things that haunted the lonely places, but Rajnish loved the quiet and the coolness. When his eyes adjusted to the darkness, he found the bushes and trees, boulders and hillocks, stood out almost as plainly as on an overcast day. The stars littered the sky like the petals scattered before the holy images in the temples, lamps lit by the gods as offerings to themselves. He moved confidently along the rutted road beside his father.

Rajnish wondered about their destination but refrained from asking his father. *Let me see if I can work it out*, he thought. *Surely we cannot be going as far as Dwarahat, for though father knows people there it will be well after dawn before we arrive. There is also a small shrine somewhere along here but the keeper will have gone home. Besides we have not brought a sacrifice.* Somewhere far off, in the patchwork darkness of the wooded hillsides, the yipping cry of a jackal arose to greet the night. His father stopped and laid a cautionary hand on his son's arm.

"What is wrong, father?" Rajnish whispered after a few minutes. "It is just a jackal calling for its supper."

"Never just a jackal, my son." Prabhu listened and when the animal yelped again, off to their right, he relaxed and started forward. "It is a favorable omen."

Omen? Rajnish wondered. *Where are we going? There is only the Shmashana, the cremation ground ahead of us, and why would we go there?*

The cremation ground loomed on their right, a flattened area of ground amongst the hilly terrain. In the starlit darkness, Rajnish could barely distinguish the broad splashes of wood ash left behind from the funeral pyres. He knew that every scrap of calcined bone was collected, so there was no need to fear stumbling across any human remains, but he still skirted the paler remains of the fires.

Prabhu led his son across the shmashana to the far side where the black shadows of the hillside and forest loomed over the bare ground. As they approached, the shadows moved, manlike, and swiftly surrounded them. Rajnish drew closer to his father, one hand reaching out to him for reassurance.

"Dakaits?" he breathed.

"Courage, my son," Prabhu replied in a low voice. In a louder one he continued, "I am Prabhu Ram, devotee of the Dark Mother. I bring my son, Rajnish Ram, to offer him in Her service."

"You offer him freely?" rumbled a deep voice from the darkness. "Knowing that he leaves here in the service of the Goddess, or not at all?"

"I do."

"Then let him approach."

Prabhu pushed his son forward. "Advance five paces, Rajnish, and kneel. Do as you are told and answer all questions." With a quick backward glance, Rajnish did as his father instructed, kneeling on the stony ground and staring blindly into the shadows.

"What is your name and age, seeker?" came the voice from the shadows.

"Rajnish Ram, sir. I am twelve years and ... and three months old."

"Who is your father?"

"Prabhu Ram, sir, of Ranikhet."

There was a pause of several seconds. "Who is your Mother?"

"Mad ..." Rajnish hesitated, as the stress on the last word sank in. "The ... the Great Mother, Kali."

"Well answered." Rajnish heard a whisper of cloth in the darkness but could see nothing and did not know if the

285

sound was significant. "Describe the goddess," rapped out the unseen voice.

"She … She has many aspects."

"What then is her color?"

"Dark, dusky."

"What does she wear around her neck?" hissed another voice.

"A … a garland of heads … human heads." Rajnish glanced to his left, seeking the owner of the new voice. Sweat beaded on his forehead though the night was cool.

"How many heads?" A new voice, to his right.

Rajnish hesitated, thinking back furiously to his visits to the temple of Kali. His father had always stressed the worship of the Black Mother and now he wished he had paid more attention. *What did the priest say*? "Fifty-one."

Again the whisper of cloth from the dark night. "Why fifty-one?"

Sweat started trickling down the back of Rajnish's tunic. The threat that emanated from the darkness was almost tangible. "I … I do not know."

The first voice spoke again. "The fifty-one heads of Kali's garland is the Varnamala. It represents the fifty-one letters of Devanagari writing. Each letter is a form of energy and all are part of the goddess. Kali is the mother of language."

His father's familiar voice spoke behind him, though all warmth had gone from it. "How is she clothed?"

Rajnish blessed the artist who had painted the huge portrait of Kali in Her temple. He closed his eyes and imagined himself standing before Her.

"She is naked except for a skirt of human hands … and … and her hair."

286

The whisper of cloth came from behind him now and very close.

"Hold," First Voice commanded. "It is sufficient. She is clothed also in Maya, the veil of illusion, and in darkness. This represents her eternal nature for she will exist even when the universe ends. Nothing defines the Great Mother – she is pure energy and being."

The questions continued, firing out of the darkness from all around him. Rajnish stammered replies and sometimes had to profess his ignorance. The whisper of the cloth came often but always the hard voice from in front of him interposed. At last the questions tailed off and silence fell. Rajnish waited but nothing happened, nothing stirred. He looked around to where he knew his father stood in the open ground but he could not see him. A chill wind blew up the valley, lifting the ashes strewn on the ground into a milky cloud in the dark air. His imagination saw shapes in the cloud and his skin crawled.

"Why are you here?"

Rajnish jumped, startled by the voice after the long silence. He thought swiftly. "To honor the Mother."

"You devote your life to her?"

"I ... I do."

"Then bow down to Kali and worship her."

In the darkness a pot shattered and fire bloomed, driving back the black shadows. The flickering light showed a female form, dusky and naked, holding a gleaming sword and the pallid head of a man. Her face was wild and staring and a glistening red tongue hung down to her chin. On the ground lay a man clothed in a leopard-skin loincloth and the woman – the goddess – had her right foot poised over the man's chest.

Rajnish froze, his mouth open and his eyes wide. A moan of terror started from deep within him but before it could burst out; his father was at his side, gripping his shoulder painfully.

"Bow down and worship the Goddess Kali," Prabhu growled.

Rajnish all but collapsed forward and from his prostrate position looked across at the goddess' foot, only a pace or two from him. As his terror mounted, he saw something strange. The foot of the goddess had a toe with a split nail. The shock stopped his scream in his throat and the realization burst over him that this was not actually Kali, anymore than the picture in the temple was actually Her. The woman was a representation of the Goddess and the man on the ground was just a man, not Shiva.

"O ... O great one, O b ... beautiful dark Mother of us a ... all," Rajnish stammered, his voice settling down as he remembered phrases from the offerings at the temple. "I bow to you, dweller in the cremation ground. O great Mother of sweet and ... and terrifying sound, I come to you in worship."

"It is sufficient," said First Voice again. "Take him back, Friend Prabhu."

Rajnish's father helped him to his feet and guided him back a few paces and sat him down on the ground facing the still forms of the man and woman. "Watch, and say nothing," murmured Prabhu before stepping back into the shadows.

The fire from the shattered pot had died down and a man came forward and scattered earth on the remnants, plunging the field back into darkness. Then a light appeared again, small and low and it bobbed along close to the ground. In its wake, candles leapt into life, the flames soaring in the still air. The chill wind had been replaced by a great stillness. Into the ring of light stepped four men.

Rajnish recognized the one in front as Abdul Azeem, one of the Muslims that worked for his father. The one at the rear too, was familiar, being Kalidas Shah, a weaver who lived in the poor part of the town. Abdul led a young man by the hand, steadying him when he stumbled, for the young man wore a blindfold. Behind him, Rajnish recognized his father, and he felt fear again.

Abdul Azeem took the young man by both hands while Prabhu removed the blindfold. The young man blinked and looked around at the ring of candles and the enfolding darkness. Kalidas Shah spoke and Rajnish knew him instantly as First Voice.

"You are here to worship Kali. Kneel, that you may offer your life to Her."

The young man knelt, and as he did so, Abdul pulled him forward by both arms, while Prabhu dropped heavily on the man's calves, pinning his legs. Kalidas Shah undid the yellow cotton sash around his waist and Rajnish shivered as he heard again the whisper of the cloth. Leaping forward, Kalidas slipped it around the young man's neck and pulled back hard. The victim struggled, but with his arms held and his legs pinned, his strangulation took but a minute.

When the executioner was satisfied, he drew the yellow sash from the man's neck and refastened it about his waist.

289

"Great Kali, Mother of the Universe, we offer You a life, taken in the prescribed manner. May it prove to be pleasing in Your eyes." Kalidas Shah nodded to Abdul and Prabhu. "Strip him and lay him face down." He turned and walked into the shadows.

The two men stripped the young man expertly and arranged his limbs, then bowed and moved out of the ring of light. For a few minutes the only object in Rajnish's sight was the prone body of the man. Then Kalidas appeared again, naked now, and from the other side of the circle, the woman who had represented Kali stepped in, naked too. The two figures circled the body, stepping lightly, bending to touch the corpse before straightening again. Kalidas picked up a small pot of paint and with a small brush started daubing the back of the dead man. Rajnish leaned forward; trying to see what was drawn there, but could not. Burning with excitement and curiosity now that the danger had passed, he shifted as if to get up and a hand descended firmly on a shoulder, forcing him back down.

"Stay," hissed Prabhu. "Stay still, on your life. He draws the Kali Yantra, the symbolic representation of the Mother's divinity." Prabhu squatted beside his son and whispered quietly. "It is midnight on the cremation ground. Kali and her consort Shiva come together in holy union. Look well, my son, for this is a sacred secret."

The two figures now swayed gently as if to silent music, facing each other over the corpse. They offered each other wine, and honeycakes and something that glinted gold in the candlelight. The tempo of their dancing increased; their arms waved up and down at their sides and legs lifted and stamped. The woman's heavy breasts bounced and swung, her wide hips thrusting the dark triangle at the base of her belly forward. The man, too, leapt and cavorted, and his penis swayed and stiffened. From the darkness, a soft and rapid beat on a small drum started and the dancing of the pair became yet faster.

Rajnish watched mesmerized. The limbs of the sweating dancers blurred and for a moment it looked as if the woman really did have four arms, so fast did she move them. Abruptly the drum ceased and Shiva lay down on his back on the body of the young man, his member erect and prominent. Kali straddled her consort and sank down onto him with a sigh of exstacy. She lifted up, adjusting her position, before dropping back down. The drum started again, slowly increasing in speed and the woman rose and fell in time to the beat. As her excitement mounted she leaned back, her naked breasts bouncing, and uttered a guttural cry of pleasure. Beneath her, the Shiva-man strained upward and collapsed, the drum falling silent at the same instant.

For several minutes they remained together, still except for the heaving breasts of the woman. She stirred, raising herself up and pulling free. The man reached up and plucked a hair from her thatch and offered it to her. On it, a drop of semen glinted in the candle light.

Prabhu sighed and put his hand on his son's shoulder again. "You have seen a union of the gods, my son. Do not regard this in the same way you would the sexual union between a man and a woman. This ceremony is holy, most sacred, and brings blessings on all who attend." He got to his feet and helped his son up, putting an arm around his shoulder and turning him away from

291

the circle of candles. "Come now, you are a devotee of the Dark Mother. Your instruction will continue but for now let us go home. No, do not look back."

Father and son left the cremation ground and started the long walk home. Rajnish was silent for most of the way, wrapped in his own thoughts. At last, he sighed and plucked at his father's sleeve.

"Father, have you killed many men?"

Prabhu raised his eyebrows, an unseen gesture in the darkness, but his voice betrayed his shock and horror. "I have never killed a man. My son, when I use the yellow cotton sash of Kali, I am offering a sacrifice to the Goddess. It is not a common killing. I thought you realized that."

"I am sorry, father, if I have put it badly and offended you. I meant to ask only if Kalidas always offers the sacrifice or do you too?"

"I will forgive you this time. Three men offer a sacrifice, as you saw tonight, but only the most senior one uses the sash. The second holds the victim's hands and the lowest pins the legs."

"Are ... are you then the lowest, father?"

Prabhu chuckled. "We are a small band, comprising three sacrificial groups. Kalidas, Abdul and I lead our groups, but of these three leaders, I am the lowest ranked."

"But Abdul works for you, and Kalidas is only a poor weaver, whereas you ... you are rich, father."

"Riches do not give rank in Kali's eyes."

Rajnish was silent for a little longer. "Who was the woman? I have not seen her face before."

292

"Nor her other parts," Prabhu laughed before he recollected he was talking to his twelve year old son. "She is the priestess of Kali from Rajapur. Kalidas requested her presence for the sadhana."

"And the man who was kill ... sacrificed?"

Prabhu paused and looked down the road toward the lights of his house where he knew his wife Madhu waited up anxiously for their return. "He was the eldest son of Kalidas."

"He killed his own son?"

"Sacrificed, Rajnish, there is a difference." Prabhu stopped and listened for a few moments to the sigh of the wind in the Chir pine forests that covered the slopes near his house. "Two weeks ago, Kalidas brought his son to the cremation ground for the ritual questioning. Unlike you, he failed, and rightfully should have been strangled on the spot. Instead the merciful Goddess granted Kalidas the honor of offering his son up as the sacrifice at the Great Sadhana."

"If ... if I had failed ..."

"I would, with regret and love, have offered you up myself."

Rajnish drew away from his father with a sob. Prabhu did not move but said in a low voice. "That was the only time I could ever have laid the yellow sash on my own flesh. You have been accepted by Kali, and you have nothing to fear from your brothers in the Fellowship while you remain true to Her. I love you, Rajnish. I always have and I always will, now let us get inside. Your mother will be worried about you."

"She knew?" Rajnish whispered. "She knew I could die and she said nothing?"

"She knew and she said nothing though her heart would break if you failed … as would mine." Prabhu gathered his son into his arms. After a brief resistance, Rajnish broke down and hugged his father, sobbing. "Come then, my beautiful son Rajnish. Come and reassure your mother, but say nothing of what you have seen, either to her or to your sisters." He led the way into the house.

Life continued much as before for Prabhu and Rajnish. The father held his place as one of the foremost traders in the town, certainly the richest and most influential. Rajnish continued his schooling and his visits to the temples in the area to learn more of the gods. If he now spent more time in the company of the priest of Kali, none remarked on it. A person, particularly a pious and devout lad like Rajnish, often found a god or goddess of especial interest and favored the chosen deity with greater attention. Kali, while of fiercer countenance than many people liked, was one of the stronger gods and a useful ally. Besides, she had her gentler side as Mother, and perhaps it was this aspect that attracted the boy.

Several months later, just before Rajnish turned thirteen, Prabhu Ram organized another trading journey down into the hot plains to the south and announced he would be taking his son with him to introduce him to the business. Kalidas Shah, the weaver, decided he would visit relatives in Rampur and asked if he could accompany the caravan for safety reasons. There were many reports of dakaits along the roads, so Prabhu graciously agreed.

The caravan, when it left Ranikhet on the road south to Naini Tal, comprised ten men – or rather, nine men and

294

a boy. Rajnish knew all the men by sight and some by name, as they worked for his father. They all, even the ones he did not know, greeted him and laughed and joked as they beat the mules into motion. When they camped for the first night near a small stream on a deserted stretch of road, Kalidas took over the leadership of the group and ordered out men along the road to keep watch. He called Rajnish over to him while Prabhu and Abdul watched in silence.

"What are we here for, lad?" Kalidas asked. "What is the purpose of this journey?"

Rajnish cocked his head on one side and looked thoughtful. "I thought it was just a trading journey, sir, until I knew you were coming. Is it to do with the Mother?"

"Go and look in the panniers of trade goods." Kalidas pointed to where they stood stacked to one side of the hobbled mules. "Tell me what goods we are trading."

Rajnish did as he was told, unfastening the catches and opening the panniers. The first two were empty, but the third contained several yellow sashes and a pickaxe, covered with writing and wrapped in blood-red cotton. He did not touch anything; just refastening the baskets and returning to his leader.

"There are no trade goods, sir, but there are yellow sashes."

Kalidas nodded. "They are called ruhmal. Do you know their significance?"

"They are used in sacrifice, sir. Does that mean … is one of … is one of them for me?"

Kalidas' mouth quirked into a fleeting smile. "Not this time, lad and not for five years at least. You must earn the honor before you are given the sacred cord of Kali. No, this time you will watch and learn."

"What … what is it I am to learn, sir?"

"We are sthaga, lad, deceivers. We find travelers and sacrifice them to the Dark Mother. You will see how it is done and observe the rituals that must follow. Stay close to your father, stay silent and do not disgrace us."

The next morning, Kalidas led the group south again, with Rajnish keyed up with excitement. As the day passed and every traveler they met was allowed to go on his way unhindered, he became quite agitated and at last broke his silence, whispering to his father.

"Why are you letting them all go, father? There have been six groups we have passed today, but you have not sacrificed any of them."

Kalidas overheard the lad and stopped the group with a gesture. "Prabhu, stay behind with Baha Udeen and Muhammad Hassan. Explain to your son one last time that I will not be questioned concerning the sacred business. If he cannot learn this lesson, then you have your two Friends with you. You know what is expected." With another curt gesture, he waved the group on, leaving Rajnish and the three men standing in the dusty road.

Prabhu grabbed his son firmly by the arm and hustled him over to the side of the road, leaving Baha and Muhammad staring unsmilingly after them.

"My son," Prabhu muttered. "Have you forgotten already that you must follow without question? You must exercise patience and tact and not anger Kalidas Shah, who is the representative of Kali."

"But I only wanted to know …"

296

"And by voicing that concern you called his judgment into question. Do not think these things are done lightly or on a whim. The Dark Mother is guiding us and she will send a sign when her chosen sacrifice appears."

"A sign? What sort of sign?"

Prabhu sighed. "This curiosity is going to get you killed, my son." He loosed his shirt and pulled one edge up slightly, revealing the yellow cotton ruhmal tied around his ample waist. "I do not want to use it on you, Rajnish, but if you cannot control yourself, I must."

"You are my father," Rajnish breathed, paling.

"And if I held back my hand I would join you on Kali's altar. Do you understand what I am saying to you?"

"Y ... yes, father," Rajnish said. "But why did we spare those travelers?"

"If I tell you, will you promise to stay silent?" Rajnish nodded and Prabhu grunted. "Alright, I will tell you. We passed six groups, the first of who included a woman. We do not sacrifice women and we can leave none alive to bear witness. The second group was too large. We only have three slayers. The third I will come back to, the fifth also. The fourth had a blacksmith among them, also a prohibited profession; and the last, the lone man, was maimed. He had a finger missing, and it would be a blasphemy to offer up a maimed sacrifice."

Rajnish listened with great interest. "What of the third and fifth?"

"The third group was perfect, two young men traveling alone. Merchants by the look of them, with gold in their purses. Yet Kali forbade it."

"How?" Rajnish looked puzzled.

"A jackal called on the left. It was a clear sign."

Muhammad shouted from the middle of the road. "What is happening, Friend Prabhu? Do you require us or not?"

"A moment, Friend Muhammad. We will be with you very shortly."

Rajnish glanced at the two sthaga standing in the hot sun, and frowned, feeling the coldness of their gaze. He turned back to his father. "And the fifth?"

"Again a likely group, but this time the wind dropped just as we were about to join them."

"This was enough?"

"Learn the omens, my son. Learn the signs that Kali sends to guide us, by observing and ask no questions. Your life depends on it."

"Yes, father. I see now what it is that I have entered. I shall be silent and respectful, and make you proud of me."

"Good boy."

Prabhu and Rajnish rejoined Baha and Muhammad and together they trotted after the mules, rejoining them by the banks of a small stream across from where the road divided in two. They found Kalidas sitting on the grass by the stream, facing the fork in the road with a brass pitcher full of clear water beside him on the right and the consecrated pickaxe of the goddess on his left. The other sthaga sat in silence a few paces behind him and waited. Prabhu motioned to his son to keep quiet and led him to a small patch of shade at the rear of the group. They waited, Prabhu anxiously keeping an eye on his son.

Three hours later they still waited, though the sun was sinking rapidly. From above them came the shrill piercing whistle of a solitary kite. As one man, the group looked up, searching the sky for the tiny dark outline of the bird. One man pointed and everyone watched as the bird of prey circled far above them. It called again and side-slipped, spilling air from its wings, arrowing down toward the setting sun. Kalidas got to his feet with the pickaxe and brass pitcher in his hands. He kissed the shining blade, then poured the water out over the gleaming iron and onto the ground, lifting up his voice in a complex chant.

"We take the right road. The goddess has spoken."

They set up camp for the night in the meadow beside the stream. Kalidas led the men in a series of rituals to cover every aspect of their brief stay – the setting up of the lean-tos, the preparation of the food and the eating of it and the breaking of the ground to bury their waste. Rajnish watched carefully, saying nothing, even when he did not understand what was happening or being said. The sthaga talked in a foreign tongue, one that Rajnish had never heard before, though he spoke several dialects and understood more. He lay down to sleep on the hard ground, wrapped in a blanket and in the midst of his companions, and prayed silently.

O Dark Mother, glorious and merciful one, make me one of your chosen sthaga. Let me honor you and obey you all my life that I too might wield the yellow cotton ruhmal in your holy service.

The next morning, after breaking their fast in the pre-dawn coldness, they forded the stream and set off down the right-hand fork in the road. The way still ran south toward Naini Tal and presently they came across three merchants camped by the side of the road. The merchants jumped up with their hands on their swords when the larger group appeared.

Kalidas hailed the men and enquired as to their destination. "We are going to Naini Tal too," he exclaimed with a smile. "My friend here is Prabhu Ram, a prominent trader of Ranikhet. Perhaps you have heard of him?"

One of the merchants, an old man with a full head of white hair, squinted at the portly figure of Prabhu for a minute before nodding his head. "I recognize him." He turned to his companions. "Put up your weapons, this man really is a merchant." Sheathing his own sword, the old man faced Kalidas unsmiling. "I will not apologize for my actions, sir, disrespectful though they may seem. There have been reports of dakaits on the road."

Kalidas smiled and bowed. "You do well to be cautious. We ourselves have seen no bandits, possibly because we are too many." He paused before adding matter-of-factly, "You are welcome to join us as far as Naini Tal. There is safety in numbers."

The old man studied Kalidas before scrutinizing the rest of his group. He nodded. "Thank you, we would be grateful for your company. My name is Mohandas Saam, this," he indicated a young man, "Is my eldest son Randeep, and the other my younger son Pandit." The two young men bowed respectfully.

Kalidas introduced himself and the others in his company, then, after Mohandas and his sons had packed up their camp, set off alongside the old man toward Naini Tal.

300

"Why is it," Mohandas asked, "That despite Prabhu Ram being the owner of this caravan, you are the one leading it? I have seen the way the other men defer to you."

"You have a keen eye, sir. I am a weaver by trade and have often had occasion to travel these roads, selling my cloth at the village fairs. My friend Prabhu desired to sell his goods in Rudrapur and Rampur but had never traveled there. I agreed, as a friend, to lead his little venture and lend him what little experience I have of the roads."

"You are a good friend indeed," Mohandas agreed, smiling. "May I enquire as to the nature of the goods you are trading?"

"Spices. Cumin and turmeric, saffron and cinnamon. Others in small quantity. Prabhu could no doubt tell you down to the last mustard grain what we carry."

Mohandas frowned. "And he wants to take them into the plains? Good Kalidas, does he not know that prices for these spices are very low there?"

Kalidas looked troubled. "No, Mohandas, I do not think he is aware of that, any more than I."

Mohandas cast a calculating gaze at the panniers on the mules. "Well, I might be able to help. After the Naini Tal fair, I and my sons are going to Champawat where there is a fair demand for spices. Prabhu Ram could either make that long and tiring journey himself, or," Mohandas coughed discreetly. "Or I could buy them myself. I would offer a good price for good quality, and you would certainly get more than you would in Rudrapur."

"An interesting thought, but what goods would you trade? Unless there is a demand for them back in Ranikhet, it would not help us."

"I would pay in fine gold."

"That is very generous of you, sir. I am sure Prabhu Ram would, with a little persuasion, be amenable to such a transaction. He is quite stingy with money. You know he is not paying me ..." Kalidas let his voice trail off suggestively.

Mohandas smiled. "You would not find me stingy in my favors. I thought perhaps two per cent, for your trouble."

"I think ten would be suitable."

The old man chuckled. "I like you, Kalidas, but not that much. Five is my final offer." Kalidas nodded with a wry grimace. "Very well, then," went on Mohandas. "I will need to examine the goods before I buy. Shall we do this now?"

"Wait until we camp for the night. Then you can examine the contents of the panniers at your leisure instead of having to rummage through them on the road."

The road to Naini Tal was poor, having suffered greatly in the past rains. The king's minister in charge of road repair throughout the kingdom had not yet sent gold to the governors of the regions, with the result that the men and mules had to negotiate several dangerous places where the cliff faces had all but carried the road into the gorges below. As a consequence, the journey lasted longer than anticipated, and they crested the last ridge before the valley of Naini, with its beautiful lake, just as the sun dipped below the mountain peaks.

"Let us camp here for the night," Kalindas cried, pointing out a pleasant meadow just off the road. "Mohandas, will you honor us with your presence tonight?"

"Gladly, my friend. The honor is ours."

While they ate, Kalindas and Prabhu kept the merchants occupied while scouts were sent out in both directions to check there were no other travelers on the road. After the meal, they sat back and drank a little wine, enjoying the peaceful evening. Mohandas looked around at the men in the little group of sthaga with a curious expression.

"You know, I have seldom seen a mixed group of Hindus and Muslims live together in such harmony. How is this achieved?"

"Why, we have a common purpose, Mohandas. When men believe in the same things, any differences are set aside. I do believe that our little band here would die to preserve our integrity."

"That is most commendable. Who would have thought that gold could bring men together?" Mohandas laughed, his sons smiling agreeably. "Now, Kalindas, Prabhu, am I to be allowed to see the contents of those panniers?"

Prabhu looked over at the scouts who had returned a few minutes before. "Hussein? Nasser? Is the Way clear?" he asked.

"It is," Nasser stated solemnly, Hussein repeating the affirmation.

"Then," cried Prabhu. "Lochan, Harshal, Baha, fetch the panniers." The men hurried to obey, setting the panniers on the ground a few paces apart. Moving

303

casually, Prabhu and Muhammad joined Baha by one of the baskets, the other men gathering in their designated groups by the others. As Mohandas' two sons were standing beside their father, Prabhu pulled at Randeep's arm and Abdul Azeem enticed the younger son Pandit to the other pannier.

Mohandas looked around the camp site with the flickering flames of the fire casting shadows out by the baskets. He saw too, that Prabhu's son, Rajnish stood well back, under the trees on the other side of the fire, rather than crowding around as any normal boy would. A faint glimmer of suspicion teased his mind.

"Why do we look at the goods out here in the dark? Let us take them closer to the fire."

A squeal of fear and pain rent the night air, echoing from the fields on the left of the road.

"The goddess speaks," cried Kalindas.

"What goddess?" Mohandas asked, his suspicions mounting. He fingered the hilt of his sword. "That was the cry of a hare. No doubt snared by a fox. Why do you say ..."

"It is time." On Kalindas' words, the men sprang into action. Lochan Thapa leapt forward and grasped Mohandas' arms tightly. At the same time, Nasser Udeen gripped the old merchant's legs firmly from behind and Kalindas' ruhmal appeared in his hands, flicking around the man's neck and pulling tight, cutting off his cry of alarm.

A few paces away, Randeep and Pandit found their life being choked from them. They struggled violently, but their arms and legs were pinioned by experts and the yellow cotton sashes did their work. Within minutes, all

304

three men lay dead. They were carried into the shadows and covered with blankets while the three stranglers went through the victims' belongings. All valuables were put to one side to be divided up later.

Rajnish watched from behind a large oak tree, his eyes wide and his mind in turmoil. His hands flexed, imagining he held the ruhmal, while his throat tightened as he imagined the feel of the sash around his own neck. He wondered whether the wife of Mohandas would weep over his death and that of her two sons.

"Let us perform Tuponee."

A large cloth was spread on the grass and Kalindas placed in the middle of it three items. First he set out a quantity of sticky brown goor, the sugar that had been consecrated earlier, before the journey, in anticipation of the sacrifices. Alongside it, he set down the sacred pickaxe, washed in pure spring water, and a piece of silver. Then he sat cross-legged on the cloth, near the middle in the position of favor, facing west. Prabhu and Abdul Azeem took their designated places, followed by the rest of the sthaga, in order of their rank, also facing the still faint glow in the sky where the sun had set. Prabhu gestured for Rajnish to join them and he sat on the grass, close by the others.

Kalidas led his men in a short prayer of thanks to their patron goddess, at the conclusion of which, the two lowest ranked members reverently took up the sacred pickaxe and dug a small pit. When they finished, they carefully washed it in pure water once more and dried it off on clean cotton cloth before placing it back on the cloth. Kalidas now rose to his feet and, taking a small handful of the goor, trickled it into the freshly dug hole, all the while chanting prayers to Kali. He thanked her for her guidance and for delivering up the sacrifice to them, and asked that much booty would come their way. The other men repeated the prayer and even Rajnish followed along as best he could.

Prabhu picked up the pickaxe and handed it to his leader, who sprinkled water on it. Abdul took up the bowl of goor and likewise passed it to Kalidas.

"Let each man partake of the holy goor." Kalidas passed among the group and pressed a small amount of the sticky sugar to every man's head, even including Rajnish. "When the time comes to taste it, lad, you will be filled with a hunger for this life." He resumed his seat and for a short time they sat in silence, hearing the crackle of the fire in the still air, the chirp of insects in the long grass, the sharp smell of woodsmoke and the subtle odors of the sacred sugar so close at hand. Their heads were filled with thoughts of the Dark Mother and her generous gifts.

"It is time," Kalidas said quietly, as if giving the signal for a sacrifice. Each man reached up and removed the sticky lump of goor from his own head and started eating it, savoring the rich, sweet taste. Rajnish too, ate the sticky sweetness and as he did so he felt within him an overwhelming urge to follow the Way of the Dark Mother, so strong it took all his control not to cry aloud with joy and determination. The other men ate in silence but the effect of the goor was the same. Grins broke out and sidelong glances and as soon as the ceremony was over, they broke into laughter, rising and hugging each other in warm fellowship. As Rajnish rose with the rest, a log fell in the fire sending up a blaze of sparks into the still night and illuminating the body of Pandit. The bulging eyes of the young man stared accusingly at Rajnish. At once, the last of the sweet goor in his mouth turned sickly and it was all he could do to not spit it out. The fervor of minutes before gushed out of him like water from a shattered jar and he felt a slow horror creep in to take its place.

The three of lowest rank, those who clasped the legs, then took it in turns to dig graves for their victims with the sacred pickaxe. The next three, those who held the hands, took sharp knives and set about cutting into tendons and flesh, cracking the joints of hip and shoulder, knee and elbow, ankle and wrist, turning the limbs back on themselves so that the corpses took up a smaller volume. The stomach cavity was ripped open so that gases of decomposition would not accumulate, perhaps raising the soil over the buried bodies. Prabhu led his son from one body to the next, explaining the procedures and the reasons behind them. Rajnish watched wide-eyed, pale and sweaty, but he hid his fear and revulsion in the darkness. The ecstacy of the goor ceremony was fading fast and he thought about his future with the sthaga with trepidation.

"Father? Wh … why are the bodies buried so well, even to disemboweling so the gases do not swell the bodies? Surely if this is a sacrifice to Kali, we should be open about it?"

"Hush." Prabhu looked around quickly and lowered his voice. "There are many who hate us and envy the love the Mother has for us. That is why we must be secret. If we proclaimed our acts they would band together and exterminate us."

"And ... and the gold? Is that offered to Kali too?"

"No, son. That is ours for Kali knows we must live to do her work. We keep whatever we find." Prabhu clapped Rajnish on the back. "That is why we seek out rich merchants. Our work is better rewarded."

When the bodies had been covered with tamped down soil and the sods of grass replaced in such a way that it was hard to tell there had been any disturbance, the sthaga retired for the night. Kalidas conferred with Prabhu and Abdul for a few minutes before coming over to Rajnish. He took the boys head in his hands and turned his heads up to face him, staring into his eyes for long minutes. Rajnish fought to control his fear, willing his trembling to stop. Kalidas grunted at last and nodded his head.

"You show a proper fear and respect for me at last. How was the goor, lad?" he asked with a grin. "Made you eager to taste it again, I'll wager. Well, you will soon enough. We hunt again tomorrow."

Kalidas turned away and went to his place by the fire. Prabhu took his son and guided him to a lesser position, further from the fire, and gave him a blanket to keep him warm during the chill of the night.

In the morning they continued on their way, passing through the green and pleasant valley of Naini, walking along the shores of the Tal or lake, to the tiny village that took its name from both. There was a fair in progress and Kalidas gave each man a small share of the spoils that they might enjoy the pleasures of the town for the morning. Kalidas did not relax, but prowled the stalls, talking to merchants and farmers, searching out the foreigners that had journeyed there from distant villages.

When they left Naini Tal just after the noon hour for the village of Bhimtal, it was in the company of two other merchants who had accepted the company of Kalidas' group to help protect their profits, which were considerable.

The road to Bhimtal was in good repair and the pace of the caravan was faster than Kalidas wished, though he tried to slow its progress, wanting another night on the road. When one of the merchants noted happily that Bhimtal was less than an hour ahead of them, Kalidas decided they could wait no longer. There had been no omen of success but the merchants' packs were full of silver and Kalidas was determined this windfall would not escape. He nodded to Abdul and Prabhu, making the secret signal to ready them.

"There has been no omen," Abdul hissed. He looked around, searching the hillsides and sky for a sign from the goddess. At that moment one of the merchants sneezed loudly and Abdul rounded on him with a cry of alarm. "An unlucky sign! We must desist."

The merchant frowned, wiping his nose on a piece of cloth. "Unlucky? What, are you superstitious?" He turned away and sneezed again.

"It is time!" Kalidas roared, snatching his yellow ruhmal from his waist and launching himself at the sneezing man. Taken by surprise, for the sneezes surely were an omen of misfortune, the other sthaga hesitated.

The sneezer snatched out a dagger and backed away, yelling out the danger. The other merchant knocked over Muhammad and took to his heels in the direction of Bhimtal. Nasser and Baha ran after him, while the others converged on the unfortunate sneezer. With a little trouble, for he managed to stab Harshal in the arm, they bound him with their arms and Kalidas placed the noose about his neck, pulling it tight.

As they lowered the body into the dust, shouts from the direction of the village disturbed them and they looked up to see a squad of the king's soldiers running down the road toward them. A mere pace ahead of them was Baha, his turban cast aside as he raced for his life. Even as they watched, bent over the body of the sneezing merchant, Baha fell and the soldiers killed him with a slash of sharp swords, not slackening their pace.

The gang scattered, though Kalidas and Lochan tried to wrest some gold from the mule panniers before giving up and dashing into the undergrowth beside the road. Prabhu clutched his son to him and as the soldiers ran up, threw down his sword and called out in surrender. The soldiers bound them both and hustled them to the side of the road as the others of the king's men hurried after the bandits.

An officer strode up, his mustaches full and gleaming beneath a scarlet turban, his uniform dusty but still grand and the gold rope of his rank catching the afternoon light. He bent over the body of the merchant and loosened the yellow ruhmal from about his neck.

"Sthaga!" he exclaimed in disgust. "Killers of Kali. I thought we had mere bandits but these …" He glared across at Prabhu and Rajnish, bound at the roadside. "Kill them," he snarled. "I would not take this scum back for trial."

A blade whispered free of its sheath and Prabhu called out, urgency in his voice. "My lord, spare my son,

310

I beg you. He is innocent of all things as I brought him with me for the first time only yesterday."

"Then he shall learn – briefly – the lesson of bad company." He nodded to the soldier. "Carry on."

"My lord," Prabhu screamed again, stumbling toward the officer. "Spare my son, I beg, and … and I will tell you everything. I know where bodies are buried."

"Hold," the officer called, halting the soldiers swing. "You know where your victims are buried?"

"Yes, my lord." Prabhu hurried on, nodding vigorously. "I know where there are bodies and … and gold."

The officer signed for the soldier to guard them well and strode toward a commotion by the side of the road. A soldier reeled out of the undergrowth and a moment later a knot of others, struggling round Kalidas like ants around a grasshopper, fell to the ground in the long grass. A blow from the flat of a blade stunned the man and he was hauled out onto the road and dumped at the officer's feet. Two other sthaga followed, both bleeding and bound.

"You know these men?" the officer asked Prabhu. When the man hesitated he added, "On your son's life."

"Yes, they are Lochan Thapa and Hussein bin Idris and … and he is Kalidas Shah."

"Sthaga? Thuggee?" The officer spat in the dust. "What rank are they?"

Prabhu shrugged. "Those two are lowly, but Kalidas is our … their leader."

Kalidas groaned and struggled onto one elbow, looking up at Prabhu with hate-filled eyes. "Traitor," he hissed. "I call on the Dark Mother to silence you. You will know no peace but her fury …"

311

"Silence him."

"... will follow you like a leopard in the night until ..." A sword hilt cracked against Kalidas' skull and he collapsed to the ground.

"Good," the officer said. "You will lead us to where the victims are buried." The soldiers returned shortly, dragging three bodies with them. Prabhu confirmed that only one was missing, Nasser Udeen, who had run after the escaping merchant with Baha Udeen, his brother, who now lay dead on the road a little distance from where they stood.

"He is dead too," laughed the officer. "Now, dump that offal by the side of the road for the kites and the jackals. We have some hunting to do." He strode off toward Naini Tal, his men falling into a triple line behind him, pushing the five stumbling bound captives along in their midst, and bringing the string of mules along behind.

They passed the night in Naini Tal village, the prisoners occupying a solid stone room half sunk into the ground, guarded continually and with the added protection of a crowd of fascinated onlookers, all eager to see the fiends who preyed on them all. The night was torture for Prabhu and Rajnish but at least Kalidas and the other two sthaga were bound and gagged. All they had to endure was their almost tangible hatred.

Mid-morning found them back at the meadow where Prabhu pointed out the three areas of disturbed soil and tamped down sod that marked the graves. A smaller pit among the roots of an oak tree yielded a cloth wrapped around gold and silver coins.

"How did you know this was here, father?" Rajnish muttered.

"I helped bury it while you were asleep."

The officer supervised the exhumation of the bodies then had the soldiers collect wood for the funeral pyres. While this took place he had the captives brought over to the tree and their gags removed.

"You are murderers," the officer said. "The penalty is death. Do you have anything to say?"

Hussein said nothing, just staring at the ground, while Lochan shook his head. Kalidas spat into the grass by the officer's feet. "I am not afraid for I have done the will of Kali. That one though," he indicated Prabhu with a toss of his head and a glare, "He will know much fear before he dies, and after, for he has betrayed the Mother and she will pursue him. My death will be far better than his."

The officer shook his head. "How is it that you Thuggee have turned the pure worship of the Mother into something foul and degrading? No, do not answer; I have no wish to debate with you." He turned to his aide. "Hang them. Strangulation is a fitting way for them to go."

Hempen nooses were quickly fashioned and dropped over three heads, the other ends of the ropes being thrown over a branch. Three to a rope, the soldiers hauled the struggling men into the air, watching them kicking and dancing on the fresh morning air that they so desperately desired in their lungs. After a short time they hung limp and still.

"Leave them there as a lesson to other Thugs." The officer turned to Prabhu who had his son's face buried in his chest so he could not see the mottled faces of the hanging men. "Now, what to do with you?"

313

"My lord knows I helped him, willingly giving up my friends for my son's sake. Whatever you do, I ask only that you spare his life. He is unconsecrated and innocent."

"Yet he may fall into evil having seen its face," the officer mused. "However, I am inclined toward generosity. You may depart in peace, Prabhu Ram of Ranikhet, with your son, but be warned. If ever the yellow ruhmal appears on these roads, I will come with my men and hang you and your whole family. Do you understand me?"

"Yes, my lord." Prabhu bowed and hurried away with his son before the king's men changed their minds. He left the meadow with the blazing pyre and ran as far and as fast as he could, dragging Rajnish with him.

That night, they camped beside the road where a small forest of Chir pine flowed down the hillside. They collected pine cones for a small fire, though they had no food, seeking its flames for heat and for the light. Shadows leaped and danced and both man and boy shivered in fear – Rajnish because of the terrible things he had seen and Prabhu because he felt the approach of the Dark One. He knew he had done the right thing to protect his son, but was terrified that his act of betrayal would bring a ghastly death to both of them. He kept silent, as he had all day, hardly exchanging more than a few words with his son. In the end, as the night wore on, they slept fitfully.

The natural sounds of the night stilled in the hour before dawn and Rajnish woke immediately, lifting himself on one elbow to stare into the darkness over the glowing embers of the fire. Something within him told him that not all was as it should be. He shook his father's arm.

"Father, wake up." As soon as Prabhu's eyes opened, he continued. "Father, there is someone or something out there in the darkness. I can hear it."

Prabhu jumped to his feet and threw more wood and pine cones onto the smoldering embers, stirring them with a stick until bright flames shot up, throwing back the night.

"Who is there?" Prabhu called. "We can hear your footsteps. Come into the light where we can see you." A dark shape detached itself from the inky shadows and moved forward.

"No, father," cried Rajnish. "Do not invite it."

The figure stepped into the light and man and boy screamed. A tall woman with dark, almost black skin stood in the dancing light of the small fire. She was naked except for the black hair that cascaded over her shoulders and breasts and a circlet of bloody hands around her wide hips. Four-armed, she carried a sword, a trident, a man's head and a bowl that caught the blood pouring from the head. The face froze their hearts as the figure turned its gaze to them. Large staring red eyes surmounted a wide mouth with protruding fangs and a blood-red tongue flickered and hung down to the chin. A golden nimbus played around the head of the figure.

"Kali, Dread Mother," Prabhu croaked. "Have mercy."

The figure spoke with a voice like the wind over a deserted shmashana and the stink of cold ash and burning bones swept over them. "You have profaned my

315

mysteries, faithless one. For that you die, now and forever, for great shall be your torment."

Prabhu fell to his knees and held onto a pine trunk for support, gasping for air. "Merciful Mother, I beg you to spare my son Rajnish. He is unconsecrated."

Fiery eyes turned on the boy and he reeled back until he leaned against a tree. After a moment, Rajnish pulled himself upright and stared back at the figure of Kali across the fire.

"You are not a god," he said, with incredulity tingeing his voice. "You are a Rakshasi, a female demon, masquerading as the goddess. I can see your inner flame." With a gasp, Rajnish slumped back in a faint, but the voice continued, cold and clear in the still air. "You shall not have the boy, for he is mine." A pale flame danced in the air in front of the boy.

The Kali-demon laughed, cold and cruel. "Who are you to contend with me, demon? Do you not know that Kali devours demons?"

"The real Kali, maybe, but you are not she. You are a Rakshasi." The cold voice paused, then, "Have you always acted as the god of the Sthaga?"

"For more than two hundred years. I have feasted well through my deception while you, brother Rakshasa, have made do with crumbs."

"Then you will not begrudge me my poor meal. Leave the boy, he is mine."

"For now."

"No. You will forsake him utterly or I will contend with you and spread the news of your deception widely. You will not find it so easy to get victims if men know your true nature."

316

Kali-demon thought it over and nodded. "He is mine though," she said, pointing her sword at Prabhu shivering on the ground.

"He was one of your followers, so I cannot dispute your right." The flame slipped back into Rajnish and took control of the fainting body. He stumbled off onto the road, with agonized screams beating at his senses as the Kali-demon moved in to feed on the terrified Prabhu.

Hours later, on the outskirts of Ranikhet and within sight of his house, Rajnish sat down by the side of the road and seemed to sleep while a voice spoke into his inner ear. A little later, he got up and ran home, in tears, crying of how bandits had ambushed them and killed everyone. If his mother, who knew of her husband's business, had doubts about her son's story, she kept them to herself and henceforth raised her son to give all the gods their dues, not just the Dark Mother.

Chapter Sixteen

I know you will think that the actions of the Sthaga, the Thuggee of Kali, are more closely allied to a demon's deeds than those of a god and indeed that is the case. I do not know if the Rakshasi I found that night near Ranikhet was the only demon who ever impersonated Kali, or whether she was but one of many, for the Thuggee were all across northern India; but what always intrigued me was the question that deception engendered. If the religion of the Thuggee was a sham, based on a false belief that made the goddess herself hated and feared, why did the real Kali never step in and restore her true worship. I have found gods and goddesses to be self-centered and jealous, not giving up their worship willingly, but thinking upon it since I left the boy Rajnish, I realize I have not seen or felt the unmistakable presence of a god for close on a thousand years.

What has happened to them? Men still worship and offer up sacrifices but it is as if the gods are no longer concerned with this world, withdrawing from physicality for some unseen purpose. This does not worry me, for I never liked gods, but it leaves a void. And a void will be filled. I have seen this already with the filling of the Kali void by a Rakshasi. I wonder if I could take the place of a vacant god. Which one would I choose? Would I be any good at it?

When I first came upon the Thugs a little after I left Arjuna and Parvati's village, I followed their bands across northern India, watching but never interfering. I tasted the minds of the dying men – rather than let them go to waste – but I possessed no-one, let not even a hint of my presence impinge on these savage minds. I wanted to see Kali and I hoped she would be drawn to the sacrifices made to her. Men died in their hundreds, then thousands, over the years. Dynasties rose and fell, as they always do, yet none of them controlled the savagery amongst them. Men died, strangled in the name of a goddess, yet she spurned the sacrifices, never putting in an appearance. Finally, I gave up my credo of non-interference and possessed a lad on the brink of his apprenticeship.

I can tell the question in your mind. I can read minds, remember. If I have slipped unfelt into you – and I am expert at this now – I know your every thought and desire. You are wondering why a demon such as me would seek out a deity famous for her destruction of demons. That is a good question; it shows you are paying attention. Unfortunately, I have no good answer.

It might be boredom. I have lived for several thousand years now and it has been a long time since I was challenged. Humans are such easy prey that perhaps I want to meet someone as strong as or stronger than me. Life seems more precious when it is at risk. Or it may be the opposite. If I want to survive I must know my enemy, and surely the worst enemy any demon can have is a god. Especially a god that excels in demon destruction.

Whatever the reason, I decided to enter a human again and see if I could precipitate a confrontation with Kali. With luck, she would be so intent on the human victim she would overlook my presence for a few vital seconds.

I entered Rajnish on the cremation ground, during the night of his initiation. I had been following that band, or at least the few in it I knew about, for a month, but that was the first time they had met. I thought about disrupting the ceremony, but I could not feel a god-presence anywhere and did not want to waste the opportunity by alerting the worshippers. Instead, I entered the lad and hid within him, observing but not controlling. I soon found out that the leader of the band, Kalidas, took himself very seriously and would brook no questioning of his authority. I also found out that Prabhu loved his son quite genuinely yet was unsure if that love was stronger than his fear of Kali. I decided to test the boundaries.

Rajnish was a quiet and studious boy, willing to watch and wait for enlightenment, but with a little stimulating I got him to ask questions and start to irritate Kalidas. I did not interfere with his beliefs yet, for I wanted to see how quickly the life took hold of him. His prayers to Kali that first night on the road showed him to be a pious lad but I also knew he had not yet seen the stranglers at work, apart from the ritualized slaughter on the cremation ground, an act that had an air of unreality for him. His reaction to the strangling of the three merchants told me he was human still. The goor ceremony took me by surprise though, as I did not think that a few rituals and a taste of raw sugar could unleash such a flood of religious fervor. Had I not been within the lad, tamping down his ecstasy, I think he would have given over his heart and mind to the dark worship, relegating his doubts as mere weakness.

As it was, fear and revulsion dominated and by a lucky chance his father led him round the graves where he looked on the dismembering and disemboweling not as a purported sacred mystery of Kali but as an attempt to

320

prevent discovery of the bodies. The gold too, he discovered, was payment for a task. The strangling had its roots in greed rather than in service to the goddess.

In the village of Naini Tal I heard gossip in the fair that king's soldiers were in Bhimtal and leaving Rajnish briefly I suggested to a man that if news were brought to the soldiers of bandits approaching, there might be a reward in it for him. Once he was on his way, I returned to Rajnish.

As an aside, I know the more astute among you will doubt my words. You think that Naini Tal was founded by the British as a summer retreat many years after these events. To an extent you are right, in that the present town was built later, but there has always been a settlement in that beautiful spot and the flat meadows by the crystal lake have been home to fairs almost as long.

I laid my plans but there is always an element of luck. If the Sthaga had not chosen to attack their victims just there, they might have passed the soldiers uneventfully, for they certainly resembled merchants more than bandits. Again, if Kalidas had escaped or been killed, my plan to have Prabhu save his son by turning traitor might not have worked. By then, I was fairly sure his love was greater than his fear, but I could not be sure.

As it was, my plan fell into place. Prabhu betrayed the Mother in the presence of Kalidas, provoking him to invoke the goddess to wreak vengeance. Now I just had to sit back and wait for the goddess to show up and while she attacked Prabhu, get some idea of her capabilities. I was certain her anger would be such that I could flee the scene without being noticed, but I had not considered the possibility of another of my kind being involved. I

321

recognized her inner flame immediately and at the same time realized I could not let this Rakshasi kill my host. I took him home and left him with a plausible story that would allay any suspicion of wrongdoing. Imprinting false memories in his brain, I resumed my normal form, unseen in the sunlight.

My first action was to find a lonely spot and spend some time thinking. I had learned two things in my years with the Thugs. The first was that the goddess Kali, if she ever had an association with this cruel sect, had cast it adrift and no longer offered them any protection. The second was that the gods were disappearing from the land. That a demon could impersonate a god for over two hundred years with impunity was staggering for it surely implied that the gods were gone from the land or no longer cared what happened. Add to this that I had not seen any sign of them in the last millennium.

Well, what was it to me? I am Rakshasa and I do what I want. Gods kill demons when they find them and a lack of gods is surely a good thing. After a bit I got to thinking about Sonaka's Eightfold Path, the tyranny of petty kings and the gentle love of ordinary peasant men and women in these mountainous realms of Garhwal and Kumaon. Did they not deserve better? What would happen to this beautiful land if the gods gave up and left? I could see the powerful preying on the weak, the greedy robbing the helpless, and the indiscriminate destruction of the forests and the animals by unscrupulous merchants and princes. It had already started and I could only see it getting worse as men realized the gods had cast the land adrift.

Could I do anything about this? Who would believe me if I said I wanted to? I am a demon. I prey on weak humans, I greedily feast on the helpless and I destroy indiscriminately. Surely this is what I do? Can I become something I am not? I think I can, for this too has already started. I rarely kill now and never indiscriminately. I have been known to protect the weak and bring benefits to those who ask. I protect this beautiful land from invaders and if I do not know what 'love' is, at least I am coming to know the meaning of 'right'. Perhaps this demon can tread the Eightfold Path, better myself and achieve nirvana. What cosmic joke would it be if a demon attained the universal godhead? Or could I do as the Rakshasi did but carry it one step further? Could I become a god?

I must think on this some more before I decide.

In the meantime, what if anything should I do about the Thuggee? My inclination is to wipe them out for they hurt what I have come to regard as my land, my people. Yet I cannot slay thousands of men when it is their belief in a false god that has led them astray. I do not want to kill again, so I must find another to do this work. The local kings, sultans and princes are not interested in this task, beyond keeping their own roads safe. A little effort nets some rewards, but a great effort becomes very expensive. No, the answer lies elsewhere and I think I know where.

For the last hundred or so years a different type of invader has trodden the plains of India, as rapacious as any who came before, but with one difference – they believe in a rule of law that precludes murder, even by their rulers. In their eyes, the world belongs to them, and

323

like any responsible landowner, it is their duty to manage the land and its peoples in a proper manner. Lately, they have decided that the mountains also belong to them and small numbers move throughout Garhwal and Kumaon, seeking out its riches for their own gain. These invaders are pale of skin and come from over the oceans; they call themselves British and they love the color red.

Word has reached me of a British officer called Captain Sleeman who wars against the Thugs in the name of his Queen and something called the Company. I will visit this man and help him with what knowledge I have, for I believe this sect should be stamped out. After that, who knows? I will certainly return to my beloved hills but I think I will get to know these British. A race that powerful could harm my hill people without thinking and that I cannot allow.

Chapter Seventeen

Reverend Samuel Pritchard tapped his pencil against his front teeth absently and looked out of his study window toward the mountains. After a few moments, he sighed and looked back to his writing tablet with its few pages of scrawled notes, then to his large leatherbound Bible open on his left-hand side. It was Saturday afternoon, the twentieth day of June, in the year of our Lord eighteen-fifty-seven and despite laboring on his sermon all week, it still was not ready for Sunday's worship. In view of the rumours of rebellion among the sepoys of the Bengal Army, Reverend Pritchard had thought to base his sermon on Matthew 24:45; "Who is the faithful and discreet slave?"

It had seemed like a good idea at the time, but after four days of scribbling notes and crossing out whole paragraphs, he just could not make the arguments stick together. He could identify the slave talked about by the Lord, and he could hold up the rebel sepoys as being anything but faithful, but could he reasonably tie them together? That was the question that was starting to nag at him. Perhaps he should just give up and drag out one of his old sermons. He doubted most of his tiny congregation would notice, though Elenore certainly would.

The Reverend put down his pencil and smiled at the thought of his wife. Though they had been married for nearly thirteen years, he still smiled and got a dreamy look on his thin bony face when he saw her, even if just in his mind's eye. They had married back home in West Drayton only days before coming out to India as missionaries. Six months in Bombay to get used to the heat and the flies, the grinding poverty and the host of foreign gods – demons, he told himself, they are just demons misleading the ignorant – then his assignment with the mission in Almora. The committee there had sent them straight to the tiny village of Ganai set in one of the principal passes between Garhwal and Kumaon. The hill country was like heaven compared to the hell of Bombay. Clean air, cooler climate and people who, while every bit as deluded by demons as their plains brethren, were unfailingly polite and hospitable. What little they had, they shared, and for nearly a year reverend Pritchard had taken friendliness for interest in the Word of God.

Then came the great festival of Shiva, the titular deity of these mountains, and every single one of his 'flock' had deserted his tiny stone church for the hill temples, chanting and singing and offering up detestable rites to their god. He was crushed and if it had not been for the strength of his wife Elenore, the Reverend Pritchard would have turned tail and run. Instead, husband and wife waited for the return of the Ganai villagers, welcoming them back as if nothing had happened, but redoubling their efforts to win the hearts and souls of this pagan people. The next year they were deserted again but the year after a widow and her young son stayed behind, possibly because the Reverend had offered schooling and food to the boy, but also possibly because the example of the Pritchards was winning through.

That was the year that Elenore became 'with child' as she delicately put it. Samuel Pritchard had intended to devote a celibate life to the Service of the Lord, but after accepting this assignment from the Missionary Society, had met Elenore, the only daughter of a country clergyman and found himself inflamed. Long walks, cold baths and hours of prayer proved of no avail and in the end, Samuel had taken the Apostle Paul's words in First Corithians to heart – "But if they have not self-control, let them marry, for it is better to marry than to be inflamed."

Elenore Shipley, a spinster of long standing in her father's parish, yearned to carry the Word of God into the missions, but what chance did a single woman have of carrying out such an assignment? The only way for a woman in the Missionary Service was as the wife of a minister, but she was thirty-five years old, tall and plain. Furthermore, her father, a simple clergyman in a poor parish, had no wealth to endow on his only child. When Samuel Pritchard happened along, she knew it for the Hand of God and accepted his proposal demurely, as befitted a well brought up lady, but her heart beat faster and she felt a sinful prickle of perspiration break out between her breasts. She did not love him, but that mattered little. She would do her duty to God and husband, in that order, and pray that a little happiness might find its way into her life, along with the expected drudgery of missionary work.

Happiness was a while coming but it arrived at last, creeping up on her unseen. She taught Sunday School for the children of the village, introducing them to Bible stories and a few of the simpler concepts of the Christian faith, trying to distract their minds from the basket of sweetmeats she kept by her desk to be handed out at lesson's end. Working with the children, she found herself desiring to be a mother, and following on the desire came the fruit. In the third year of their ministry a boy was born to them, christened Charles Albert after the grandfathers and raised strictly but with love by both parents. Now, at ten years of age, he studied with one or other of his parents every weekday morning, helped with the numerous tasks around the church in the afternoons and aided his mother in running the Sunday School.

Samuel Pritchard leaned back in his chair and contemplated his life with a certain smugness. Thirteen years in the ministry and already he had a dozen stalwart converts from paganism and twice that showing interest. They had warned him in Bombay that it would be a difficult task ... the distinctive sound of a horse's hooves, metal shoes on the stone of the road, interrupted his train of thought.

The Reverend pushed his chair back and stood up. He walked across the uneven hardwood floor to the window and peered out, craning his neck to glimpse the gate and the small section of road visible through the break in the stone wall. The clop of hooves sounded again and this time the tread of feet marching in unison followed it. *Soldiers? Why are they here?* He hurried to the front door and out onto the verandah as the horseman turned in through the gate, followed by a squad of about twenty soldiers.

The rider wore the red coat of the regular army with the two pips of a full lieutenant. The face that looked out from under the rim of a topee sported a blond lock of hair falling over the eyes and a full mustache in a reddened face. The lieutenant grinned as he spotted the Reverend on the verandah and touched the tip of his swagger stick to his topee.

"I say, you wouldn't be Reverend Pritchard, by any chance?"

"That is correct, lieutenant. How may I help you?"

"Well, I'd actually like a word with you, sir, if you don't mind."

"Of course. May I offer you some refreshment? Tea, perhaps?"

"A cold drink would really hit the spot. It's deuced hot today … er, pardon my language, Reverend."

"I do not believe in strong drink before sundown and then only in moderation, but I can offer you some cold water if that would be acceptable." Samuel turned and clapped his hands for the servant hovering in the doorway behind him. "Khalim, bring tea for one and a jug of cold water with a glass." He gestured toward a table and chairs on the wide verandah. "Please join me, lieutenant."

The officer nodded and turned in his saddle, looking back to where the squad of soldiers was just entering the mission compound. "Naik," he called crisply. "Fall the men out and avail yourselves of the shade by the wall. Be ready to move out in, oh, two hours." He swung his leg and dismounted, leading his mount forward and tying the reins loosely to a verandah post. The horse immediately lowered its head and started cropping the rough grass of the patchy lawn. The lieutenant clattered up the steps and swept his topee off with one hand, running his other hand over his fair hair to coax it into a semblance of order. "Lieutenant James Dunbar, Third Bengal Lancers, presently seconded to a detachment of the Sirmoor Battalion in Almora, Reverend." He stuck out his hand and shook Samuel's.

329

The Reverend offered Lieutenant Dunbar a chair and, when Khalim appeared with the drinks, handed him a glass of cold water, the outside dripping with condensation. "Don't stand on ceremony, Lieutenant. You look as if you need it."

Dunbar grinned. "Thank you, sir." He upended the glass and drank thirstily, lowering it with a heartfelt sigh of appreciation. "Now that really did hit the spot. Could I, er ..." He waggled the glass suggestively.

"Of course. Khalim." Pritchard seated himself and poured a thin stream of weak tea into a cup and added a spoonful of raw sugar, stirring it briskly. He sipped the steaming liquid and put the cup back in the saucer before turning back to the lieutenant. "May I enquire as to the nature of your visit to Ganai? We seldom see another European in these parts and now we find a British officer in our midst."

"Not a social call, I'm afraid, Reverend. You've er, heard about the mutiny?

"A little. We received a letter from the Mission in Naini Tal about a month ago. They said it would probably blow over in a few weeks." Samuel looked keenly at his guest. "That's why you're here? Because it hasn't blown over?"

"That's right, sir. Meerut and Delhi fell to the rebels within days. Now it's spreading and it seems the whole native army is affected." Dunbar caught the Reverend's involuntary glance toward the sepoys sitting in the sparse shade of the stone wall. "Don't worry, sir. My lads are loyal. I have a good Naik in charge of them."

"You didn't come all this way just to bring me the news though."

"No sir. I have orders to escort you and your family to Almora where you can be protected. Just in case the trouble spreads to the hills."

"I see. And how long do you envisage this ah … sojourn with the army will last?"

"I don't know, sir, and that's God's honest truth, pardon the expression. I don't expect it'll be long, not more than a month or two. As soon as our boys get stuck into them, they'll fold. They're only natives, after all."

"Well, I'm sorry you've had a wasted trip, lieutenant, but I'm not going. I cannot leave my flock for that length of time."

"Please reconsider, Reverend. If not for your own sake, then for your wife and child." Dunbar lowered his voice despite no-one being within earshot. "There have been reports of … of atrocities."

"The people here love us, lieutenant. This is the safest place for us."

"Will you not at least put it to your wife, sir?"

Samuel smiled. "If it will put your mind at rest." He turned and clapped his hands for Khalim again. "Where is the memsahib?"

Khalim bowed his turbaned head. "She is in the church, I believe, Reverend Sahib. Arranging flowers I am thinking."

"Please find her, Khalim, and tell her we have a visitor."

"Yes, sahib. At once, sahib." Khalim backed away before turning and hurrying off.

A few minutes later, during which Pritchard and Dunbar shared a companiable silence, quenching their respective thirsts, Elenore came hurrying over the compound with a boy in tow. When she caught sight of the lieutenant's red coat she slowed and her hands automatically brushed at her hair and tugged at her long dress. The men stood as she stepped up onto the verandah and Dunbar bowed as Pritchard introduced his wife.

"Delighted, ma'am. I just wish these were happier circumstances."

Elenore said nothing but one eyebrow lifted slightly.

Dunbar coughed delicately and nodded toward the boy hovering at the edge of the verandah.

"Ah, my son Charles Albert," Pritchard said with a slight smile. "Come here, Charles. This is Lieutenant Dunbar of the Third Bengal Lancers."

"Good afternoon, sir," Charles said quietly. "I am pleased to meet you."

Dunbar nodded to the boy pleasantly before looking pointedly at the Reverend.

"Run along now, Charles. This is grown-up business."

"Yes father ... mother. Sir." Charles turned and walked the length of the verandah before breaking into a run. He leapt off the verandah and landed on all fours on the rough grass of the compound.

"Charles, be careful," called his mother.

Charles pretended he hadn't heard and wandered off toward the sepoys sitting in the shade of the stone wall. They looked up as he approached.

"Good-day to you, young sahib," said one of the sepoys with a grin. "Have you come to give us cold water or tea like the Lieutenant Sahib is presently enjoying?"

"Watch your tongue, Prakash," the Naik rapped out. "Show some respect for the sahib."

332

"Ah, young sahib," said another sepoy. "You must be paying no attention to us, please. We are just thirsty, having marched many miles today."

"I'm sorry," Charles said. "I did not think of that." He turned and glanced back at the house. "I suppose I could get you some, or get one of the servants to."

"Of course," muttered Prakash, in Hindi. "Let the servants do everything."

"I did not quite get that," Charles said with a frown. "I'm learning Hindi and the hill dialects but I'm not sure ..."

The Naik got to his feet and loomed over Prakash. He swore at him colorfully in Gujarati before turning back to the boy. "Please excuse his ill manners, young sahib. He is a badmash and I will make sure he gets guard duty tonight. We do not need water, as we have brought a sufficiency with us."

"Thank you, Naik. I am Charles Albert Pritchard, the son of the Reverend here. Will you all be coming to church tomorrow morning? Father gives some smashing sermons."

"I do not think we will be here tomorrow, Charles Albert Pritchard Sahib," the Naik said with a faint smile. "But even if we were, we are Hindu and Muslim and so could not attend."

"Oh, father wouldn't mind. He says we Christians have a duty to show everyone the right way to worship God. Why, when we came to Ganai it was just us – well, I was born a couple of years later – but father and mother have converted lots of people who used to be Hindu." Charles frowned. "No Muslims though. What do

333

Muslims believe in? Do they have lots of funny gods too?"

"Young sahib," the Naik said quickly. "It is not good to ... to be making light of other people's beliefs. It might upset them."

"Oh, well I did not mean to do that. I thought if you came to church tomorrow you might see how good it is and want to con ... to learn more."

"Then we will think upon your words and if we are here tomorrow, and if we judge it right to do so, then we will come and see your Christian God."

"Good." Charles looked beyond the Naik to the stacks of muskets by the wall. "I say. Are those Enfield rifles? Can I look at them?"

"I am thinking those guns are army property, young sahib, and it might be proper to get the Lieutenant Sahib's permission first."

"Oh, well, I suppose I could." Charles pouted and looked toward the verandah. His face brightened as he saw the officer come down the steps and stride towards him, adjusting his topee as he came. He ran to meet him, an eager smile on his face. "Lieutenant Dunbar, can I have a look at your guns? I asked the Naik but he said they were army property and I must ask you, so I am."

Dunbar looked down at the boy and frowned. "Eh? Er, look ... er, young Pritchard, I'm rather busy right now. Run along off to your parents, there's a good chap." He strode past Charles and addressed himself to the Naik as the men scrambled to their feet, Prakash leaving it as long as he dared. "We are staying the night, Gohindar Ras. Get the men settled in their tents at the far end of the compound."

The Naik saluted smartly. "Very good, sir. I will have your tent put up immediately, so that you ..."

"No need, Naik. I will be staying in the main house, and dining there. The Reverend says you may bring the men around to the kitchen at dusk where every man will be given a bowl of rice." He touched his riding crop to the edge of his topee. "Carry on then."

Gohindar saluted again and turned to the sepoys, barking out a string of orders that had them marching in double time with their packs and muskets toward the end of the compound. In no more than a few minutes, the tents were set up and a camp fire started to brew water for tea.

Night fell and the sepoys gathered around the fire, eating their bowls of rice and vegetables, mixed with a little goat meat bought from the villagers. They drank mugs of hot sweet milky tea, having obtained fresh milk and a small block of goor from the same source. Tobacco changed hands too, and soon bluish clouds of scented smoke wreathed their heads as they talked.

"Our brothers are already victorious in Delhi," Prakash said softly. "Are we to sit quietly while others free us from these foreign chains?"

Abdullah glanced across to where the Naik sat by himself, his tent separated from those of the sepoys by twenty feet, as befitted his rank. His back was to the men and he sat staring at the lights of the main house, within which a piano created soft music.

"Softly, brother, we do not want the Naik to hear us."

"You think I am afraid of the Naik? He is no better than the British for he obeys them without question."

335

"I am thinking you jump to attention whenever the Naik yaps," Vasu observed. "Are you perhaps claiming the right to wear a red coat too?" The man jumped to his feet and began strutting back and forth. "I am Subedar Prakash. You will polish my boots, by golly, or I will have you shot at dawn."

A howl of laughter greeted Vasu's clowning and Prakash scowled. "And will you think it so funny when you lose your caste because of the British? Or you, Abdullah, or you Haamid? What will you say when they make you profane Allah's name?"

"What are you talking about? What have you heard?"

Prakash made a show of looking at the Naik, then at the lights of the main house. Everyone was silent, their eyes all turned in his direction. The only sounds were the crackle and snap of the fire, the faint tinkle of the piano and somewhere a dog barked. Wood smoke mixed with the subtle leftover odors of their dinner and wafted into the delicately pine-scented hill air. He leaned forward, drawing every man inward slightly as they strained for his words.

"The British are trying to make every Muslim forswear his faith, every Hindu to lose his caste."

"That is impossible," Haamid declared. "I pray five times a day and follow every rule laid out to guide me in my worship. No-one can make me change." Echoes of agreement rose and fell while Prakash's eyes glittered in the fire light.

"Does anyone here have a cartridge?"

"Why?"

"Give me one, and fetch one of the rifled muskets and I will show you."

336

"You are not going to shoot anyone, are you?" Vasu asked nervously. "Not even the Naik?" He pulled a greased cardboard cartridge from his belt.

Abdullah got to his feet and trotted over to the stacked muskets, bringing one back to the fire. "Here," he said, holding it out to Prakash.

"You keep it. Now take the cartridge from Vasu." Prakash waited for the munition to change hands. "Abdullah, you have been a sepoy for five years. Show us what you do when you load the musket."

"You are wanting me to load the musket? I must ask you why?"

"I want to show you something. Do not worry, Abdullah, I will not let you hurt anyone. Yet," he added, under his breath.

Abdullah shrugged and put the rifle butt on the ground, the end of the barrel reaching nearly to chest height. He raised the cardboard cartridge to his mouth and bit off the end, tearing it open with his strong white teeth. He started to pour the gunpowder down the barrel.

"That will be enough," Prakash said quietly. "Put the rifle on the ground." He waited until Abdullah was standing with just the cartridge in his hand. "Now tell me, Abdullah. What is on the cartridge that makes it slippery and keeps away the damp?"

Abdullah looked at the cartridge and shrugged. "Grease."

"What type of grease?"

He sniffed it. "I do not know. Butter?"

"It is a mixture of pig and cow fat. The British use this deliberately so that we will all defile ourselves."

337

Abdullah's mouth dropped open in horror and he threw the cartridge away into the darkness. "If that is true then I have tasted of the flesh of pig. I am ritually unclean."

"I too," Haamid cried. "For I also tear open the cartridges with my teeth."

"We all do," Narendra said. "We are all trained to do so. But I am unclean because the fat of a cow has touched my lips. I am no better than a chamar, a leather-worker. I am become one of the Dalit, untouchable."

Vasu wailed, raising his voice in lamentation, several of the other sepoys joining in.

"What is going on here? Why is it you are making all this noise? You will disturb the sahibs." The Naik pushed through to the camp fire and stood looking around at the distraught faces. "What is the matter?"

"Ah, it is the good and faithful Naik, Gohindar Ras," Prakash said, rising to his feet and staring belligerently at the non-commissioned officer. "I was telling the men of the regard the British have for our beliefs."

"What are you talking about?"

"The cartridges, Naik," Vasu cried. "They are greased with cow and pig fat. We are all unclean."

"That is nonsense," Gohindar replied crisply.

"Nonsense, is it?" Prakash asked. "Then why is it our brothers in Meerut and Delhi have rebelled because of this atrocity. I tell you the British will not be satisfied until every one of us is made into a god-eating Christian."

"Do not listen to this man." Gohindar swiveled on his heel and looked at each sepoy in turn. "You know Prakash is a trouble maker. He tells lies, for it is well known that after the sepoys at Meerut refused to use the cartridges, the British officers agreed that the men should grease their own cartridges with beeswax or vegetable oil ..."

"Why would they need to do that unless they really were using pig and cow fat in the first place?" Prakash interrupted. "For years we have all been defiling ourselves while the British laughed at us. Well, no more. I say we kill the British officer, this Dunbar Sahib, and march to join our brothers in Delhi. Together we will kill every British person and sweep this accursed oppressor out of our land."

"That is treasonable talk, Prakash. You will cease it right now or I will bind you to await the sahib's pleasure."

"You are no better than a trained sloth bear, Gohindar Ras, for you dance by the roadside to the British officer's tune. You know what the British are trying to do. It is your country and your faith too. Help us. Rise up with us and remove these chains that bind us." Prakash talked quietly but fervently, seeking to persuade now, rather than confront.

"No, for I have heard what your brothers are doing. Over two hundred British women and children killed in Kanpur. I do not make war on the innocent, and I will not let you do so." Naik Ras rapped out a command. "Vasu, Narendar. Bind this man and put him under arrest. He will be tried tomorrow by Dunbar Sahib."

"Brothers, help me. Unless we act the British will remove our caste, make us unacceptable to our gods." Prakash turned and started haranguing the men. "Take your muskets and kill the Naik and the officer. Kill the

339

white man, woman and child also, and any who would stop us."

Gohindar Ras, finding that Vasu and Narendar had not obeyed him, grabbed hold of Prakash himself, and tried to wrestle him to the ground.

"We must help him," Abdullah cried hoarsely, but the others hung back, unsure of whom he meant. With a curse, he leaped forward and dealt the Naik a stunning blow on the side of his head, loosening his grip on Prakash.

"Kill him," Prakash yelled, drawing his knife.

"No," Abdullah said firmly. "The Naik is one of us. When he sees our success, he will join us. We should tie him up and leave him in one of the tents while we deal with the Dunbar Sahib and the Reverend Sahib."

Prakash grumbled but Abdullah's suggestion carried weight with the other sepoys who felt no anger toward their Naik, who only six months before had been a fellow sepoy. They tied him securely and gagged him, lying him down in one of the tents before gathering around the camp fire once more.

"Get your muskets and load them," Prakash ordered. "Then let us take our first step toward freedom."

The sepoys were silent for the most part, feeling more fear and anxiety than anger, but the issue of the cartridge grease troubled them. If truly the British had set out to defile them, then that act must be purged and what better way than by blood? They trooped over to the stacked muskets in ones and twos, bringing them back to the fire to load.

Haamid took out a cartridge and looked at it irresolutely. "How are we loading these guns?" he asked. "I am not wanting to bite these cartridges anymore."

"Fool. Tear them open with your hands."

The sepoys loaded the guns and strutted around feeling much bolder for having them in their hands. Prakash pulled a brand from the fire and brandished it over his head.

"Follow me," he yelled. "We shall kill all the British." He ran off across the compound toward the Reverend's house and a moment later the sepoys followed, shouting and cursing to keep up their courage. One or two delayed long enough to grab other brands before following.

Numerous lights still shone behind lace curtains in the house and the sound of the piano greeted the rebellious sepoys as they mounted the steps and surged onto the verandah. The music faltered and died, and a few moments later a door was flung open. Lieutenant Dunbar stood in the doorway, backlit by the several oil lamps in the parlor. His red coat was unbuttoned at the neck and he carried a half empty whisky glass in one hand.

"What the deuce is going on out here? Naik, is that you?" Dunbar stared at the lead figure on the verandah. The flaming torch half lit the bearer's face and threw the rest into shadow.

Prakash threw out one arm and pointed at his lieutenant. "There is the British dog," he howled. "Kill him."

Abdullah pushed past, his rifle musket raised. "I will do it. I will kill him."

341

Dunbar dropped his glass with a curse and pulled his service revolver from its holster. The musket and the revolver went off at the same instant. The musket ball zipped wasp-like over Dunbar's shoulder and the crash of breaking glass followed on an instant. Dunbar's bullet found its mark and Abdullah screamed and fell back. The lieutenant snapped off another three shots into the darkness, missing Prakash who ducked back quickly, but wounding two other sepoys. He then stepped back into the parlor and slammed the door, wincing as chips of wood flew from balls slamming into the thin door.

"Reverend, get down on the floor with your missus if you please." He saw one of the servants hovering near the broken glass of a sideboard. "You, Khalim is it? Get the boy, the young sahib quickly. Get him dressed."

A burning brand shattered a window and flames licked at the curtains. As the Reverend scrambled across to beat at them with his jacket, a ragged volley of musket fire blew the other windows out, smashing oil lamps and glassware, sending splinters of wood viciously flying. The room plunged into darkness, lit only by the fires, which though small, gained strength by the moment.

"Reverend," Dunbar called urgently. "Is there anywhere we can go? Somewhere less flammable?" He dug out a few spare bullets from a small clip on his belt and reloaded his revolver.

"There's the church. It is made of solid stone."

"That'll do. Where is it? Easy to get to, I hope."

"Across the compound, on the village side."

Dunbar swore. "We'll have to chance it, we cannot stay here." Musket fire, random and inaccurate, peppered the outside of the building, the few that found the open

342

windows humming viciously across the room. The flames grew and licked up the walls, filling the upper parts of the room with black smoke. "Here's how we are going to do it. Reverend, you will collect your son and lead the way out the back, keeping to the darkest part of the compound. Mrs Pritchard, you will organize the servants to gather what medical supplies, food and water you can quickly find and follow your husband closely. I will bring up the rear, offering what protection I can." He brandished his revolver grimly.

Khalim pushed open the parlor door. "I have the young sahib ready, Reverend Sahib, Memsahib."

Mrs Pritchard scrambled through the door, pushing Khalim and her protesting and excited son ahead of her. "We'll meet you in the kitchen."

"Do you have any guns in the house, Reverend?"

"Only a fowling piece, but I could never fire on another human being, sir."

"You leave that to me. Get it, and as many cartridges as you can find. Hurry, man. We don't have much time." Dunbar waited a few minutes after the Reverend left the room before raising himself up to peer through the smoke and flames into the night. He saw the flash of a musket and felt the ball sizzle through the air near his head. Squeezing off two shots, he was rewarded by a scream, and he ducked back down, scrambling for the door. "That'll hold them a moment," he muttered.

Everyone was waiting in the kitchen. Dunbar quickly checked the bags and baskets, throwing out a tin of tea and another of sugar, but adding a plate of cold boiled potatoes from the pantry. "We won't be brewing up tea. We need things that don't take much preparation. Forget the pots and kettle. Is that all the water? It will have to do. Medicines? Cough syrup won't be much use, ma'am. Bring some extra cloths for bandages. Muhammad, bring a couple of lanterns and matches. Right, is everyone ready? You know what you are doing?" Dunbar doused the oil lantern and opened the back door cautiously, peering out into the darkened compound. "Thank God I have idiots in my command. They are all round the front looking at the fire." He motioned to the Reverend. "After you, sir, as quickly and quietly as you can."

Reverend Pritchard ran out into the darkness, holding his son by the hand and carrying his fowling piece. Mrs Pritchard followed, clasping the bag of medical supplies, with Muhammad and Khalim close behind, laden with food and bottles of water. Dunbar brought up the rear, his revolver in hand, walking sideways to face the front of the compound and the milling mutineers. Slowly, the little party crossed the compound in the shadows, angling across toward the main gate which was in full view of the burning house.

Pritchard halted at the edge of the shadow and waited for the others to catch up. "There's no cover," he whispered to Dunbar. "We'll be in full view all the way to the gate."

"Can't be helped. Walk, don't run, and above all, keep quiet. There is enough going on that they might miss us unless a sudden movement catches their eye, or we make a noise. Get going now."

"What about your red coat, lieutenant? It's a bit obvious isn't it?"

Dunbar drew himself up. "It is the Queen's uniform, sir," he said stiffly.

Pritchard shrugged. "Fair enough. Here we go then." He calmly walked out into the light, the roaring flames from the house casting long black shadows to their front and right. Behind him walked the others, pace after pace, closer to the gate.

Dunbar, watching the mutineers as he walked, saw a man turn and look towards them for several long seconds before turning back to the fire again. He made no outcry and Dunbar sighed with relief.

They were within yards of the gate when Charles, walking beside his father, let out a piercing scream. Everyone froze and for a heartbeat or two the only sound was the roar of the flames. A musket cracked but Dunbar ignored it as a sepoy stumbled out of the shrubbery on the other side of the gate, his turban awry and blood streaking one side of his face and staining his beard.

"Leave him to me," Dunbar yelled, pushing the Reverend toward the gate as he leapt forward. "Run, all of you. Get to the church." He leveled the gun at the man stumbling toward them.

"Lieutenant Sahib, do not shoot. It is I, Gohindar Ras. You must flee sir." He stopped and looked at the Pritchard family as they ran past. "The ... the men, Sahib, they have mutinied, just like in Meerut."

Another musket cracked and the ball hit the wall a few feet away, ricocheting away with a waspish whine. Dunbar ignored it and the sound of running feet, concentrating on the face of the Naik who stood swaying in front of him. "Gohindar," he said softly. "Are you with me?"

"I am, Sahib. To the death."

345

Dunbar whirled and fired, one of the sepoys throwing up his arms with a despairing cry before crashing to the ground. He altered his aim and fired again, despite the musket ball that plucked at the lapel of his red jacket.

"I am thinking we should leave, Sahib," Gohindar said. He looked toward the deserted gate. "Perhaps we should be following the other sahibs?"

"Capital idea, Naik. Pick up that musket there and let us depart." Dunbar waited as Gohindar grabbed the fallen musket and a few scattered cartridges before running for the gate. He followed, snapping off another shot as the mutineers pressed forward again.

"Where are we going, Sahib?" Gohindar asked. "Are we heading for the cover of the hills?"

"For the church. It's about two hundred yards up there, now shut up and run." Dunbar demonstrated by racing off into the darkness of the road.

The Naik followed more slowly until musket balls started kicking up the dust around his feet. Then he caught up with the lieutenant. The church was a small square building made of rounded river stones mortared together into a sturdy structure. The open windows held no glass but had steeply sloping timber awnings designed to cast shade and keep the rain at bay. A single thick oak door gave access to the interior and the Reverend stood in the black opening, his white shirt glimmering slightly as he beckoned to Dunbar and the Naik. Behind him, the first faint buttery glow of an oil lantern lit the gloom within.

Dunbar and Gohindar ducked inside and pulled the door closed behind them. They dragged a heavy oaken pew across the stone-flagged floor and wedged the door shut.

Mopping at his brow with a crisp white handkerchief, Dunbar turned to face the people in the church, their faces pale and alarmed in the sputtering light of the single oil lamp. He grinned, seeing the uncertainty when they glanced at the Naik. "Don't worry, this is Naik Gohindar Ras. He's already had a disagreement with those bloody – pardon my French, ma'am – mutineers. He's a good man in a fight."

"I'm glad you are with us, Naik,' Pritchard said. "Lieutenant Dunbar, this is my church but I think it would be best if you took charge of the defence." He beckoned to Dunbar and guided him around the small stone chamber. "As you can see, it could be easy to defend or else a deathtrap. One entrance, a small window at about chest height at the front and two others each side but high up. At the back there is just the plain altar and two small windowless rooms where I store the Bibles and hymnals."

Dunbar considered. "No water supply, no latrines. Please don't take this personally sir, but we will be pissing in your church before long."

Pritchard grimaced. "Perhaps we should use one of the small rooms?"

"My thoughts exactly. We'll set one up as living quarters for your wife and son and the other as a latrine. I don't suppose you have any spare paper?"

"Having gone this far, I think I can spare a couple of the hymnals." He caught the lieutenant's eye. "Just use them with reverence."

Dunbar grinned. "A laugh always make a situation less grim, I always say."

"Sahib," Gohindar called softly. "There are men out on the road. I cannot see them, but I can hear them."

"Take the lamp back to the storeroom." Dunbar strode quickly to the small front window where Gohindar stood and peered cautiously around the edge.

"See where the stone wall ends, Sahib? I am thinking they are crouched down behind it."

"Then they know we are here," Dunbar said grimly. "Well, it may come to a fight. What do we have in the way of weapons, Naik?"

"I have the musket rifle, with nine cartridges. The Reverend Sahib has his little hunting gun with four cartridges and you have your revolver, sahib."

"With eight bullets. Not much to fight a battle with. Twenty-one ways of killing our enemies and maybe as many as eighteen of them left out there. I know I killed two. Maybe I wounded some." Dunbar turned from the window and sat down on the pew that blocked the door. He looked curiously at Gohindar, noting the bloody scalp wound and the bleeding marks of ropes at his wrists. "What happened to you? You were obviously with the men when they mutinied. Are they all as steadfast as that damn Prakash?"

"They asked me to join them and when I refused they tied me up. They are not very skillful at tying knots, Sahib. As for ringleaders, there are very few. Abdullah maybe but the others will follow them like sheep."

"Not Abdullah," Dunbar replied with a note of satisfaction. "He will be burning in his own special Muslim hell for breaking faith with the Company."

Pritchard came over and joined them by the door. "What's happening?" he whispered. "I feel like I should be doing something."

"Well, unless you want to try killing a few mutineers, I suggest you do what you do best. A few words to Him upstairs wouldn't hurt."

"Lieutenant, I would remind you that we are in the House of the Lord. Sometimes your language borders on the blasphemous."

"Pray for me then, Reverend. I have other things on my mind, like keeping us all alive."

Pritchard stared at the red-coated soldier before turning and striding up the aisle of the little church to the altar where he knelt in the shadows and bent his head in prayer.

"A strange man," Dunbar murmured. "Stay by this window, Gohindar. I will check on the others. Do not shoot unless you are certain of killing the man. We do not have nearly enough ammunition to satisfy me."

"Yes, sahib." Gohindar paused and looked around the darkened church. "Is this really the house of your God, as the Reverend Sahib said? It seems like something one of our ascetics would inhabit, without statues and pictures and no offerings left on the altar."

Dunbar paused and turned back. "That's what the Reverend would have us believe, Gohindar. For myself, I believe God is more likely to be found in the forests and the plains … and especially these beautiful mountains." He grinned, his teeth flashing pale in the dim light. "Now keep a sharp eye out, I have no wish to meet any gods before my time."

"Yes, sahib," Gohindar repeated, turning toward the window. He waited until the lieutenant was at the other end of the little church before adding, under his breath, "I do not think there is much danger of meeting any gods tonight. The Christian God must be out walking the hill trails, for I do not feel his presence in this pile of stones."

The night passed peacefully enough. The mutineers kept out of sight for the most part. Once or twice, Gohindar saw a fleeting form in the darkness but, mindful of their small stock of ammunition, refrained from chancing a shot. Toward dawn, after there had been no sound from outside for an hour, Dunbar woke the Pritchards' two Muslim servants and put them on guard duty, allowing Gohindar and himself to catch a little sleep. The flagstones were hard and cold, with a chill breeze blowing down off the mountains but at least they were spared the worst of the wind in their little stone structure.

Dawn flushed the grayness from the sky with delicate tones of pink and yellow. As the light grew to the point where one could tell the difference between a black thread and a white one, the Muslim definition of dawn, Dunbar saw activity on the road outside and knew that the mutineers were gathering for an onslaught.

"Enemy in sight," he called. "Clear the decks for action."

Pritchard approached with a gruff "Good morning" and risked a glance out of the front window. "What should I do?"

"Same as before, Reverend. Take everyone back into the storeroom and guard that. Take your fowling piece and see if you can find the will to use it."

"I cannot kill my fellow man, Dunbar. I am a man of peace."

"Think about what they'll do to your wife and child if they get past the Naik and me."

"They are coming, sahibs," Gohindar called. He raised the musket and fired, the explosion reverberating off the stone walls of the church. "I hit him, sahibs." He ducked back and ripped at a cartridge with his teeth, reloading the musket quickly.

Dunbar drew a bead on a running man with his revolver and squeezed the trigger gently, nodding with satisfaction as the man collapsed without a cry. He swung toward another one but as he fired, a musket ball slammed into the wall next to him filling the air with tiny shards of stone and peppering his face. His own shot missed and he swore, running his hand over his face, smearing blood over it in a grotesque mask.

A ragged volley ripped through the open window and ricocheted off the stonework. Screams came from the back room and Dunbar yelled out "Anyone hurt?"

"It's alright," Pritchard called back. "A near miss."

When the musket fire died away, Gohindar risked another look and almost immediately another shot. Sheltering behind the wall of the church again, he reloaded. Dunbar scanned the narrow view from the window and frowned.

"Where are they? I can hear them but I can't see them."

"I am smelling smoke, Sahib."

Dunbar looked up to the rafters and the dim recesses of the high ceiling. "Reverend?" he called out. "What is the roof made of?"

351

"Wood shingles. Cypress, I think. Why?"

"No reason. Just wondering." Dunbar caught the Naik's puzzled look and shrugged. "No point worrying the woman and child, there's nothing we can do about it."

Pritchard came out of the back room and ran over to the front of the church, doubled over. He carried a bottle of water and some bread and cheese. He handed them to Dunbar. "You are worried about fire, aren't you?"

Dunbar nodded. He bit into the bread and cheese and passed it to Gohindar. "Gohindar can smell smoke," he said around his mouthful. "I did not want to cause alarm but they may be firing the roof."

"And if they are? What can we do?"

"Absolutely nothing, so let's just wait and see." Dunbar accepted the food back from Gohindar and took another bite.

Pritchard considered for several minutes. "How long do we wait? I mean, how long before rescue arrives? You were supposed to bring us in. What happens when we don't turn up?"

Dunbar took a long drink of water before answering. "Good question. Let's see. Today's Sunday. Nothing on God's good earth is going to shift you on a Sunday, so they will assume we left first thing Monday morning. It's about a day and a half to Almora, bringing us to midday Tuesday. They will wait at least until Thursday morning before there is any major concern. If we are lucky they leave on Friday, arriving here Saturday." Dunbar smiled wryly. "Rescue is about a week away."

"Can we last a week?"

"Not a hope, old chap. We have food for about four days if we ration ourselves and water for two. That's if

352

they leave us alone. My guess is they have fired the door and will rush us when it burns through."

"Then what?"

"Use your imagination, Reverend. We take as many of them with us as we can before they kill us."

"Dear God," Pritchard muttered. "There must be something we can do." He turned and wandered back to his family, muttering to himself.

"There is smoke coming under the door, Sahib. I am very much worried that you are right in your surmise."

"D'you know any good Hindu gods to pray to, Gohindar? My god doesn't seem to be listening. Not even to the good Reverend."

"There is one who might, but he is a very small god, Sahib, and may not have much power in this situation in which we are finding ourselves."

Dunbar grinned. "No matter, pray away. What's his name anyway?"

Gohindar hesitated. "He sometimes goes by the name of Pashupati but he says he has not been a god very long."

"Really? Well, the name is not as important as the deed. Ask your god if he will aid us."

The wood of the door started to buckle and blacken and billows of smoke poured through the gap at the bottom. Dunbar and Gohindar drew back to near the altar and piled the pews up in two uneven stacks, one across the entrance to the storeroom where the others sheltered, and the other by the altar.

"Now's the time to use that fowling piece, Pritchard."

"I told you I will not kill a man."

"Then you and your family will die. Give it to one of your servants then. Maybe one of them is prepared to defend you."

A segment of the door fell inward with a crash and a shower of sparks.

"Get ready," Dunbar growled.

The remains of the door slammed open and several men rushed in, their muskets leveled and bayonets fixed. Behind him Dunbar heard the sharp report of the fowling piece but he could see no visible effect. Then he was firing and men fell, to be replaced by others. The muskets roared and he felt a ball strike his side, scoring a line of fire across his ribs. A musket flashed beside him, then Gohindar pitched backward onto the flagstones and lay still. Dunbar cursed and fired again but his aim was spoiled by the onrushing steel of the bayonets, one piercing his upper arm and a musket butt ramming into his chest. He went down, his revolver skittering over the stone floor and he saw the fowling piece grabbed from Khalim's hands. Screams erupted from the little room and he saw the servant Muhammad stagger back with a bayonet thrust in his gut. Pritchard grappled with a sepoy and others leapt onto his wife and son. A musket butt descended on his head and Dunbar collapsed face down on the flagstones.

Vasu yelled in triumph and raised his bayonet high, preparing to stab down into his red-coated foe. Other sepoys pulled the stack of pews in front of the storeroom apart and hauled out the defenceless people. They threw them to the floor with savage yells of delight.

"Hold!" Prakash knocked Vasu's arm up and strode to face his men. "We do not kill anyone."

354

"What are you talking about?" asked Haamid. "That is what we came to do and many of our brothers lie dead. I say we kill them all."

Prakash held his head and closed his eyes for a moment, as if thinking. "And I say we do not. Who is leader here, Haamid? Do you think to see yourself as Subedar?"

"Why not, if you are losing your courage?" Haamid strutted in front of the men. "What do you say, men? Will you follow me, or …"

"Silence!" Prakash screamed. His eyes bulged and his hand closed convulsively around the stock of his musket. "I will not be questioned …" A musket shot crashed out and Haamid collapsed backward with a bloody hole in his chest. Prakash strode up to the body and kicked it violently.

"Does anyone else dispute my decision?" Nobody answered. "Good. Tie them all up securely and put them in this little room. Then stack these … these benches over the entrance." He watched as his orders were carried out. "Raju, go and get Dunbar Sah … the officer's horse and bring it here."

Vasu looked at Prakash with alarm and some curiosity. "What are you planning, Prakash?"

"Are you my Havildar that I must tell you what I am doing?"

Vasu shrugged and turned away, careful to keep his musket averted. "I am just thinking that …"

"Do not. Leave the thinking to me, Vasu, all of you." The sound of running feet and of trotting hooves came from the road outside. "I have something that needs to be done. While I am gone, nobody is to stay on guard over these prisoners. They are to be left alone. You will go back to the camp in the compound and stay there until I return. You may occupy yourselves by tending to our dead and wounded. Do you understand?"

"But what if the prisoners escape?" The sepoy who asked blanched as Prakash swung his musket toward him. "I … I understand," he stammered.

Prakash watched the sepoys leave the church and start wandering up the road toward the compound. Villagers were up and about now and several were standing about fifty yards away, watching what was happening. Prakash called out to them in the local dialect. "Do not be concerned. There has been some fighting but it is over now. There will be no church meeting this morning so there is no need to enter this building." He turned away, knowing they would enter as soon as he left. Swinging himself up onto Dunbar's horse he ordered Raju back to the compound and dug his heels into its sides. Within minutes he had galloped through the village and off onto the road to Almora.

The day passed relatively quietly. Within minutes of Prakash's departure, the villagers entered the church and released the prisoners in the tiny back room. They tended to their wounds and fed them, then, as the sepoys remained in the Mission compound, smuggled the Sahibs, the Naik and the Pritchards' Muslim servant to the village and hid them. As they trooped out of the church, stepping over the charred and ashen remains of the door; Gohindar Ras plucked at Dunbar's coat.

"Sahib, what has happened? Has he gone?"

"Prakash? Yes, he took my horse and scarpered. The other sepoys are back in the compound for some reason."

Dunbar did not accompany the others to the village. "I have to keep an eye on the sepoys. There's no telling what mischief they'll get up to."

"You don't have a gun," Pritchard observed. "They'll kill you if they see you. Come to the village with us. Rescue should only be a week, you said so yourself."

"Duty, old chap. Don't worry, I'll be discreet." Dunbar took off his red coat and bundled it inside out under his arm.

Toward nightfall, he saw the sepoys cremate the fallen soldiers, the fires lighting the compound like day. Afterward, the mutineers returned to their tents and slept, without even setting sentries. Dunbar considered creeping in and stealing a musket and ammunition, but decided the risk was too great. The personal danger was acceptable, but if he failed, the sepoys could go on the rampage again and they might kill the missionaries this time.

Gohindar brought him food and a mug of hot sweet tea at dawn and together they watched the mutineers. The sepoys became increasingly agitated as morning became afternoon and there was no sign of their leader Prakash. Arguments broke out and a few fights erupted. Dunbar hoped that if things got sufficiently out of hand, there might be an opportunity to intervene and wrest control away from the mutineers.

The sound of horses' hooves sounded faintly on the road from Almora. Dunbar looked at Gohindar in alarm. "Has Prakash brought more mutineers? It is too soon for rescue."

Gohindar listened again. "Those are cavalry mounts, sahib, ridden fast by people who know their business."

"You are right. Come on." Dunbar raced down toward the road, shaking out his coat as he went. He burst out of the scrub as a large detachment of mounted soldiers appeared, galloping up the road from the village. At their head was a cavalry major, his Risaldar by his side. The major reined in hard as he caught sight of the two men by the side of the road. As the riders slowed he waved the Risaldar on toward the compound before turning to the disheveled man in a stained red coat.

"You are out of uniform … Lieutenant."

"Yes sir. Sorry sir." Dunbar saluted crisply and held it until the major returned it. "Lieutenant Dunbar, sir. This is Naik Ras."

The major glanced at the Naik, then back to Dunbar who was finishing buttoning his coat. "Porter's the name. Second Bengal Lancers under Colonel Creighton. By a stroke of luck we'd just got into Almora when your messenger arrived." A volley of shots from the compound did not even make his eyes flicker. "I think we've cleaned up your mess for you, Dunbar."

"Thank you, sir. Er … what messenger?"

"That sepoy you sent. What was his name, Prakash or something? He reported a mutiny and then had the audacity to claim to be the ringleader. Well, we locked him up smartish and got over here as fast as we could. Where are the Reverend and his family?"

"In the village, sir. I sent them there for safety and came out here to watch the mutineers."

"And you took off your coat so it wouldn't be seen?" Major Porter asked. "Good show." He looked toward the

358

compound. "We'll get you a mount and then we'd better see about escorting the Reverend back to Almora." He turned his horse and trotted off toward the Mission compound.

"What the hell was that all about, Gohindar? What would make Prakash turn himself in?"

Naik Gohindar Ras grinned. "I am thinking my little god Pashupati answered my prayers, by golly."

Chapter Eighteen

The British called it 'The Indian Mutiny' and retaliated with a savagery that made many who had not supported the uprising listen to the murmurings that continued under the noses of the foreign overlords. In the minds of Indian patriots, the years of 1857 to 1858 became known as the 'First War of Independence'. There was no way that First War could have succeeded though. The country was too disorganized; the British, though only some thirty-five thousand strong within India, had the resources of an Empire to call upon. The rapidity with which they crushed the uprising spoke of their determination and ability.

I was torn in opposing ways that year. For twenty years I had stayed close to British officers, possessing them on occasion, but more often just laying low and keeping an eye on their actions. Captain Sleeman was the first British officer I knew, my Lieutenant Dunbar about the fiftieth. I have to say that in the British, as in my own countrymen, there are good and bad. Some, like Sleeman and Dunbar, were decent men who did their best for the people around them. They endeavored to leave the world a better place for having been there. I cannot fault them on that, though they did show an annoying tendency to treat us 'natives' as nothing more than overgrown children. I came to see that this paternalistic view was commonplace and stemmed from their odd idea that they were inherently superior to every other race. Their holy men, people like the Reverend Pritchard, were even worse. They honestly believed that their Trimurti; their

Brahma, Vishnu, Shiva; whom they call Father, Son, Ghost, was actually an Englishman.

I should explain that Britain is made up of several nations but the highest of these are the English who can be likened to our Brahmins. Their warrior caste seems to be mostly nations they call Irish or Scottish. They have a Dalit caste too, an untouchable, whom they call 'colonial' and the disdain of the English for these untouchables is immense. Yet even these colonials are thought to be superior to the humble Hindu and Muslim of this beautiful land. Only those British who come from England or who have been trained and educated in England are eligible for the highest positions in our land. In the middle are the British who are not English, and at the bottom are the rightful inhabitants of India. I was confused when I first heard these ideas and if my explanation does not help you then the fault is mine for I must still be confused.

Why then, if I believe so much in this land that gave rise to me, did I support the British and help them in the uprising? Perhaps because, having possessed so many officers and sepoys, having access to so many ideas and influences, I could see a wider landscape. Perhaps I delude myself, but I believe that if the uprising had not been put down quickly, the anger of the British would have crushed India's fledgling independence. There would have been such a reign of horror and misery instituted by the reconquerors of our land that hundreds of years may have passed before freedom came. India was divided in 1857 into religions and princely states and warring factions. We had not learned to think together, to act in unity.

I possessed Naik Gohindar Ras a year before the uprising, when he was still one of the ordinary sepoys. As such, he was privy to much of the disquiet and grumblings that had been eating away at the men's morale for so long. I cannot say for sure whether there was any basis for the belief that the cartridge grease was contaminated by beef lard or pig fat. Certainly some cartridges were greased with the products of unclean animals but I could never find a mind that unequivocally admitted to doing it deliberately. Some senior officers knew of the sometime contamination but dismissed concerns as overblown and unimportant. Cow and pig were not unclean for a Christian so Muslim and Hindu concerns took on a flavor of unreasonableness.

Following on from the belief that the British intended this profanity was another incident that had not yet touched the hill stations. Salt was carried up from the sea at great expense and with great effort. A tax on salt incidentally produced considerable revenues for the British but the trouble arose when it was noticed the salt had a reddish tinge. Some immediately thought of contamination, not with fat but with blood. This was one more attempt by the perfidious British to profane the two great religions of India. There was no factual content to this rumor, however. The reddish tinge came from ochre which had been used to mark the bags.

Gohindar Ras benefited from my presence within him. I have learned that there are two methods of possession, each with their advantages and drawbacks. If I move in quietly and dig deep, hiding in the inner recesses of mind and body, I can remain undetected indefinitely. Unfortunately, this limits me if I am trying to find out things beyond the immediate range of the person's senses. The other way is to make my presence known, dipping into memory and emotion at will. The drawback here is that a person has an unreasoning fear of being possessed by a demon and fights me every step of the way. It is an unequal battle, of course, but I do not want to be ever vigilant in case my desires and actions are compromised. So I have developed a ruse. I pretend to be a god.

Now you may not think that is much of a ruse. A Christian or a Muslim, wedded so strongly to the idea of a single deity, would immediately assume I was a demon, afrit or djinn and seek to expel me. Exorcism piqued my interest when terrified men first tried it, bringing in their priests and holy men to invoke their god, seeking to drive me out. The Christian and Muslim god was not listening, or else he cannot act outside of the lands of his own peoples, but he did not trouble me. I withdrew from my possession, not because I was driven out, but because I could not hope to achieve anything with all that noise going on. So the priests claimed success, the possessed was freed of a demon and a lot of money, and I learned much. The gods really have withdrawn from this beautiful land, leaving me free to become the god of my choosing.

I told Gohindar Ras that I was a minor god and that I required the use of his body for a while for my own unspecified purposes. I offered him inducements of course, and he quickly saw the benefits that could result from my presence. In fact, I brought him promotion, helped him win at dice by subtle manipulation of his hand and arm muscles, and opened his eyes to a wider world than his squalid village and the army barracks at Almora. I even saved his life twice. The first time was on patrol when a bandit shot at him. I grabbed control of his muscles and flung him to one side, the musket ball passing within a finger width of his head. The other time was in the Haldwani barracks when cholera swept through the army lines. Gohindar collapsed, squirting watery diarrhea and doubling up with severe cramps. I have cleansed the little boxes of a man's body before, sweeping out the dust that invades them. This time, my knowledge had grown and I knew the boxes to be cells and the dust to be invading organisms, bacteria that lodged in the walls of my host's intestine and produced those deadly symptoms. It took a day, but I was intimately associated with Gohindar's gut and I do not need rest. The doctors were amazed at his swift recovery and put it down to their own clumsy ministrations.

Gohindar knew better though, and it was from that day that he truly believed me to be a god. He fell to his knees and worshiped me as Rudra the healer. Though Rudra is also ruler of the demons and an aspect of Shiva, I did not welcome being identified with this 'black and furious' god, a dealer in violence. I informed Gohindra, manifesting myself by bringing a leopard out of the forest to lie down at his feet, that I was a gentler aspect of Rudra and that I preferred the appellation of Pashupati, lord of animals. I further told him, not wanting to be a dishonest deity, that I had not always been a god and that he should not always rely on me to save him. He must learn to care for his own body and life.

As a start, I revealed to him the contaminated water source that housed the cholera bacterium. He took this knowledge to the Regimental Sergeant-Major, one of the bad British who can see no good thing ever coming from a native. He dismissed the idea of a water-borne disease as 'poppycock' and had it not been for one of the junior doctors recently out from London where he had worked under Doctor John Snow, the cholera might have killed many more. The young doctor made the connection and identified the source of the contamination, earning him the commendation of the Colonel. Generously, the doctor revealed the source of the information and Gohindar was promoted to Naik in Dunbar's platoon of sepoys.

As I have said, I was privy, through Gohindar, to a lot of the rumor and discontent within the ranks of the sepoys. When my host was promoted to Naik, that comradeship he enjoyed with the common soldier was lost. They saw Gohindar starting up the slope toward command and resented it, cutting him out of their grumblings and discussions. Then Prakash was transferred from a Delhi command a scant month before the uprising and started his work within the ranks of basically loyal troops. Not being able to listen in, I missed the significance of Prakash and was taken by surprise when he instigated the rebellion in Ganai. I declined to interfere, not lending Gohindar my strength and vitality, as I wanted to see what would happen. Only if his life was threatened would I step in.

As it turned out, he was not in any real danger as Prakash was the only sepoy with a desire to shed blood. The others were pulled in by the excitement but at the early stages still had proper regard for the native officers set over them. Alone in the tent after Gohindar was tied up and left unconscious, I awakened him and burst his bonds, suggesting he warn Dunbar immediately. Gohindar had a great respect bordering on love for his Lieutenant and wanted to blindly follow his lead and I was content again but when the fire was set and the sepoys charged the church, I knew I had to act. Besides, gohindar actually prayed to me to save them. I did not want any of the little group to die, but I could not save Muhammad. I suppose I was not a very effective god but I was new to the profession.

As the group in the church was overwhelmed, I saw that one man was pivotal. Prakash held all the power and I knew the hate in him would lead to the shedding of blood, so I left Gohindar and entered the rebel leader.

His own actions threw him into confusion, and this led in turn to a great anger. When Haamid questioned him he lost his temper and killed as casually as one might crush a tick. I controlled him a few moments later and did not let up for the rest of that day. I had to get the sepoys to leave their captives unguarded, so I intimated to Prakash that keeping the foreigners separate would lessen the chances of any of the sepoys getting ideas of his own. I then forced him to ride Dunbar's horse to Almora, and to his horror, let him watch as I surrendered 'our' body to the authorities, admitting everything. Leaving Prakash whimpering in terror of the rope, I returned to Ganai before Major Porter had even started out on his rescue mission. I had a Naik to look after.

Watching him though, as he waited with his lieutenant, I knew my intimate association with him was over. It was time to be a god and go out into my mountainous realm and do godly things. I would be Pashupati, Lord and Protector of Animals, and if people also mistook me for Dhanvantari the Healer, I would not object.

Are our actions truly our own, or are we guided into the paths we take? When I first fled through these glorious mountains and valleys of Garhwal and Kumaon, on my way to Mount Kailasa, so many centuries ago, I had noted that radiant beauty, Nanda Devi. I knew then she was a part of my life and I was drawn to her again, fifty years after the Mutiny.

Chapter Nineteen

Nanda Devi, Goddess of Bliss of the Himalaya, stood proud and tall, her snow-covered towers of rock ripping a thin trail of cloud from the azure sky. Below her, gathered around like courtiers or worshipers, stood a dozen or more searing pinnacles of rock, each a massive upthrust of stone that awed the minds of men who looked upon their beauty, yet each less imposing, less magnificent, than the soaring beauty of the Goddess.

Pandalis, a short, wiry mountain man, a Pahari, of rugged good looks and indeterminate age, stood on the trail that led up through the low rhododendron and broadleaf forest of the lower slopes and stared up through the gaps in the foliage toward his first glimpse of the dazzling whiteness of Nanda Devi. He smiled, showing perfect white teeth, and his deep-set brown eyes sparkled with pleasure. Stroking his jet-black mustache, the same color as the wavy locks on his head, he murmured a few words of greeting before resuming his upward climb.

The man seemed to move leisurely, yet his legs measured out the distance, his paces devouring the trail as it wound up through the trees, into areas of low scrub and then out onto a broad slope of tussock grass and loose scree. He looked up once more, but Nanda Devi hid herself behind the intervening walls of rock that were her first bastion of defence. Seemingly impregnable, like the stone walls of a great city, the rock face towered above Pandalis, rising sheer and precipitous. He searched the rock face, noting the presence of tiny plants clinging to the surface, a faint shadowing in the stone that spoke of a crevice, a crack, maybe just a hair-thin split that allowed tenacious life a tenuous hold. He knew he could use these cracks, these minute toe and finger holds to scale the great face for, he admitted to himself, his skill was great, but today he chose the easier, if still demanding, climb up the river pass.

Pandalis turned away and set off along the path that now skirted the cliffs, heading northeastward, away from the rushing Rishi Ganga River, and toward the trail from the village of Lata and the narrow Dharansi Pass. Many passed this way, even beyond the Pass, but few managed the rigors of the trail beyond the second barrier of the Rishi Gorge, the inner defences the Goddess had thrown up to preserve her privacy and sanctity. At the proper time, every twelve years, a procession of devout worshipers would brave the altitude and precipitous path to honor the Goddess in her inner fastness, but that time was not yet. Pandalis knew that when he attained the inner basin with its pristine meadows, he would have the place to himself. Alone, he would commune with the Goddess who had always been a part of his life.

The path he followed intersected the one from Lata and he turned eastward toward Dharansi. The land steepened and presently he found himself climbing, clambering up the rough track and over tumbled boulders, the loose stony soil slipping beneath his sandaled feet. Though his breath came no faster for his exertions, Pandalis stopped often, drinking in the cool air and the vistas that slowly unfolded beneath him. He came across a tiny streamlet cascading down the steep slope, its meager waters jostling and leaping as if enthusiasm could make up for its lack of size. Kneeling beside the water course, Pandalis stared into a pool between the rocks, admiring the colored pebbles stirred by the vigor of the water's passage. He scooped a handful of the cold liquid and sipped, not thirsty, but appreciating its crystal purity. Rising again, he murmured thanks to Nanda Devi and moved on.

Dharansi Pass was barren, a lip of worn rock between the shoulders of the ridge, the path leading on through tussock grasses and low herbs toward the pastures that lay between the two walls of defensive rock. Footprints of goat and sheep, scattered droppings, told of the passage of small herds into these grasslands ahead of him. Mentally, Pandalis shrugged. He would prefer to enjoy the solitude of the valley that lay before him, but the shepherds relied on these pastures for their survival and he would not begrudge their presence. To one who fostered the proper frame of mind, solitude could be found within a chattering crowd.

The flocks grazed a mile or two further on, feeding contentedly on the rich meadow plants. The goats, for that is what this flock proved to be, raised wary heads and contemplated the stranger entering their domain, then with a bleat of recognition; one old buck recognized Pandalis and trotted toward him. The goat stretched upward, nose quivering, and then lowered its head to butt the man affectionately. Pandalis smiled and rested a hand gently on the animal's head for a moment before moving on, leaving the goat staring after him in bemusement. The goatherd, a young lad of few years but greater responsibility, approached slowly and bent his head, hands together.

"Namaste, Pandalis. It is good to see you again."

"And you, Johar. Namaste, and peace be with you. Are you alone up here?"

The lad nodded. "Just me and my goats, Pandalis." He grinned and pointed back down the trail to where the old buck still stood staring up at them. "Rama remembers you."

"I remember him too, Johar. I was treading these paths before either of you were born."

"Are you hungry? I have some bread and cheese."

"Thank you, but no. My hunger is satisfied by the sight of the Goddess of Bliss. I will leave you to your duties."

"Namaste, Pandalis." The lad bowed again. "There is another man ahead of you, a sahib."

Pandalis raised his eyebrows. "A white man? An Englishman? Is he alone?"

"I do not know what race he belongs to, Pandalis. They all look alike to me with their pale skins and red faces, but he was polite and spoke our tongue well."

"When did you see him?"

"Ten days ago, in Lata. He purchased cracked barley, some butter and tea. He said he was climbing to Dharansi and left before I, so I presume he is somewhere ahead of me."

"Did he say his name? Was it Longstaff?"

Johar shrugged. "He did not say and who am I to question a sahib? Do you know this 'long staff'?"

"I was here with him and other Englishmen two years ago when they tried to find a way up the Rishi Gorge." Pandalis smiled. "I managed to obscure the path sufficiently and they gave up."

371

"Why do the sahibs come? Is it to worship the Goddess?"

"No. They look at all this," Pandalis waved a hand at the surrounding pillars of rock and snow that lanced the blue sky, "and believe it is just rock to climb and conquer. They have no understanding and little appreciation."

"One could pity them," Johar ventured.

"Indeed. Well, perhaps I will find this traveler and talk with him. May the Goddess protect you and your herd, Johar." Pandalis took his leave and walked on up the path that followed the rushing Rishi Ganga River toward the towering ramparts of the Gorge, still many miles away. He found the Englishman, for that is what he proved to be, where the land starts to rise steeply once more.

The Englishman had made a temporary camp by the side of the trail, at a point where it dipped toward the turbulent waters of the Rishi Ganga. He sat on a boulder with a battered metal mug in his hands, steam arising from the hot tea, and looking out over the river toward the cliffs of the inner rampart. A stone clattered softly on the path above him and he looked round quickly. When he saw the mountain man, he rose to his feet, revealing a long thin body clothed in a red plaid shirt, khaki shorts and battered hiking boots. Thin gray hair sprawled sparsely over the spotted dome of his skull and he looked out through watery blue eyes.

"Namaste," the Englishman said in a thin but clear voice. "May the peace of the Goddess be upon thee," he added in the local dialect. "I have little to offer but you are welcome to what I have."

372

Pandalis greeted him in turn. "Thank you. Perhaps I might be permitted to enjoy the warmth of your fire?"

The Englishman moved away from the boulder and gestured for Pandalis to sit. "Tea?" he asked. "I have just made some."

Pandalis inclined his head in gracious acceptance and took the small shallow pannier that the Englishman produced from his pack, pouring the hot dark liquid from the pot resting in the embers of the small fire. He sipped and nodded appreciatively before setting the pannier down.

The two men sat in silence for a time, though neither looked in the least bit uncomfortable. At last, Pandalis stirred.

"Why do you come here, Englishman? Is it to climb our mountains, to set your little flags on their summits?"

"No. I would not desecrate their purity by setting foot on them. I come merely to see them and, if the Goddess of Bliss permits, to sit at her feet and contemplate her beauty."

"I am amazed, Englishman, for I thought that all your kind came to claim our land, seeking that which could be carried away, setting your flag, your king and your God over that which remains."

The Englishman smiled ruefully. "My people do tend to do those things, but not all of us. I am a stranger in your land and I beg your hospitality that I may see wonders."

"Not all who seek wonders are grateful afterward," Pandalis murmured. "What is your name, Englishman?"

A raised eyebrow … "You are direct, unlike most Pahari I have met. However, that is no bad thing between men. My name is Wilfred Banks."

"You are British Army?"

"Once, when I wore a younger man's body. Now I wander these hills, seeking enlightenment." Banks looked at the other man, his pale blue eyes seeking meaning in the Pahari's dark brown ones. "May I ask your name?"

"Pandalis."

"I am honored to make your acquaintance, Pandalis."

"And I yours, Wilfred Banks."

Banks paused and for a few moments appeared to struggle in his mind. "Forgive me if I presume upon our recent acquaintance but I note that you do not call me 'sahib' like every other nat … member of your race."

"'Sahib' is a word of subservience, and I am subservient to no man. We are given names that others may know us. We have exchanged ours and I see no need to bow before you, save as I would to any man who showed me kindness."

"Well said, Pandalis. I, too, have no need of princes or lords or any that would raise themselves above their fellow men. I seek no honors, no titles."

Pandalis nodded and sat silently for a bit, while the embers of the fire burned down to ash. "You said you came to sit at the feet of the Goddess of Bliss. Are you not a Christian, Wilfred Banks? My understanding is that Christians believe all other forms of worship to be false."

"Then perhaps I am not a Christian, for I believe there are many paths a man might take. The path of Christ is one, that of Muhammad another, and the Way of

374

Buddha yet another. I would not presume to believe any one of these is right and the others wrong."

"Yet the first two follow one God and Buddha none. What then of the myriad Hindu gods?"

"You know better than I that Trimurti represents the three aspects of godhead – creation, sustenance and destruction – and that all other gods are but lesser aspects of the three. God, whatever men choose to call him or her, is the universe and all creatures are called back to oneness in the end."

Pandalis laughed. "You sound like a Buddhist teacher I once knew. Do you follow the Eightfold Path?"

"I try, but I am an old man and I fear I will not have much longer in which to perfect myself."

Pandalis scanned the man sitting in front of him, noting the slack, spotted wrinkles of skin stretched over the spare frame of bone. The hands of the man betrayed a faint tremor and he knew the man was indeed old.

"Eighty-three," Banks said softly, in answer to the unspoken question.

"In this life."

"You believe we are born into another?"

"So we are taught."

Banks sighed. "I hope you are right, though I have never spoken with a man who has lived before. I would like to be young again, to enjoy these beautiful mountains. Maybe if God is merciful I will be born as a Pahari like yourself."

"You would not want to be as I am, Wilfred Banks. But that is in the hands of such gods as there are. I, too, have never known a man who lived before but I have known one or two that were holy enough that they might achieve that destiny."

"You have traveled far in these hills?"

"And outside them on occasion, though never outside India. I feel myself drawn back to Garhwal and Kumaon whenever I stray. This is my home, especially Nanda Devi."

"You live here?"

Pandalis grinned, showing white teeth. "Only the gods live on the high peaks. I come here as often as I can, as I have always done ever since I first was granted the sight of her flawless beauty."

"Tell me about it – how you first saw her."

Pandalis sat in silence for a long time, so long that Banks started to think he would not answer. At length, he stirred and looked away over his shoulder toward the position of the hidden mountain. "It was a long time ago, so long I think it must have happened to another man, or else I have truly lived before. I remember the plains and fleeing one who would kill me. I journeyed far and came at last to these mountains where Nanda Devi spreads out her glory. My enemy still pursued me so I fled onward, but later I recollected the beauty and returned. I always return to the crystal air and the pristine snows."

"You have the spirit of a poet, Pandalis."

"I am a simple man, Wilfred Banks. And what of you? When were you blessed by the Goddess of Bliss?"

Banks sighed. "I hesitate to admit it for I must surely lessen myself in your eyes. I came to your country as a young man, a soldier in the service of Queen and Country. After twelve years I found myself in Almora at the time of what is called the Mutiny."

"Did you know a Captain Dunbar?"

"Dunbar?" Banks screwed up his thin face in concentration, his pale eyes unfocusing. "It has been a long time ..."

"It is of no importance. Please go on, Wilfrid Banks. Tell me of Nanda Devi."

Banks nodded. "You can see Nanda Devi from Almora, a white peak rising in the distance as part of the ramparts that protect the land of the gods. I fell in love with her at first sight. I yearned to travel to the high hills and get to know this beautiful land but I was posted to Delhi after the Mutiny was put down, and thence to Madras, Kalicutt and Mandalay. When my term in the army expired I tried to return to the hills but I had signed up in England, so to England I must return. I found what employment I could and dreamt of Nanda Devi, of walking the paths of her hills and valleys, especially here in her very lap."

"Now who is the poet, Wilfrid Banks?" Pandalis chuckled. "Go on. How did you return?"

"I retired in eighteen eighty-eight, twenty years ago next month. I had a small amount saved so ..."

"You had a wife? Sons?"

Banks shook his head. "There was a girl once ..." He fell silent for several minutes before shaking his head again. "She was the daughter of a general and I was a lowly Captain without prospects. It would never have worked." The old man smiled. "If I had married her I would never have had the freedom to return to India. I booked passage to Bombay and landed six months later with fifty pounds and a change of clothes. I set off for the hills on foot and I have been wandering ever since."

"But you have waited twenty years to visit Nanda Devi?"

Banks stared at the Pahari in amusement. "Did I not say I fell in love when I first saw her? This was my first destination, but I could not get close. Her companions guard her jealously – Dunagiri, Changabang, Mangraon, Maiktoli, Trisul. I have walked completely around her, seen her from every angle, searching the cliffs and precipices, the ravines and rubble slopes for a way in, but until three years ago I could not even get this far. I followed Longstaff, Mumm and Bruce as they forced the Dharansi Pass in their first attempt but they were blocked by the Rishi Gorge. Two years ago I studied their routes again but with no greater success. The same last year. This year I mean to find a way through the gorge to the headwaters of the Rishi Ganga where it springs from the flanks of Nanda Devi."

"Many have died looking to force the gorge," Pandalis observed.

"I know, yet it can be done."

"Are you sure? Perhaps the gods keep the inner valleys secret for a reason."

Banks shook his gray head. "The Goddess would not reveal herself if she did not want to be approached. She is looking for a man of courage."

"And you are that man?"

"If the Goddess wills it."

"Then if you will permit, Wilfred Banks, I will accompany you a little way that I may observe your efforts."

The setting sun lit up the clouds and snow-covered rock walls of the eastern edge of the great massif and the shadows of the lower curtain wall of Dharansi and Malathuni spread out over the valley floor. The chill air became suddenly colder and Banks set about making camp in the lee of a cluster of large boulders above the spray of the roaring Rishi Ganga. There was little wood available in these heights but Pandalis found dry twigs of juniper and crumbled droppings of goat and deer. The fire burnt sullenly and gave off acrid smoke, but it heated the two men during the night as they huddled beneath the raw and icy clear night skies, the stars blazing down like crystals of ice swept by the wind from Nanda Devi's slopes.

They shared a blanket and as the Englishman slept, Pandalis looked at him carefully, examining the thin body and bony face, feeling the man's age. He frowned, knowing this foreigner did not have the strength to survive what lay ahead.

Banks woke in the early dawn to find Pandalis crouched by the rekindled fire, stirring a small pot of tea mixed with cracked barley and butter. The smell awoke his taste buds and he felt a rush of saliva to his mouth. Murmuring a greeting, he tossed the blanket aside and slowly climbed to his feet, grimacing at the pain in his stiff joints and aching muscles. He went to one side, behind the boulders, and urinated before walking slowly to the edge of the river where the calmer water had congealed into a thin rime of ice. He washed, tossing the frigid water into his face, before tottering back to the small fire. Accepting a cup of the tsampa, he spooned the hot cereal into his mouth with shaking hands.

"You are not eating, Pandalis?"

"I did so before you woke."

Banks nodded, though he eyed the level of the porridge in the pot doubtfully. He scraped up the last smears with a bony finger and waved away the offer of more. "Time we were moving on. I want to be at the foot of the gorge while there is still some light."

With his battered rucksack on his back, Banks stood in the bright morning sunlight, soaking up the meager warmth while he stared toward the rim wall and the jagged slash of the gorge. He set off up the trail, maintaining a remarkably fast pace for such an old man. Pandalis had no difficulty keeping up though, following a dozen paces behind the Englishman and keeping a watchful eye on him, especially where the track became steep or narrow. Their journey proved uneventful and they brewed tea in a small glade sheltered from the chilling northeasterly breeze off the Rhamani glacier. They reached the bottom of a great slab of rock broken from the cliff face in the late afternoon, as the long shadows from Dharansi reached out for them.

Banks pointed up at the cliffs. "The path lies there, I am convinced of it. See where the track hugs the cliffs before heading into the gorge? There are slabs of rock like this one, steeply sloping, and the track no more than a hint across the slippery surface. Lose your footing and nothing will stop your slide into death."

"And then you are through the gorge?" Pandalis fixed his dark eyes on Bank's pale blue ones.

The Englishman laughed thinly. "The slabs are but the first obstacle. Then comes the staircase, a narrow path more suitable for a mountain goat than a man, thinning to a mere crack in places. It angles up the sheer wall of the gorge. That is as far as I have been, Pandalis, but there was a chimney at the end that may lead upward. I mean to try it."

"A chimney, Wilfred Banks?" Pandalis asked. "What do you mean? Has someone built a house there?"

"A chimney is a vertical crack in the rock big enough to get into. They can be climbed with care."

"Would it not be easier to follow the course of the river? You know that goes through to the uplands. Maybe the chimney and the staircase do not."

Banks shook his head. "Nothing can live in the Rishi gorge bed. It would be like trying to climb a raging waterfall. No, this is the only path. Now," he looked around in the fading light. "We need to make camp. I intend to be climbing at first light."

The Englishman held fast to his determination and at first light breakfasted on more tsampa and checked his boots and clothing. "I have no ropes or climbing equipment, Pandalis. Today is the culmination of my life. Either I succeed in my attempt or I die." He smiled and clapped the Pahari on the shoulder. "I thank you for your company, but I go on alone. Think of me next time you see Nanda Devi. One way or another, I will be with her." He turned away and without a backward look set off on the path skirting the cliffs to the slabs at the foot of the Rishi gorge.

Reaching the narrow gash in the rock wall, Banks cast a swift look at the raging torrent of the river, the boom and roar of the water drowning out any other sound, before turning back to a studied contemplation of the first of the steep slabs. He nodded and stepped up onto the rock, scuffing the soles of his boots across the surface, feeling the tiny grit particles slip and slide. Cautiously he started up the steep slab, leaning in toward the stone, one hand trailing across it. His eyes were almost unfocused as he worked his way upward and across, moving more by feel than by sight. An hour later he reached the crumbled edge of the slab and stopped, examining the next one for foot and handholds. He did not look down, knowing he was already far above the rushing river with nothing between him and death but a sheet of steep smooth rock.

The second slab was steeper but a faint flaw in the grain of the stone had produced a miniscule, raised ridge, no more than a millimeter or two in height and often less. It was to this ridge that the sides of his boots clung, the friction between the surfaces being the only thing that held him upright. Slowly, like a gecko on a wall, he moved across and upward, his palms spread and pressed to the smooth rock to add a tiny bit of extra grip. The far edge of the slab had crumbled against the next one at some time since his last visit, the raw rock showing up as a gray gash against the weathered brown of the rest of the slab. He tested the broken surface cautiously before putting his weight on it and when it held, leaned back between the two slabs and closed his eyes. Slowly, the trembling in his limbs faded as stressed muscles gained a respite from their recent strain.

You're never going to make it, old boy, he thought. *Yes, I am*, he answered himself. *Think positively. Think about Nanda Devi.*

Banks took several deep breaths, willing himself to be calm, before opening his eyes. The sun was hidden by the rock wall above him and his view was limited by the tall cliffs of the opposite side of the ravine, so close he felt he could reach out and caress them. He risked a quick

382

look down, then up at the narrow gash of blue sky far above him. From the position of the shadows he estimated it was close to noon already. *Time to be moving on, old boy.*

The third and fourth slabs were marginally easier to cross, the angle being less and the presence of myriad inclusions in the structure of the rock giving him purchase. He made faster time, pushing himself against the progress of the sun and he almost paid the price. Crossing between slabs he threw his weight onto a foothold without properly testing it and it crumbled beneath him. He fell forward onto the rock face, spreadeagled, feeling gravity relentlessly overcoming friction. Digging in his fingers, he felt a nail rip and tear, the pain almost unnoticed as panic flared in his mind. He slipped half a metre and the tip of one boot caught in a crevice, halting the downward movement. Motionless, Banks clung to the steep slab and fought for calm. Without relaxing, he closed his eyes and thought of the Goddess of Bliss, high above him, until the sweat cooled on his body and the first tiny shivers warned him of an approaching chill. He opened his eyes and looked cautiously around, noting cracks and bumps, planning his next moves with care. The track – a slight indentation in the surface of the rock – lay across his thighs, yet the journey to reach it took him an hour. Once there, he set off again, feeling a weakness now in his limbs that he recognized as hunger.

I'll eat when I reach the staircase. Just this slab and one other.

Golden rays of late sun stabbed up the gorge by the time Banks eased himself off the last slab and onto the relative comfort of the narrow ledge. With a shuddering sigh he slipped the battered pack off his shoulders and lowered himself gratefully to a sitting position, feet dangling over the immense fall that ended in the spray of the river so far below. Even here though, the boom and roar of the water almost deafened him, the sound rebounding off the canyon walls. He scraped tsampa from his small pot, wincing as his exposed nail bed rasped against the coarse barley fragments. Despite the meager sustenance, he felt new strength trickling back into exhausted limbs and he hoisted himself back onto his feet, ready to face the next challenge.

Now he truly raced the fading daylight. He could never hope to conquer the gorge before nightfall, but unless he found a secure place to sleep, he would surely fall to his death. For a while the ledge continued, irregularly rising and falling as it snaked across the cliff face, then abruptly ended where a recent small avalanche had carried away the rock. The shallow chute left by the falling debris was no more than a few metres wide but the surface was treacherous. Pebbles cascaded past him as he looked.

Banks took a firm grip on the rock with his right hand and pushed his right foot firmly up against the rock face before carefully extending his left limbs outward, into the chute. His fingers scrabbled gently, feeling for a hold but finding nothing. He reached up, trying again, then lower down, but the chute was smooth beneath a thin layer of crumbling debris. Pulling back onto the ledge, he knelt and examined the rock again.

There, a slight ridge where the ledge has been carried away. And there, half a body length further

384

down, a toehold, and another. Banks measured distances and depths in his mind, estimating and calculating the odds. The light faded and he knew he had minutes left. He could not hope to return to the base of the slabs, and if he stayed on the narrow ledge he would sleep and fall to his death. There was no choice, no decision to be made, so he lowered himself from the ledge, hanging on by his fingertips and stretching out his left leg toward the first hold.

Darkness had fallen by the time he reached the other side and he moved by touch alone. The ridge that guided his bleeding fingertips suddenly widened out into a gutter and then into the ledge again and he hauled himself up, falling face down onto the uneven surface in exhaustion. His legs still stuck out over the precipice however, so after a few minutes he scrambled cautiously to his feet and started inching along the ledge, his palms flat against the wall and his feet shuffling forward, feeling his way in the stygian darkness where starlight failed to penetrate. Only the relentless boom of the raging river and the rasp of uneven rock on tender fingertips gave him a sense of existence.

In the darkness he cracked a shin against rock and nearly fell, reeling back against the cliff face to steady himself. He reached out a hand to investigate the obstruction and found a large, jagged boulder blocking the ledge. It only felt about waist high but Banks debated the wisdom in trying to climb over it in the dark. Instead, he felt around the edges and found a deep crevice between the boulder and the vertical rock wall on his right. The ledge itself was broad at this point, perhaps two feet across, so he decided to spend the night there. He fumbled in his rucksack and pulled out a spoon. Around this he tied a strap from his rucksack and lying down on the ledge; thrust his arm deep into the crevice, pushing the spoon and strap ahead of his fingers. At full stretch he turned the spoon sideways, wedging it and by applying some tension to the strap, made sure it would stay in place. He then wound the end of the strap that was still attached to the rucksack around his arm and, fitting the pack awkwardly under his head, sprawled himself on the ledge snug up against the cliff. Exhaustion took over within seconds and balanced precariously above several thousand feet of empty air, he slept.

Banks awoke near dawn, though the light in the canyon was only marginally brighter than full night. He stirred and yawned, wondering where he was until he reached out a hand and felt nothing. Shivering, aching in every muscle and his joints crying out for relief, he sat up, the sudden movement darkening his vision as he started to faint. The strap still tied around his right arm pulled him up short, preventing his tumble forward from the ledge. He grabbed the boulder and hung on while his mind and body got to grips with his situation. *Not good, old boy.*

Leaning back against the boulder, he undid the strap and pulled the spoon out from the crevice. Dawn arrived and he waited patiently for the shadows to abate, knowing it would be hours if ever before sunlight touched this deep in the ravine. He would have to leave soon, but not before he ate and took stock of the path ahead. *You're too old, old boy. Eighty-three is no age to be scrambling around mountains.*

"Sod it," he said out loud, and grinned at the sound of his own voice. "This is all that's kept you alive all these years – finding a way to reach Nanda Devi. Well, you're almost there now, so stop dithering and get on with it."

Banks opened his rucksack and rummaged inside, pushing aside a packet of tea and another of cracked barley. The butter, wrapped in a cloth, had melted despite the chill air and leaked into his pack. He sucked the grease off his fingers and pulled out his pot of tsampa, forcing the last of the sticky mess down his throat. Retieing the strap, he slipped it over his shoulders and stood cautiously, eyeing the boulder in front of him. He grinned ruefully when he spied a broad section of ledge a few feet further along. "Such is life," he muttered. "Well, first things first." Unbuttoning his flies, he directed a thin stream of urine over the edge of the cliff, watching as his water broke up into drops, droplets and mist to vanish before it had fallen half a hundred feet.

The track that led past the boulder, 'vaikunth seedi' or staircase to heaven as it was sometimes called, angled upward now, narrowing and broadening, at times becoming no more than a broad crack. Banks managed to negotiate the obstacles, though the trembling in his limbs was more noticeable than the previous day. He stopped at increasingly frequent intervals, pressing up against the shadowed cliff, his breath rasping in a dry throat. *Why didn't I bring water*, he asked himself. *Because you thought you'd be at the top by now, you fool*, he answered. Looking up, he saw the blue strip of sky that beckoned to him, marginally larger but still distant. He started out again.

The staircase ended abruptly, but a few feet above him the rock face folded upon itself, forming a narrow half tube that rose upward. Water had evidently formed it

387

over many years as the rocks were smooth and worn though dry at the moment. The day was passing swiftly, so Wilfred Banks did not hesitate, moving his pack around to his chest. Reaching up, he gripped a protrusion and hauled, his boots seeking out and finding holds until he found himself in the tube of the chimney. He leaned back against one wall and pressed his boots against the opposite one, increasing the pressure from his legs until he was quite secure. The cliff face was at his left hand and open air to his right, but as long as he could maintain a minimum pressure on his back and his boots, he would not fall. He started upward, walking slowly up the chimney wall, easing his back up, his bony shoulder blades grinding against the uneven rock. Stopping often to rest, he made slow but steady progress, the blue sky above slowly broadening out and he started to feel hopeful that the chimney might extend all the way to the top.

It did not. As the shadows deepened and a few resolute rays of the setting sun pierced the deep ravine, Banks came to the top of the chimney where a large rock stood out from the cliff surface, affording him a place to rest. A chute, a depression in the rock, continued another fifty feet more, but the walls were not of sufficient depth to allow his present mode of travel. There were handholds though, so he would have to climb again. Where the shallow chute petered away to nothingness, a slight overhang hinted at another ledge. Banks looked at it grimly and flexed his thin arms, knowing he would have to haul himself up those last few feet by the strength of his arms alone. He slowly turned and found holds, transferring the rucksack to his back again. "Gecko time again," he murmured.

The fifty feet to the overhang took an hour and dark shadows clothed the canyon walls as he clung below the lip of rock, straining his eyes to search out the vital holds. *There ... and there.* If he could hold his weight by his fingertips for a few moments he might be able to grab hold of the ledge. He moved, swiftly, his legs thrusting him upward and his fingers gripped, loosened, gripped again and his hand shot over the edge of the ledge and held. Bringing his other hand up, he hung from the lip at full stretch, gasping, and his heart pounding. Slowly, his feet scrabbling for some slight purchase, he hauled upward, his fingers cracking and nails tearing under the strain. His elbows bent outward and his head came level with the lip. He gasped with relief as he saw there was indeed a ledge there. With a cry of exertion he swung one leg up and got a foot onto the ledge. The foothold gave momentary relief to his aching hands and he panted hard, gathering his last reserves of strength. His heartbeat thundered in his ears, louder than the distant rush of water, then it faltered, raced and slowed again and his vision blurred.

"No! God, help me, please." Banks pulled himself up violently, blindly, feeling his chest rasp against the lip of the ledge. *Almost there, one more ...* His foot slipped off the ledge and his body swung, pulling him off, his fingers fighting to hold on but failing. He fell.

The rock at the top of the chimney, fifty feet below, broke his fall and his back. A scream of pain shattered the rushing night and Banks blacked out, not feeling a thing as his body slipped into the chute of the chimney and continued its downward plunge.

Consciousness returned and Banks found himself wishing it had not. Surprisingly, pain was not his immediate concern; in fact, there was no sensation at all below his waist. He looked in the general direction of his feet but saw nothing. Trying to move his feet met with no success either and he grimaced. "You've got yourself in a spot of bother this time, old boy." He coughed and felt a freshet of blood course down his chin. His right hand would not respond but with his left he felt his unshaven face and the warmth of fresh blood. Moving his hand down his body, he came across something sharp sticking through his torn shirt, the fabric cold and sodden around it. He investigated gingerly and concluded it was a broken rib. No doubt the other end had pierced a lung. *End of the line, old boy.* His hand dropped back and brushed against the rock wall. *I'm on the ledge*, he thought. *Can I push myself off? It'd be quick at least.* He tried, pushing with his one good hand but as his body twisted toward the long fall, bones grated and pain flooded his upper body. Screaming weakly he collapsed back and slipped into unconsciousness once more.

An open tube of rock hung above him, framed by blue sky. Banks stared at it for a long time, wondering what it was and whether it was important. At last, his brain started working and he recollected the chimney, realizing that he had by some lucky chance – *lucky?* – fallen through it to the ledge beneath. He slid his eyes to the side as for some reason he just did not have the energy to move his head, and found he could see most of his body. His right arm appeared to be missing but as he had

390

not yet died of blood loss, he was moderately certain it was still there, either twisted beneath him or hanging over the edge of the cliff. *Why couldn't I have followed it? I'd be dead now and past all this. Well, I dare say it'll come soon enough.* He looked up at the blue sky again and thought of the pristine snows of Nanda Devi. *Will my soul rise up out of this cleft? I'd like to see her again.*

The day faded into night and Banks smiled, knowing this must surely be his last night. He could not possibly survive to see the dawn. His lower body was unfeeling and the rest of him lay numb from the chilling cold, his last bodily resources fueling his brain as he clung to life. Closing his eyes, he awaited the end. A little later he opened them again. Death was being recalcitrant and it seemed there was more in store for him. His gaze wandered in the gloom, across the ravine to the far walls, up the chimney to the invisible sky, and back down the staircase. "Won't be long now," he whispered. "I'm starting to hallucinate."

A faint blue light had appeared far down the cliff face and a long way to the side. Banks estimated it was about where the slabs met the start of the staircase. *What is it?* he wondered, forgetting his statement about hallucinations. The light came closer, bobbing and weaving as it followed the staircase ledge. It did not stop when it reached the breach in the trail but drifted out over the precipice until the ledge resumed. Banks stared at the blue glow as it stopped near his feet, feeling no fear, only a great curiosity. "Hello," he murmured. "Are you an angel come to take me to heaven?"

The light flickered and expanded, forming a dark figure in the midst of the light. "It is I, Wilfred Banks –

Pandalis." The Pahari bent over the body on the trail. "You are badly hurt, Englishman. Do you want me to take you back down?"

Banks tried to laugh but the laugh brought on a coughing fit and the movement ripped something inside. He gasped with pain and fresh blood dribbled from his lips. "I am dying, Pandalis, though death is a long time coming."

"It will come when it is ready. Do you want me to carry you down?"

"No. I would rather die here, where I am closer to the Goddess."

Pandalis looked up the rock face and gestured. "This is your chimney? It does not look too hard."

"It's not. It's the overhang at the other end that beat me." Banks' voice drifted away for several moments. "So close. I was so close ..."

"Would you like me to carry you to the top, Wilfred Banks? Then you can see the Goddess before you die."

"You could do that? How? And how did you climb up here in the dark?"

White teeth flashed in a grin in the darkness. "I am a man of the mountains, Wilfred Banks. Have you forgotten?"

"Even so ..." Banks panted, feeling the cold creep into his shoulders and neck. "I thank you for your offer, Pandalis, but it would not be the same. I wanted to reach the goddess by my own efforts."

"It is so important to you?"

The figure of Pandalis, limned by the strange blue light, faded from sight and the gloom swept in again. A tear oozed from one of Banks' eyes. "I've lost it, old boy,

392

imagining Pandalis here with me." He looked up the chimney again and saw every crevice, every rough surface, as clearly as if the sun shone on the rock. "How very curious." Rising to his feet, Banks slid the rucksack, sodden with blood, from his back and dropped it over the edge, watching as it fell. Despite the night, and the blood-darkened fabric, he followed its course all the way down to the river. With a smile, he reached up into the chimney and climbed.

Banks felt young again, his muscles responding to the demands put upon them and his fingers and feet gripped the holds without hesitation as he scaled the cliff in a steady movement. Throughout it all, he felt detached, as if watching someone else climb the rock face, but at every difficult part he felt his own decision take hold. The overhang held no fear for him, or much of a challenge. He gained the new ledge and moved along it confidently, every rock and crack standing out in clear detail. When the ledge vanished, he took to the sheer wall and climbed it smoothly, clinging to minute blemishes in the structure, swinging out hand over hand to conquer the overhangs. *Am I dead? Is this all the last desire of my dying brain?* He shrugged mentally and climbed on; knowing this was what he had been born to do. *I'm coming, Goddess. Wait for me.*

Dawn was graying the eastern sky when he at last stepped out of the gorge onto the low, wind-swept vegetation of the upper valley. Somewhere out there, still hidden by the darkness, lay Nanda Devi, Goddess of Bliss. He had succeeded in conquering the Rishi Gorge.

Banks looked around and saw a jumble of rocks on a slight rise a few hundred feet away. He felt tired, deathly

393

tired, but there would be a good view of the mountain from there when the sun rose. Dragging feet that did not want to move, he staggered and stumbled to the rocks and arranged himself carefully, sitting up against a large flat boulder with his face to the growing light. He coughed again and felt the tear inside him pour fresh blood into his lungs. Fighting for breath, he coughed and spat to clear his mouth.

"I ... I wish Pandalis was h ... here. I'd rather die with a fr ... friend beside me."

"I am here, Wilfred Banks. I have been here all along."

Banks slid his eyes sideways and saw the Pahari sitting beside him, staring out to where Nanda Devi stood darkly massive against the still gray sky. "Did you carry me, Pandalis? I said I wanted to do this myself."

"It was your skill and your knowledge that conquered the cliff face, Wilfred Banks. I just lent you a bit of strength."

"That's alright then." Banks closed his eyes and panted. "I'm not going to last ... my friend. Dawn is coming too slowly."

"Behold, Wilfred Banks," Pandalis said quietly. "The Goddess comes in her glory."

With an enormous effort, Banks opened his eyes to a staggering vista. Golden light burst out from the eastern horizon, surrounding the great mountain in a lurid glow. But instead of Nanda Devi being lost in shadow as the dazzle increased from behind her, the mountain itself seemed to pulse with an inner light, the snows of her slopes showing up brilliant white. Streamers of cloud rushed out from the high peak, pink and gold and white, making the dying man gasp with the wonder of it. The face of the Goddess formed on the snow slopes, smiling at the dying Englishman and a hand reached out, wispy and tenuous.

"Come to me, Wilfred Banks," the Goddess seemed to say. "Be at peace in my arms."

Banks struggled and lifted his left arm toward her, a smile cracking the dried blood on his face. He felt himself lifting out of his broken body and hurtling toward the gentle face on the snows. As he merged with the Goddess, his mind slid into darkness and his body fell to the side.

Pandalis sat for over an hour in silence, watching the real dawn creep slowly into the high valley. The peak of Nanda Devi was lost in cloud, almost invisible from where he sat, but he smiled anyway, wishing the Englishman well. After a while, he rose and busied himself with the frail body beside him, washing the blood from the smiling face, arranging the limbs and covering the remains with a tall cairn of rocks.

"Be at peace, Wilfred Banks," he murmured. Turning from the cairn, Pandalis started slowly up the valley toward the eternal snows of Nanda Devi.

Chapter Twenty

I buried the Englishman, Wilfred Banks, beneath a cairn of stones in the high valley within sight of the mountain he so loved. I buried him because he was a Christian, rather than a Hindu, and while I am not familiar with the funeral rites of his faith, I do know that they shun the cleansing fires of cremation. Well, each to his own. I placed him within the earth where his mortal body will decay and rejoin the great circle of life. Where his spirit went, I cannot say. I have said before that as far as I can determine the spark of life that is man does not long survive his death, but this may be just because I can no longer detect it. The belief that man survives death and is reborn must come from somewhere. Perhaps some god divulged this secret long ago to his worshipers and the knowledge has been passed down from father to son. Christians, if I understand them correctly, do not believe in reincarnation, yet still believe they survive in some form. According to them, a man is judged by his deeds and is consigned by his god to heaven or hell. I have always thought that is very unreasonable, for how can any man, however saintly, achieve nirvana within one lifetime? Even the Buddha had lived many times before. And if a man commits evil deeds for a lifetime of fifty years, does he deserve an eternity of torment?

I do not know if the spirit of Wilfred Banks continues on somewhere, but if he does, I hope he escapes the Christian fate. Perhaps his embrace of the Goddess of Bliss there at the end was sufficient to bring him under the sway of our friendly Hindu gods. They will judge his deeds and his intent and assign him another life. Maybe in this next one he will be a man of the mountains and live close to the gods.

He was a brave man and worthy of being a Pahari. He fought with a strength and tenacity far beyond the limitations of his body. He was eighty-three, yet he clung to life so fiercely, waiting and hoping that somehow he would yet achieve his life's ambition though his body lay broken and bleeding. Yes, I helped him up that last few hundred feet, but not by carrying him. I possessed the Englishman as I have so many before and read his intentions, stimulating muscles no longer connected to nerves, blocking the considerable pain and enabling his human eyes to see as a demon does. He climbed that cliff using his own skill and knowledge. All I did was enable him to drive his broken body one last time.

I touched his mind there at the end too, for I saw his life slipping from his broken body like water through an ill-woven basket. I saw the mountain in the early dawn through my heightened senses and took pity on him. Rather than let him see a mist-shrouded mountain, I conjured for him a vision of Nanda Devi. It was a simple matter as all I did was stimulate his needs and desires, tickling his optic centres so he saw what he wanted to see. It was all very straight forward except for one thing – the Goddess herself. I did not think to form an image of her in my mind as I knew him to be a logical man, if an obsessed one. Why would an Englishman think to see a foreign god in the side of a mountain? The face of the Goddess took me by surprise, especially as I saw her myself and not through his eyes. I did not form the image in the Englishman's mind – did he somehow form it in mine? If so, it shook me, for the image survived the old man's death by several seconds. As Wilfred Banks slumped down, the eyes of the Goddess image turned and held me. I felt she knew me for what I was and accepted it. A great calm descended and if the gods had decided to annihilate one more Rakshasa from the world, I would not have resisted. Perhaps her acceptance means I have become a god after all. Not a full-fledged god, but a godling at least. I must think on my future actions.

This brings me to another consideration. If I am a god now, even a very minor one, could I have saved Wilfred Banks' life? I have saved men before, being able to sweep the cells clean of foreign invaders, the animalcules that cause a man to sicken and die. I can even prevent toxins entering the bloodstream from ingested food and knit broken bones. It bothers me that I sat beside the Englishman at the end and let him die when perhaps I should have tried to heal him. Other gods do it. I have possessed many Christians and Muslims and know that their god not only heals but can raise men from the dead. It happens in Hinduism too, so should I have at least attempted it? What could I have done? I could have healed broken ribs, mended torn lungs and gut, fought off the infections accelerating within him. His right arm was shattered in several places, yet I could have achieved that too. What I could not do was heal his torn spinal cord. Almost severed, he had no control from the waist down. I was able to bypass the nerves while I inhabited his body but unless I stayed there the rest of his life he would have been a cripple. And it would have been a short life, for his age lay heavy upon him. I know of no way to stop the river of a man's life from flowing to its end.

So I let Wilfred Banks die and walked away from his graveside toward the Goddess and the mountain. I searched the untouched snows, but if she had existed there before, I could find no sign of her now. I left the high valley, descending over precipices that no man could climb until I stood once more in the foothills, among the warmth and bustle of teeming mankind. I took on the form of Pandalis again, for I had grown fond of this image, and wandered. I crossed my Himalayas from Nanga Parbat in what would one day be Pakistan to Namche Barwa in Tibet. I visited Mount Kailasa again, this time without disturbing the peace of any of the pilgrims, and journeyed south to the plains of Mother Ganga. I stood where the Khandava forest had once flourished and visited a shrine of Krishna, reasonably certain that he was not there. I sacrificed to Kali – not the Rakshasi who usurped her worshipers – but to the true goddess, praying for her blessing. I did not feel her presence, there in her temple, but perhaps she heard me anyway, for I am at peace.

Despite my distant wanderings, I returned to my beloved realms of Garhwal and Kumaon. It is here I belong, and if I am to be a god to any people, it is to the strong, resilient men and women of these beautiful hills and valleys that I will devote my powers.

I frequented a beautiful, forested hill near Champawat for a few years, living and walking with the beasts, and lending my protection to the villagers nearby. They soon became aware of the presence of a handsome man that walked the trails through the forest or sat at the edge of the cultivated fields, speaking to no-one, but to whom the animals deferred. This could mean only one

399

thing to them – that Pashupati, Lord of Animals, was among them. They left me offerings of milk and rice, or chapattis, or flowers, and in return I kept the deer from raiding their crops or the leopard from killing their goats. The villagers boasted of the god on their hill and pilgrims came, hoping for a blessing. A priest built a small shrine in a grove of banyans and made a living collecting sacrifices. I did not begrudge him his living for what use had I for food? The villagers offered it anyway and it was not right that it should be wasted. Then the sick started to arrive at the shrine and I healed a few. My reputation grew and other priests arrived, setting up a shelter for the sick and tending them as best they could while they awaited the intervention of the god. When the priests affected a cure, I was given the credit anyway, for it was my holy hill, and who was to say I had not healed them? Soon, a town sprang up, devoted to the worship of Pashupati and Dhanvantari, the healer of the gods.

The hill became too noisy for me and I decided to leave. One would think that in the absence of the god (me) the healings would cease and that animals would once again pillage the crops. For some strange reason neither of these things happened, and if anything, the fame of the hill increased in my absence.

The world was changing even as I hid myself away in Kumaon. The British ruled, fairly for the most part, but they were still foreigners and would one day have to leave. Sixty-three years before, a few men had tried to wrest control of their own country from the grasp of this power and failed, for the masses were not ready for that responsibility. Now, the winds of independence were blowing again, but India is vast and her peoples many. It would be years yet before India was united. Names like Gandhi, Nehru and Jinnah were spoken in the streets, but the rule of the British was still strong and I knew I could not yet hide away in the hills. I left my refuge and journeyed west to a small village I had visited before, now grown to a town on the shores of a beautiful lake or Tal. Surrounded by forested hills, the climate was cool and pleasant and attracted many British families, seeking refuge from the stifling plains of the Indian summer. I came to Naini Tal on a hot summer's day in the year nineteen-thirty by British reckoning.

Chapter Twenty-One

Allahabad lay sweltering under the pale sun of the Indian summer. The rains were delayed, the only sign of their impending appearance were the frequent thunderstorms that flickered on the evening horizon, but no rain fell to break the crippling heat. The temperatures continued to mount as May turned into June and the business in the city almost came to a halt from nine in the morning until late afternoon. Even the lean, mangy pariah dogs ceased their perpetual round of scavenging and lay panting in whatever scraps of shade they could find. The only potential relief from the heat was the breeze that intermittently blew from the southwest, the expected source of the rains. It was a hot breeze though, as if from an oven, and it stirred up the pale dust, lifting it high in the air to paint the blue summer skies burnt yellow and coat every object with a patina of age and neglect.

Two small English girls lay on their beds in their shaded bedroom and stared at the electric fan turning lazy circles on the ceiling. The bright sun filtered through foliage and window shutters to paint part of the floor and one wall in barred and flecked patterns, reminding them that a world of excitement and exploration lay just beyond their walls. The creak of the fan beat a counterpoint to their boredom and somewhere deep within the house they could just make out the murmur of voices.

"Are you awake, Pippa?"

The older of the two girls opened her eyes. "Of course I am. Who wants to sleep in the middle of the day?" She rolled over on her bed and looked across the room to the other bed where a smaller girl sat cross-legged on the flower-patterned eiderdown. "You want to play a game?"

The younger girl shook her head. "I want to go outside. I hate being locked up for an afternoon nap. That's just for little girls," she added fiercely.

Phillipa laughed. "But you are a little girl, Maud."

Maud poked out her tongue. "I hate you," she hissed. A moment's silence followed before the younger girl slipped off her bed and ran to her sister, sitting down beside her and regarding her with a solemn expression. "No I don't, Pippa. Please forgive me. It was a horrid thing to say." Phillipa smiled and in an instant, Maud was hugging her older sister. She straightened and her grin slipped. "I'm nearly as old as you anyway, only two years and three months younger."

Phillipa smiled again and sat up. "You are perfectly correct, Maud. You'll catch up with me in no time." She ran her hands over her long skirts, smoothing out the creases.

Maud looked askance at Phillipa, unsure whether her sister was making fun of her. "So can we go outside?"

"Why ask me? Mother sent us to our room to rest. You'd better ask her."

Maud frowned. "Mama's not well and you know how she gets when she has one of her headaches. If we didn't tell her …"

"What about Ayah?" Phillipa knew that the children's nurse asleep in the next room was unlikely to awaken, but she enjoyed leading her little sister on. Maud had a quick wit and a sense of adventure bordering on the irresponsible, and Phillipa loved setting her problems and watching how she overcame them.

"Pooh. Ayah would sleep through a thunderstorm," Maud retorted. "We can tiptoe past her without a problem."

"Then where? If we try for the verandah, we have to pass mummy's room."

"She'll be asleep too."

"But the dogs won't be."

Maud frowned in concentration, thinking about their mother's eight cocker spaniels. The dogs adored her and refused to be parted. When she retired to her room with one of her headaches, the dogs always accompanied her – and they were light sleepers.

"The only other way out is down the hall to the front door," Phillipa went on. "Majeed will be on the front porch. He always is when all we memsahibs are asleep." Majeed was the major-domo of the household, ruling the servants with a rod of iron. Nothing happened within the house without his knowledge.

"It'll have to be the window then," Maud sighed. "I hate the window. There's that long drop and those horrid prickly bushes."

Phillipa grinned, knowing all along that the window was the only choice. "It won't be so bad. I can go first and catch you if you like." She got up from her bed and walked over to the window, throwing open the shutters to let a flood of light and heat into the room. The verandah, which surrounded three sides of the house, stopped short of the girls' room and there was a drop of nearly six feet from the windowsill to the dry drifts of leaves and parched earth beneath the plumbago bushes planted under the window. Phillipa looked out cautiously in case any of the servants were in the garden despite the heat, but none were.

"The coast is clear," she whispered.

Maud hooked one leg over the sill and looked down into the wilted plumbago bushes. "There'll be lizards,' she grumbled.

"Then let me go first. I told you I'll catch you."

By way of an answer, the younger girl swung her other leg over and held her skirts tight around her legs. "Here goes." She pushed off the sill and half fell, half jumped into the shrubbery.

The noise of her landing sounded very loud to Phillipa and her eyes darted to the door of their room but nothing stirred in the house. She looked back to see Maud standing on the brown remnants of the lawn picking fragments of plumbago bush from her clothing. Squinting up at the bright sun, she ducked back inside the room to emerge a few moments later clutching wide straw hats. With a flick of her wrist, Phillipa sent them skimming toward her sister before climbing out the window and jumping in a flurry of skirts and petticoats.

Maud giggled as her older sister extricated herself from the plumbago and joined her on the dry lawn. "I could see your undies."

Phillipa blushed and busied herself setting her straw hat over her unruly hair. "You shouldn't have been looking," she said primly.

Maud giggled again. "Come on." She grabbed her hat from the ground and set off across the small strip of dead grass and onto the baked clay and gravel of the long driveway. After a moment, Phillipa joined her.

The heat was fearful after the cool of the bedroom. The baking ground made their feet feel as if they walked on coals, the fire burning straight through the leather soles of their shoes. Waves of heat blasted down at them from the glowing sun wrapped in dust, meeting the reflected pulses from the hard earth. Sweat broke out almost immediately, staining armpits and beading on foreheads and face, trickling down their necks.

"This is silly," Phillipa muttered. "It's too hot to be outside. We should go back."

Maud took no notice and marched on, so Phillipa just shrugged and followed along, as she always did. Maud was the younger girl, but when it came to adventures, she took the lead.

An old mulberry tree grew near the ruins of the old stables, surrounded by patches of long, dead grass and weeds. The girls looked anxiously at the ruins before they passed. The servants claimed a cobra lived in the ruins and came out in the cool of the evenings to warm itself on the hard baked clay. Perhaps in the heat it was cooling itself under the dappled shade of the mulberry. They ran quickly past and out of the gate onto the long wide road that led in one direction to the town, and in the other toward the church and the road that led to the railway station. Maud turned immediately toward the church.

"We're not going to the church, are we," Phillipa grumbled. "It's boring there. There are only old headstones to look at and you know Reverend Burkhart doesn't like children there without a grown-up."

"I thought you liked looking at old graves," Maud said, staring at her sister in surprise. "You got all weepy last time when we found the headstone of that baby girl."

"Did not. Anyway it was sad."

"Well, we're not going there today. We're going somewhere much better."

"Where?"

"You'll see." Maud broke into a run for a few paces before pulling up and fanning her face with her straw hat. "It's awfully hot, but there'll be shade there. No water though, do you think we should have brought some?"

"How could we have got to the kitchen without waking someone?"

The stone walls of the little churchyard came in sight, the stonework enclosing a large wooden church and scores of headstones standing miserably in the dusty heat, the black shadows cast by the grave markers looking like open pits. A few scraggly trees cast meager amounts of shade, inviting the girls to stop and rest but they hurried past in case the Reverend saw them and asked what they were doing.

The road curved to the east after it passed the church, running on full tilt toward the railway station. That was where the girls could not explain their presence should they be questioned. They were allowed as far as the church if their Ayah was with them but never past it unless with a parent. Today, the road was deserted, not a single person stirring in the rippling air of the furnace. The only thing that moved was a solitary kite circling far above them. Even the insects were stilled, keeping a lethargic silence in the bare brown bushes and long grass of the fields. Maud and Phillipa ran, despite the heat,

407

their feet kicking up puffs of white dust, coating the polished leather of their shoes and the hems of their dresses.

"Where are we going?" Phillipa wailed.

"Down here, hurry." Maud pointed down a lane that passed through a small stand of mango trees. She darted into the grove and her sister followed.

The shade of the trees was heavy. After the brilliant heat of the day, the grove was almost gloomy, sucking in the light and smothering it. A heavy sweet-sour smell of rotting fruit hung in the cooler air and butterflies flitted past, coming to rest head down on the rough bark of the trees.

"That's better," Phillipa said, removing her straw hat and mopping at her face with her hankie. Her brown hair hung in wet straggles and she shook her head, trying to fluff them out. Spatters of sweat stained the dried leaves at her feet. She looked around at the grove of trees and the thick leaf litter under them. "Is this why we came? It's cool but there might be snakes in the leaves."

"Probably," Maud said offhandedly. She stood at the far end of the grove, staring out into the brightness beyond. "This isn't what we came to see though. That is." She pointed.

Phillipa walked over to her sister and shaded her eyes against the glare. "That old gate and stone wall? Why? What is it?"

"The cholera cemetery."

"What?" Phillipa grabbed her little sister and swung her round. "Are you mad? We could catch something – cholera probably. We can't go in there."

408

"Course we can." Maud shook free and took a step out into the sun. "Peter Hopkins at school told me about it. He and some friends went exploring and found tombs and statues and stuff."

"You can't believe him, he's a boy. Boys lie. Besides, even if he did, how do you know he won't get sick?"

"Because his father told him cholera comes from water. There's no water round here."

Phillipa looked around at the parched landscape with a sinking feeling. It was becoming obvious that Maud was going to go into the cholera cemetery and unless she felt like explaining to her parents why she'd let her, she would have to go too, to keep an eye on her headstrong little sister.

"Come on, then." Maud ran toward the gate in the old crumbling wall of the cemetery. "Look, it's not even locked." She tugged at the rusty bars of the leaning gate, pulling it open with a creak, and slipped inside. Phillipa opened the gate a little further and joined her, standing alongside and staring.

The cholera cemetery lay bleak and empty, a dry wasteland of stone and tangled, dead vegetation where nothing moved. Maud moved forward slowly, her eyes gleaming with excitement. Phillipa followed, and as they advanced on the rock outcrops, the mounds resolved suddenly into crumbled walls and yawning crypts, everything the color of dust and weathered bones.

"I don't like it," murmured Phillipa. "There's nothing to see here. Let's go ..." Her eyes opened wide and she pointed to one of the old tombs and shrieked. "There's someone there."

409

At the end of the shattered tomb, just where the tangle of vegetation met the sliver of dark shade cast by the walls, stood the pale figure of a man in a long gray robe. The man's head faced toward them, seeming to stare intently at the two young girls, his arms stretched out in a wide curving arc. Both girls froze, their breath coming in hurried pants as they felt panic rise in them.

"Who is he?" Maud whispered, a tremor in her voice. "Why doesn't he move?"

Phillipa, who had been on the verge of grabbing her little sister by the hand and taking to her heels, looked more intently at the man. "Why doesn't he move?" she repeated and advanced a few steps, squinting against the glare. Abruptly, she laughed. "Because he can't move." She turned and grinned at an incredulous Maud. "It's a statue of an angel. What we thought were arms are his wings."

They came closer and examined the statue, running their fingers over the weathered and lichen-covered stone as if to reassure themselves.

"You see, we're having an adventure already. Isn't this more exciting than resting in our stuffy old bedrooms?"

"A few moments ago you were ready to pee, you were so scared," Phillipa observed, feeling like she might have to duck behind some bushes herself.

"I was not," Maud said indignantly. "That's a horrid thing to say." She flounced off along the wall of the tomb.

"Where are you going?"

"To find some more adventures. Are you coming?"

Maud led the way deeper into the cholera cemetery, along the ghost of paths still graveled and straight but tainted now with the disregard that nature has for the works of man. Weeds and matted grasses choked the paths and the once tidy shrubs and trees that had comforted the families of the victims with their soft beauty were now wild and straggled, a vision of a world in which the men, women and children buried in this place were forgotten, ignored by the living. Over everything lay the heat of the Indian summer, pressing down like a dusty suffocating blanket. They found a tomb in better repair than most and walked around it to find the family name.

"James Miller," Phillipa read out from the weathered inscription. "Died in seventeen ninety-three, aged forty-one; his wife Edith, the same year, aged thirty; their children James, Thomas, Edmund, Flora, same year." She shook her head. "Little Flora was only two."

Maud looked at her sister sharply. "Are you going to cry?"

"No, of course not." Phillipa took out her hankie again, now completely dry, and blew her nose quietly. "She didn't have much of a life, did she?"

"I 'spect she's in heaven with the angels though."

The next tomb was in worse condition, with its inscription cracked and incomplete. They could make little sense of the weathered words and moved on, deeper into the cemetery. Maud was enthusiastic, running from tomb to crypt to tiny grave enclosed by rusted iron railings or broken wooden palings, eagerly searching out the names or, if they were missing, any unusual feature. An army of stone angels guarded the dead, their lifeless eyes looking out at a wilderness of neglect.

411

"I'm bored and hot," Phillipa complained. "Let's go home, Maud. We'll have to soon anyway, before daddy gets home."

"One more, Pippa, please."

"We've looked at dozens already and it's boring here. We should go home," Phillipa added firmly.

"One more, and then we'll go, I promise." Maud looked around at the crumbling ruins and dead landscape. Secretly, she wanted to go home too, but it would never do to let her big sister win the argument. "That one." She pointed toward a tomb that was sunk deep into the ground, only a foot or two of wall showing above the dead grass. Tall trees surrounded it, and though the leaves hung limply in the heat-rippled air, they still managed to trap a small amount of shade beneath them.

"There could be snakes in that long grass."

"Pooh, you just don't want to go." Maud picked up a broken piece of wood nonetheless, and advanced cautiously, poking the grass as she went.

Phillipa sighed and used another stick to beat at the grass as they crept along a narrow path toward the sunken tomb. "Who made the path? And look, there are footprints. Dogs, I think."

"Wolves," Maud said, her eyes wide. "Or tigers."

"I think dogs are a lot more likely. I hope we don't meet any though, some of those pariah dogs can be vicious."

The tomb, despite being sunk in the ground, was in poor repair. Three great stone slabs that had once covered the grave were lying sprawled and broken, only one of them still in place. One side wall had collapsed inward, an avalanche of broken stone and crumbled earth fanning

412

out in a steep cone to the floor of the crypt some eight feet below. The edge of the slope reached deep into the shadow cast by the remaining roof slab and they could make out nothing in the blackness. The footprints of the dog continued down into the crypt, having compacted a thin trail in the loose earth.

"It's his lair," Maud breathed in excitement. "A wolf's lair. He's waiting down there for nightfall so he can come up and kill a goat or something." She shivered deliciously. "Or maybe a baby. I've heard they snatch native babies."

"I'm sure it's only a dog, or at worst a jackal. And they're not going to snatch anything. Now, we've seen the tomb, so let's go home."

"In a moment, I want to see it, whatever it is. It'll be asleep now, so if we're quiet ..."

"You? Quiet?" Phillipa shook her head. "Hey, what are you doing?"

Maud climbed on top of the remaining roof slab and peered over the edge, staring down into the inky blackness. "There's something down there. I can see a shape ... oh!" The little girl clutched at her hat without success as it fell into the pit, gliding down to land just inside the shadow, on the edge of the earth slide. "Pippa, my hat." Maud scrambled to her feet and ran to the far edge of the slab and jumped to the ground, running round to the top of the slide.

Phillipa ran to intercept her and grabbed her arm as she started down the slope, dragging her back out of the tomb. "What are you doing? You can't go in there."

"I've got to get my hat."

413

"Don't be silly. What if there really is something down there? A wolf even?"

Maud fell silent, thinking hard. "You said it was only a dog at worst," she said at last. "I'm not afraid of a dog. I want my hat and I'm going to get it." She tried to shake her sister's hand from her arm.

"You are not going down there," Phillipa said firmly. "What would mummy and daddy say if they knew I just stood here and let you go into a place where there might be anything?" She took a deep breath and exhaled noisily. "I'll go."

"Oh, Pippa, would you? For me?" Maud looked up adoringly at her big sister. "I mean, even if it's only a silly old dog, you're awfully brave."

"Well, I can't let my little sister go, can I? But first we have to find out if there is anything down there."

"How? We can't see."

"We could throw a few stones."

They searched unsuccessfully in the long grass for stones and in the end resorted to hardened lumps of clay and mortar from the decayed walls. Despite a small barrage of missiles, nothing stirred in the shadows and the only sound in the hot stillness was a cicada in one of the trees.

"Alright, there's nothing there. I'm going down." Phillipa climbed over the broken lip of the tomb and started down the slope, her feet kicking up clouds of dust as the leather soles of her shoes slipped in the loose debris.

"Be careful, Pippa," Maud called.

Phillipa did not reply, concentrating on the foot of the slope, her sister's straw hat, and the black shadows

414

beyond. She stepped onto the floor of the crypt and with her eyes fixed on the blackness, bent and felt for the hat. As she gripped it and straightened up, something moved in the deepest part of the shadow. A shape, and something gleamed, two things, red like embers. She screamed and turned, scrambling up the slope on hands and knees, the straw hat clutched tightly in one fist.

Clouds of dust obscured the tomb and Maud called out shrilly. "What is it, Pippa? What's wrong? What did you see?" Then she screamed as a pale figure staggered out of the tomb and stumbled toward her. Opening her mouth to scream again, she suddenly recognized her sister under the blanket of dust, and shut her mouth with a click of teeth. A moment later she felt like screaming again as her sister spoke.

"Run, Maud, run. Quickly, before it … oh, God, no." Phillipa ran past her sister and started back down the overgrown gravel path toward the gate and the grove of mango trees. Maud cast a horrified glance at the yawning tomb with the cloud of dust still billowing out of it and bolted after her older sister.

Phillipa fled as if something horrible was after her and she was through the iron gate and into the mango trees before Maud caught up to her, despite the smaller girl being the faster runner. She grabbed Phillipa's arm, evoking another scream from the older girl's throat. Maud screamed too, taken by surprise, and burst into tears.

"What is it, Pippa? You're scaring me."

Phillipa stared wildly. Her mouth moved but no words came out. After a few moments, she shuddered and held out her hand with her sister's battered straw hat. "Here's your hat, Maud. Try not to drop it again."

Maud's sobs slackened and she stared at her sister, the tears cutting runnels in the caked dust on her cheeks. "What happened? What did you see?"

Phillipa stared back, her mouth moving awkwardly as if she was just learning to speak. "Nothing. I just saw shadows." She looked around and stared up and down the road. "Which way's home?"

Maud pointed, not taking her eyes off her sister.

* * *

"I don't understand, doctor. If there is nothing physically wrong with the girl, why is she ill?"

Doctor Whitfield hummed and hawed for a few moments before replying, feeling for the stethoscope that minutes earlier had been around his neck. "Perhaps I was being … hmm … a bit optimistic there, Mister Haye. When I say there is nothing wrong with her, I meant there is nothing … ah … obviously wrong with her." He located the stethoscope in his jacket pocket and fingered it, gaining reassurance from the symbol of his profession. "She is, well, a little on the hot side but that could … ah … just be the sun. I understand she was out in it this afternoon?"

Edwin Haye nodded, darting a look at his wife Pearl who sat on a plump sofa nursing her head with one hand. Her cocker spaniels lay on the carpeted floor close to her feet, their attention riveted on their mistress. "My daughters decided to leave the house during their afternoon nap. Reverend Burkhart found them on the

416

road outside his church a little after three. They, or at least my younger daughter Maud, were raving about some large dog or wolf. He took them into his house and telephoned me immediately. They were in a dreadful state, covered in dust and I judged them to be dehydrated. That's why I called you."

"Hmm … well, best to be on the … ah … safe side. A touch of the sun, I expect. Keep them cool and … hmm … give them plenty to … ah … drink. Dehydration can give them headaches, so if they do get … ah … headaches, give them half an aspirin. But … hmm … plenty of fluids should do the trick."

"And the listlessness? Maud is fine despite being out in the heat too, but Phillipa just lies in her room staring at the ceiling and not saying anything."

"Heat affects… ah … all of us differently. Natives are untroubled by … hmm … heat that would drive a white man mad … hmm. I expect she will be … ah … fully recovered in a day or two."

"This dog they mentioned. Could she have been bitten?"

"Rabies, you mean? Ah … no. You would not see … hmm … symptoms for at least … hmm … ten days. She wasn't bitten, was she? I didn't see a … hmm … bite."

Edwin Haye escorted the doctor to the door and watched as he climbed into his car and drove off before going back in to his wife. "Bloody man. With all his hmms and ahs I don't believe he has the faintest idea what's wrong."

"Don't swear, dear. I'm sure he knows what he's doing. Phillipa will be right as rain in a few days, you'll see. Now, I can feel my headache coming on again so

417

I'm going to have an early night." She got to her feet and, surrounded by dogs, left the room.

Edwin looked in on the girls before retiring to his study to read. Maud was curled up with a book, while Phillipa lay on her back with her eyes open and unmoving.

"Hello daddy," Maud said. "Are we going to be alright? Did the doctor say?"

Edwin smiled. "Right as rain in two shakes of a lamb's tail. You just got a bit too much sun. I think a couple of days around the house with lots of fresh lemonade and rest, and you'll be ready for new adventures." He glanced across at Phillipa who lay as if ignoring them. Sitting down on Maud's bed, he lowered his voice. "Where did you go this afternoon anyway? Burkhart ... Reverend Burkhart said you were on the road outside the churchyard. Were you looking at the gravestones again?" Maud shook her head, glancing across at her sister and Edwin smiled reassuringly. "You're not in trouble, either of you, even if you've been somewhere you shouldn't. I just need to know in case ... well, maybe Phillipa scratched herself on something or an insect stung her ..." He looked at his young daughter's eyes carefully as he casually added, "Or she was bitten by a dog."

Maud hesitated. "We went to the cholera cemetery, daddy. It was my fault, I made Pippa go and now she's ... she's ..."

"Shh. She'll be alright. Just tell me what happened."

Maud told her father, the words coming slowly at first but gathering strength and speed as the tale progressed. There were many non sequiturs and asides,

418

but Edwin listened patiently, not interrupting but sometimes nudging his daughter's mind back on track. "Now she just lies there and won't even talk to me." She grasped her father's hand tightly and searched his face for reassurance. "Is ... is she going to die, daddy?"

"No, Maud," Edwin said firmly. "You both caught the sun and it has affected Phillipa more. I promise you, you'll both be fine in a few days."

As it turned out, her father was half right. Maud was back to her usual energetic self within two days, but Phillipa, while able to leave her bed, remained lethargic, sitting around the house and conversing in monosyllables. Her slight temperature did not abate and Edwin started to entertain fresh thoughts about the possibility of rabies. He refused to call Doctor Whitfield, but made the journey in to the city hospital where after an hour's wait, a young Indian doctor came out into the waiting room to see him.

"Let me see if I am understanding you correctly, Mister Haye. You are thinking a rabid dog may have bitten your daughter five days ago and that she is exhibiting signs of the sickness?" Doctor Subhash Deep offered his visitor a chair and sat down next to Edwin. "I can be reassuring you immediately, Mister Haye. From the symptoms you describe, she is most unlikely to be contracting rabies. It has an incubation time ... you are understanding incubation time?" Edwin nodded. "Good. Then you are also understanding that it is too early to be diagnosing this disease." He held up a hand as Edwin opened his mouth. "I am also a father, Mister Haye, and I am understanding your concern, but if she is running a temperature it is not because of rabies."

"Then why?"

Doctor Deep shrugged. "Who can say? You could bring your daughter in for tests, but we are not a well-equipped hospital. It is most likely a local infection. Is she having any scratches on her skin from her outing?"

"A few, but none of them deep and they are healing."

The doctor nodded. "If that is so, then she will get better. The other area that is concerning me is her lack of energy. It is seeming to me that a twelve year old girl should not be sitting around the house not talking. Perhaps something is scaring her or she cannot be forgetting her experience because the days are continuing to be hot."

"What are you suggesting, doctor?"

"I am thinking you should be taking her to the hills, Mister Haye. Do you have a place you could be staying? Friends, maybe?"

Edwin nodded. "We usually go up to Naini Tal in the summer. We have a cottage there. The only reason we are still in Allahabad is that my wife is unwell."

"Then I am strongly suggesting you should be taking your family to Naini Tal, Mister Haye. The cooler, purer air will be helping both your wife's and your daughter's health and the change of scenery will be taking the girl's mind off her experiences."

* * *

The road to Naini Tal curved in from the southeast heading up to the old stone Post Office close by the lake shore. Edwin Haye had brought his family up by steam train from Allahabad, but the metre-wide gauge train only reached as far as Kathgodam, the trains not being powerful enough to attempt the steep climb into the Himalayan foothills. They transferred to a car owned by a close friend of Edwin's for the forty kilometer journey up the dusty switchback road to Naini Tal. The servants, with the bulk of the luggage and eight frantic spaniels, howling the loss of their mistress, would follow in bullock carts, expecting to arrive two days later. The car, a nineteen twenty-eight Austin Seven Saloon, made short work of the hill road despite its rutted and pockmarked surface and Maud found it enormously satisfying to ride in style past the gawking men and women plodding up and down the road. She waved gaily until her mother told her quite sharply to stop making a public spectacle of herself. Phillipa sat quietly throughout the trip, train and car, uttering a simple 'yes' or 'no' to any question.

The air grew cooler as they ascended and the dusty face of the sun blossomed into a golden disk set in a beautiful pale blue sky. The hills, clad in fresh green forests, farms, meadows and paddy fields, rose around them and as the car labored to ridge tops, they glimpsed the far-off splendour of the high Himalayas. Edwin knew some of the peaks and he pointed them out as they came in sight.

"There's Nanda Kot, and Trisul – glorious mountains in their own right. A whole lot of other peaks too that I can't identify at this distance, but my favorite, the Queen of them all, is Nanda Devi. There, see that great pyramid?"

"Have you climbed it, daddy?" Maud asked.

Her father laughed. "No-one climbs a goddess, Maud, and that is what people believe she is – the Goddess of Bliss."

"Edwin, dear, please stop filling the girls' heads with nonsense. Reverend Burkhart would be horrified to hear you call a mountain a goddess."

They drove on in silence for a while, until Edwin said quietly. "No man has climbed Nanda Devi, and I don't believe anyone ever will. She is said to be surrounded by impregnable cliffs."

"What does 'pregnable mean?"

"Never you mind, Maud," her mother said sharply.

"It means they can't be climbed," Edwin replied with a grin.

The cottage the Haye's owned lay in a quiet lane beneath Government House in the southern part of Naini Tal. Cottage was really a misnomer as the large bungalow sprawled over a flattened area of the hillside, surrounded by a broad, shadowy verandah. The property was called Rose Cottage, named for a few straggly rose bushes planted beside the gravel path that led up to the broad front steps. Maud's mother had planted them, long before Maud could remember, but as she only paid them any attention in the summer months when the Haye's, in company with many other reasonably well-to-do families, migrated to the coolness of the hill stations, they grew lank and ragged for most of the year.

A gardener looked after the lawns and shrubbery and two housemaids attended to the cottage, but they had other employment through the rest of the year. They were hard at work getting house and garden into shape as the car pulled up at the gate, but downed tools and came running to meet the family. Amid great chattering and bustling, the few bags in the car were carried up to the house and one of the maids hurried off to find the cook.

By nightfall, every member of the family was ensconced in their rooms and their meager belongings unpacked. After dinner, they sat out on the wide verandah and looked out at the dark lake and the scattering of lights from the other houses. So dark was the night, and so clear the sky, that it was hard to tell where the hills ended and the sky began, the blaze of stars merging imperceptibly with the house lights, until it seemed as if they were surrounded by space, a firmament of stars burning all around them.

Despite Maud's quiet protests, Phillipa shared her room. Over the last week, the older girl had withdrawn into herself more and more, growing more sullen and less responsive. Several times, Maud had woken in the night to find her sister standing by her bed, staring at her with glittering eyes. Sometimes, the older girl could be led back to her own bed, where she would roll over to face the wall and immediately fall asleep. Other times, she would grin, baring her teeth, and Maud, shivering with fright, would have no recourse but to switch the electric light on and sit watching Phillipa until the dawn.

"Daddy, please don't make me sleep with Pippa," she whispered. "I like having a room of my own up here."

"Phillipa needs you. She's still sick and I don't want her to be alone."

"She scares me, daddy. Sometimes she ..."

"She's your sister, Maud. Remember that. Family comes first, personal wants second. You are sharing a room with Phillipa and that's an end to it."

The first night passed without incident and the next morning, after breakfast, Maud set out to explore the garden. It was swiftly accomplished as Abdul the gardener was as fanatical about cleanliness in his surroundings as he was in his personal life. In between prayers, he dug and clipped, watered and mulched, until the garden, instead of being a haven for animals and small girls, became instead a tame paradise filled with ordered plants, a few birds and the ubiquitous insects. The only exceptions were the memsahib's roses. Under strict instructions to leave them alone, Abdul regarded the plants as a personal affront to his faith and his job. He avoided them entirely, pretending they did not exist.

However, even these diseased and insect-ridden plants were only a momentary distraction for a small girl and Maud joined her mother and Phillipa on the lawn for morning tea.

"Your father's gone into town to organize deliveries of groceries. I thought we might go for a walk after lunch. There are some very nice walks around here."

"I know, mummy. We went on them last year."

"Then you will remember how educational they were as well as uplifting the spirits." Pearl glanced at her older daughter. "Phillipa in particular might benefit from seeing God's handiwork."

The walk took them up the hill toward Government House. On the way they passed the Church of Saint Nicholas, Saint Joseph's School and Saint Mary's Convent. Her mother pointed out the sights and lectured them both on the proper place of church and government in an ordered life and how they could both, despite being girls, rise in society. "When the time comes, your father and I will find you good husbands. A properly educated young woman is an asset to any ambitious young man.

424

Times are changing, girls, and you must be ready to take your places in the Great British Raj."

"Yes, mama," Maud said, though she had her own ideas about her future and they certainly did not include boys. Phillipa said nothing, just plodding along stolidly behind her sister.

"I think we might move up here permanently in a year or two," Maud's mother went on. "There are some fine schools for you two, and the cooler weather is better for my health."

Maud's spirits lifted at the thought of getting away from the hot dusty heat of the Ganges plain and enjoying the cool, moist forests of the hills. She dropped back, letting her mother walk ahead before taking her sister by the hand. "Hear that, Pippa. We are moving up here. Won't that be fun? There's a lot more to explore here."

Phillipa stopped and turned to her sister, tears trickling from her eyes. "Heh … hep me," she whispered.

"What are you doing?" Their mother had looked back and saw Maud talking and Phillipa crying. "What are you saying to her?"

"Nothing, mummy. I was just saying what fun it would be to live here and she started crying. I didn't say anything else, honestly."

"Well, whatever it was, you upset your sister and you know she's ill. We will return to the Cottage immediately. Maud, you walk in front where I can keep an eye on you."

Maud opened her mouth to protest but thought better of it. She turned and started back the way they had come, after glancing once more at her sister. Phillipa had stopped crying and instead grinned broadly, one eye

425

drooping in an unmistakeable wink. Maud controlled a cry of horror and hurried off, her mother calling to her to slow down.

The bullock carts arrived in the late afternoon, disgorging more servants, a horde of dogs and mountains of luggage. For an hour, all was chaos, with people tripping over bags and dogs and the noise driving Maud's mother to her room with a headache. The spaniels went wild exploring the sights and smells of the garden and Abdul raced around after them, shouting at them when they stopped to dig in his flowerbeds or squatted on his carefully-tended lawn. Eventually, they got the energy and curiosity out of their system and disappeared inside to gather adoringly in their mistress' bedroom.

That night, Maud dreaded the moment when they would be sent to bed. She dawdled, took a very long time in the bathroom, and then insisted on saying 'goodnight' to each dog. When she started with the servants, her mother clapped her hands in annoyance and ordered her straight to bed.

Phillipa was waiting for her when she opened the door and peered in. She sat in her bed, staring at her hands which lay in her lap. "Hep," she slurred, without looking up. "Hep me."

Maud shivered but went and sat on the end of her sister's bed. "How can I help you, Pippa? I don't know what's wrong with you."

Phillipa lifted her head and once more her eyes were filled with tears. "Pray," she said clearly. For an instant she was the old Pippa that Maud loved, and then the older girl put back her head and howled with grief, the cries

426

rising in pitch and volume until shrieks of anguish filled the house.

Edwin burst into the room, a walking stick in his hand. Behind him, his wife tried to control the dogs that leapt and barked, slavering and howling with fear and rage as they lifted their voices against the screaming girl in the bed.

Maud ran to her father and cowered behind him, crying. He passed her roughly back to her mother and yelled for Abdul and the maids. Together, they fought the howling girl into a semblance of calm, her cries dying down to whimpers. Suddenly, Phillipa started to convulse, blood gushing from her bitten tongue.

"Send for the doctor," Edwin roared. "Hurry!"

Abruptly, Phillipa spasmed and fell sideways, her eyes rolling up in her head. He limbs went limp and she collapsed into her father's arms. By the time the local doctor arrived, an old man by the name of Featherston, the maids had changed the sheets and remade the bed while Edwin cleaned the blood from his daughter's face. He sent the maids out but stayed as Doctor Featherston made his examination, explaining the whole situation and his fears in short, terse sentences.

"No. Despite the convulsions it is not rabies, Mister Haye. Be reassured on that point at least."

"If it's not rabies, what is it?"

"I'd say she contracted something from the cholera cemetery. Not cholera either," the doctor added hurriedly. "To tell the truth, I don't know. All we can do for now is treat the symptoms, which means keeping her calm and keeping her cool. Featherston removed a thermometer from the girl's armpit and examined it. "A hundred and three. That's not good. She should be in a hospital."

Edwin grimaced. "The doctor at the hospital in Allahabad recommended we bring her here. That was before this latest turn of events, though."

"Well, keep her as cool as you can with moist towels under a fan. Give her half … no, a full aspirin every four hours, and I'll come back and see her in the morning."

"How do I give her aspirin if she's unconscious?"

Featherston nodded. "Dissolve one in water and rub it into her gums a little at a time. She'll absorb enough to be effective. Do not let her drink unless she is fully awake. She could choke."

The two men went out into the hall, calling the maids in to sit with the unconscious girl. The noise from the dogs prevented talk, so they entered the drawing room. Doctor Featherston gestured at the telephone. "If you don't mind, I'd like to call my wife. Let her know I'm alright."

"Of course, I'll be out the front, trying to quieten those bloody dogs. I don't know what's got into them." He left the room and closed the door.

Featherston dialed and spoke briefly with his wife. "I'll be leaving in a few minutes … yes, a cup of tea would be lovely … yes, see you soon." He replaced the receiver and ran a hand through his thinning gray hair.

"Please, are you going to make my sister better?"

Featherston saw a tear-streaked face staring up at him from a chair in the corner of the room. "Hello, I didn't see you there."

"Are you going to make my sister better?"

428

The doctor smiled. "Of course. Why, she'll ..." He stopped and frowned. "What's your name?"

"Maud, sir."

"Well, Maud, I'm going to try very hard to make your sister better, but to be honest I don't know what's wrong with her."

"She asked me to help her, but I don't know how."

"She did? When was this?"

"Just ... just before she screamed and fell over. She said, 'Help me' and 'Pray'."

Doctor Featherston nodded and ventured a small smile. "Perhaps you should do that then. Pray."

Maud frowned. "Pray to God?" she asked doubtfully.

"Are you a good Christian girl, Maud?"

"Sometimes. I go to church on Sundays with mummy and daddy and ... and Pippa, but I look out the window and wish I was outside, playing." Maud's tears brimmed over. "Is God punishing Pippa because I want to play instead of being good?"

"I don't think so, Maud." The doctor grinned. "I used to fall asleep in church," he confessed.

Maud gaped, reassessing the man standing in front of her. "So if I pray, God will help me? Even if I've been bad?"

"I expect he'll listen to you Maud. Everyone ... well, most people pray in times of trouble. To whatever god they believe in." Doctor Featherston looked at his watch. "I've got to go, Maud, but I'll see you in the morning. Be brave and pray hard."

Maud sat and looked at the open door after the doctor left. She heard his car drive away and a few moments later, her father came in and picked her up.

"Bed, little one." He saw his daughter's terror and hastily reassured her. "You'll be sleeping in another room tonight. Juleep and Mandah are taking it in turns to keep Phillipa cool." He kissed Maud's forehead and put her to bed in another bedroom, leaving a bedside light on before he went out.

Maud lay awake a long time, listening to the sounds of an active house and wondering just what was happening to her sister. "I'll pray for you, Pippa. Just like you want me to. But I'll pray to every god I can 'cause I'm not sure Jesus will listen to me." Smiling, she turned over and shut her eyes, falling asleep almost immediately despite her anxiety.

The next morning, Maud looked in on her sister as soon as she woke, but there was no change from the night before. Over breakfast, served in the kitchen by cook, she mulled over a course of action. She had tried approaching God in prayer directly a few minutes before but she felt selfconscious, awkward. *Perhaps I should get people who know what they are doing to pray for me.* She resolved to call on the vicar at the church of Saint Nicholas that morning. *Who else? What about the other gods*? She thought hard for many minutes, not noticing as cook took her plate and cup away and wiped down the table in front of her.

Walking out into the garden, she looked around for the gardener and found him muttering as he removed dog excreta from the lawn. Maud ran over and interrupted his work. "Abdul, you're a …" She stopped, not really sure what to call his faith. Her father had called him something once, a … a … "Are you a muscle man?" she asked hesitantly.

430

Abdul looked at the small girl suspiciously. "Am I what, little miss?"

"A muscle man. Daddy says you worship a different god from Jesus."

"Ah, I see," Abdul said, nodding his head, his expression solemn. "You ask if I am a Musselman, a Muslim. Yes, I am, little miss."

Maud smiled. "And you worship a different god from Christians?"

"I worship the One True God, Allah."

"Not Jesus?"

"No, little miss. You should ask your father about these things, it is not for me to instruct you in the Faith."

Maud nodded. "I can do that, but you pray, don't you? I've seen you on your little mat."

Abdul cringed at the thought that this girl child had watched him as he bowed down in worship, but hid his horror. "I pray to Allah five times a day as the Prophet instructs."

"Would you pray for my sister Phillipa? She asked me to and the doctor said I should try every god, not just ours."

Abdul raised his eyebrows. "They asked for Allah's help?"

Maud nodded, telling herself it really was true. "You are the only one who can ask your … ask Allah. Will you ask him to make Pippa better?"

Abdul stroked his beard and mustaches thoughtfully before nodding. "If it pleases Allah, he will listen to my prayer."

"Oh, thank you, Abdul." Maud almost threw her arms about him but controlled herself at the last minute.

431

Instead, she dropped into an exaggerated curtsy and ran off toward the gate. She slipped out onto the road keeping an eye out for her parents. If a servant saw her it would be a few minutes before her mother or father could be told, and she would be out of sight before then. She headed up the hill toward the Church of Saint Nicholas.

Vicar Jones was a young man with blue eyes focused on souls rather than the bodies that clothed them. Anything that drew men (and children) back to God, pleased him, and this child's request brought a smile to his lips.

"Of course I'll pray for your sister, Maud. Did your parents tell you to come and see me?"

Maud shook her head. "Phillipa said so, and Doctor Featherston." She thought she had better not say anything about asking Abdul for Allah's help.

From Saint Nicholas' she ran to Saint Mary's farther along the Mall. She stood hesitantly outside the church grounds before going in. Sometimes her mother talked about Catholics in a very uncharitable way when she thought her daughters could not hear. Maybe the Catholics have a different god, she thought. She marched into the church and braced Father Murphy in the tiny sacristy as he folded freshly laundered robes.

"And what would you be wanting, little girl?" Maud told him. "Well, sure and you have yourself a big problem, child." He fixed the girl with a glittering eye. "Are yer Catholic, child?" He sighed as Maud shook her head. "I thought I hadn't seen yer at Mass. What are yer then? A Protestant of some type, no doubt."

"Daddy says we are C of E." Maud frowned. "Does it matter?"

"Completely," Father Murphy replied. "And not at all. We are all God's children, especially those that have strayed. Away with you then, Maud. I'll be mentioning your sister at Mass tonight. I can't say fairer than that."

"Thank you." Maud bobbed into another curtsy and ran out of the church into the warm sunshine. That's three, she thought. Jesus, Allah and … and the Catholic one. What else?" She looked at a passing Hindu woman and wondered what god she worshiped. The woman would not stop and answer her questions but hurried on, wrapping her sari and shawl tightly about her.

Maud did not give up, wandering along the Mall, gradually getting further away from home. Cottages and gardens gave way to scrubland and forest. As the road climbed, deodar and oak gave way to ringal and rhododendron forest. People stopped and listened to the little girl but they either shook their heads or pointed back toward the Christian churches, thinking she was asking the way to her own god. She started to get very tired and sat down on a clay bank near a clump of bamboo where the road started dipping down toward the now invisible lake. Looking around, she was slightly worried to find that the bamboo or ringal forest stretched out around her and that she did not know where she was. Getting to her feet once more, she dusted off her skirt and stared up and down the road, trying to work out which way she had come. The road and the forest looked very much the same.

"Are you lost, little miss?"

The voice came suddenly from behind her and Maud swung round with a half-suppressed cry, knowing that the road had been empty a few moments before. "What …

433

where did you come from?" she asked the old man standing before her.

He was thin and wiry with jet black hair and a large mustache. His dark eyes penetrated deeply into her and sparkled as if amused by what they saw.

"I hear that you are seeking gods. Our gods. May I ask why a little Christian girl is looking for Hindu gods?"

"My sister is very ill and the doctors don't know what is wrong with her."

"Why do you not ask your Christian god for help?"

"I have. And the Catholic one and the … the Muslim one."

"And now you want to ask the Hindu gods to help." The old man cocked his head on one side and stared in a disconcerting way. "What do you think is wrong with her?"

"I don't know." Maud felt like crying. She was hot and tired and this strange old man kept asking her questions instead of giving her answers. "She is hot and sits still a lot. Sometimes she howls and screams. She looks at me like … like someone else is looking out of her." And then suddenly, between one heartbeat and the next, she knew what was wrong with her sister.

"The dog. There was a dog, or at least it might have been. Maybe it was a jackal or a wolf," she rambled. "In the cemetery. It attacked Pippa and she screamed and climbed out of the tomb and she's been odd ever since." She rushed on with her story, filling in fragments and back-tracking as she thought of something else. "That's it; it must be … isn't it?"

The old man nodded gravely. "Strange things happen, little girl. I could tell you stories that would keep you awake at night."

"Please. What do I do?"

"You must pray to Dhanvantari, healer to the gods. And to Pashupati, Lord of the Animals in case it really was a dog or a jackal or a wolf."

"Just pray?" Maud looked doubtful. "How do I pray? I don't know any Hindu prayers. Do they understand English?"

The old man grinned. "They are gods are they not? But you cannot just pray, you must offer up a sacrifice at their shrines on the Ayarpatta Hill."

Maud's heart sank. "A sacrifice? Of what?"

"Flowers, child. What did you think? The Lord of Animals wanted one of his own sacrificed? The Healer wanted a death? What do they teach you in your faith?"

"Sorry," Maud mumbled. "I thought that was what a sacrifice was."

"You are forgiven," the old man said, smiling. "You must offer up the most precious flowers you have, speak your request clearly, addressing the gods by name and then return home without looking back. Can you do that?"

"I ... I think so. What were their names again?"

"Dhanvantari the Healer, and Pashupati."

Maud repeated the names several times, committing them to memory. "Where is their shrine?"

The old man pointed further up the road. "Fifty paces on ..." He looked at Maud for a moment with amusement crinkling the corners of his eyes. "Seventy paces on is a small track marked by a white stone. Follow

435

it up the hill until you come to the road that leads to the reservoir. Look for a very tall deodar tree. The shrine of Dhanvantari lies beneath it."

"And that of Pashupati?"

"The Lord of Animals has no shrine here as he does not need one. The forest lies all about him and is his shrine. Say your prayers to both and they will hear."

"Thank you," Maud said. "I will go home and get some flowers immediately."

"Lay two whole flowers, the very best you can find, on the ground at the shrine, then as you walk home, drop petals behind you so the gods can find your sister."

Maud opened her mouth, then thought better of her action and closed it again, thinking that she had better not ask the question. After a moment, she shrugged mentally and asked it anyway. "How can two gods who know English not know where my sister lives?"

The old man looked at her solemnly without speaking for over a minute. "You are asking the gods to do you a great service, little miss," he said quietly. "Can you not do a very small thing for the gods?"

Maud blushed and hung her head. "Yes, I'm sorry. I 'pologize."

"Go then and gather your flowers. Pray for your sister."

"Will you come with me? Help me?"

The old man shook his head. "I have other things to do, little miss. This you must do alone, if your love for your sister is great enough." He turned and wandered off up the road.

Maud watched him until he turned the corner and disappeared. "It is," she whispered. "I love Pippa." She ran off in the opposite direction and soon found herself back in familiar parts of the Mall.

After lunch, Edwin took the car and drove into the town again to consult with Doctor Featherston. His wife gathered her eight spaniels about her like sycophantic courtiers and went to her room. Maud crept into the bedroom where her sister still lay unconscious, one maid dabbing her hot face and body with a cool flannel, the other working a woven punkah with a cord tied to one foot.

"What's wrong with the fan?" she asked.

"It is broken, memsahib," Juleep said, ceasing her labors as punkah-wallah for a moment. "The lecetricity has gone."

"No electricity?" Maud tried the light switch but with no effect. She shrugged and looked across at her sister. "I'm getting help, Pippa," she said quietly.

"Pardon, memsahib?" Mandah asked.

"Nothing." Maud left, closing the door, and tiptoed down the hall to listen at her mother's bedroom door. All she could hear was her heavy breathing and a soft ripping sound as one of the spaniels broke wind. "Bad dog," she muttered. She looked for Abdul the gardener next and located him sharpening knives in the little shed at the back of the garden. Leaving him to his labors she went back inside the house and took a pillow case from the linen closet before creeping out the front door and down to her mother's rose bushes.

Despite the neglect of the last few months, the straggly stems bore a bountiful crop of flowers, from bud to full-blown bloom. First, she selected the best two she could find, a huge red tea rose and a white bud, and broke

437

the stems, putting them on one side. Then she opened up the pillow case and systematically started stripping every petal from the bushes. By the time she finished, the pillow case was only half full but she knew it would have to do. *I'll just have to drop the petals farther apart.*

The track leading up the Ayarpatta Hill by the white stone was lying in deep shade by the time Maud got there, the sun having dipped below the hill, though there was still plenty of daylight left. She hurried, feeling slightly scared as the ringal forest lay silent about her. Every now and then she would stop and listen, hoping to hear reassuring noises of people, maybe a woodcutter or a farmer heading homeward. Even some birdsong would have been a relief, but all she heard, very faint – so faint it may have been imagination – was a soft footfall on the dry bamboo leaves of the forest floor, off to one side. She wavered in her determination for a few seconds, before turning and running up the path as hard as she could go. Minutes later, she burst out onto the road leading to the reservoir and there, not fifty yards away, stood a very tall deodar.

The shrine of Dhanvantari was like many hill shrines, a simple house-shaped structure of wood, only large enough to hold a small statue of the god and a scattering of offerings, rice and saffron, milk and strings of flowers. Maud lugged her sack of petals across the open space under the tree to the shrine and gazed at the blank eyes of the statue. *It's only a statue. How can it help*? She thrust her doubts aside and opening the pillow case, took out the two intact roses. The larger one she placed among the offerings before the god. *It's his shrine after all.* The white bud she placed a few paces away, at the edge of the open space. Clearing her throat self-consciously, Maud addressed the gods.

"Dhanvantari and Pashupati, my sister Pipp … Phillipa is sick. Very sick. I bring you an offering of the best flowers in my mother's garden and ask that you heal her." Nothing happened. The only sound was that of a gentle breeze in the branches of the deodar. "Please." She hesitated, but could not think of anything else to say, so she turned and walked away, feeling let down.

At the edge of the clearing, she dropped her first rose petal, counted out five steps and dropped another. Crossing the reservoir road, she walked steadily down the forest track, dropping petals as she went. She resisted the temptation to look back, despite a very strong feeling that she was being followed. The feeling grew as the pillow case emptied and by the time she passed the white stone and set off at a run down the Mall, she was sure the footsteps she had heard earlier were back, louder and nearer. The old man's injunction not to look back was forgotten – nothing on earth would have induced her to turn and confront the thing she knew was close on her heels. Trembling with fright, she raced past cottages and into the lane where her home stood, scattering the petals from the bottom of the case. The last few she left at the gate, ducking inside and slamming the iron catch shut. She stood panting in the dusk until one of the maids came out to fetch her inside to face her mother's anger over the stripped rose bushes.

That night, without her supper, Maud lay down on her bed and looked across to her sister. The electricity was still off, the line having come down somewhere to the south. The air was hot, despite the elevation, and Edwin

439

had the girls' beds carried out onto the verandah where they could catch the cooling effect of the gentle breeze off the lake. The mosquito netting tucked around the beds hardly stirred and Maud lay wakeful in the dark, watching Phillipa across the breadth of the verandah. The older girl lay motionless. Earlier that evening, she had woken from her sleep and taken a little nourishment, and now she lay awake too, staring up at the ceiling, though not giving any sign of cognition.

The stars slowly wheeled across the sky, a scattering of jewels that shed so faint a light that even after her eyes became accustomed to the dark, Maud could only make out the other furniture around her as dark shapes. Night birds cried on the hill behind the house and once a leopard called up in the ringal forest. Some animal scratched its busy way across the iron roof and something slithered in the dry earth beneath the verandah. Maud fell asleep at last, wondering whether any of the gods would really help her.

She awoke minutes or hours later, she had no way to tell. The moon had risen, a broad half coin of silver that threw a path of light down the verandah and between the two beds. Into that path of silver light, moving noiselessly, loped a huge gray wolf. It slowed as it came level with the beds and looked toward Maud, its eyes glittering like shards of mica, its breath hot and smelling of blood. After a few minutes, its glowing eyes blinked and it turned toward the other bed. The great shaggy head stretched forward and it sniffed the older girl, the fur on its hackles rising, and a low growl issuing from its throat. Moving closer to her feet, the wolf stood at the foot of Phillipa's bed and stared unwaveringly at the girl.

Maud lay rigid with fear; certain this was the wolf from the tomb. Somehow it had followed them up from the cemetery in Allahabad and was now going to kill her sister, then her. She tried to scream, to call for her father, but her limbs were paralyzed, her throat remained closed. All she could do was watch, and as the hours passed, the wolf just stood there, staring at Phillipa, a barely audible rumble its only sign of life. Not even its flanks moved as it breathed. So still did it remain that if Maud had not seen it arrive, she would have thought it a statue. Phillipa lay quietly, the only sign of life was a shudder that racked her body every now and then, but despite her paralysis and the knowledge that this creature of the dark places was here to kill them both, Maud felt her fear slowly lift. The moon slipped round the sky but the silver light path across the verandah remained, illuminating the wolf and ... something else. Maud felt her fear come crashing back. At the head of the bed, where Phillipa's face stared at the ceiling, a shape was forming. A fog, light and misty, vaguely blueish, swirled around Phillipa's bed and slowly solidified into the lean, hungry body of a jackal. It sat on the boards between the two beds, leaning forward intently, staring back at the gray wolf. The jackal grinned, showing its teeth. A red tongue lolled from the open mouth and the eyes glittered red in the dark head. The wolf turned its gaze from the girl to the jackal and fixed its gaze on the other animal, otherwise remaining motionless.

The night passed slowly, both animals staring at each other across the few paces that separated them. As the eastern sky grayed, leaking light across the landscape, the wolf slowly and with a stiff-legged gait, advanced on the jackal. The smaller animal arose, and snarled, deep and throatily. In total silence, the wolf sprang and its jaws closed on the jackal's throat, bearing it to the ground. The jackal convulsed, its claws scrabbling loudly against the floorboards before collapsing and shuddering. When all movement ceased, the wolf loosened its grip and turned to stare at Maud.

As the first rays of the morning sun broke over the hills to the east, throwing a beautiful glow of gold over the cottage, the wolf and the body of the jackal at its feet faded, dissolving as if they were mist blown by the breeze, until they were gone.

A sudden noise made Maud cry out and she swung to face her sister's bed. Phillipa was sitting up. She had thrown the mosquito netting to one side and she was looking around her in growing consternation. Seeing her younger sister, she gave a cry of delight.

"Maud, I've had the strangest dream."

Maud yelped and threw herself across the verandah, hugging her sister delightedly. "You've been sick, Pippa, but your better now," she gabbled. "I prayed and … and I sacrificed and the gods answered my prayers."

"Whoa. Steady the buffs, Maud. What are you talking about? And when did we come up to Naini Tal? I don't remember anything after the cemetery. Did I get too much sun? Tell me what's happening."

After breakfast, while Doctor Featherston and her parents were examining Phillipa, Maud wandered up the Mall road again, hoping to find the old man. To her delight, he was sitting by the side of the road in the place she had seen him the day before.

"There you are," Maud said. "It worked."

442

"I thought it might. You said a prayer from the heart and scattered the flower petals properly. The gods heard you."

Maud stared at the old man, wondering how he knew these things. She gulped and stuttered before forcing out her question. "Who are you? Really? Are ... are you a god?"

The old man laughed. "I have been called many things, little girl. Do I not look like a man to you? Surely the gods are tall and handsome, strong and full of wisdom?" He laughed some more, then wiped his eyes on the ends of his sleeves. "My name is Pandalis."

"I am pleased to meet you, Pandalis. My name is Maud ... Maud Haye."

Pandalis got to his feet and made a slight bow. "Stay away from broken tombs and lonely graveyards, Maud Haye." He turned and set off up the road.

"Will I see you again?" Maud called out.

Without turning, Pandalis called back. "Only the gods can say, Miss Maud. Only the gods."

Chapter Twenty-Two

I think becoming a god has made me blind. I started life as a demon and I know from legends and stories and even my own experience that other demons exist. In fact I met one not so long ago – what was it, a century and a half ago? The female demon that impersonated Kali led me to my apotheosis, yet I never really considered the likelihood of coming across another one. The Kali-demon is out there somewhere unless the real Kali has hunted her down and killed her. Can demons truly die, I hear you ask? Oh yes, without a doubt. Gods are powerful, more powerful even than I, who only aspire to be one. I have no doubt that were I to meet a real god face to face, I would die a swift death. So I mind my own business, wander these beautiful hills and mountains, and seek to better myself. Maybe if the teachings of the Buddha are correct, I will one day reach nirvana and attain godhead. Then, I will lose individuality and no longer be in danger.

I arrived in Naini Tal that summer, before the heat started, and reveled in the cool, fresh breezes off the lake, the myriad paths through the hills and the luxuriant forests of oak and pine, deodar, ringal and rhododendron. The town itself had grown since last I saw it. In fact, the Naini Tal I visited at the time of the Thuggee was only a village at the north end of the curved lake. In eighteen-forty, the British had made it one of their hill stations, large numbers of army officers and their families building cottages and bungalows in and around the village, expanding over the years along the eastern shore to the southern end where the road ran down to Kathgodam and the railhead. Churches followed, and schools, until the town became an outpost of the dying British Raj in the foothills of the Himalayas.

There were still many native tribesmen in the region, devout and hardworking and it was an ideal place for a struggling young god to set up business. I wandered the trails in the guise of the old Pahari, Pandalis and effected many cures as a healer. Where people looked to me as the source of their healing, I directed them to the shrine of Dhanvantari under the tall deodar on Ayarpatta. I had built it myself and offered up the first sacrifice soon after I arrived. If Dhanvantari himself was watching, I did not want to incur his enmity by taking credit in his name, so I steered people toward him and as he did nothing, I cured in his name. I think we were both satisfied for he never bothered me. Pashupati too, for I managed the animals in the area, guiding them away from crops as best I could and luring hunters away from them.

I stayed close to the Hindu population, generally leaving the British alone. I liked individuals among them but as a race they had outstayed their time in India. One day soon they would leave and India could forge its own destiny, follow its own gods, free of alien influence. There was one man who lived in Naini Tal, an Englishman known as 'Carpet Sahib', who was one of the better ones. He occupied a cottage near Ayarpatta but put out his hand to help anybody in need. His reputation was made by the time he came to Naini, for he was a great hunter. Now, one would think that would not be a mark of favor, but he limited himself for the most part to hunting maneating tigers and leopards and without a doubt saved hundreds of lives over the years. This

445

Corbett man was held in high regard by government officials and though he later went overseas and died there, many years later a National Park was formed in his name. I worked with him on many occasions, in various guises, and we had some interesting talks on wildlife and its management. He had an intuitive knowledge of the forests and I belive this knowledge saved his life on more than one occasion.

The only other English person I came to know in Naini was a young girl. Gripped by a personal grief and unable to find solace within her own beliefs, she reached out to the Hindu gods. *What could I do*? Gossip spreads like a forest fire in the dry season and within hours of her starting her quest, news had reached me. I appeared to her in the ringal forest and listened to her tale, which intrigued me. Her sister had been exposed to some infection, down there in the cholera cemetery of Allahabad, an infection that had targeted her nervous system. Well, I could cure those – sometimes – and I was willing to try. However, the girl was reaching out to the gods, so the gods must answer. I instructed her on how to appeal to Dhanvantari the healer and I threw in Pashupati as well, as the image of the dog in the tomb was prominent in her mind. Yes, I went into her mind. Just for a few moments to get her disjointed story clear in my mind. I did not even feed from her energies as I have found an alternative to taking what I need.

A quick aside then, as I do not want you to think I was still demon enough to feed off unwilling humans. A strange thing happens when a human offers up a prayer or a sacrifice to a god. Part of his mind goes out and the energy of his being is offered freely to the deity. If a man offers a sacrifice to me as Pashupati or Dhanvantari, I am offered more than the rice, or flowers or incense. He offers me his being too, and I absorb some of it. You could regard it as payment for the service I perform, but however you regard it, it has now been many years since I have fed off an unwilling life and many more since I killed men to sustain myself. I will not kill a human again.

So, back to the girl. I instructed her to find flowers and borrowed a story from her mind, a story of children lost in the forest and scattering bread behind them. She ran off to get the flowers and I waited, invisible, for her return. When she came, I followed her, as a wolf padding softly through the ringal forest. Reaching the deodar, the girl made her sacrifice and I followed her home.

That night, as the moon rose, I went to her, prepared to enter the house and possess her sister. Instead, they slept on the verandah and I padded down the avenue of silver light to the girl's bed. She was awake and watching me in a wash of fear. I stilled her limbs and turned my attention to her sick sister. I was amazed to find a demon in possession of Phillipa's body.

"Who are you?" I asked of the demon curled up in her head. (Remember that a demon has no physical substance and can exist in the whole of a body or just part of it, as it pleases. Also we do not talk as humans do, being able to communicate in silence).

It sat there and stared out of the girl's eyes at my wolf shape for several minutes, apparently unaware that the form standing before it was a construct of my mind. "My name is Ravana," it said at last. "Beware lest I fall on you and destroy you."

447

"You are not Ravana. He was the demon-king of Lanka thousands of years ago. You are a demon and possibly old but you are not he."

"That is the name I go by," he said sulkily. "Leave me alone."

"What happened to falling on me and destroying me?"

"I have no quarrel with you," Ravana said. "This is my prey. I found her."

"But I have a quarrel with you while you are in her body. This girl in the other bed asked me to rid her sister of an infection. You are that infection."

"You are a demon yourself," Ravana said slowly. "I can see your flame. Why does a demon take orders from a human? Why do you not possess her and use her?"

"She does not order me. She petitioned me through prayer."

"People pray to the gods, not to demons. Are you mad ... or do you think yourself a god?" Ravana laughed and uncurled, stretching out into the rest of Phillipa's body.

"Whatever I am, I try to do what is right and I know that it is not right for you to possess that girl."

Ravana laughed again. "A demon with morals. What is your name, o demon who would be a god?"

"Pandalis, but that is not relevant." I fixed my fiercest stare on Ravana. "Will you vacate that body willingly, or must I force you?"

"You think you could?" Ravana stared back and I felt the ripple of his flame pass through mine as he examined my capabilities. "Well, perhaps you could, after all." He shrugged mentally. "If she means that much to you, I will

448

exchange sisters. You take this one and I will possess the smaller one over there." The eyes of his host flicked casually toward Maud. "She is awake and watches us, though her fear is great. How can you still her without possessing her?"

I was not about to give away any of my secrets so I did not answer. Instead, I sent a tendril of my being inside Phillipa's lower body. It was answered in an instant as Ravana hurled his not inconsiderable strength against mine. We fought, as furiously as any two human warriors in battle, though our watcher saw nothing and Phillipa felt little. I was stronger and more experienced than this demon – I could feel that from our first touch – and I should have been able to overcome him within minutes. My weakness lay in my reluctance to let any harm come to my patient. I shielded her from as much harm and pain as I could while I stubbornly fought my way up her body, grappling with Ravana through arteries and nerves, organs and muscles, forcing him up to his refuge of last resort in Phillipa's brain. Here I found the girl herself, frightened and whimpering in the dark recesses of her mind, watching the two demons that fought for control of her body. Hours passed as I first isolated Ravana from the physical part of Phillipa and then gradually forced him out.

He emerged as a swirl of mist, shot through with blue streaks of his anger, and coagulated into the form of a jackal beside the girl's bed. My own form as wolf now confronted him, for I had not relinquished my guise even as I fought him through the channels of our human prize.

449

"You have defeated me," he panted, his jackal tongue lolling. "Let me go and I will depart, seeking victims elsewhere."

"No."

"Why not? We are both demons, you know as well as I that we exist by preying on men. I will withdraw from this place and leave this girl for you."

"I do not trust you."

Ravana grinned. "You wish me to swear an oath?"

"On what? You have no honor and you believe in no god."

"Then we are at an impasse."

I had a problem. I had forced the demon out of Phillipa but I could not prevent his reentry or possession of Maud. Had our positions been reversed, I have no doubt he would destroy me without a thought, but my conscience – that new-found and troubling addition – told me it was wrong to kill. I could not attack him, but I could defend myself.

"You are right," I said, allowing a touch of resignation and defeat to show. "I will accept your promise. Go from here and trouble these people no more." I did the equivalent of lowering my fists and turning away, though the girl probably saw no change in the wolf's stance. At once, Ravana saw his chance and his power lashed out at me. Had my strength been a whit less, he might have succeeded. However, once his initial thrust was blocked, I turned on him and overwhelmed him. I sprang and gripped him by the throat and what took place invisibly was no less final. I drank of his flame voraciously, feeling his strength feed me and his being, his individuality dwindle to nothingness.

I stood over the fallen carcass of the jackal, Ravana's chosen guise, waiting for the last flickers of life to leave him. The first light of dawn arose in the eastern sky and as it did, he faded from sight. I followed, for my work was done and the little girl's prayers to Dhanvantari and Pashupati answered.

The old Pahari man reformed in the ringal forest, for I was interested to see whether the girl had guessed at my identity. She had, but no child needs to meet a god face to face, so I turned her enquiry away and left her.

I left Naini Tal not long after and set off on my wanderings again. Times were changing rapidly in India as the country lurched inexorably toward its independence. I was interested in whether this could be accomplished peacefully or whether the British would fight to retain their Empire. In the end, I was in Garhwal when independence arrived. Although the hill tribes were less fired up than their southern brethren, the aftermath of passionate feelings spilled into bloody deeds as a great country found itself divided.

Chapter Twenty-Three

The little village of Charangat sat astride a ridge about thirty kilometers north of Kalsi and fifty kilometers from Mussoorie in the District of Dehra Dun in the newly formed State of Uttar Pradesh in the equally newly formed Union of India. Charangat was remarkable for only two things; the first being that its population of two hundred and two men, women and children almost exactly matched the national average of eighty-one percent Hindu, thirteen percent Muslim and equal percentages of Christians, Sikhs and Buddhists; the second being that in its five hundred year history there had never been a case of murder or violent death within its boundaries. Even in times of war, when opposing armies marched through the hills bent on pillage and slaughter, the inhabitants of Chandragat had offered hospitality to all. Its grinding poverty had discouraged looting and the easy-going nature of its people offered no cause for violence.

Both claims to fame came to an end on the night of August the sixteenth in the year nineteen forty-seven. It was not a foreign army that ripped the community apart, but its own smoldering bigotry that had grown within the minds of men over the years, finally bearing poisonous fruit even as their country achieved its long-awaited independence.

Greater India, which stretched from the Afghan border to the lands of Burma in the east, had been home for centuries to two of the great religions of the world, Hinduism and Islam. Although the two could exist in harmony and often did, there was always a suspicion in the minds of believers from either camp that they were unjustly treated. In the long fight against the British to achieve independence the two religions fought alongside one another but when it came to dividing the spoils, consensus could not be reached. Despite the efforts of Mohandas K Gandhi to see that the Muslim minority was not disadvantaged in the new independent India, the Muslim-dominated districts to the west and east could not find common ground with the Hindu-dominated center and in the interests of peace, a partition of India was proclaimed.

The mainly Muslim districts of Punjab, Sindh, Baluchistan, the North-West Province and Bengal became part of the Dominion of Pakistan, while the bulk of the country became Hindu India. Many Muslims chose to stay in the areas they called home but many millions migrated westward. These refugees from an increasingly hostile homeland met millions of Hindus streaming eastward, eager to be among their fellow religionists. Bloody battles broke out and disputes raged over areas near the border where approximately equal numbers of Hindu and Muslim lived. The Princely States became part of India or Pakistan mostly on the whim of their ruler, but this decision was not always amicable. The ruler of Kashmir was a Hindu, whereas the majority of his subjects were Muslim. When he opted to join the union of India, violence erupted. Kashmir is still a disputed region.

Charangat, on its little ridge away from the main trade routes, missed the violence and bloodshed in the lead-up to Partition and when the Day of Independence finally arrived, joined in the days of celebration. It was just unfortunate that the Great Day happened to fall on a Friday. Mondays and Thursdays are days of fasting in the Muslim communities and the day before Independence was no exception. The three Muslim families of Charangat spent the daylight hours fasting with the heads of the families, Nasser Musharraf, Liquat ul-Haq, and Hussein Ali Khan leading wives and children in the day's prayers.

Friday dawned bright and clear. Dawn prayers were followed by a small meal and preparations started for the celebrations. The whole population was to meet in the middle of the village where speeches were planned by the chief and elders, the children would sing, and a great feast would be eaten. For days, women had been cooking food from the tithe put aside by common assent. Drink was present in abundance, from the thin, sour beer brewed locally to the cases of bottled beer brought in on the backs of willing villagers. The Muslims of Charangat did not partake of intoxicating drink, of course, the Prophet, peace be upon him, having declared such things *haram*. Nevertheless, they displayed forebearance and tried not to look too disapproving when the others in the village imbibed. As a treat, Mohindar Vishnu Patel, the village chief, had dug into his pocket and bought five cases of Coca-Cola, enough for every child and youth in the village to have a bottle. These were cooling in the stream that lay below Charangat, alongside the much more plentiful beer.

Mid-morning arrived and the village center seethed with activity. The elders were determined that their community would not be shown up as provincial and backward. Carpenters constructed a stage for the speakers, festooned in bunting of orange, white and green, the new national colors. A flagpole was erected in the open space in front of the stage, from the top of which hung a rather bedraggled Union Jack. Although the British flag had never officially flown above Charangat, the elders had decided it would be a particularly symbolic gesture if, at the stroke of noon, the flag of the Raj descended and the new flag of hope and Independence rose into the skies. They ignored the fact that India would then have been independent for twelve hours, very conscious that the eyes of, if not the world, at least Mussoorie and the district of Dehradun would be upon them. Gopal Chandra Shah, a farmer of Charangat, had a wife who was the sister of a man who had once helped the aunt of an editor for the Mussoorie Gazette. Favors had been called in and the reporter, Vinayak Rao, now sat in the shade of the fig tree beside the stage in the middle of the village, sipping on a cool beer and fanning his face with a sweat-stained hat, unsure as to just what he had done to deserve this assignment. He had promised his editor a thrilling account of the day's activities and the elders of the village that he would write a favorable report on the Independence Day celebrations in Charangat.

"Not that it'll be printed," he grumbled to himself. "Nothing ever happens here and nobody cares about these stupid little villages." Rao hailed one of the women and persuaded her to fetch another bottle of beer. When she fetched one from the stream, he pressed the cool bottle against his forehead, sighing with the relief. His headache had come on quite suddenly on the way to Charangat and showed no signs of abating.

455

Midday approached and the crowd in the village center swelled. Already, the elders of the village were seated on the stage, staring out over the crowd and striving to look nonchalant, as if this sort of thing was something they did every day. They failed miserably, fidgeting and sneaking surreptitious looks at the notes they had made for their speeches. The village chief, Mohindar Vishnu Patel, liked to think of himself as thoroughly modern and had brought in a small petrol-driven generator to provide power to run a microphone for the speeches. He now carried the microphone on its stand over to a battered old truck that had somehow traversed the rutted roads up to Charangat. Trailing a long wire from the microphone, he thrust the head close to the warped hood of the truck as his son Madanlal enthusiastically leaned on the horn. The amplified blast made people jump and several women screamed, the noise being taken up by the children who yelled and shouted as hard as they could. The sound carried the length of the ridge and into the valleys on either side, bringing the remaining population running.

Patel carried the microphone back to the stage and carefully set it up again. He stood behind it and waited for silence, his patient stance eventually attracting the interest of everyone, and conversation died away. Ignoring the inevitable cries of babies, Patel lifted his arms and addressed the crowd.

"Citizens of Charangat, today is a day unlike any other you have seen. All our lives we have lived under the rule of a foreign power." He gestured dramatically at the flagpole topped by the limp Union Jack, and every eye followed him. "But no more. On this day, the fifteenth of

456

August, nineteen forty-seven, we have cast off these chains and have risen up as a new India, a Union of India in which every Hindu can be proud." Patel paused and scanned the crowd, beaming with pride. He saw Nasser Musharraf frowning and realized his gaffe. "Every Muslim too, of course," he added, drawing attention to his omission. "Now, before we start the celebrations which will culminate in the raising of the glorious new flag of India, we shall hear a few short words from the beloved elders of our village." As he finished, his son Madanlal started applauding, aided by several of his friends. The clapping spread, rippling through the crowd, despite thirsty looks that were cast on the crates of beer stacked in the shade.

The first speaker, a portly middle-aged storekeeper named Shankar Rastriya Vaish, rose to his feet and nervously approached the microphone. Not being used to the latest technology, he leaned close and shouted his first words, the crash of sound startling him so much he jumped and the crowd roared with laughter. Making the best of it, he forced a nervous smile and mopped his brow, restarting his speech from several feet away. His first words were lost until one of the other elders got up and repositioned the microphone.

Vaish rambled on for twenty minutes, talking about how a Union of India would be good for trade, based on Indian goods rather than British goods. His arguments were based on dubious facts and he drew far-fetched conclusions from them, the whole tenor of his speech reflecting dreams of economic glory rather than cold hard reality.

457

Patel glanced at his watch, adding up the minutes and estimating the time left before the planned noon ceremony. Unless Vaish finished soon, they would be running late. He shrugged, disguising the gesture by re-crossing his legs and keeping a look of rapt attention on his face. *How many people have watches anyway*, he asked himself. *The rest won't know we are late*.

At last, the storekeeper's speech limped to a halt. Vaish stood at the microphone in silence for a minute, obviously searching for something else to say. He shook his head and ventured, "Long live the Union of India." The crowd broke into loud cheers and Vaish returned smiling to his chair, letting Gopal Chandra Shah take his place.

Shah talked about farming and crops, being a farmer and the son of a farmer. He spoke of lentils and beans, of corn and amaranth, and of the poppy crop that grew far up the hillside. The reporter, who had been half-asleep in his chair under the fig tree, pricked up his ears at the mention of opium and thought to himself that the editor of the Mussoorie Gazette might after all be interested in his article. He started scribbling in his notepad.

Chandra Shah gave up his spot to Suryadev Nathuram Kamath, a carpenter, but a man who could claim two whole years of high school education. As a child, his parents had died of a sickness and he had gone to live with a relative in far-off Delhi. The relative was a lawyer and had put Kamath into school with his own son. Two years of education at St Stephen's College had not wrought much effect on the youth as he preferred the nightlife of the city and the company of hooligans to the study of books. His faith suffered in a city dedicated to

458

self-interest and under the influence of a man tainted by Marxism, tossed his beliefs and his gods aside, striving to follow pure socialist reason. A near arrest curtailed his increasingly bad habits and under pressure from his lawyer relative, he had apprenticed himself out to a cabinet maker and learnt much of the ways of wood. Ten years later, Kamath returned to Charangat and opened a small business, marrying and raising a large family in the process. Now the richest man in the village and a lot of the surrounding countryside, as well as being the most educated, he was consulted on a variety of issues.

Kamath spoke on the benefits of a good education, hinting that a good deal more than two years had been spent acquiring his knowledge and wisdom. He deplored the superstitious beliefs of the uneducated man and lost no opportunity in encouraging people to send their children to school.

"Now that India is independent," he said. "She must take her place proudly among the nations of the earth. We can no longer afford to be known as a nation of servants, of shop-keepers, of peasant farmers. We must educate ourselves and become lawyers, judges, teachers and scientists. I, myself, could have done this, being educated in Delhi by one of its foremost jurisprudence practitioners ..." Kamath lost his audience at this point, which was perhaps just as well, as he had left the truth behind for that shadowland construction that reflected what he might have become. "I left the city to return to the village of my birth that I might help my less fortunate brethren. I implore you, as we stand at the bright doorway of a glorious future, to cast aside those superstitions that hold you fast, to throw away this unreasoning belief in a supernatural being to which you can pray, and grasp the strong staff of knowledge." His next words precipitated bloodshed – not then, but soon. "Let knowledge be your god, not Brahma, not Vishnu, nor Shiva, nor Allah, nor Buddha, nor Jesus. They are all false gods." He sat down smiling, content that he had helped his village.

Most of Kamath's audience did not hear his last statement, or if they did, did not pay attention to it. Nasser Musharraf was one that heard and understood and he stiffened, staring at the stage. He waited for Patel to repudiate the statement, but when the Chief did not, rising instead to deliver his own speech, Musharraf knew he must act to defend the Holy Name of Allah. He gathered the Muslim men around him and dispatched his son Abdullah to order the women and children away.

Patel's eye caught the swirl of movement as the Muslims pushed through the crowd and for an instant held the peace of his village in his hands. He let it slip away as a feeling of annoyance overcame him. The words of his speech died away and he called out petulantly.

"Nasser Musharraf, why do you lead your people away? Do you not want to celebrate India's independence on this glorious day?"

Musharraf halted, his sons lending moral support as they stood and glared at the villagers. "I cannot stay and hear the True God slandered. I am not a violent man so rather, I will take my people away so you may continue your celebrations."

"Stay at least for the raising of the flag, Musharraf. This is your country too that we honor."

"It is past the noon hour and we must offer up the Jumu'ah, the noon prayers, on this our holy day."

Kamath leapt to his feet and tried unsuccessfully to take the microphone from Patel, finally leaning over the railing of the stage and yelling at the tall, bearded Muslim. "What is more important? To offer superstitious prayers or to honor the flag of your country?"

The young Muslims roared with anger but Musharraf shouted above their clamor. "The Prophet, peace be upon him, warns us against idolatry, urging us to worship Allah, the Benificent and Merciful, in purity and truth. You, Suryadev Nathuram Kamath, along with your fellow Hindus, worship idols; and now you wish to add a flag to their number. Neither I, nor my family, nor any of my people, will worship this flag of yours." He turned, and with his sons and the other men, strode through the crowd, shoving aside anyone who was slow to move.

Kamath stared after them, pale and quivering with anger. "Then if you will not honor India's flag, go back to Pakistan, for you do not belong here," he yelled.

Patel started appealing for calm and after a while, by virtue of the fact that he had the microphone and could shout louder than anyone else, managed to quieten the crowd and resume his interrupted speech. He struggled on for nearly twenty minutes but his heart was not in the platitudes written in his notes and he gave up. Signaling the children, Patel led the villagers in a ragged rendition of the new national anthem as the limp Union Jack was lowered and the crisp new Union of India flag rose in its stead. A volley of cheering broke out, the Hindus who now totally dominated the crowd in the middle of the village, leading the celebrations, though the Christian

461

couple with their infant daughter, the Sikh husband and wife, and the two Buddhist monks also showed their patriotism by clapping. Only the Muslims, twenty-seven of them, refrained from the celebration, being at that moment in their cramped *masjid*, offering up the two *raka'ah* of the Friday *dhuhr* prayers.

As was proper, Nasser Musharraf first gave a short sermon or khutba, in which he dwelled on the insidious presence of idolatry and false worship all around them. It was only thanks to Allah, the Benificent and Merciful that they had escaped being present when the flag, which until then had escaped their notice as being an idol, had risen above them. "Even now," he said, "the false worship of the perfidious Hindu threatens our very existence here in Charangat."

Musharraf, being not only the eldest of the Faithful, but also the best educated, having once studied under an Imam in Lahore many years before, had been elected Speaker, or khatib, by the acclaim of the Muslim men. The women, of course, had no say in the matter, as the study of the Qur'an was very properly the duty of the men. Women concerned themselves with the home and let their menfolk guide them in the avoidance of sin.

Following the sermon, the women and girls departed from the main room and crammed into a smaller windowless chamber where they could perform the rituals without fear of contaminating the men as they approached Allah, the Benificent and Merciful, in prayer. Musharraf, as khatib, led the communal prayer, after which the women hurried off to prepare a meal while the men and youths gathered in the courtyard of the masjid to talk about the days occurrences. The sound of raucous

462

celebrations intruded on their quiet talk and several of the young men cast angry eyes toward the street.

"We should not be standing here talking while the infidels bring shame on our village," Ali al-Abbas muttered. A young man without skills, he had drifted up from Dehradun a month before and stayed to help Liquat ul-Haq with his bakery as the unfortunate man had no sons of his own, only four daughters and, as every man knows, daughters are only useful in the home, not in business.

"You are right," Muhammad Khan agreed. "But what are we to do? There are only nine able-bodied men in the masjid."

Muhammad Musharraf scoffed. "Are we women to be frightened by a few Hindus? Did not the Prophet, peace be upon him, say that the Faithful are armed with Righteousness? Father, you act as Imam. Am I not right?" His brothers, Abdullah and Jamaal joined in, entreating their father.

Nasser Musharraf stroked his beard thoughtfully and looked around at the eager faces of his three sons, and the two young single men without family, Ali al-Abbas and Houd Is-Haaq. "The Prophet, peace be upon him, did so speak. Yet I would counsel patience, a virtue that the Prophet, peace be upon him, also prized highly."

"Listen to the Imam," Faris Ghasaan growled. He worked his jaw as if chewing something in his toothless mouth and scowled at Jamaal, who stood nearest him. "I saw troubles in my younger days down in Delhi. The Hindus are too many."

463

"And you are content to sit in the sun and talk, old man," Jamaal retorted. "The fire has gone out of your belly."

"Jamaal, you forget yourself," snapped his father. "No son of mine talks to an elder that way. You will apologize at once."

Jamaal bowed his head, giving way to the authority of his father and begged the old man's forgiveness. Faris Ghasaan hemmed and hawed, but glad of the attention, grinned toothlessly and accepted the youth's apology.

The young men bowed respectfully to their fathers and the older men, and excused themselves. Musharraf admonished them not to cause trouble and let them go.

Muhammad Musharraf led the other youths and young men out into the street. "We shall be obedient to the will of my father," he said. "But he will see that it is not us that start the fight. The Hindus will start it ... and we will finish it."

"What are we going to do?" Muhammad Ali Khan asked anxiously.

"Nothing at all. Just follow me." The young Musharraf led the other five young men down the dusty street toward the sounds of revelry. As they sauntered into the open place around the fig tree and the stage, those nearest them edged away, becoming a lot less boisterous as they kept a wary eye open for trouble. The main groups of revelers were still unaware that the Muslim youths were back and kept up the singing and dancing. Bottles of cool beer passed from hand to hand and children ran, weaving through the crowd laughing, a handful of pi-dogs at their heels.

A young Hindu, Prabhat Nanda, drinking in the company of his friends, saw the young Muslims and called out loudly. "Muhammad, have you come to join in the celebrations?"

"I do not worship idols," Muhammad said calmly. "I leave that sort of thing to you, for you have many false gods whereas we have only the One True God."

Digambar Gujral and Gangadhar Kapil joined their friend Prabhat, their faces no longer smiling. "Who are you to insult our gods? Get out of here and leave us alone."

"I would like nothing better but it is you who invited us," Muhammad said, pointing at Chief Patel. "I stay only to tell you that your gods are nothing more than hunks of stone and wood." A murmur of horror raced through the crowd and heads turned toward the young Muslims with the strutting figure of Musharraf's son to the fore. In the silence, his words rang clear and were heard by all as he pointed to the flag of the Union of India flapping in the breeze at the top of the flagpole. "That flag that you worship is nothing more than colored cloth. It will not feed you, clothe you or give you shelter. It is worthless." He hawked up phlegm from his throat and spat in the dust.

A cry of outrage and anger shattered the quietness after his words and a bottle arced overhead to thud into the dust near the young Muslims.

Jameel and Abdullah ran forward to grab their brother and hustle him away as more bottles flew toward them. "Are you trying to get us all killed?" Abdullah hissed. The others in their group were already edging backward, and as the front row of Hindu men surged

465

forward, they took to their heels and raced back up the street toward the masjid and their little group of houses. The three Musharraf youths were close behind, and twenty paces further back ran the Hindu men, screaming for blood.

The elders of the masjid were standing outside in the street, still discussing the day's events when the mob appeared. After a moment of frozen disbelief, they roared for wives and children to get indoors and lock the windows. The elders disappeared inside Musharraf's house, being the closest, as the youths arrived and slammed the doors shut after them, bolting them even as a volley of empty beer bottles shattered against the outside walls.

"What has happened?" Liquat yelled.

Nasser Musharraf made sure his wife, his youngest son and three daughters were safe before turning to his eldest son. "Muhammad," he said, the muscle beside his eye flicking spasmodically. "What have you done?"

His brothers Abdullah and Jamaal stepped back, knowing from experience of the sign of anger growing in their father. Muhammad swallowed, looking pale, his bravado evaporating in the face of supreme authority. After a hurried glance toward the door where rocks were now thudding, he faced his father. "I have done nothing."

Somewhere in the house, glass shattered and a woman screamed. Nasser cocked his head and listened for a moment before turning his attention back to his son. "Does that sound like nothing? Our family is in danger. What have you done to provoke this unruly behavior in our neighbors?" He took a step toward Muhammad and leaned close, lowering his voice so only his son could

466

hear. "Do not lie, for Allah the Benificent and Merciful abhors a liar. Tell the truth, however grievous, and I will honor you as my son."

Muhammad dropped his head. "Yes, father. But I have told the truth. I did nothing but … but I said things."

Nasser sighed. "Words are as dangerous as deeds, my son. What did you say?"

"Only the truth, father. I spoke no lies."

"Then tell me."

"I … I said Allah was the only True God."

The elder Musharraf nodded and stroked his beard again. "You spoke the truth, but the Hindus know our beliefs. That would not arouse them. What else?"

"I said their gods were made of stone and wood and therefore false."

"Again true, but stupid to say so in front of intoxicated men." Nasser narrowed his eyes and looked at his son carefully. "Was there anything else?" The tic near his eye started up again and Muhammad gulped.

"I said their flag was worthless and … and I spat on the ground."

"You are a fool!" Nasser screamed, and slapped his son's face, rocking the youth back on his heels. The others gathered in the room stared with shocked expressions at this public display of anger before averting their eyes. For an instant, Muhammad's fist clenched at his side and a spark of fury flashed in his eyes, then he bent his head.

"Forgive me, father. I only tried to do as you exhort us to do at prayers – to hold Allah's Name sacred, above all others."

Nasser Musharraf glared at his son, and then stared around the room, slowly becoming aware that he had shamed his son in front of almost the whole Muslim community of Charangat. He thanked Allah, the Benificent and Merciful, that at least the women had not witnessed his shame. That would have been insupportable.

Pitching his voice so it carried above the shouts from the street, he addressed the whole room and his eldest son. "The flag - any flag - may be an idol for ignorant men, but only a fool tells a mob that they are wrong. My son, I believe you acted with the best of intentions, desiring that Allah, the Benificent and Merciful, be held above all other gods, for He is the One True God. For this I forgive you, without reservation." He turned away to face the other elders and youths. "Now I must somehow make matters right with our neighbors, for we must continue to live in Charangat, among these men who hurl bottles and insults at us. Muslim and Hindu have lived in peace in this village for hundreds of years. I would not see that peace end over something so stupid."

"You are not going outside, are you?" Liquat asked anxiously. "They will surely kill you."

Nasser Musharraf smiled. "No, I will go to an upper room and call down to them from a window. In the meantime, I would be honored if you would accept the hospitality of my house." He turned and clapped his hands softly, calling, "Jameela!"

After a brief delay, his wife hurried into the room, straightening the burqa that enveloped her from head to toe. Only a glimpse of her slim hands hinted at the beauty that lay beneath the blue garment. Nasser gazed fondly at his wife of twenty years, his eyes softening momentarily as she hurried to him and bowed submissively.

"Bring food and drink for my guests."

"At once, my lord," Jameela murmured. She hurried off and once outside the room, called to her daughters to come to the kitchen at once.

Nasser excused himself and hurried upstairs to his bedroom window which looked out on the main street. He eased the shutters open and stared down at the scenes of chaos on the street below. Shattered glass lay scattered almost in drifts by the walls of his house, and a mob of about twenty youths kept up a steady barrage of rocks. As they bounced off the wooden walls, small children darted in to collect the missiles, delivering them back to the throwers. The older men and women stood further back, watching the actions of the youths but neither helping nor hindering them. Nasser thought this was a good sign and opened the shutters wide and called to the chief, whom he could see in the crowd.

"Vishnu Patel. Why do you allow this to happen in Charangat? Disperse these rowdy men or send for the police."

At once, a youth yelled and pointed, and a shower of rocks crashed against the upper story, several flying through the open window. Nasser ducked aside and called down again. "Vishnu Patel. Call these men off and let us talk."

The shouting outside died down and the rattle of rocks ceased. Nasser could hear voices outside and after a few minutes, Patel called up to him.

"There will be no more rocks thrown, Nasser Musharraf. Come down and let us talk this thing through like civilized people."

Nasser leaned out of the window and saw that the rock-throwing youths had retreated and that Patel and the other elders now stood in the open semi-circle in front of the house. The reporter, Vinayak Rao, stood a little to one side, scribbling with his pencil in his battered notebook.

"I think I will stay up here for now, Vishnu Patel. I am not sure I feel safe among the men I have known all my life."

Patel held his hands up in an exaggerated shrug. "Things have got out of hand, Musharraf, but the fault does not lie on just one side. Your son said some very bad things." The crowd behind him muttered, and one man called out, "We should hang him for blasphemy."

Patel swung round on the crowd. "Enough! Go to your homes or go back to the celebrations. We will have no further talk of violence here. Imam Musharraf and I will discuss the problem together sensibly and come to a peaceful solution. Go now." The crowd thinned and drifted back toward the meeting place, with much grumbling and muttering, but after five minutes the only people in the street were the elders and the reporter.

"I will come down," Nasser called. He walked downstairs and after hurried reassurances to his family and friends, stepped out into the street with Liquat ul-Haq and Hussein Ali Khan. They stopped a few paces from the elders and regarded them warily. "Well?" Nasser asked. "You have us here. What needs saying?"

"Your son should be whipped for blasphemy," Vaish sputtered. "That needs saying for a start."

"No-one will lay a hand on my son," Nasser grated.

"Um, excuse me," the reporter said hesitantly. "I am a stranger to your village, but I feel I should point out that strictly, there has been no blasphemy."

"What do you mean?" Chandra Shah retorted. "We were all there. We heard it."

"There was no blasphemy," Nathuram Kamath said. "You cannot slander that which does not exist."

"Don't you start again, Kamath. Your speech did not help. We all heard Musharraf's son."

"I was there too," said the reporter. "And he certainly denigrated our gods and the flag, but as the lad is not of our faith, he cannot really be said to blaspheme. I would suggest the lesser charge of disturbing the peace would be more accurate."

Kamath laughed. "Now that is sensible. I agree."

"It is utter nonsense," Vaish said. "You are putting his remarks in the same category as ... as singing drunkenly in the streets."

"I'm inclined to agree with Vaish," Shah added. "The result of his words and the spitting, don't forget, was much greater than drunken singing."

"About on the same level as throwing stones at houses and damaging property," Nasser interposed dryly. "Do not lose sight of the fact that damage has been done to my house."

"That is true," Liquat added. "And the women and children have been put in fear of their lives."

"Perhaps we can agree that the short tempers of youths have been responsible for both sides of this

471

mischief?" Patel turned from his fellow elders to Nasser and the other Muslims. "An insult has been answered with some violence."

"Were it not for the intoxication of your youths, none of this would have happened," Hussein said. "The Prophet, peace be upon him, warns against the evils of intoxication. We can see today that he is right."

"Alright, I will agree that alcohol played a part too," Patel soothed. "But please remember that there has never been trouble between Hindu and Muslim in Charangat. We must make an effort not to let it start now. Our struggles as a nation to achieve independence only succeeded because Hindu and Muslim could work together peacefully. Can we not reach some compromise?"

"Perhaps some recompense to the Imam for the damage to his house?" Rao said quietly. "And an apology for the remarks made?"

"You!" Vaish snapped. "Shut up. You are not even from this village."

"Nevertheless," Chandra Shah mused. "It might be a solution. Musharraf, do you wish to be paid for the damage done to your house?"

"It would be just."

Patel nodded. "I think we can discuss this and reach a reasonable figure. What about an apology? Will your son Muhammad apologize for his words?"

Musharraf consulted with his friends in a whisper before replying. "It would depend on the form of the apology. I cannot allow him to apologize for something if it allows the Name of Allah, the Benificent and Merciful, to be slandered."

"Then there's an end to it." Kamath threw up his hands in disgust. "Don't you think your Allah, if he is supposed to be so powerful; can look after his own reputation? It's superstition like this that drags our beloved country down."

"I will disregard your words, Nathuram Kamath," Musharraf said quietly, "Designed as they are to raise dissension and discord." He addressed Patel. "What words must my son use in this apology? I must approve them first."

"I had not given it much thought," Patel confessed. "I suppose something along the lines of ..."

"I unreservedly apologize to the people of Charangat if my words and actions have caused distress." The reporter read from his notebook, his words clear and firm. "I spoke and acted without thinking and I am sorry for the anger they have caused."

Patel looked at Rao in amazement, then at his elders. "It sounds alright to me. Would that be sufficient?" Shah nodded and Kamath scowled before reluctantly agreeing.

Vaish shook his head. "He said our gods were false, made of stone and wood. How can an apology like that make up for that insult?"

"He is a Muslim, Shankar Vaish," Rao said quietly. "The lad was brought up to believe just that. He is only saying what he truly believes. Truly, his only sin is youth – he did not think before he spoke."

"Put like that ..." Vaish grumbled. "I will go along with it if everyone else agrees."

Patel nodded. "Good. And you Musharraf? Does that apology meet with your approval? It does not say anything against Allah."

473

Musharraf thought for a moment. "It will do," he nodded. "When?"

"If you will take my suggestion," Rao said. "Today is too soon, drink claims the minds of too many. Tomorrow morning will be worse as hangovers will rule most people. However, if we brought the two groups together under the fig-tree at dusk tomorrow, then everybody will disperse immediately afterward to evening prayers or their meal. There should be no time for trouble."

"I thought you were supposed to report the news, not make it," Kamath said.

Musharraf agreed with the form of the apology and the time. With a gesture of respect, the three Muslim men bowed and retreated back inside their house. Patel and the others walked back to the renewed celebrations.

"Say nothing about our discussion yet," Patel warned. "I do not want the hotheads to have time to raise objections."

Kamath drew the reporter to one side and found a beer for them both. "I know your profession is to use words, but you came up with the wording of that apology very quickly. How did you do it? Have you done this sort of thing before?"

Rao shrugged. "I'm not sure exactly. It just seemed a sensible thing to say." He upended the bottle and drank. "You didn't help matters much. What were you trying to do, aggravate the situation?"

Kamath scowled. "More problems have been caused by religion than anything else in history. I can see no good reason to believe in gods of any persuasion." He put down his bottle and started gesturing to highlight his points. "What does religion do? First, it separates people, turning one man against another; second, it provides a life of comfort for people who never do a stroke of real work – priests, I mean; and third, with a god to blame or look to for support, a man need do nothing to help himself. I have worked hard for what I have, but so many of my neighbors, all god-fearing men, just sit back and pray. They would be better off buying a lottery ticket; at least they would stand a chance of improving their lot."

"So you really do not believe in the gods?"

"Have I not just said so? I can see no evidence for gods, so why should I believe in them?"

"You make a good argument, Nathuram Kamath." Rao finished his beer and pulled up a chair. He sat down and watched the festivities for a few minutes before gesturing at the surrounding hills. "The loggers are hard at work in this area, seeking out all the best timber, I see."

Kamath dragged his attention back from the revelers. "Eh? Oh, yes. Another good example of men making a living by their own hard work, not relying on superstitious nonsense."

"There is still a lot of thick forest around though. I imagine there must be wild animals too ... tigers perhaps?" Rao smiled apologetically. "I rode here on my bicycle and I will have to return tomorrow at dusk. I would not like to meet a tiger."

Kamath laughed. "People say there are tigers, but I think you will be safe enough. I have never seen one."

"What, never? Surely you must have seen signs like scratch marks, tracks or the remains of a kill?"

"I am a city and town man, Rao. I do not go into the forests if I can help it."

475

"So you have never seen a tiger, ever?"

"That is what I said. Why? Where is this conversation going?"

"How do you know tigers exist, if you have never seen one?"

Kamath stared at the reporter. "Are you mad? Of course tigers exist. I have just never seen one."

"You said the same things of gods – that you do not believe in them because you have never seen one."

Kamath gaped, then turned back to the celebrations. "That is a ridiculous argument. It is not the same thing at all."

Rao smiled and drained his beer. "Yet who knows? One day you may see a god and you will believe." He stood and put the bottle back into the wooden crate with other empties. "I think I will look around some more, Nathuram Kamath. I bid you good day."

Kamath watched the reporter walk away through the crowd and snorted. "Idiot," he muttered. "Stupid argument too, there are no gods so how could I see one?" Reaching for the crate he opened another bottle and drank thirstily, dismissing Vinayak Rao and his ideas from his mind.

The Independence Day celebrations reached their peak that night, by which time most of the adult male population of Charangat, and some of the females, had overindulged. Saturday morning dawned overcast, with a chill wind of the mountains, but few people stirred before mid-morning, and when they did, it was quietly, loud noises making them cringe. The only people behaving normally that morning were the Muslims, Buddhists and Sikhs, all of whom abstain from alcohol. Many Hindus

476

do not approve of drink either, but as the previous day was a very special occasion – for after all, how many times does your country attain its independence? – most felt that represented sufficient dispensation.

Muhammad Musharraf was up at dawn like the others in his community, and after prayers, sought the company of the other young men. His father had ordered him to apologize to the infidel the next evening, and his anger was steadily growing. He feared his father enough to bottle it up, but in the company of his peers, he let his fury show.

"How can he possibly agree to this? An apology – for what? Did I not speak the truth? Abdullah, Jamaal, Ali, Houd? Support me here." Even in his anger he did not look at the other Muhammad, son of Ali Khan, for he knew that youth was always timid.

"We were there, Muhammad," Houd Is-haaq agreed. "You spoke the truth." Ali al-Abbas nodded his agreement.

"And what of you, my brothers? Do you say I lied?"

"Of course not," Jamaal assured him. "It's just that … well, father said it was not the right thing to do and …"

"And that is why you must apologize," Abdullah finished. "Not because you told lies but because it upset the sensibilities of our Hindu neighbors."

"Why should I care about them? They are polytheists and idol worshipers. Why, they are not even People of the Book like Thomas and Lakshmi Patwari, the Christians. I can forgive Christians their idols for at least they try to worship Allah the Benificent and Merciful,

477

though they have been sorely led astray. The Hindus though … no, I cannot apologize."

"Muhammad, you have to," Jamaal pleaded. "You saw how angry father got last night."

"Yes, I saw," Muhammad hissed. His hand rose to his cheek and he flushed with the remembered shame of his father's blow. "My father forgets the teachings of the Prophet, peace be upon him. When one's religion is oppressed by the infidel, one must strive to overcome them. I invoke *jihad*. I will not rest until I have avenged this slight on the Name of Allah."

Muhammad Ali Khan had been trying to follow the tirade of his namesake. "But you have been oppressing them with your words and … and by spitting. What slight are you avenging?"

The eldest son of Musharraf just stared at his friend. "You are no warrior," he said at last. "You do not understand."

"You will still have to apologize, brother," Abdullah said softly. "*Jihad* or no, father will make you."

"We shall see. Go now, all of you. I have things that I must do before tonight."

Across the village, another group of youths discussed the same event. Vishnu Patel was a widower and his son Madanlal had his own rooms at the back of the house. His father's duties kept him busy and out of the house much of the time, and without a mother or sisters, Madanlal found he could do pretty much as he pleased. Today, he had some of his closest friends around and they sat in the courtyard at the rear of the house, sipping on beers and smoking cigarettes.

"Well, at least he is being made to apologize," said Gangadhar Gujral. "I thought for a while he was going to get clean away with it."

"He might as well have," Prabhat Nanda said morosely. "Our elders are cowards, begging your pardon Madanlal. They have caved in to the wiles of that cunning old goat Musharraf."

Madanlal shrugged. "That one planned the whole affair if you ask me. You noticed how he waited for my father's speech and led his people out just to cause a disturbance?"

Dattatraya Sharma nodded and belched loudly. "Prayers are a weak excuse as everyone knows those Allah-worshipers are allowed to pray anytime from noon until dusk. It was a deliberate attempt to cause offence."

"And then that fucking Muhammad stirred things further," Nanda added savagely. He ground his cigarette butt into the dirt and lit up another one.

"Nanda, that is terrible language," Gangadhar said. "Where did you learn it?"

"In the market place at Mussoorie last year. I heard a British soldier use it." Nanda grinned. "Effective, isn't it?"

Gangadhar shrugged. "No doubt, but nasty. Maybe now the British have gone, we won't be hearing it again."

"Getting back to Musharraf and his son," Madanlal said patiently, "What are we going to do?"

"Do we need to do anything?" Dattatraya asked. "I know his behavior was offensive but if he's apologizing publicly, what else can we do?"

"Plenty. We can make sure he never does it again."

"How?"

479

"Before I answer that, let me ask you a question – all of you." Madanlal put down his beer and flicked his cigarette away, leaning forward conspiratorially. "What would be the reaction of the village if he repeated his insults, maybe even expanded on them?"

"They'd fuckin' tear him apart," Nanda grinned.

"Yeah, except for that 'f' thing, I'd agree with Nanda," Gangadhar said.

"So how are you going to get him to repeat his insults if he has come to apologize?

"You'll see. Just back me up is all I ask of you. Will you do it?" Madanlal's three companions nodded.

The sun set over Charangat and the brightness of the day faded toward dusk, that time when a black thread and a white one can no longer be distinguished. Nasser Musharraf stood with his three sons at the lower end of the meeting place, looking across to where the stage still stood near the fig tree. The elders of the village were seated and the villagers stood in an expectant huddle, waiting for the words that most hoped would heal the rifts that had opened up between neighbors. Above them, atop its flagpole, hung the flag of the Union of India, the mandala in its central band of white hidden by its folds. Several large torches burned, throwing a ruddy light over the faces in the crowd and the bright glare of an electric arc light hurled its brilliance from one side, near where the portable petrol generator chugged. Patel saw the four Muslim men waiting and came across to them.

"I thought light would be preferable to the microphone," Patel commented, clasping his hands nervously in front of him. "Er, the others of your people are not attending, Nasser Musharraf?"

"I decided the fewer were here the better. I do not wish to appear confrontational."

Patel nodded. "Very wise. Well, er, shall we go across?" he led the way across the dusty place to the stage. "I will say a few introductory words first, then your son Muhammad says his apology, he salutes the flag and we can all go home."

Nasser looked across at the Hindu and stopped abruptly. "What do you mean, he salutes the flag? Nothing was said about this before."

"Nathuram Kamath thought it would be a nice touch to end with. There is no problem is there?"

"Opinion is divided on this point," Musharraf admitted. "Some say that to salute a flag is to honor the state which it represents above Allah the Benificent and Merciful. Others say it is a gesture signifying nothing more than respect."

Patel listened patiently. "And what do you say?"

Nasser Musharraf pondered. "If the flag was offered as an object of worship, I would have to refuse, but if it was solely to show respect for our country, then I have no objection."

"Excellent." Parel smiled broadly and gestured. "Come; let us get on with this."

"Do I not get a say in this salute, father?" Muhammad asked in a low voice.

"Be guided by me in this, my son, as in all other matters."

The small party mounted the stage and took their seats while Patel addressed the assembled villagers. "Fellow citizens of Charangat, we are gathered here at sunset on the day after our great feast of independence, to

481

heal the wounds in our village caused by hot heads and drink. Some things were spoken that should not have been and some actions performed that should not have been. The damage caused by members of our village have been paid for out of local taxes and now, to heal the hurtful words comes a youth known to us all, Muhammad Musharraf. I ask you please to listen to him carefully and with forgiveness in your hearts. Remember that for centuries, Hindu and Muslim have lived together in Charangat in harmony. Do not let this inestimable record end today." He turned to the Muslim family and smiled, putting out his hand. "Muhammad, please address us."

Muhammad arose and with a quick glance at his brothers Abdullah and Jamaal, strode to the front of the stage and looked out over the crowd for several minutes, saying nothing. The assembled villagers waited, but as the silence drew out they began to fidget and mutter.

"Well, are you going to say something?" someone called.

"Yes. Yes!" Muhammad yelled back. "I am going to say something. Things were said yesterday by a great many people, some things good and true, other things bad and lies. My father, the elders of the *masjid* and the elders of this little village want me to read something to you, an apology, so I will." He took out a piece of paper from his jacket pocket and unfolded it.

"It says, 'I, Muhammad Musharraf, apologize to the people of Charangat if my words and actions have caused distress. I spoke and acted without thinking and I am sorry for the anger they have caused.' These are the words written down for me to read to you, and I have done so." He crumpled the paper and tossed it aside.

482

"That is the apology?" Vaish hissed. "He did not even sound sincere. Let him apologize from his heart."

Patel leaned over to whisper to Nasser, but the growing murmur of outrage from the crowd meant he had to speak loudly. "He is right, Musharraf. He must say it from his heart or it is worthless, just words written down and read quickly, without meaning."

"Muhammad. Apologize again. This time properly, as I instructed you." Nasser spoke urgently, aware of the mood of the crowd.

Muhammad stared at his father for a moment, then at his brothers, before turning back to face the villagers. "I will speak again," he shouted. "But not to apologize. I have done that already, as I was instructed to do. This time I speak from my heart, and my heart tells me I must worship Allah, the Benificent and Merciful, and his prophet, peace be upon him. I cannot stand idly by and see the True Faith besmirched by infidels, by polytheists who ..."

Nasser leapt to his feet. "Muhammad, be quiet. I order you as father and Imam."

"... worship gods of stone, of clay, of wood. Gods who are part animal, gods with many arms and limbs. They are not gods but djinn, afrit, demons ..."

"Kill him!" screamed a voice from the crowd. At once, violent voices erupted all round the stage and shadows leapt and danced in the bright electric light as people shook fists and waved sticks. "Kill him," the voice screamed again and the crowd surged forward.

Nasser Musharraf grabbed his eldest son by the arm, trying to drag him back, and Patel leaned out over the

483

stage railing and remonstrated with the crowd, telling them to calm themselves.

"Kill him!" Madanlal Patel ran out in front and pointed up at his father. "Do not protect him. He is evil, like all of his people. He must die for his insults to our gods." Madanlal gestured and his friends joined him, adding their voices to the clamor.

Muhammad shook off his father and reached into his jacket, pulling out a small snub-nosed gun. He pointed it at Madanlal and tugged on the trigger. The crack of the gun cut through the roar of the crowd and left an echoing silence in its wake. Then a woman screamed and everybody started shouting again, some people pushing forward, others trying to get away. In front, just under the stage, Gangadhar Gujral lay on his back, his unblinking eyes staring at the night sky in mild surprise.

Nasser cried out in agony and stumbled forward, clutching for his eldest son, but Abdullah and Jamaal were quicker, throwing their arms around their brother, trying to wrestle the gun from him.

"Let me go!" Muhammad shrieked. "I must kill the infidels, Allah commands it." He fought and bit, snapping off another two shots at the milling people below. One wounded Madanlal, but the other zipped over the heads of the crowd.

Jamaal grabbed the gun and pulled, ripping it free of his brother's hand as it went off, the bullet creasing Jamaal's scalp and burying itself in his father's neck as the man came up behind. Nasser Musharraf collapsed to the floor of the stage with a strangled cry, his hands vainly trying to stem the bright red blood pulsing out between his fingers.

484

"Nasser, no!" screamed Vishnu Patel. Chandra Shah grabbed his chief and dragged him back out of harm's way.

"He has shot his father!" Vaish cried, pointing but not attempting to help. The noise from the crowd shut off as if a great door had slammed shut, isolating the stage from the rest of the world.

The three brothers swung round, their faces pale with shock and horror. The gun slipped from Jamaal's hand and fell to the stage, skittering along the planks until it fell to the dusty ground at Madanlal's feet. The young men stood around their dying father, trembling, not knowing what to do.

Jamaal fell to his knees and cradled his father's head, attempting to put his hands over the bubbling wound, but all he managed to do was cover himself in blood. "I'm sorry, I'm sorry, I'm sorry," he babbled, tears pouring down his cheeks. Abdullah knelt and put his arm around his younger brother, clasping him close as Nasser Musharraf shuddered and fell back in the pooled blood. Muhammad just stood and stared at his dead father and blood-spattered brothers.

The others on the stage stared too, but their minds were in turmoil. Elders Vaish and Shah retained enough common sense to realize the trouble must be halted before anything more happened. Already the crowd, which had been dispersing, was regathering, drawn by the tragedy on the stage. Now, instead of anger, murmurs of grief and sympathy started to be heard.

Shah grapped Kamath's arm. "Find policeman Narayan. We must apprehend these killers."

Kamath forced a snort of derision. "Killers? Look at them. They are small boys now. Besides, where is the gun?" He stared at Chandra Shah's blank look. "I will go and find him. You and Vaish stay here. Try and prevent any further violence." Kamath turned and ran down the steps at the back of the stage. At the bottom he bumped into the reporter Vinayak Rao, who was starting up the steps.

"Good, someone with a level head." Kamath grabbed Rao and steered him through the margins of the crowd. "We must find the policeman."

Madanlal ignored the throbbing pain in his left arm where the bullet had ripped a hot furrow through his bicep. He stared down and the gun lying in the dirt, then back up at the stricken figures on the stage. One of the Muslim youths had shot their father. Stooping, he picked up the gun and turned it over in his hand, wondering whether it had more bullets in it. *Gujral, my arm, a miss and the father*, he thought. *How many do they hold? Is it six like in the Western movies?* With a grin, Madanlal hefted it and slid his forefinger round the trigger.

Holding the gun by his side, pointing at the ground, Madanlal circled the stage and climbed the steps, ignoring his friends. As he reached the top, Chandra Shah moved to intercept him, to turn him back, but Madanlal lifted the gun and Shah hurriedly backed away.

Vishnu Patel sat on one of the chairs at the edge of the stage, crying unashamedly. He had lost a friend and grievous though the personal loss was, he felt the breakdown of the village unity far more. Lost in his misery, he did not see his son Madanlal mount the stage, cross to where the brothers stood weeping over the body

486

of their father, and raise the gun, pressing it against Muhammad's chest.

"Blasphemer," Madanlal hissed. "You have insulted the gods of India and now you die." He pulled the trigger.

Muhammad barely heard the words, or the click of the hammer on an empty chamber, but he looked down anyway, striving to equate his good intentions with the horror that had overtaken him. "What ... what ...?" His brother Abdullah saw the gun and yelled, pushing at the man holding it. The man staggered and swung the gun round, and Abdullah heard the empty gun click again. The sound enraged him more than if a shot had been fired and he threw himself at Madanlal. The two stumbled across the stage until they hit the railing, which snapped under their combined weight, precipitating them to the dusty street several feet below.

The impact jarred Abdullah and he struggled to his knees, forcing his eyes to focus. He saw Madanlal lying beside him, unmoving, and the gun a few feet away. Taking a deep breath, he lurched sideways and grabbed the gun, rising shakily to his feet in triumph a few moments later. "I have it, brothers." He shook the gun above his head. "I have it and they will not ..." A heavy bamboo staff slashed behind him and caught him on the back of his head, crushing his skull. Abdullah was dead before he hit the ground and he never saw the bystanders hurl themselves on Prabhat Nanda and bear him struggling to the ground.

Across the open space, Kamath and Rao heard the roar of anger and the triumphant scream of a youth, abruptly cut off. They stopped and looked back at the scene, brightly lit by the incandescent lighting.

Comparative silence fell and a tension seemed to lift, people's shoulders slumping as they turned away.

"I think it is over," Kamath said. "Maybe the policeman is in the crowd already."

"I could not stop it," Rao muttered. "Nobody asked me."

"Eh? Of course you couldn't, none of us could." Kamath swung round and stared into the shadows at the edge of the street. A woman's cries, racked with grief and despair, came softly on the breeze now that the shouting by the stage had died down. "Come on." Kamath trotted over, Rao close behind him.

In the dark, close by the mudbrick wall, knelt Lakshmi Patwari, one of the town's Christian converts. Her husband Thomas was nowhere to be seen, but in the crying woman's arms was their two year old daughter, Isabel, her dress soaked with blood. She looked up as Kamath and Rao arrived, her face streaked and racked with agony.

"Shots," she gasped. "One hit her. Please." Lakshmi held out the shuddering body of her child. "Please save her."

Kamath took the child and laid her down on the ground, ripping her dress away to reveal a small hole in her chest. Blood pulsed weakly from it and the girl struggled to breath. He turned the child over and wiped at the blood high up on her back. "No exit hole. The bullet is still in her."

Rao crouched down and leaned close, murmuring so the mother would not hear. "Is that bad?

Kamath shrugged. "Who knows? I know a bit of first aid but nothing that would help in a case like this. The

488

bullet has hit an artery, I think, also her windpipe for she struggles to breathe."

Lakshmi Patwari leaned over and laid a trembling hand on Rao's arm. "Help her, please," she sobbed. "I beg you."

Rao nodded. "Let me look."

"Do you know medicine, Rao?"

The reporter did not answer but took the little girl from Kamath and slid a hand under her back. He knelt very still, bent over her for several minutes, until Kamath reached out and shook his shoulder.

"Rao? What are you doing?"

"You missed the bullet. Here it is." Rao brought his hand out from under the girl's back and dropped a bloody pellet of metal onto the ground. "I do not think the bullet touched anything important. See, she is better."

The blood that had pulsed from the wound slowed to a trickle and the girl's breathing eased. Rao passed the child back to her sobbing mother and stood up. "She needs to see a doctor immediately, a hospital maybe."

Kamath rose and nodded. "I'll organize the truck. We can get her down to Mussoorie by dawn." He helped Lakshmi Patwari to her feet and, shouting for attention, managed to get the truck organized very quickly. Little Isabel Patwari was not the only one transported to the hospital that night, but she was the only one Kamath found himself caring about. He looked round for Rao as the truck started up but the reporter was nowhere to be seen.

The doctor at the hospital declared himself thoroughly mystified by Isabel's wound. He drew Nathuram Kamath aside and questioned him in some detail. "It is obviously a bullet wound but there is no trace of it in her."

"Well, of course not, doctor. It came out of her back. I have it here." Kamath dug the piece of metal out of his pocket.

"I'm sorry; Mr Kamath, but that cannot be the projectile. It did not come out of the child's back. There is no exit wound." The doctor went on to say that the aorta and trachea had been damaged but somehow had resealed themselves. "I cannot understand how, medically speaking, she survived. There is not even any infection. She is a very lucky girl. I understand her parents are Christian? Well, as a good Hindu, I am not sure I believe in the Christian god, so all I can say is that some god took care of her last night." He grinned and clapped a shaken Kamath on the shoulder before walking back to his patient.

Kamath went looking for the Mussoorie Gazette offices and camped on the doorstep until Vinayak Rao cycled up on Monday morning. He looked blankly at Kamath, shaking his head, as the village elder fired questions at him.

"I'm very sorry; Mr Kamath, but I don't know you. I think you must be mistaking me for somebody else." He listened patiently to Kamath's involved explanations and submitted to further questioning but all he could say was that he had been out cycling in the hills all weekend, and that he was very glad that the little girl was better. "It sounds like your village has been through a lot in the last few days. I think they are lucky to have you working to bring all factions back into harmony." Rao turned away

490

and started to lock his bike to the railings outside the newspaper offices. He hesitated.

"I've just remembered something." Rao looked at Kamath with a puzzled frown. "I feel I should ask you if you have seen the tiger yet." He shrugged and entered the building, leaving Kamath – who did not believe in gods as he had never seen one – staring after him.

Chapter Twenty-Four

Those of you who have been following my story will realize that I possessed the reporter Vinayak Rao. I spent the months and days before Independence Day wandering the roads and villages of Uttarakhand, soon to become part of the State of Uttar Pradesh. I watched the people, looking to see how they would take to this great new adventure opening up from them. For the most part, they welcomed the opportunity of self-governance, though many expectations of what life would be like in the Union of India were totally unrealistic. Those who saw the power and the privilege of the British passing to them were disappointed, for most of that went to the politicians in Delhi. In the beginning days of August though, hopes were high as people looked at their neighbors and wondered which of them would hold the greatest power.

Muslim and Hindu coexisted in India for centuries, for all that Islam was a relatively new religion still fired up with proselytizing zeal. Hinduism was old when Islam was born and displayed tolerance for this new faith. Many beliefs had or would walk on Indian soil – Buddhism, Christianity, Sikhism, Jainism and others that seized hold of a handful of men's minds. Of these, Islam arguably had the most influence on the people, for Muslims are a people burning with a desire to glorify their god and his prophet. This led them into conflict, for no faith will stand to see itself persecuted and downtrodden for long. Wars erupted and millions died over the centuries, but as far as I could tell, none of them survived the dissolution of their body, let alone achieved the paradise or rebirth their faith promised.

That is not to say that relations between the two great faiths of India were always abrasive. Men of good will were prepared to coexist amicably, showing tolerance for the other. Many believed India should be a country for all Indians, irrespective of their faith, but it was not to be. The Muslims drew apart, torn by jealousy of the Hindu majority, fearful of what would happen to them as a minority. On the day before the Union of India came into being, the Dominion of Pakistan was formed, a nation of Muslims on the western and eastern borders of the Sub-continent.

I sought out the islands of harmony in a nation that was tearing itself apart and came to the village of Charangat. A microcosm of the nascent nation, Charangat was a village without a violent past. Hindu and Muslim lived in harmony here, I was told, and wanting to see for myself, made the short journey.

I came across the reporter cycling along the potholed roads and talked to him in my guise of the old Pahari tribesman, Pandalis. I found out his destination and that he was expected. An unexpected stranger in a small town is always noticed and often people do not behave in the same way, so I took the opportunity that presented, slipping quietly into the man's mind. I have got quite good at this over the years, and Rao was not aware of my presence. He was very surprised and a little alarmed at my sudden disappearance but I controlled his surging adrenaline and he calmed down very quickly, shrugging the memory of the old man aside.

I stayed hidden, only interfering enough to guide him to places I wanted to be, to people I wanted to see, and occasionally to say things I wanted him to say. You know the events of that weekend, but may be curious as to why I did nothing until the end. Well, I have learned that it is best not to interfere with a man's chosen course in life. When I was younger, a mere thousand years or so, I did whatever I wanted, reaping lives from the harvest burgeoning around me. As I discerned the pointlessness of my demon existence I became less bloodthirsty, striving eventually to follow the Eightfold Path of the Buddha, in the slim hope that one day I might achieve divinity. I know, I am still a demon and at most I can be a counterfeit god, but what do you care? The dream has stopped me killing and now I help humans where I can. Surely that means something?

Anyway, to return to my non-interference in Charangat, all the people involved, Hindus and Muslims both, relied on their own gods and were more concerned with defending their own views on what their gods desired than in finding a way out of the problem. Muhammad Musharraf could not see past what he saw as a slight on his god, and Madanlal Patel was the focus of the Hindu population's suppressed fear. Could I have saved lives? Yes. I could have taken over Muhammad's body and forced a genuine-sounding apology, but what would that have achieved? I would have to leave him sooner or later and when I did, his hatred of his own action would have sparked violence. If I prevented Madanlal from inciting the crowd, his loathing of Muslims would have broken out again later. No, there was only one life I could save that night, that of Isabel Patwari, and only because her mother asked me to.

I am proving to be quite human in some ways, am I not? It must be the effect of living in so many of them.

The girl's mother had no way of knowing I was in Rao, and if she had, her Christian faith would have rejected a demon's help out of hand. But I chose to believe what I wanted to believe, that she prayed to me for help and I gave it.

It was not hard, not for one such as me. I slipped from Rao into Isabel, pushed the bullet past the spine and through the tissues of the back, sealing the wound instantly. The aorta was split and her trachea ruptured – she was seconds away from death. I held the tissues closed and accelerated healing, expunging the bacteria I found at the same time. Her blood volume was low and her heart under strain so I spent a while balancing her blood pressure and heart rate to achieve a relatively stable equilibrium. I also temporarily stimulated her bone marrow into abnormally high levels of blood cell production and adjusted her hormone levels. Several minutes were all it took. I withdrew into Rao's body again and held up the bullet.

Nothing further could be achieved in Charangat, so I left Kamath organizing the hospital journey and Patel managing his grief, and accompanied Rao out of town. It was the late evening, but a demon's vision made the road as bright as day and a demon's presence kept him safe from wild beasts.

Only one other thing remains – Nathuram Kamath. My first impression of him was of a pompous, abrasive man who cared more for his own opinion than of the feelings of his neighbors. Being a reporter – well, being in a reporter – I had the opportunity of delving into the backgrounds of people without actually entering them. An interview is a clumsy way of finding out what a person really thinks but it was interesting so I amused myself. Kamath was quite fascinating. His years in Delhi under the influence of the Marxist had turned him into a socialist without really giving him the strength to follow it through. He returned to Charangat and lived a capitalist existence but still disdained the peasant workers his new beliefs should have had him support. It also destroyed his faith in his gods, but I judged this was more because he felt deserted by them than any lack of willingness to believe. I decided to probe a bit and used that old argument about still believing in things though not discerned.

Later, he witnessed an apparent miracle when Isabel Patwari cheated death and I could not resist having Rao mention the tiger just when Kamath was feeling most bewildered. He had seen a god at work; could he deny a god's existence? I suppose you want to know whether Kamath found religion, returned to the faith of his fathers. I do not know because I did not stay around to find out. I stayed with Rao long enough to help him write a very good piece on the Charangat troubles for his editor. He was as surprised as his editor as I had suppressed his memories of the weekend. His reaction to Kamath was genuine, he really did not remember the man.

My purpose in leaving so abruptly stemmed from the conversation on tigers and gods Rao had had with Kamath. Rao remarked on the state of the forests and the effects of the loggers. Despite traveling the hills and valleys for millennia, I had not noticed the depredations of the last century. Men were coming into the hills and stripping them of their largest trees, destroying the forests and wildlife and ruining the lives of my people. I decided to see for myself and look for a way for my people to help themselves.   I ended up in the Chamoli district of Garhwal.

Chapter Twenty-Five

The mountains that danced attendance on Nanda Devi – admittedly a slow stately pavane that spread over millions of years – were bare-breasted in rock and ice but clothed around their hips in a rich, full tapestry of forest. For untold thousands of years they stood untouched save where some natural disaster spawned by thunderstorm or earthquake ripped through the verdant covering leaving, for an eyeblink, naked soil and rock. The forests healed and within a few generations of the short-lived humans that crept up from the hot plains, the sweep of woodland was once more unbroken. Deodara and chir pine, oak and ash, fir and spruce, maple and *Cornus*, all had their place, nestled in the broad river valleys or rocky gorges, clinging to steep-sided hills or windswept ridges, they grew where the gods had set them and man was incidental to the design of that great 'abode of snow' the Himalayas.

Man came of course, for even gods cannot prevent man going where he pleases. He came in ever growing numbers and cleared land to grow crops, to foster the sweet grass that fed his cattle and goats, and harvested the forest for food, timber and medicines. For long ages, the impact of humans was minimal, but his numbers grew and multiplied and he pushed ever further into the pristine wilderness. Kings of Garhwal and Kumaon fought over the land and its harvest, followed by Moghal emperors and the British, each more rapacious than the last, eager to wrest whatever they could from its soil. Then came independence for India, but the plundering did not stop. Instead of the spoils ending up in the coffers of alien rulers, they now found their way into the banks of businessmen in the big cities; men who had no connection to the soil and cared nothing about the peasants who slaved for them in the hills.

The town of Koti sits on a low swell of land near the Koti River, a minor tributary of the rushing Alaknanda. If you had business there, you would take the train to Rishikesh, then by road some two hundred kilometers to Gopeshwar in the Chamoli District of Garhwal. From here, if the weather is good and the roads are in good repair, you can travel a little further up the Alaknanda, to the town of Chamoli. If, as would probably be the case, the road gangs have not yet cleared the latest land slips and gaping holes in the road, you can proceed on foot, likely with many pilgrims heading for the holy temples of Joshimath and Badarinath. About a day's journey past Chamoli, a rope and wood bridge crosses the Alaknanda River at the mouth of the Koti River and here you bid farewell to the pilgrims, turning up the narrow valley and heading northwest. The trail here is narrow and winding and climbs steeply through open woodland and scrub, alive with bird calls and, though you cannot see them, with animals. Possibly, at one of the places where a small stream crosses the trail, you might see the spoor of a tiger or leopard pressed into the mud.

About a day's walk up from the rope bridge you will happen upon farmland, terraced fields set into the steep hillsides and find small herds of goats or a handful of cattle grazing the sweet grass under the watchful eye of a young boy. Another half an hour and you walk, quite suddenly, into the town of Koti. It boasts a main street with a town square, many stone houses including a community center, a doctor, several stores and a temple dedicated to Shiva, though you may offer to any of the gods there and the priest will be happy to oblige.

There are forests around Koti, though the richest of these, with the biggest trees is another ten kilometers further upriver. The nearer stands have been cut over many times and are little more than scrub. The men of Koti, as in so many towns and villages throughout Uttarakhand, are predominantly farmers, and the women tend to everything else that needs to be done. Aside from the never-ending round of work bringing up children, cooking and cleaning the family home, they must card and spin wool, weave and dye clothing, gather firewood and search for and prepare medicines from the plants they find in the forests. Over the years, trees had been felled by the townsfolk and by outside interests, and as the forests receded from the township, the women found themselves having further and further to walk each day to collect medicinal plants and fuel. The stand of tall trees and relatively undisturbed forest ten kilometers above Koti is the last in their valley, and the women are acutely aware of its importance.

Seven years before, a small stand of mountain ash was felled by the men of Koti, on the promise of good prices when the lumber was sold by the timber company, Robinson and Bose. They were paid, but it was less than half of what they were expecting. A representative of the company made the long trip up to Koti to explain the realities of a competitive market economy, but failed to placate the angry hill people. They found a lawyer and took the company to court. Seven years later, the town could no longer afford the drawn-out legal battles and had all but given up hope of seeing their money. Robinson

500

and Bose, on the other hand, now cast avaricious eyes on the forests above Koti. They sent another representative to the town to make the men of Koti an offer for the best timber trees.

The *panchayat* or council of Koti town met in the community center to hear the words of the timber company's spokesman and to decide on a course of action for the townspeople. Mohan Das, the *sarpanch* or council leader stood and briefly glanced at the other elected members, the *panch*, and the gathered townspeople before addressing the timber representative.

"We have heard your words, Subir Ram, and the offer your company Robinson and Bose has made but before we decide on this matter, I would like to ask my fellow *panch* members if they have any questions or comments."

A chair scraped back and a weather-beaten farmer, Govind Bisht, got to his feet, fixing the company man with a steely glare. "Why should we believe a word you say? You came to us before and bought our timber but then refused to pay." He sat down again with a grim look.

Subir Ram nodded and, without getting up, addressed the hall. "That was seven years ago and the representative who drew up the contract has been fired."

"Then where is our money?" Kalika Lalit asked. The herder had been a member of the original *panchayat* that approved the felling of the ash trees and he felt the failure to secure payment as a personal affront. "If he has been fired, then why is the company not honoring his agreement?"

"It is not a matter of not honoring the agreement," Ram said evasively. "There is some disagreement as to exactly what the terms of the contract were."

"There is no doubt in our minds," Govind Bisht growled.

Storekeeper Atma Prabhad stood up. "Subir Ram, would you be as good as to tell us again exactly what trees your company wants from the forest? I know you have told us but just so we are all clear in our minds."

"Certainly, *Panch* Prabhad." Ram got up and went to the charts sitting on the stand at the front of the hall and shuffled through them to find the sketch map of the forest. "Here is the forest, and here you see marked the positions of the largest trees. Ten of them are ash, six are oak and the rest are deodar cypress. Thirty in all. Now, we have marked these trees already ..."

"Mr Ram," Govind Bisht interrupted. "Why these trees? When they fall they will do much damage to the surrounding ones. Can you not take smaller ones on the edge of the forest? Perhaps more than thirty to make up."

"I'm afraid it doesn't work like that. Smaller trees have less useful wood and more waste. It is the largest trees we need and are willing to pay for."

"Ah, yes," Atma Prabhad nodded. "We come to the price. Please continue Mr Ram."

"The different types of trees are worth different amounts, so we are offering a sum for all thirty trees." Ram looked around the hall smiling, building up the expectation though he knew he was just repeating the price already offered. "Robinson and Bose Timber Company of Uttar Pradesh are willing to pay the sum of nine thousand five hundred Rupees for the thirty trees. I might add that you are not required to do anything else to earn this vast amount of money except agree."

"That is a great deal of money," Mohan Das said slowly. "If the Company is willing to pay so much, how much more are the trees actually worth?"

"Well, of course they are worth more," Subir Ram replied. "But you must remember that the Company is paying the loggers to cut them down, also the mill workers must saw them up and the salesmen sell them to the manufacturers and cabinet makers. There are many links in the chain and as I'm sure you realize, the Company deserves to make a profit."

"Are we getting a fair price though?" Gujar Bhushan asked. "As leader of the Artisans' collective, I know how our crafts are bought for very little up here in the hills and for very much more to the tourists in Delhi and Bombay. Maybe it is the same with our trees."

"You will not get a better price elsewhere," Subir Ram said sharply. "Robinson and Bose are being very fair, but if you wish to cut down the trees yourself you can transport them to the plains, mill them yourselves and sell them." He smiled, knowing his alternate proposal was preposterous. "It would be very expensive for you to do all this, of course, whereas Robinson and Bose already have these things set up. That is why they can offer you such a good price."

"Even so," Gujar Bhushan muttered. "Maybe we should look elsewhere before agreeing."

"Where else can we look?" Mohan Das asked. "There are few companies willing to come this deep into Chamoli. I say we need to vote on this proposal."

503

"Do I not get a say, *Sarpanch*?" The last figure at the *Panch* table stood and adjusted her shawl before facing the audience. "You all know me, Vimala Shamsar. I am spokesperson for the Women's collective and I have been pushing our *panchayat* to improve health, education and women's rights for many years …"

"Sit down, old woman," called a male voice from the back of the hall. "We have heard it all before."

"And you will continue to hear it until there are changes made," Vimala continued. "As for this proposal to cut down our trees, we have heard a lot about how many rupees we will get, though we are still waiting for the rupees we were promised seven years ago. What we have not heard about is what the loss of our trees will mean for the women of this town."

"Vimala Shamsar," Mohan Das said quietly. "We are talking about something that will benefit the whole village, not half of it. We have heard the women's views before, now it is time to vote."

"It is time to vote when every *panch* has had a say, *Sarpanch* Das. I know the rules as well as anyone, and I have not yet had my say."

Mohan Das sighed and sat down again, rolling his eyes. "Very well, but please make it brief."

"I will be as brief as I will be, Mohan Das." Vimala turned from the *panch* members and addressed the audience again. Though nearly half the population of Koti was female, less than a quarter of the seats were occupied by women. Though technically equal, in actuality a much greater burden was placed on women who still had to care for the children and keep house for the men. The males had leisure time to sit around and

504

discuss the issues and it was no accident that only one of the six people of the *panchayat* was female.

Vimala came down off the low stage to stand before the townspeople. "Work in Koti is divided between men and women, but it is not divided equally. Men work in the fields, tending crops or watching over the herds so they do not stray, but women do everything else." She raised a hand to quell the rumbles of anger from some of the men. "But I am not here to talk about this. You have heard me speak of it before ..."

"Many times!" called a man, bringing a ripple of laughter from the audience.

"... and I will speak of it again, but not today. Today I speak for the women of Koti in relation to our forest. A man thinks in terms of what he can raise to sell, to bring in money to buy things like bicycles and transistor radios and tee shirts. A woman, who is concerned with the home and family, thinks long term, of the endless cycle of life and how a little can be made to go a long way." A murmur of agreement arose from the seated ranks of women. "But what is the forest? A man looks at it and sees trees which can be cut down and sold, animals that can be hunted for food or to sell. He sees it as a source of money. A woman sees it differently."

Vimala stopped and looked back at the stand with the sketches used by the company representative. "I think I can show you what I mean." She walked back onto the stage and approached the stand. "I am sure Mr Subir Ram will not object to me using the back of one of his drawings."

Subir Ram looked flustered. "Well ..." He glanced at the *sarpanch* for support.

Mohan Das nodded. "Let her finish."

Vimala smiled and took the marker pen, turning one of the sketches over. She drew a vertical line down the middle and drew a stick figure of a man on one side at the top, and the figure of a woman in a sari on the other. "I know not all of you can read and write, so I will try to outline my points with a little drawing." She pointed to the man figure. "What is it a man wants? Money." She wrote the word 'Rupee' under the figure and then added the dollar symbol, '$'. "You will all recognize what this means," she said with a laugh.

"Now, what does the forest mean to a woman? First it means food, for while the men cultivate the fields and herd goats and cows, we search the forest for the many small fruits, edible plants and tubers, and mushrooms that add spice and flavor to the meals we prepare." Vimala wrote 'Food' under the symbol of the woman, hesitated and drew a stylized apple. "This will have to represent food, although apples do not grow in the forest. Next we gather fuel. Every man expects a hot meal on the table when he gets home at night, but how many appreciate how he gets it? We must scour the ground for fallen wood and twigs, bringing bundles home for cooking and heating." She added 'Fuel' to the chart and drew a little fire beside it. "Fodder is another thing the forest means to a woman. Although the men and boys take the goats and cattle out to graze during the day, what are they to eat at night? They must have sweet grass and branches cut from forest trees, another thing the women of Koti must collect every day." The word 'Fodder' and a picture of a leafy branch joined the other reasons on the chart. "Let me talk about fibres now. Every woman weaves baskets and mats for her house. Where does she get these fibres? In part, from plants that grow in forests." 'Fibre' and a woven basket were quickly added. "And last, we come to medicines. If we cannot afford medicines that come from the doctor, and not all of us can spend money on such things, particularly if we have a large family; then we must go to the forest when a child falls sick. There are many plants we can use, but they grow only in forests. Nowhere else." Vimala added 'Medicine' and thought for a moment before adding a smiling face. "A healthy child brings joy to all," she explained.

Mohan Das got to his feet and clapped his hands a few times. "Thank you, *Panch* Shamsar. Your little speech has been most entertaining." He gestured at the drawings on the chart and chuckled, drawing an echo of laughter from the men in the audience. "Now, perhaps we can move onto the vote."

"I have not yet finished, *Sarpanch*," Vimala said coldly. "You are required to hear me out."

Mohan Das sighed theatrically and sat down again, waving a hand in resignation.

"Thank you." Vimala turned her back on the *sarpanch* and addressed the hall again. "Our men of Koti work hard, but they walk for half an hour to reach the fields every morning, rest at the hottest part of the day and in the evening walk home for another half hour. Once upon a time, when forests surrounded Koti, the women could do the same, though even then they seldom had time for a midday rest. I am old now and my husband has long gone back to Mother Ganga ..."

"What a pity the custom of *suttee* is no more." The voice issued from a group of young men at the back of the hall.

"That remark shames you, Suresh Dutt," Vimala said, shaking her head. "If your parents had instilled respect for elders in you, you would be a half way decent man."

Dobhal Dutt erupted to his feet. "Are you saying I have not brought up my son in a proper manner? If your husband was alive he would ..."

"Sit down!" Mohan Das thundered from the stage. "I will not have my *panch* members interrupted by outbursts. Your son is ill-mannered, Dobhal, and we can see who he learns it from."

Dobhal Dutt sat down again amid laughter and a little jeering. "Go on, *panch* Shamsar," called another man. "We are listening."

Vimala nodded and waited for the noise to die down. "When I was a young wife," she said. "I could walk to the forests in minutes and find everything for my husband; my family and my home, for the forests were all around Koti. As time went by, the trees were felled and the scrub that was left was of little value. Some could be cleared to create pasture, which is good, but it meant I had to walk further to find food, fodder and fuel. Then the new forests were cut, and the ones after that. Now we have to walk for two hours just to get there. If you cut these thirty trees, it will not mean the end of the forest, but many more trees will be damaged as they fall, and having cut these thirty, will Robinson and Bose be back next year to cut thirty more? Are we to lose the last patch of forest in our valley? Where will the women of Koti go then? What will happen to our town when there is no more fuel to be had?"

Vimala turned back to her seat with a considerable amount of applause accompanying her. Mohan Das stood and called for quiet then announced that it was time for the vote.

"Could I say one more thing, *Sarpanch*?" Subir Ram asked. "It will only take a moment." Mohan Das hesitated but as no other *panch* member raised an objection, nodded.

"Thank you. That was an admirable speech by *Panch* Shamsar, and on the face of it, she puts a good argument. The world is changing though, and nobody wants to be left behind by progress. She says there will be no more fuel, but she forgets that with progress there will soon be electric power to all the towns. You will not need smoky fires when you can have clean electric heaters and cooking stoves. Soon a good road will be built to Koti and the world will come to you, to buy your produce. Soon everyone here in Koti will be rich enough to buy all the food you need, you will buy milk and meat from the stores so you will not need fodder, strong plastic baskets to replace the fibre ones. Medicines will be available for all at the hospital that is certain to be built in this growing town. Good people of Koti, the trees are but the start of this wonderful process." Ram cleared his throat and smiled. "This was to be a surprise, but I think perhaps I could tell you now. The Robinson and Bose Timber Company have decided to make every family in Koti a payment of one hundred rupees for the small trouble that was caused in the past."

509

An incredulous uproar broke out; people shouting and firing questions at Ram and the *panchayat*. Subir Ram stood grinning, waving the noise down. "My friends," he continued. "All that you need to do to collect the money is for the head of the family to present himself at the company offices in Chamoli the day after tomorrow and you will collect one hundred rupees each in cash."

Mohan Das shouted the meeting to silence and when at length the hubbub dropped to a level where he could speak, asked Subir Ram the question uppermost in his mind. "This payment of a hundred rupees for each family, it is in addition to the nine thousand five hundred for the trees?"

"Yes, *sarpanch*."

"And does it depend on this *panchayat* agreeing to the contract on the trees?"

"No, it does not," Subir Ram said. "However, the company is showing you it is your friend. In the spirit of friendship we hope that you will look favorably on our proposal."

"Then it is time to vote."

"Vote 'yes'," called a man from the audience. A roar of approval went up, though few women joined in.

"This money is a bribe," Vimala called. "Do not sell yourselves, people of Koti."

"You will get your share, Vimala Shamsar, do not fear," Subir Ram replied with a laugh. "Come down to Chamoli with the rest and get your rupees."

Mohan Das turned to his *panchayat*. "If you vote to accept the offer from the timber company, please raise your hand." Every hand rose except those of Vimala

Shamsar and Gujar Bhushan. Under the gaze of the other four *panch* members, Gujar raised his hand too.

"Carried," Mohan Das said with a smirk of satisfaction. "Five votes to one."

The meeting ended and the crowd dispersed, the men chattering excitedly, making plans on how to spend their money, whereas the women, for the most part, hurried back to their families.

Vimala stood beside the main door and stopped two women as they left, drawing them to one side. "Anjali, Nisha, find the others. The collective meets tomorrow morning at nine."

"At nine we will be on the road to the forest, Vimala," Nisha said. "You know that."

"Tomorrow is different. The men will leave at dawn for Chamoli." Vimala forced a reassuring smile. "Manohar will not beat you, for he will not be here."

Nisha bobbed grudging acceptance. "If he leaves, I will be there." She ran off toward her house.

"There's nothing we can do, is there?" Anjali asked. "The men will squander the money and the forest will be cut down."

"There's always something we can do," Vimala said firmly. "Do not lose heart. We will win this yet."

"How? The *sarpanch* will sign the agreement and that's that."

Vimala's shoulders slumped. "I don't know, Anjali, I don't know."

The next morning, just after dawn, the men of Koti gathered in the town square where Mohan Das and Subir Ram addressed them briefly once more. The men shivered, though they had their jackets firmly wrapped

511

around them, for the morning air was chilly. Mist blanketed the fields and the sun shone like a dull red stone, giving little light and less heat. Somewhere a tardy cock crowed and the village sounds came muffled to the crowded street.

"Every head of the household can make a claim for the hundred rupees, but you must be there in person," Mohan Das called out. "By my count, that should be fifty-three people, yet I see many more people here this morning."

"I am taking my sons with me," said Shabhra Lal. "I am wanting them to see my triumph as I claim my money." A chorus of agreement broke out from other men near him.

Subir Ram laughed. "That is good. This is a proud day for the men of Koti for they have won a great battle." Several of the men puffed out their chests so as to look important. "Just make sure that you can all identify yourself to the company clerks. The money will only be paid to the head of the household."

"How am I to do that?" one man asked. "I do not have anything that says I am who I am. I know who I am and so do my friends."

"I will vouch for anyone who does not have identification," Mohan Das said reassuringly. "Now let us depart. The sooner we leave, the sooner we get our money."

"And what of you, Vimala Shamsar?" Subir Ram called, seeing the old woman on the edge of the crowd. "Are you joining us in Chamoli? A hundred rupees is yours too. You are head of the household now your husband is dead."

Vimala shook her head. "The money is a bribe to get us to do what is wrong. I will not collect it."

Subir Ram shrugged. "As you wish." He pushed through the throng to where Mohan Das stood waiting. "To Chamoli!" he cried, waving his arm. The crowd surged after them, down the valley road.

Within an hour, the village lay almost deserted under the gathering strength of the morning sun. The only males to remain in the village were old men too frail to make the trek down to Chamoli, and young boys. These youngsters collected their family's livestock, cattle or goats, and started them on the road to the pastures. Bells clinked in the thinning mist, mingling with the cries of the boys, the lowing of cows and the bleating of goats.

Vimala, and her helpers Anjali and Nisha, started gathering the women of the collective toward the meeting hall. Nisha was quiet, nursing her bruised face, but she determinedly found the late-comers and hurried them along. Vimala stood at the door and counted each woman in, keeping a tally in her head of who was there and who was not. She finally closed the doors on forty women, before turning and sweeping her gaze over despairing faces.

"Do not lose heart," Vimala said quietly. "After all, it is only thirty trees. That is not the whole forest."

"Only thirty this time," Kavita corrected. "Next time another thirty, the time after fifty, then a hundred. The timber company will not stop until every tree is cut down."

"Then we must stop them. It is our livelihood we are talking about."

513

"Stop them how?" a young woman called Rati asked. "Are we to get lawyers to fight in the courts?"

"We do not have the money to pay lawyers," Vimala pointed out.

"You should have taken the hundred rupees, Vimala Shamsar."

"A hundred rupees would not buy a lawyer for a day. No, we must find another way."

"How? Should we attack the wood cutters when they come? Our husbands will prevent us. Should we fight our husbands too?"

"I do not want violence," Vimala said, shaking her head. "But I cannot see any way round it. Unless we stole their axes somehow."

"There is another way." A very young voice spoke from the back of the hall. Heads turned and Vimala rose on her toes to peer over the women.

"Who speaks? I do not recognize your voice."

The ranks of women parted to reveal a young woman, hardly more than a girl, clad in a brilliantly colored green sari and deep yellow shawl, a gold bangle at her wrist and a stud in her right nostril. A bright red *tilaka* glowed on her forehead.

"Who are you, girl? Vimala asked. "You are not from this town. How did you get in here? I was at the door and did not see you. This is a meeting of the women's collective."

"I am Durga Shakti. I know how you can defeat the timber company."

Vimala laughed. "You do? You have a name of power but what would a young girl like you know of the ways of timber companies and men?"

514

The girl smiled and walked forward to stand beside the older woman. "Do you think you are the only women in the hills to face the loss of your forests? This is happening everywhere. Forests are being cleared of the trees that hold the soil and the land is washing down the rivers to the distant sea." Durga's voice was gentle but it carried effortlessly to every woman in the hall. "There is a way to stop them, though. It calls for courage and determination, but that is something that a woman must show every day of her life. Be strong, my sisters, and we shall overcome adversity."

"She speaks truth," Nisha said. "A woman must be strong just to survive, and a woman alone can achieve very little."

"What do you know of forests, girl?" Vimala asked, with a biting edge to her voice. "From the look of you, you come from a rich family and have never done a day's work in your short life. Who are you to teach us?"

"I would not presume to teach you," Durga replied. "And I do not have rich parents." She held up the folds of her sari and examined it as if seeing it for the first time. "This is only cloth. Do you judge a person by her garments or her youth, women of Koti? Should I go elsewhere and leave you to lose your battle with the wood cutters?"

Vimala hesitated, before bowing her head. "I am justly chastised by a woman half my age ..."

"A quarter, more like," Anjali said with a grin.

Vimala laughed, several of the women joining in. "A quarter then. Durga Shakti, will you tell us what you know?"

"Chipko," Durga said.

515

"Hugging?" Nisha frowned. "If you think hugging our husbands will save the trees …"

"Not your husbands. Listen. The Forestry Department announced an auction of over two thousand trees in the Reni forest, which like Koti, overlooks the Alaknanda River. Who remembers the flood of nineteen seventy?" Half a dozen women put their hands up. "It would not have affected you here for you still have some of your forests, but in the villages below forests that had been cleared, the rain ate away at the bare soil and hillsides fell. Many people died and countless more suffered the loss of family members, houses, farms and businesses. This is what happens when you cut down forests. The land washes away."

Durga walked over to the huge oak table that the *panchayat* used for its meetings and climbed up on it, sitting down and delicately arranging the folds of her sari around her. She faced her audience, and from her elevated position could see every face. "I was in Reni when Chandi Prasad Bhatt – a great friend of the land, someone they call an environmentalist – came to talk to the village. He talked of how the forest and the land is holy, of how the gods gave it to men so they could use it, but use it wisely, so that every generation could benefit. He told of what happens when forests are cut down, when greedy men look for short term gain ahead of the future of the children. With the forests gone, the floods come, and people die. Those that are left are poorer, but the men who cut the trees for money are far away enjoying their wealth while the hill people starve." Durga paused, but every woman in the hall remained silent, awaiting her next words.

516

"Then Chandi Prasad told us of the Chipko Movement and how it could defeat the tree cutters. 'It is simple,' he said. 'You hug the trees.'"

"Hug the trees," Vimala said, her voice flat. "I hoped you had something sensible to say, some idea that we could use ..."

Durga slipped down off the table and strode quickly across to the older woman. "You are an axe-man. You cut trees for a living."

"What are you talking about?"

"Here." Durga grabbed a short bamboo cane standing near the dusty blackboard. "This is your axe." She spun around and scanned the front row of women, her eyes stopping at Nisha's bruised face. Durga's eyes glistened and she reached out a hand and gently stroked the young woman's hair. "You shall be the tree, damaged but standing strong. Yet only the love of your sisters can help you." The girl beckoned to another woman. "What is your name?"

"Rati," the young woman said shyly.

"Do you love your sister here?" Durga pointed at Nisha.

Rati blushed and hung her head. "She is not my sister."

"Every woman in Koti is your sister. Will you help her?"

Rati nodded.

"Very well then." Durga stepped back and she cried out excitedly. "Here are the wood cutters hired by the timber company." She pointed at Vimala standing to one side with the bamboo rod dangling in one hand. "They have come to cut down this beautiful tree." A finger

517

stabbed toward Nisha. "Only Rati can save her." She whirled toward the young woman. "Remember Chipko – hugging. Save your tree. Hurry. Before the axe arrives to strike her down."

Rati stared wide-eyed at Vimala then with a tiny cry, rushed at Nisha and embraced her, hugging her close, with tears in her eyes.

Durga grinned. "The axe-man arrives but he cannot strike the tree because Rati is in the way. He will not strike because he sees his own mother, his own wife or sister or daughter standing before him and he feels shame."

Vimala tossed the cane aside and pursed her lips thoughtfully. "And this works? You have seen it work?"

"The company that won the auction to cut down Reni's trees arrived one day in a bus with axes and saws. The Government, perhaps in an agreement with the company, announced a compensation for land taken by the military in the war against China, and the men of Reni rushed to Chamoli to collect their money, leaving the village and the forest defenceless. Only the women remained. Then Gaura Devi, the leader of the Women's collective in Reni, when she heard the bus was coming, collected as many women as she could and led them to the forest. They pleaded with the men, asking them not to cut down the trees, and explained why. 'The forest is our life,' they said. When the men moved toward the trees, the women embraced the trunks and the men backed away. One had been drinking and he threatened the women with a gun. Gaura Devi stood up to him, saying the forest was her mother and that he would have to shoot her first."

"And it worked? Did they win?"

"The fight is not yet over, but the government is now aware of the threat to the forests and has halted all logging in the Reni forest. So yes, the women of Reni won – and so can you. All you must do is stand up for yourselves and the forests that must remain alive if you are to survive."

The women gathered around Vimala, Nashi and Rati excitedly, chattering and hugging in a sudden release of sisterly affection. Kavita cried out that they should elect Durga Shakti to the *panchayat* of the Women's collective so that she might continue to advise them. A chorus of agreement sounded but when they looked for the girl she was nowhere to be found.

"She is a modest girl," Karishma said. "Being properly brought up; she has slipped out of the hall and gone home."

"And where is her home, Karishma?" Vimala demanded. "Do any of you know? Have any of you seen her before today?"

Rati laughed nervously. "What are you saying? That she is a ghost?"

"Don't be stupid," Vimala snapped. "She is obviously one of these … these environmentalists come to warn us about the timber company ..."

"And tell us about Chipko," Nashi interrupted.

"That too."

"Then why did she leave so suddenly?"

Vimala shrugged. "How would I know? Now," she clapped her hands loudly until the chatter subsided. "What are we going to do? It seems, if the events at Reni are true, that the company has lured the men away from Koti so they can bring in the loggers."

Anjali frowned and raised her hand until Vimala nodded in her direction. "But if the town *panchayat* has agreed to the sale of the trees, why do they need to wait for the men to leave?"

"I don't know, but it seems like a big coincidence."

"Maybe they are going to cut down more than thirty trees. Durga said the Forestry Department sold two thousand at Reni. The men would stop them doing that, wouldn't they?

The discussion went on a while longer but they could think of no better reason for the luring away of the men from the town.

"How do we stop them?"

Rati grinned happily. "By Chipko."

"Agreed," Vimala said. "But what I meant was how do we know when to be up at the forest? The road through Koti is not the only way into our valley."

"We must post lookouts on all the trails to warn us of the loggers' approach."

By noon, the lower road and the three tracks over the ridges to Koti and the upper valley were staffed by young girls. Rati volunteered to organize the youngsters and make sure that they were never alone on watch and that they were relieved every few hours. Young minds were easily distracted and no-one wanted the loggers slipping past unseen if a girl slept through boredom or tiredness. The sun crossed the zenith and slipped westward, the boys returned with their flocks and herds, but there was no sign of the company men.

The old men of the town, left behind with the women and children, complained loudly that the women were neglecting their duties. 'Where is the fodder you should have collected?' they asked. 'And the firewood to cook our evening meal?'

Some of the women relented and pooled the fuel stocks of the town, organizing meals for everyone in the town square. The girls came in from their lookout duties and the women led the children in songs and told them stories. Were it not for the absence of the men, it would have seemed like one of the festivals of the gods. The priest of the temple of Shiva made offerings to all the gods at the several altars of the temple. Being less worldly than most men, he knew of the sacred trust given to men to care for the abode of the gods.

When the fires burned down and the children and old men had all been put to bed, Nashi and Vimala sat on the steps of the meeting house and smoked a cigarette, staring up at the star-strewn sky.

"We should have put lookouts on the tracks after the girls came in," Nisha said. "The loggers could sneak past us in the night."

"What could they see out there?" Vimala replied. She inhaled, turning the tip of her cigarette a bright red. "Our men will be down in Chamoli." Smoke gusted out as she talked. "They will collect their money tomorrow and start back again. I think the loggers will come by noon tomorrow at the latest."

They came just after dawn, when the grass still sparkled with dew and the mist from the river valley swirled lazily over the road. A child, a girl of eleven, ran up the main street of the town and disappeared into her house, crying out that men were coming up the road toward Koti. Her mother ran for the meeting house where Nisha greeted her bleary-eyed by the door.

"What is it, Mala?"

"They are coming. My daughter Gita saw them on the road."

Nisha nodded. "Rouse everyone, Mala. Get them all here quickly." She ducked inside the building and hurried over to where Vimala slept on some mats at the back of the hall. She shook the older woman awake. "They're here."

"Here?" Vimala stared uncomprehendingly at the young woman bent over her. "Oh, you mean coming." She struggled to her feet and adjusted her clothing. "Don't just stand there, Nisha. We must rouse the collective."

"Mala is already doing it. Listen."

From outside in the square came the sound of many voices. Vimala walked out onto the meeting house steps and addressed the women and children gathered there, even as others ran up. "The loggers are coming," she cried. "Now is the time to try Chipko." She went on to order the women to collect as much cold food as could easily be carried – chapattis and rice mainly – and bottles of water. "Now we must run to the forest if we are to get there before the men."

They set off up the road that led to the upper valley, running as fast as they could, but it soon became apparent that not everyone could travel quickly. The children tired, as did the older women, Vimala included, while the younger women and older girls ran onward, widening the gap.

Vimala called them back. "We must present a united front to the loggers. It will do no good to arrive in ones and twos."

Anjali shook her head. "It will also do no good if we arrive so late that they have already chopped the trees down. Let us younger women run on to slow them at least until everybody can get there."

Vimala grimaced, but knew the young woman was right. "Go then, and do what you can. We will follow as quickly as possible." Anjali grinned and, hitching up her sari, ran off, followed by a dozen women and girls. Vimala ordered the rest of the group to sit down by the road side and feed the youngsters.

Ten minutes later they set off again, walking this time, in a steady pace that ate up the kilometers but without exhausting the children. As they drew near to the forest, Vimala's heart clenched for she saw men moving at the forest edge and thin tendrils of smoke rising through the leaves.

"They are burning the forest!" cried one of the women, and they started running up the last stretch of road. As they passed a stunted deodar cypress, a figure darted out from the side and grabbed Vimala by the arm, calling to the others to stop.

"This way, quickly." Nisha waved at the women and children to follow and led the group into the forest down a sun-dappled path that led deep into the woodland. She stopped them under cover of the forest and explained the situation breathlessly.

"The loggers have marked the trees they intend to cut down and have started fires to make tea. They will eat a meal before they use their axes, so we have time."

"Where are the others?"

"By the closest marked trees – and Anjali is watching the men."

A burst of laughter and deep voices raised warned them of the proximity of the loggers, so stressing the importance of keeping the children quiet, Nisha led them all quickly to where the others waited.

"What do we do now, Vimala?"

The old woman thought hard. "Let a woman and a child guard each of the marked trees ..."

"We do not have enough people for that," Nisha interrupted.

"We don't? How many trees are marked?"

"At least a hundred. You were right, Vimala. This is why they got rid of our menfolk."

"Then guard the nearest ones. I will go and talk to the men. Maybe they will listen to reason."

"I do not think they will," Nisha said. "But I will accompany you anyway."

The two women made their way to the camp where Anjali joined them from her post behind a large bush. "You are just in time," she whispered. "They are getting ready to start work."

Vimala took a deep breath and prayed silently to her gods before stepping out into the small clearing where about twenty men stood and sat around two small campfires. Already, the fires were out and sizzling as earth was scraped over them, smothering the embers. Nobody took any notice of the three women and Vimala stood at the edge of the clearing, uncertain as to their next actions.

"What are you waiting for?" Anjali asked, her voice carrying clearly across the open space.

Several men turned and stared at the women. "What 'ave we got 'ere?" asked one, a short man with a large paunch. He laughed, and took a few steps closer. "Wimmin from th' forest. You come up from th' town tah give us a good time, then?" More men turned, stopping what they were doing to see what was going on.

Another man, a tall balding one wearing a jacket like the ones favored by Jawaharlal Nehru, guffawed. "Have you looked at them, Rajiv? They're old women – well, that one on the left'll do me – you can have the others."

"Alright, alright, what's going on?" An older man carrying a clipboard and pencil pushed through the crowd of men and stopped short when he saw the three women. "Who are you and what are you doing here?"

"I am Vimala Shamsur, *panch* of Koti and *sarpanch* of the Women's collective. These are my assistants. Who are you? You are trespassing in the forest of Koti that belongs to the citizens of that town."

The man snorted derisively. "I am Sunderlal Dev, foreman. If you were truly a *panch* member you would know that the trees of this forest have been sold to the timber company Robinson and Bose. We have come to cut down those trees, so we are here legally."

"You tell 'em, boss." A chorus of agreement rang out.

"We will not let you cut our trees down," Vimala said. Insects chirred in the undergrowth and birds called in the silence that greeted the old woman's words. The sour smell of wood ash clung to the clearing, mingling with the lingering odors of the recent meal.

"How are you going to stop us?" asked the man with the clipboard at length. "My men have axes and saws for the trees." He leered at the women's clothing. "Are you hiding guns under those saris? Well, we have guns too." Two men brandished old shotguns in the air. "There is no way you can stop us, so go home and do your household work. Leave men's business to men."

"Mr Dev, these forests are more than just timber and money to us. The women of Koti, no doubt like your mothers and sisters and wives, must look to the land for a living. We come up here every day to gather firewood and fodder for the animals, fibers and medicines. If you cut down the trees, the forest will disappear and we will have nowhere to go. Then when the rains come the soil will wash into the river and we will not even be able to grow food for our children."

"You talk as if we are cutting down the whole forest," Sunderlal Dev laughed. "We have only come to cut down thirty trees."

"Then why have you marked over a hundred?" Nisha yelled. "Our men only sold thirty to the company but you will take the whole forest unless we stop you."

The foreman looked down, clearly uncomfortable. "We are only doing what we are told to do."

"Come on, boss," Rajiv whined. "Let's get on wiv it, if we is goin' tah."

"Yeah, three women can't stop us."

"Alright," Sunderlal Dev called out, reaching a decision. He turned to the men and waved them forward with his clipboard. "Let's go and do what we are getting paid for … but nobody hurt the women," he added as he saw Rajiv and Bina, the tall balding man step toward the youngest woman. "You two get your axes and follow me."

"Back to the trees," Vimala crisply commanded, seeing the younger women off before turning and following at a fast walk. They reached the first of the marked trees, a small group of two oaks and an ash, only moments ahead of the first loggers.

"Three to a tree," Vimala called out. "Link hands; hug those trees like you would your children." Women and girls ran for the trees and after a few moments of confusion, joined hands around the trunks of the marked trees. Vimala, Nisha and Anjali positioned themselves in front of the trees while the other women milled uncertainly, some of them embracing unmarked trees. "The rest of you wait. If they move toward a marked tree, hug it."

"Ah, come on, woman," Dev complained as he approached the first tree. "Tell your friends to move out of the way. We're going to cut it down and we don't want anyone to get hurt."

"No-one will get hurt," Vimala reassured him. "If you just lay down your axes and go away."

"That is not going to happen." The foreman called up three burly men and told them to remove the women from the first oak. As they moved in, the women started screaming and the men stopped, looking questioningly at their boss. "Go ahead, but don't hurt them."

"Your men are committing assault, Sunderlal Dev. If you do not call them off immediately, I will charge you with the crime to the police in Chamoli."

"They are interfering with these men as they try to do lawful work. Your charges will fail. Remove the

527

women!" Dev called. The three burly men seized the women and carried them away from the tree, kicking and screaming.

Vimala gestured and three more women ran from the waiting group, linking arms around the oak again. Dev angrily called up three more men but as soon as they hauled the women away, another three ran in.

"There are more of us," Vimala said, satisfaction creeping into her voice. "What will you do when every man is assaulting a woman and there are none left to wield an axe? There will still be women around the trees."

One of the captured girls screamed again as the tall, balding man grabbed her round the waist and Dev yelled at him. "Let them go. Let them all go." The women ran back to the others.

Dev scowled at Vimala then nodded suddenly. "Dobhal," he called to one of the men. "Take ten men and head for ... the far group. You understand which trees I mean?" Dobhal nodded. "Start there and work back toward us."

As the men shouldered their axes and saws and set off at a run, Vimala called out for half the women to follow them. "Anjali, go with them. You know what to do." The young woman nodded and quickly picked out a dozen women and a handful of girls, racing off after Dobhal's men.

"It will not work, Sunderlal Dev. The women will hug the trees no matter where your men are."

"We are only trying to do our job, woman. Would you be happy if someone stopped your husband or father or son from doing their work?"

"Would you be happy if men laid hands on your wives or mothers or sisters and forcibly dragged them away?"

The foreman's face flushed and the muscles of his jaw clenched. He looked at the fourteen women left, nine of them hugging the trees, then at his nine men, calculating. Nodding, he walked over to his men and quietly outlined his plan. "Go!" he yelled, and ran for the group of women, his arms spread wide. Three of his men ran to the ash tree and grabbed the women, dragging them away. As three more women started for the tree, four men raced forward, joining Dev and preventing the women from helping while the remaining two, Rajiv and the bald man, raised their axes and stepped forward, grinning.

Nisha yelled and the women round her oak let go and ran for the vulnerable ash tree, dodging the men as they tried to herd them away. One woman slipped through the cordon, then another and suddenly, the two men with axes changed direction, racing for the now-deserted oak.

"Back!" Vimala screamed. She hitched up her sari and raced for the unprotected oak, ducking under the upraised axe of the bald man and throwing her arms around the tree. The man cursed and backed away.

Sunderlal Dev examined the situation around the trees with interest, a smile growing on his face. Of the fourteen women, six protected the other two trees and three were held by his men. The leader-bitch faced the two axemen, leaving just four women free to interfere. However, he had nine men at his disposal. Three held the women captive, two axemen stood ready, and four faced the free women. That meant that he could remove the

529

bitch and his two axemen could complete their job. Once the women saw one tree felled they would lose heart. He smugly swaggered across to face Vimala.

"Last chance, woman. Step away from the tree."

Vimala shook her head. "No."

"As you wish." Sunderlal Dev leapt forward and grabbed Vimala by one hand, throwing his weight back and dragging her forward, her other hand losing its grip on the bark. At once the bald man moved in and swung his axe, the blade biting deep into the trunk. He wrestled it free and stepped back and around the tree, turning to face Rajiv, who also got himself into position and prepared to swing his axe.

Vimala screamed and fought against Dev, struggling to free her hand. "Nisha, help me!"

Nisha let go of the ash, leaving it in the charge of the two other women and ran to her *sarpanch*. Beside her, only a pace or two away, the loggers swung their blades. Getting into a rhythm, the bald man and Rajiv rained blows on the tree trunk, with each axe blow chips of wood and bark spattered outward. Nisha threw herself at the foreman, her nails seeking his face.

Dev tried to ward off the woman's attack with one hand while still holding fast to Vimala. The old lady kicked him hard, her bare foot connecting with his knee, and he cried out in pain, releasing her hand. She stumbled back, turned, and lurched toward the oak, clasping it as Rajiv's axe swung round again.

Instead of the solid thunk of iron into wood, the blow made a sound like a wet branch snapping. Rajiv stared wide-eyed at the head of his axe embedded deep in the woman's thigh.

530

Vimala felt the blow and thought one of the men had kicked her. She looked down and instinctively drew back, the movement loosening the axe's hold on her flesh. Blood erupted, swiftly soaking her sari, and she collapsed sideways, her fingernails ripping on the bark as she fell. Agony washed over her and she screamed – a high wailing cry that died into ragged gasps as she arched her body against the pain.

Nisha let go of Dev and stared in horror for a moment, before throwing herself down beside her friend, cradling her head, unmindful of the blood pumping out over both of them. The other women looked on, not knowing what to do, and as the men backed away, crowded close around the dying woman.

Vimala fluttered her eyelids as she fought to focus on Nisha's face. The pain had receded until it felt like something happening to someone else. Forms moved about her and she licked her lips, forcing her mind to form words.

"W ... why all ... here? Guard ... trees."

Nisha sobbed and held her close. "They've gone, Vimala. The men have run off. We've won but why did it have to be this way?" Around her, most of the other women and girls were crying, though some sat several feet away, refusing to look at the blood-stained scene.

"Ss good ... hugg ... works. Chipko." Vimala struggled for breath and her hand sought Nisha's. "Is night?" she gasped. "Dark."

Nisha did not reply, just hugging her friend and rocking back and forth, her tears pouring down her cheeks.

A few minutes later, Vimala suddenly squeezed Nisha's hand and a smile crept onto her pallid face. She took a deep breath and her voice strengthened. "Look, Nisha, a light. The ... the men have come from the village. It will all be ..." Her muscles went suddenly limp and her head lolled back.

Nisha and Anjali kept vigil by the body of their friend, carrying her away from the blood-soaked ground around the wounded oak and laying her down on a bed of fallen leaves. The other women and girls returned to Koti to prepare for the arrival of the men and to bear the devastating news. Rati and Kavita returned later in the day with a clean sari and water, and helped the other two women to bathe Vimala's body and clothe her in fresh garments.

Several men arrived from the village hours later, as dusk was approaching. Mohan Das stood over the body of his *panch* member for several minutes, before turning and staring at the four women sitting on their heels nearby.

"What have you women done? Was it necessary for Vimala Shamsar to die? And for what – trying to protect trees that we had sold to the timber company?"

Nisha raised her tear-streaked face. "She did not die trying – she died succeeding."

"The men had a right to fell the trees," Mohan Das yelled. "She had no cause to stop them."

"They are our trees," Anjali said. "We should protect them."

"And they were going to cut down many more trees," Rati added. "Look for yourself how many are marked."

532

Mohan Das frowned, then accompanied by Govind Bisht and Kalika Lalit, walked off into the forest. The remaining men set about making a stretcher out of saplings and strips of bark. They had just finished when Mohan Das returned.

"I counted over sixty before I stopped," he said quietly. "The company was planning to cheat us."

"What will you do?" Nisha asked.

"I don't know but I think I must call a meeting of the *panchayat*. We must discuss whether we can do business with Robinson and Bose."

"You would even contemplate it? Remember you will have to have another of the women's collective as a *panch* member. Do not think you can do just as you please."

"You, Nisha?" Mohan Das smiled. "You think you can oppose me?"

"I or one of my sisters. Whoever they elect as *sarpanch*. We have won once, Mohan Das, we can do so again. Chipko is a force to be reckoned with and women are finding their strength. Do not think we will let Vimala Shamsar die in vain."

533

Chapter Twenty-Six

Time is moving faster, for gods as well as men, or is it just that the pace of change is accelerating? It seems but yesterday that the hills moved to the slow sway of men's lives as they did what they and their fathers and grandfathers had done before them. Farmers and herders grew food, men made the things they needed out of metal or wood or clay, priests wandered the land, women raised children. Petty kings ruled and went to war, subjugating tiny parcels of land, killing a few men, exacting a few taxes, before turning once more to the seemingly endless routine of everyday life. Over the ages, new peoples came to Uttarakhand, bringing new ideas and new things. Then suddenly, it seemed, in this last century, population swelled and the flood of inventions swamped even the hills, from cars and trains to electricity and plumbing, to transistor radios and tee-shirts.

As these things happened, the land suffered. More people led to a greater demand on the forests and the farmland. The cutting down of the forests started slowly. Wood cutters and charcoal burners had little effect, but once the people of the open plains and foreigners became aware of our natural wealth, there seemed to be nothing that could stand in their way.

Except the hill people themselves. I think it is a mistake to attribute high ecological principles to those who lived before. They certainly believed that the gods created the earth and everything in it and that the bounty the earth provided was a gift, but they had no concept of limited resources, or of the catastrophes that could result from ecological abuse. The knowledge just was not there, and their numbers were so low that they could exhaust no more than local resources. When drought or flood threatened, they appeased the gods. When famine or sickness took its toll, they shrugged their shoulders and got on with their lives. It had never happened before, so how could the hill tribes know that stripping the hillside of its vegetation cover would lead to landslides and the loss of valuable topsoil. They had always relied on the forest for food, fodder, fuel and medicines, taking a tree now and then for wood, so how were they to know that suddenly removing a lot of trees, particularly of the same sort, would rip a hole in the interwoven fabric of the local ecology.

A knowledge of ecology as a science started elsewhere but it was embraced by the hill people, especially the women. I am not saying that women are inherently more sensible or intelligent, able to grasp ecological concepts more easily than men. I am not saying that men are greedier by nature or that women are more selfless. However, the division of labor between the genders meant that men farmed the fields and women farmed the forests. As the forests disappeared, women found themselves walking further and working harder, whereas for men the labor input of daily life remained the same. I suppose it was natural that when the ecology movement started, the women of Uttarakhand should be the first to respond. The Chipko Movement struck a chord and many women saw for the first time that their own actions could benefit society. No longer were men the only ones to achieve things outside the family home.

I was there in the early days, watching and listening. Back in the fifties, Chandi Prasad Bhatt was a young man among many others who helped the people of his homeland develop economically and fight the abuse of strong drink. When the war with the Chinese to the north broke out, the government built many roads into Uttarakhand and following hard on the heels of the road builders came the trucks of the logging companies. Laborers from the plains were brought in by contractors and Chandi Prasad helped organize labor co-operatives, including the local use of the forests. The big companies tried to halt the competition and shut the locals out of the market, out-bidding them in the auctions. Illegal logging blossomed, compounding the problem. Then the floods began as the topsoil washed away in the monsoon rains.

Chandi Prasad and others realized the cause and petitioned the government to halt clear-felling, but they did not listen. The ecologically minded groups debated how to stop the loggers themselves. Many ideas were put forward, from outright terrorism to destroying the trees themselves to prevent the companies from profiting. I'd like to be able to say that hugging was my idea, but it was not. The most I did was try to turn people away from violence as a solution. Chandi Prasad himself came up with the idea of hugging trees, and a few weeks later in the Mandel forest near Gopeshwar, Chipko as a policy was adopted.

The word spread, and here I could help. I adopted the disguise of a young woman – I was a lot less intimidating and far more acceptable to meetings of women's collectives – and set about spreading the word to out of the way villages and towns. I took the name of Durga Shakti – the feminine energy of the supreme goddess – and tried to persuade women to adopt the passive resistance of Chipko. When I had introduced the idea, I left, for I had decided that as befitted a god, I would not interfere unless asked. As it happened, in Koti as elsewhere, the women succeeded quite well on their own.

I know, you are saying 'a woman died, how can that be called a success?' but consider this, the logging was halted, which was what the effort was all about. Vimala herself considered the sacrifice worthwhile. I know, because she told me.

Now that caught your attention! I have always said that the flame of a human existence does not burn strongly enough to survive the death of the body. I am glad that I qualified that statement by saying I had never seen one survive, and I have been present at the deaths of thousands. Never, that is, until some sixty-five years ago on the slopes of Nanda Devi when it seemed as if the mind of an Englishman survived for a time. Vimala Shamsar was different.

I followed the women up to the forest as an invisible flame, watched the events unfold, and was ready to intervene if called on. Alas, an increasingly secular society only calls on the gods as a last resort. Vimala lay dying and at the end, caught sight of me, the blue hovering flame piercing the gathering darkness in her mind. To say I was startled by what happened next would be to put it mildly. One moment I was alone, watching a brave woman dying, and the next moment, two people looked down at a dead woman.

"Who are you?" Vimala asked, her eyes wide. Although she existed solely as a flame, force of habit

537

clothed her in a body and sari. "Are you a god or a demon?"

"I mean you no harm," I said, marveling at her continued existence.

"Have you come to … to take me to the next life?"

"No."

Vimala looked down at her body and the wailing women. "We won, didn't we?"

"Yes. Here as in other places throughout Uttarakhand."

"It was worth it." She turned and cocked her head as if listening, but I heard nothing. Smiling, she turned back to me and said quietly, "Bless you," before drifting off into the forest.

I never saw her again and I am unsure of just what I did see that day. Did I conjure her form in my mind's eye because I felt guilty about letting her die, or have I become more sensitive with the years, finally being able to see that humans have a spirit that lives on beyond the dissolution of mortal flesh? If so, does this mean I have refined my own spirit and in reality, become more god-like? Of course, this episode raises further questions for me – disquieting ones. Has my solitary existence, living among humans who I once preyed on, tipped me over the edge into insanity? Am I insane? How else would you define a demon who thinks he is a god? Have I become delusional, desiring to find others in the spirit realm and conjuring one? Or if I allow that this human actually survived death and I saw her and spoke to her, then why now and never before? Is somebody or something guiding me, leading me? Where to, and why? She listened to something I could not hear. Who spoke to her there in the forest that caused her to offer me a blessing?

Deeply disturbed, I fled the valley of the Koti River and journeyed to the one place where I have always found peace and solitude – the snows of Nanda Devi. Alas, even these beautiful high meadows and ice fields have suffered at the hand of man, and everywhere I walked I found the detritus and garbage of mankind. What is it that leads a man to seek out the wild and pristine places of the earth, perhaps even where few people have been before, and leave his trash behind? I found a babbling brook that cascaded over water-worn boulders, down from the Trisul glacier, and in its ice-cold crystal waters I found plastic bottles and the rusting remains of tin cans. For a few moments I considered returning to my old ways and wreaking a horrible revenge on the despoilers, but I calmed. This mountain belonged to another, and if it was her will to allow this horror, then it was not my place to act for her. I asked forgiveness of the Bliss-giving Goddess and departed, again wandering over hills and valleys of beautiful Uttarakhand. But now my eyes were opened and my heart heavy, for I saw the evil things that man in his greed was doing to the earth. Money had replaced the gods and the things men would do for money made me weep. There are many places in Uttarakhand that are still of great beauty, but being a god or demon I have a longer sight than man, and I dread to think what this land will be like in another five hundred years or so.

To cheer myself, I sought out the company of the wild beasts of the forest, deciding to shun man for a while. The beasts, unlike man, live in harmony with each other and there is something clean and natural about the tiger and his prey, the fish hawk patrolling the rivers and the small flocks of blue-winged Sivas hunting the bushes for insects. Life and death abound, but it is clean and open, and for several years I kept to myself. Until one day I found myself following old trails I have walked on before, down through forest and grassland to the shores of Naini Tal, now crowded by humans. It held memories for me, but memories were not what I was after, so I traveled westward, to a new lake, one created by man. Surrounding it was a reserve, a national park, named for that old hunter and conservationist I had known in Naini – Jim Corbett. Despite thousands of visitors each year, nobody was allowed on foot in the park, which suited me, so I struck off alone in my old guise of the Pahari hillman, Pandalis. Most of the Park has no roads and few trails, so I knew I would meet no-one, be disturbed neither by officials nor by tourists. Or so I thought.

Chapter Twenty-Seven

He came riding from Ranikhet, his bicycle rattling and squeaking over the hill roads, his long legs straining with the effort to climb the ridges, recklessly relying on the brakes as he free-wheeled down the steep inclines. His blond hair blew in the wind and his cheerful, rather ruddy face gleamed with the sheer joy of the experience. Twenty-three years old and fresh out of university in Australia where he had graduated with a Master's degree in biology, John Stevenson was determined to make the most of his two months in India. Knowing no-one, and traveling alone, he had perforce picked up a smattering of the local tongue, at least enough to get by on with a lot of smiling and simple English among the friendly hill people.

Uttarakhand was his sole destination, not only because of its renowned beauty, but also because he had family ties to the area. His grandmother had been born in Allahabad in nearby Uttar Pradesh and had often spoken with great fondness of her own grandparents' house in Mussoorie, her childhood in Naini Tal and growing up in Almora. John had visited all these places, but the real excitement had come from seeing the places where the legendary Jim Corbett had hunted man-eating tigers and leopards. Armed with battered paperback copies of the books, John tracked down the sites, reveling in the thrill of being on the spot where the Rudraprayag man-eating leopard met its fate, where the Chowgarh tigers roamed, where the Thak man-eater was killed. John's father had introduced him to the India of Rudyard Kipling and Jim Corbett and the tales had caught his imagination. His father's other passion had been butterflies – first collecting them and later photography. This latter pursuit interested John also and was the last of the reasons he had come to India.

After six weeks of traveling the hills and valleys of Garhwal and Kumaon, John had arrived at the great tiger reserve in the southern hills, where the first rampart of the snow-bound Himalayas rear up from the hot plains of the sacred Ganga River. John had visited the Park already, as an official tourist, but now he was on his way back, by bicycle, knowing he was about to do something illegal. He was going to sneak back into the Park alone and spend the last week of his holiday cycling through the forests and grasslands, following the game trails and camping alone and without the protection of a fire, all to follow his third reason for coming to India – butterflies.

Butterfly watching might seem like a strange pastime for a grown man, but it was a lot more serious than the simple collecting and photography in which his father had indulged. John had taken a general biology course at university, majoring in entomology and had then followed up with a master's degree studying the egg-laying habits of the *Aristolochia* swallowtails of northern Queensland. When he returned from his trip to India, John intended to enroll in doctoral studies before finding a job in a research station somewhere. This trip was a holiday, a break from intensive studies, but it also served to feed a fascination with India and its butterflies.

The road from Ranikhet switch-backed along the course of the Kosi River, winding through countryside where some eighty years before the Mohan man-eater had held a reign of terror. The river flowed west before turning abruptly south, where the road split. The main branch followed the river, heading down to Ramnagar, but the other, smaller road turned north toward the Mohan Forest Rest House and the Durgadevi Gate. John had not been alone on the Ranikhet – Ramnagar road by any means. A steady stream of motorized traffic passed in both directions, interspersed with foot traffic and the occasional bullock cart. Since the turnoff though, the traffic had been a lot lighter, being limited mainly to tourists and Park officials. He knew he was safe enough until he reached the Gate, the official entrance to the tiger reserve, but if he went that way, his presence would attract the attention of the Rangers and that was something he certainly did not want.

Cycling past the Mohan Rest House on its knoll of grass surrounded by forest, he casually averted his eyes from the tourist group gathered on the verandah drinking tea and listening to a talk by one of the Rangers. He felt the ranger's eyes slide over him, but kept pedaling, his eyes scanning the forest tree canopy as if looking for birds. Half a mile further on, and out of sight of both the Rest House and the manned checkpoint at the Durgadevi Gate, he found what he was looking for. A game trail plunged across the dirt road and disappeared into the thick Sal forest to the left. With a quick glance up and down the road, John hopped off his bike and led it onto the trail, quickly pushing along until he was out of sight of the road. He stopped and listened, dreading the sound of pursuit or the sharp voices of the rangers. Walking alone in the tiger reserve was strictly prohibited and half-humorous signs along the crocodile infested rivers and tracks through the Park told of the prosecution that would be inflicted on survivors. John intended the latter but not the former.

Standing silently in the Sal forest, John listened to the calls of many species of birds, starting up again after his initial disturbance of their habitat. He paid them little attention, not knowing their names, though on his official visit to the Park a week earlier he had dutifully photographed them and joined in the activities organized for the benefit of the dedicated bird watchers in the tour group. Instead, his eyes flicked over the sun-dappled vegetation, following the gliding path of a pair of Common Sailor butterflies. The black and white banded wings, coupled with the glide and flick of their flight, looked lazy, but he knew from experience how hard it was to sneak close enough to get a decent photo of one. He had managed it though, a few weeks back and the image captured by his Fuji digital camera was already lodged in his hotmail account, safe in cyberspace along with hundreds of others. John smiled at the sight of the Sailors, telling himself it was a good omen for his venture.

Pulling out his battered notebook with the sketch map of the park, John estimated his position and worked out the course he should take when the game trail allowed him. The forest was still open, the rough-barked sal trees rising to form a canopy, metres above his head, the dim light that filtered through letting only a few shade-tolerant ground-cover plants survive. The lack of undergrowth made cycling easy but it also meant he was visible if he came too close to a road. Shrugging, he set off, pedaling quickly along the trail, heading roughly west, then north-west through the mixed sal and pine forest.

About an hour later he emerged without warning onto a dirt road. He ducked back into the denser undergrowth along the roadside and dropped his bike behind a bush, crouching down and listening. Nothing man-made stirred in the hot afternoon, the only sound being the whirr and buzz of insects and faroff, the belling of a sambhar buck warning of the presence of a predator. Little grass yellow butterflies tumbled across the grass verges of the road and high in the blue sky above wheeled a solitary kite.

John debated whether to follow the road westward toward the Gairal Forest Rest House or to continue northwest across a narrow strip of forest to the Ramganga River. His destination was on the far side of the river so he would have to cross it sooner or later, but not all places were equally safe. The only time he had crossed it was further down-river, near the confluence with the Mandal River. The deep pools were the haunts of crocodiles, but on elephant-back it had proved no problem. It was possible though that the upper reaches of the Ramganga would be shallow enough to wade. That decided him, and after checking the road again, he quickly wheeled his bicycle across and into the scant cover of the forest again. The strip of forest was thinner than he thought and a few minutes later, John stood at the edge of the sal looking across a broad plain of tall brown grass toward the silver ribbon of the Ramganga River.

"Damn," he muttered, the sound of his own voice making him a little self-conscious, but also reassuring him. "Anything could be in there. Tigers, snakes and elephants, oh my." He snorted with laughter and pushed into the grass.

The tall blades were brown and dry in the hot sun, breathlessly waiting for the monsoons which was still at least a month off. Shriveled grass made his passage easier and before long he happened on another, broader game trail that led in the general direction of the river. He mounted his bike and pedaled along leisurely, enjoying the pleasant feel of the air on his face, drying the sweat staining his plain green tee-shirt and patched denim jeans. Far ahead, down the avenue lined by head-high grass, John could see the round gray mass of a boulder, apparently marking the bank of the river.

As he got closer, the boulder moved, changing shape, swinging round to face the approaching cyclist with ears spread wide and trunk upraised to taste the air. John braked suddenly and stood stock still as the elephant moved slowly toward him, its trunk questing.

What the hell do I do? he thought. A moment later, *The wind. What direction is it?* Glancing at the swaying tops of the grass blades he saw that the wind cut across the avenue from right to left. *If it can't smell me, I'm safe.* John smiled with relief before realizing the elephant was still closing on him and there was not enough room on the trail for both of them. He started to turn and stopped, wondering whether, if the elephant charged, he could out-distance it. *I have to remain down-wind and keep quiet. Elephants have poor eyesight – I think.* He eased slowly to the left, picking his way as quietly as he could into the tall grass at the left side of the path.

The elephant stopped and directed its senses toward the stealthy footsteps, a frustrated whine escaping from its open mouth. Something was there but there was no scent of danger. It started forward again, moving slowly now, trunk swaying and sniffing at the hot air.

John knew he could not risk any more sound so stood stock still, his bike turned with him, to face the path. The elephant ambled into sight, its little eyes staring without seeing, its ears spread to catch any sound and the tip of its trunk twitching and up-raised to detect the slightest odor of danger. For a moment the elephant's right eye stared right at John, less than five metres away as the elephant came alongside, before moving away and out of sight down the trail. He waited, counting slowly to himself and promising five minutes before he moved. Five minutes came and went and he decided another five could not hurt. In the end it was nearly twenty minutes before he walked slowly and stiffly out into the middle of the path. The elephant was nowhere to be seen so, shaking slightly, John wobbled off on his bicycle toward the river.

The Ramganga River ran swiftly and noisily over fist and head-sized boulders, its clean waters bubbling and rushing over the stones. John waded in, slipping and tripping over the rocks, leaning on his bicycle for balance as the water crept upward. It was no deeper than knee-height, too shallow and rushing for crocodiles, cool and refreshing in the hot afternoon sun. In mid-stream he stopped, rummaging in his pack for his water bottle. He poured out the tepid fluid, submerging the bottle beneath the river's flow and letting the fresh water gurgle and bubble in. Lifting it, he drank deeply and poured the rest over his head and shoulders before refilling the bottle and putting it back in his pack.

The far side of the river comprised a shingle and sand bank stretching back over many metres toward a low swell of scrub. A hill rose almost immediately, and behind it, others stood in ranks, already in shadow from the westering sun.

I need to find a place to camp for the night.

John followed the course of the river, keeping to a narrow strip of grass that bordered the scrubby edges of the forested hills until he came to a place where the river swung away from the hills and the grass opened out into a wide floodplain. Somewhere to his right, lost behind the sea of grass and nestled in a patch of fern-draped forest, stood the Loharchaur Forest Rest House. He debated whether to look for it, trying to balance the increased safety of being near other people with the increased risk of detection. After a few minutes he decided the risk was too great, continuing downriver toward the arm of sal forest that stretched out from the hill slopes to grasp the silver river. Here, he hoped, he would find somewhere secure to spend the night.

Deep shadow obscured the forest by the time he found a decent sized banyan tree, its buttressed roots rising up out of the leaf litter like low walls. He broke a small branch from a nearby shrub and swept the leaves away from a triangular enclave between the buttresses, until he got down to bare, dry soil. Fixing the bicycle across the entrance to his campsite, he unpacked his pack and spread a thin ground sheet and lightweight sleeping bag. The light was fading, but he spent several minutes going over his digital camera in its waterproof case, his spare memory cards and batteries, making sure that everything looked intact. Putting them back in his pack, John brought out his meager food supplies – bread, goat's cheese and dried fruit – and had his supper, staring into the dark forest as he chewed and planned his course for the next day. The bird calls and the scream of a troop of langurs deep inside the forest almost broke through his concentration, but he pushed the distractions aside, concentrating on how he would avoid the tourist groups in the well-traversed area he would be in tomorrow.

When it got too dark to see, John stowed the rest of his food in a heavy plastic bag and lay down, drawing the sleeping bag up around his head to keep out the mosquitoes. His repellent did not seem to be doing its job and before long his face was covered in itching welts. The darkness beneath the trees was almost absolute, only a gray glimmer of light filtering through from the direction of the river.

After the chorus of bird and animal cries as they prepared themselves for sleep, there was a subdued interval when the forest seemed to die down to a murmur. Then the forest awoke to its nightly activities, when animals foraged and hunted under cover of darkness. John lay awake for a long time, jumping at every noise and forcing himself to find a reasonable explanation for every cry, every rustle and scurry in the dry leaves, every soft footfall that passed by. He knew from experience that large animals can pass quietly by while sometimes very small ones make a racket completely out of keeping with their size. Smiling, he recalled a visit to New Zealand two years before where, as a zoology student, he had been invited to visit Kapiti Island, a bird sanctuary off the west coast of the lower North Island. He had sat in the dense 'bush' at night with the Ranger and heard the approach of what sounded like a herd of goats. Switching on his flashlight as the herd burst upon him, John was astounded to see a solitary Kiwi, the symbol of New Zealand, poking about in the leaf litter. A wingless bird the size of a small chicken, it had stared at him for a moment before crashing off into the undergrowth.

Here in the Indian night, John wondered at the noises he could hear and the sizes of the beasts making them, but he did not worry. From all he had heard, the large predators, tigers and leopards, steered clear of people. A lot was made of man-eaters but John suspected there were very few of those around. Certainly, in the last five weeks of tramping the haunts of legendary man-eaters he had heard nothing of current ones. The mosquitoes had abated somewhat, so he rolled over and went to sleep.

The next morning, John awoke to the sound of elephants trumpeting. He hurriedly packed up his belongings and wheeling his bike, went to investigate. He stood at the edge of the forest and looked out over the grass toward the river, where swirls of mist still clung wetly to the grass. The emerging sun shone a deep orange through the mist, highlighting something multi-headed, bobbing along at the top of the grass. Despite knowing what it must be, John stared, forcing his mind to comprehend. Three elephants walked in line near the river, their bodies obscured by the long grass. Each of them wore a harness of wood and rope and perched on their backs were half a dozen people. Their heads were the ones he could see bobbing above the grass. Although it was very unlikely anyone could see him, John drew back into the cover of the trees.

"Nicely timed," he murmured. *I can follow them at a discreet distance and they'll take me exactly where I want to go.* John relieved himself and rubbed the sleep out of his eyes before trundling his bicycle back down to the river. The dew on the grass soaked his jeans and his shoes, a pair of battered old no-brand sneakers, squelched as he walked. The air smelled clean and crisp with every so often a whiff of elephant. Once, the odor grew suddenly stronger and he stopped, listening. Only bird calls broke the silence and he walked on cautiously, coming across a boulder-pile of steaming dung in the middle of the path. It was so fresh that no flies had yet found it and john knew he was as close as he dared get. Hunkering down on his heels to wait for the elephants to get ahead, he pulled some bread and cheese out of his pack and ate, watching the first insects spiral in to take advantage of the fresh dung.

The sun rose higher, burning off the river mist and drying the dew. The path led down to the Mandal River, a smaller water course that was almost dried up at the end of the dry season. Another couple of months, after the first monsoonal rains deluged the Siwalik Hills and the river would become a rushing torrent, fordable only on elephant-back. For the moment though, it ran ankle-deep and John had no trouble following the elephants across to the west bank. This side of the river was in the Corbett National Park proper, as opposed to the buffer zone of forest and grass around it. The Park was regularly patrolled by rangers in jeeps so John would have to be extremely vigilant from now on. Luckily, he was following an elephant tour, which might well be the safest place to be. Three elephants meant three rangers, so perhaps there would not be any others nearby. There were small hamlets across the Mandal River, and it was possible he could be seen by one of the inhabitants, but unless they stopped him, all they could tell a ranger was that they had seen a white man. With luck, he would be in and out again before it ever got reported.

The Maidavan chowkri is a popular lunching spot, where the tourists exchange elephants for jeeps, ready for the steep climb to the Kanda Forest Rest House atop one of the ridges of the Siwalik Hills. John remembered his own trip only a few days before, the rapid, jouncing ride over rough roads, splashing through small streams as they roared up the steep road. The drivers were not stopping for anyone, least of all a butterfly enthusiast trapped among fanatical bird watchers. Never mind that he thought he had seen a very rare butterfly and never mind that he had paid his park fees like everyone else. There was a timetable to keep and the majority wanted to push on. Maybe if he had been in the rear jeep, the driver might have been persuaded, but the lead jeep had the others pressing close behind and the ranger wanted to keep his speed up for the steep climb.

That would not happen this time. He would find the stream, and with luck, the butterfly. Many species were territorial, John knew from his studies, and would return to a place unless badly disturbed. He hoped *Teinopalpus* would be no different.

As the track curved toward the Maidavan chowkri, John left it, pushing into the untracked sal forest again, and taking advantage of the lack of undergrowth to curve round in a wide semicircle. By the time he judged himself to be west of the chowkri, the sun was high in the sky and he stopped for lunch, knowing that the jeep trip to Kanda would not start before early afternoon. He did not want to misjudge it and arrive at the stream crossing

552

before the jeeps passed. To while away the time, he moved closer to the road where a large *Lantana* thicket grew, the dark green glossy ovate leaves of the bush being liberally sprinkled with clusters of the red, orange and yellow flowers. A number of butterflies flew in the sunshine, swarming round the thicket. Taking out his camera, John started to take pictures.

Lantana is an introduced weed from the Americas that has escaped cultivation and now spreads everywhere, choking out native plants wherever it takes hold. John knew it from Queensland where it was classified as a noxious weed. Despite his environmental leanings, though, he also knew of its value as a nectar plant for adult butterflies, so it was with mixed feelings that he set about taking butterfly pictures.

Many of the butterflies flying around the thicket were species that occurred throughout Southeast Asia and Australia, although often as different subspecies. So even though the Common Crow butterfly hanging from a dead twig with wings folded was a familiar sight from Queensland's riparian forest, John took its picture, moving close and using the camera's zoom function to get a decent close-up. Plain and Blue Tiger butterflies were present, as was the Common Bluebottle. John knew them all from Australia, where they had different common names, but he was a scientist and recognized the similarity by referring to them by their scientific names – *Danaus*, *Tirumala* and *Graphium*.

Other less familiar butterflies were present too; including some John did not know the names of. He concentrated on these, creeping as close as he dared and zooming in. So intense was his concentration that he was

553

totally unaware he was being watched until he looked up and saw an old man looking at him from the edge of the clearing. *Shit*! he thought. *Is he a ranger? Can I convince him I'm with the party at Maidavan*?

"Hello," John called out, forcing a nonchalant note into his voice. "I didn't see you there. Is it time for the jeeps to leave for Kanda?"

The old man ambled over and looked John up and down with dark, piercing eyes. "What is it that you are doing, if I might ask?"

John shrugged. "This? Just snapping a few pics of butterflies. That's allowed, isn't it?" Now that he was face to face with the stranger, he could see that the old man was not a ranger. He had no uniform for a start and he was far too old anyway. "Are you from a village near here?"

The man shook his head. "I have been here before, but not for many years. What is that you are holding?"

"A Fuji digital. It's an old model but all I can afford. It does a reasonable job but ..." John saw the look of incomprehension on the old man's face. "A camera," he amended. "I'm taking pictures of butterflies."

"Ah, I understand. I have seen a camera before. Perhaps you have other pictures of butterflies I could look at? Holiday snaps?" The old man grinned, revealing a full set of pearly white teeth.

John smiled now, warming to the old man. "It's not that type of camera. I don't use film so I don't have snaps. It's ... it's digital ..." he trailed off, not knowing how to explain the workings of the camera when he didn't really know himself. "I take the picture, and then I can see it on this little screen here." He turned the camera

554

round to show the small screen and the picture of a feeding *Graphium sarpedon*.

The old man peered at the tiny screen, his eyebrows knitting in concentration. After a few minutes he nodded and pointed to where a similar butterfly hovered over another panicle of *Lantana* blossoms.

"Yes, good," John exclaimed. "Well, I must be getting along. I expect you have to get back to your village too. Which way is it?" He waited expectantly for the old man to point a way. Whichever way it was, John planned to be going the exact opposite way.

Instead, the old man just smiled again. "You are not with the other tourists are you? You ride a bicycle, following the elephants but out of sight. I saw you all morning from when you crossed the Mandal River."

John looked away, chewing his lip. "Are you going to report me?"

"If I do not, what will you do?"

John stared at the old man for a minute or two, trying to decide whether he had more to lose by telling him the truth or misleading him. Eventually, he sighed and gave in to his conscience. "I sneaked into the park to take a photograph of a special butterfly. I was here with other tourists last week and I saw it then – I think – but the rangers would not stop and let me photograph it so ... here I am."

"Why would you go to so much trouble for a butterfly? Is it worth a lot of money? Will you be selling it to the newspapers for many rupees?"

John shook his head and laughed. "No money. I just want to prove it is here in Corbett Park. It shouldn't be, it's too far west, but I'm sure it's here. I saw it." *I think,* he added silently.

"Then I will help you find it."

"Er, look, that's very kind of you but I'm fine by myself."

"You will teach me about butterflies and I will protect you from the wild animals that inhabit this place," the old man stated. "Perhaps I may be permitted to push your bicycle, or even ride it? I rode one once, though it was many years ago and I may have forgotten how."

"You never really forget," John said, and burst into laughter. The idea of this old man protecting him from wild animals was absurd, but maybe it was the other way round; he wanted the young foreigner to protect him. Well, he was a likable enough old guy, it could not hurt. "Okay then ... er, what's your name?"

"Pandalis."

"Is that a common name? I think I've heard it before."

"I do not think so."

"Well, I'm John Stevenson. I'm pleased to meet you, Pandalis." John shook hands with the old Pahari tribesman, feeling the strength in the gnarled and weathered hand. "The bike is over there, behind that bush."

John led the way, striking northward to intersect the Maidavan-Kanda road. Pandalis trotted alongside, pushing the bike and asking many questions about butterflies. Over the next half hour or so, John had just about exhausted his knowledge of Indian butterflies and was turning to generalities of behaviour and structure, telling him about anecdotes from his childhood, when

556

Pandalis suddenly stopped dead, holding out an arm to alert his companion.

"Wait, John Stevenson." The old man cocked his head, listening for a few moments, before pointing off to their left. "We must go this way."

"Why? The road lies straight ahead and I need to see where we are." John started forward again.

"We cannot go ahead, John Stevenson. Ahead is a tigress that has killed a wild pig. She is lying up in a thicket nearby and will resent being disturbed."

John turned back to look at Pandalis, eyebrows raised. "How do you know that? You can't possibly have heard that or," he sniffed the air, "smelled it."

"I have known tigers for many years, so do not ask me how I know. I ask you to go this way," Pandalis pointed to the left again. "We will come to the road shortly, but by another route."

"Okay. If it means that much to you." John set off in the direction the old man indicated and for a time they walked in silence. As they walked in a wide circle through the sal forest, they cut across the breeze and unmistakably, the scent of carrion drifted to them. "Something's dead."

"As I said, John Stevenson, there is a dead pig."

John grimaced but said nothing. A little later they came across the road, a single-lane dirt road almost overhung by the trees on either side. "I'm not sure exactly where we are, but I think we are just short of the hill up to Kanda. If it wasn't for the trees we could probably see it."

"I am sure you are right. I will go and see." Pandalis hopped onto the bicycle and pedaled away up the road, weaving a bit to start with.

"Hey!" John ran after him a few steps and stopped when he saw he had no hope of catching the old Pahari. *Damn the man*, he thought. *He's made off with my bicycle.* He shrugged and started after him at a brisk walk, settling his pack more comfortably between his shoulderblades. *Well, so what if he has stolen it. I'm close enough now to walk.*

The day was pleasantly warm beneath the intermittent shade of the overhanging trees and butterflies flitted and danced in the sun spots. For a time, John amused himself attempting to herd a Blue Pansy butterfly along the road. A medium sized insect with brown, white and blue markings, it would bask in a sunspot on the road until he was almost on top of it before flicking up and flying rapidly away for twenty or thirty paces before settling again. John knew it probably had a favorite stretch of road to patrol, so tried to push it past, into the territory of another Blue Pansy. He was interested to see what would happen. It did not work. The butterfly flitted past him and back the way he'd come. John grinned and continued on his way.

The road started to climb slightly, just enough to make the trees seem to grow at a slight angle to the roadway rather than on the perpendicular. *I was right, I am near the hill.* A distant growl came from behind him and John turned, listening, trying to block out the birdsong and insect hum. The noise grew louder and he suddenly realized it was the sound of the tour jeeps. He looked into the open forest on either side and dashed for the cover of a nearby thicket, dropping to the ground behind it. Too late, John considered the possibility of snakes in the leaf litter, but only a small lizard scurried out as he crashed down.

Moments later, the first jeep came in sight, moving quite slowly but raising a small cloud of dust from the dry road, the fine particles drifting to cover the roadside vegetation. Another jeep passed, the occupants scanning the sides of the road but no-one called out in surprise or pointed. The dust had almost settled before the third jeep arrived, moving much faster than the preceding two, racing to catch up. John remained behind his bush for a few minutes longer, waiting until the sound of the vehicles died away and the normal chorus of bird and insect life resumed before coming back to the road.

A hundred metres farther on and around a bend in the road, John found Pandalis sitting on a low bank with the bicycle propped at his feet. The old man was leaning back against the stump of a tree with his eyes closed and a cigarette in his mouth. He opened one eye as John approached. "You were right, John Stevenson, the hill is just ahead and there is a stream at the bottom in case you are thirsty."

"Cigarettes are bad for you," John muttered, almost chagrined at being proved wrong about the old man.

"I know. Sometimes I smoke one for the taste." Pandalis stubbed out the remnant and tucked it away into a pocket of his jacket. "Would you like to rest or shall we wait until we get to the stream?"

"Were you just sitting here when the jeeps passed? They'll report you at Kanda and come back to find us both."

"Nobody sees me unless I allow it, John Stevenson. Come now," Pandalis said, scrambling to his feet and brushing his trousers off. "Let us be going."

John nodded, and smiled; glad the old man had not stolen his bicycle. "It's just John. Forget the surname, Pandalis."

The old Pahari cocked his head, a twinkle in his deep brown eyes. "If you wish it, Just John." His mouth quirked and he grinned, slapping his thigh with mirth. "You see, I am keeping company with Englishmen too much, I think. I am telling their jokes now."

John grinned and lifted the bicycle from the bank. "Very good, Pandalis, but I'm not English, I'm Australian."

"Australian? Where is this, John?"

"Australia, Down Under. It is a big dry country far to the southeast. We don't like to be mistaken for English."

"You think you are better than English?" Pandalis frowned.

"Not better, though I can't stomach whinging Poms. Just different, Pandalis. We do things differently."

"Then that is alright. Shall we find the stream, John? You look as if you are thirsty."

The stream was a small one, hardly more than a soak that cut across the road in a slurry of sandy mud before losing itself in the forest to the west. A little to the east of the road, the stream sprang from the rock in a tiny moss-covered rivulet, tumbling down a score of feet to a small pool. The water was clear, cool and very tasty, and John drank his fill before splashing his head and shoulders and refilling his water bottle. While he did so, Pandalis sat cross-legged in the shade and watched him.

John turned, stifling a contented belch with one hand and gesturing toward the streamlet. "You are not thirsty?"

Pandalis shook his head. "I need for little."

John sat opposite the old Pahari and rummaged in his pack, drawing out a plastic bag with his food. "You will break bread with me?"

"For the sake of friendship, John, not for hunger." Pandalis accepted a piece of bread, refusing the cheese, and nibbled on it as the other man ate. The forest lay silent around them except for the ever-present hum of insects and the muted splashing of the tiny rivulet.

"Forgive me if I speak out of turn, Pandalis. I do not know your customs, but what is it you do for a living? Your knowledge of English is remarkable."

Pandalis smiled. "Thank you, John. It is best if a man volunteers information but the English ... forgive me, Australians ... have great curiosity, so I will indulge you." The old man sat silently for a few moments. "I am a wanderer, without home or family save for these mountains and its people. I work as I need to, when the opportunity arises, but I have no profession, no trade, unless you count ..." Pandalis broke off and smiled.

"Unless you count what?"

"Maybe I will tell you later."

John nodded. "Fair enough. Will you at least tell me where you learnt to speak English so well?"

"I have worked for Englishmen and listened to them, talking with ones who would give an old man the time." Pandalis' eyes lost their focus. "There was an English Captain once, and a Lieutenant – later a climber and a hunter." The old man laughed and turned his piercing

561

eyes on the young Australian. "The hunter, the last of these, was the very Jim Corbett for whom this Park is named."

"You're kidding? Corbett left India after Independence. That was, what, nearly sixty years ago? That would make you at least eighty and you're not that old."

"I age well, John."

"That's for sure. And if the hunter was later, how old were you when you knew the Captain and, what did you say, Major?"

"Lieutenant Dunbar, and I was a grown man."

"Then you'd have to be closer to a hundred. No way." John frowned suddenly. "Is this some ... some story or ... or fable you are telling me?"

"You think I am lying to you?" Pandalis watched the young man closely but John did not meet his eyes. He sighed. "I am not lying but if I told you my secret you would not believe me."

"Try me."

"Will you respect my customs enough to let me tell you in my own time?"

"Okay," John said grudgingly.

"I promise I will tell you before we part company. Now, shall we go and look for this butterfly of yours?"

The soak at the bottom of the hill where the small stream crossed the road was almost devoid of butterflies, although there were a few prints in the soft mud at the edge of the water, near where the tyre tracks of the jeep entered and left the stream. Pandalis pointed some of them out.

"Jackal, and there is pig. Some birds and here a large lizard."

"Well, there aren't many butterflies, but this isn't the place I was after. It's further up the hill." John stepped across the muddy patch and, pushing his bicycle, started up the hill road as it weaved up the side of the ridge. He noted Pandalis trotting alongside, seemingly untroubled by the climb despite his age.

"You have told me that butterflies seek flowers and each one has a special plant that the caterpillars eat, but why are they wanting water? Do they not get enough from the flower nectar?"

"They're after minerals," John panted. "It's a behavior called puddling and a lot of butterflies do it. Mostly ... mostly whites and yellows, but some nymphs and swallowtails too."

"And this butterfly you seek –it puddles?"

"Yes, that's where I saw it, as we splashed through the next stream up the hill. There was a bunch of yellows on the mud with a few other splashes of color, including the Emperor. That's one of its common names – the Emperor of India."

"Do you have a picture of it so I can know what it looks like? I can help you look."

"Not unless you can read my mind. No, I know what it looks like and I can more or less describe it to you, but I think the easiest way is just to look for a large dark green, brown and yellow tailed butterfly. See anything like that and you call me."

"I will call you, John."

They reached the second stream by late afternoon. This watercourse was larger than the one at the bottom of

563

the hill and where it crossed the road, the packed dirt had been firmed and strengthened by gravel and boulders brought up from the riverbed of the Ramganga. Despite the stones, however, there remained several stretches of sunlit mud and sand criss-crossed by animal footprints. On these, groups of lemon-colored butterflies sat like scattered *Cassia* blossoms, their long thin probosci unfurled and probing between the grains of sediment. Every few minutes, a ripple would pass through the assembled insects and several would lift off the ground, resettling moments later. Sprinkled among the lemon butterflies were splashes of other colors, red and black and white, with occasional flutters of blue and black.

John laid his bicycle down in some long grass near the road and, taking off his pack, took his camera out. He checked it over thoroughly before moving closer to the fluttering clouds of butterflies.

"It's not here." John could not keep the disappointment out of his voice.

"Did you not say it is a rare butterfly? You might not expect to see one immediately. We must wait for it."

"Makes sense. I saw it when the jeeps passed and that was not long after midday. Maybe it only comes down in the hottest part of the day."

"I shall make us a camp, John. Over there, I think." Pandalis pointed. "Somewhere we cannot be seen."

"Okay, I'll be along in a little while. I'll hang around in case it comes back."

John squatted near the sand and mudbanks, his eyes roaming over the gathered butterflies. He took a few pictures of the massed insects and even a short video, though he knew it would run his batteries down. Playing

564

it back, he nodded with satisfaction when he saw he had captured the ripple effect perfectly. The sun sank behind the ridge and the shadows swept swiftly over the stream, the butterflies disappearing within minutes. John arose and stretched, putting his camera back in its case.

Pandalis had found a small level spot on an otherwise steep hillside and had cleared it of leaves. The ground underneath was firm and dry and looked inviting to someone who was just starting to realize how tired he was. The only troubling aspect was the small fire burning in the middle of the cleared patch.

"Won't a fire be seen at night?"

"Nobody travels these roads at night and out there is only the Ramganga Reservoir. Nobody will see us, John."

John was glad of the fire, and the company, as it grew dark. He felt more exposed out there on the hillside than between the buttress roots of the banyan and a cool wind was blowing through the sal forest. Sweet, cool water from the stream washed down toasted bread and cheese. Pandalis refused to join him in his meal but when pressed, accepted a piece of dried fruit.

"What will you do when you go home to Australia, John? Will you show everyone your picture?"

"If I get one, yes. I'll put it on my website so anyone who is interested can see it." He then had to explain what a website was, then the Internet, followed by e-mails, chat rooms, computers and everything else that arose from those topics.

"And these things are here in India too? I must look into this." Pandalis took another piece of dried fruit and chewed it slowly. "If I was to look at your website, John, what would I find?"

"Well, you'd find my butterfly pictures and some of the places I have been, the people I have met. I have a page with some of my grandma's paintings – she was born in Allahabad and before I came here I was looking at some of the places she lived. She liked Naini Tal the best, I think. Leastways, she told some great stories. Anyway, she liked painting, so I have some of those there." John paused for a moment. "Let's see, what else? Oh yes, I have a link to my dad's website. He writes novels."

"What is a novel?"

"You don't know what a novel is?" Pandalis shook his head. "Okay, a novel is a story, a long story that is written down and printed in a book. You know what a book is?"

"Yes, John. Books have reached Uttarakhand," Pandalis said with a smile.

John blushed and looked away to hide his embarrassment. "Sorry. Well, my dad writes these long stories and makes money when people buy his books. I really envy him his talent. I wish I could write."

"Why don't you? Surely a man who has been to university and has traveled knows how to tell a story."

"Hmm. Well, I was good at essay writing at uni, but we were given topics to write about. What could I write about as a novel?"

"You could tell the story of your hunt for the Emperor of India."

John laughed. "That would only make a very short story."

Pandalis laughed with him and changed the subject, shortly bidding him goodnight and curling up at the outer edge of the firelight. John remained awake for some time, thinking about many things but coming back to his trip to India, tying it all together, wondering whether he should try making a short story out of his travels.

"Nobody's interested in a story about butterflies," he muttered. "People want excitement and adventure, villains and beautiful women." He yawned and curled up in his sleeping bag, drifting off very quickly.

John was up at dawn the next day and was out at the soak while the sun was still drying the dew. Few butterflies were about, so he wandered up the road toward Kanda for about an hour, then back again. He took many pictures of birds and a hurried one of some small mammal as it darted across the road. The image was blurred and he debated whether to delete it but in the end decided to keep it. *Maybe it won't be so bad on a big screen.* Patches of *Lantana* sprinkled the roadside as well as a few other flowering shrubs he did not recognize. Some butterflies were starting to emerge as the air heated and he stopped by one patch for about half an hour waiting for a perfect specimen of a Common Rose, *Atrophaneura aristolochiae*, to move close enough to photograph. Finally it did, and John snapped half a dozen decent pictures.

He was back at the stream by mid-morning, where butterflies were starting to congregate on the mudbanks once more. Yellows and whites mainly, though a few Bluebottles were scattered among them. John did a rough count and made a few notes, also jotting down the identity and location of his butterfly pictures. Presently, Pandalis joined him by the side of the stream and put a ripe mango down beside him.

"I found a tree with a few missed by the bats. I thought you might like one."

"Fantastic. I love mangoes." John split the skin and peeled it away from the soft yellow flesh, sticky juice running down his fingers. He slurped up a mouthful and strained the flesh out from the many fibers in it. "Bloody delicious," he commented as he placed the skin and the large, sucked seed onto the sand near the water's edge. He saw Pandalis' question in his eyes. "Some butterflies are fruit feeders and will come to fallen fruit. It's worth a try." John bent down and rinsed his fingers and his mouth, drying the former on his jeans and the latter on the sleeve of his tee-shirt, before retrieving his camera and retreating a few steps to the grass verge to wait.

The sun rose higher in the sky and the mud beside the stream slowly dried. As the sunlight and the moisture shifted, the clouds of butterflies slowly drifted also. The whites and yellows were constant, a few continually leaving and others darting in to replace them. Swallowtails and Nymphs also came, fewer but gaudier, catching the eye. John took several more pictures but he was on edge all morning, continually looking around at the surrounding forest, scanning the tops of the trees.

"The Emperor is a canopy flier," he explained. "They don't often come down to the ground so this soak may be my best bet. On the other hand, I'd hate to miss one sitting in a tree above my head."

Noon came and went and John looked anxiously at his watch, then down the hill road. "The jeeps will be coming through soon. I hate to leave here but we are going to have to."

"We will hear them coming long before they get here," Pandalis said calmly. "There is a green and brown butterfly, John. Is it your Emperor?"

"What? Where?" John followed the old Pahari's pointing finger and saw a large butterfly sitting on a leaf about six metres above him. It had its wings folded and displayed only a mottled brown aspect. "I can't see any green." He raised his camera and took three shots. "It's too far away," he said as he examined the images in the screen. Even with maximum zoom, you can only see a shape."

"Perhaps it will come down. I could throw a stick at it if you want."

"That might scare it away altogether. No, we'll wait." John sat down on the grass and switched his camera off to save the batteries, keeping an eye on the motionless butterfly as he did so. Far away, he heard the faint growl of car engines. "Oh, Jeez, not now." He leapt to his feet again and stared down the road, then back to the tree just as the butterfly dropped, then flew rapidly down in a wide spiral to land on the stream edge near the other puddling butterflies. It flexed its wings, opening them out wide and folding them, revealing olive green, jade and dark brown with splashes of yellow. John gaped and fumbled with his camera, not wanting to tear his eyes away from his quarry.

The noise of the jeeps grew louder and John raised the camera, peering through the viewfinder as the butterfly opened its wings again. He pressed the shutter button to the half setting to let it automatically focus.

569

Nothing happened. Again. "Shit! What's wrong with it?" John gave up and pressed the button all the way in, hearing the whirr and click of the photo being taken. He rapidly took three more, the roar of the jeeps loud in his ear as they approached. Pandalis, with surprising strength for such an old man, grabbed him and threw him to the ground just as the first of the vehicles raced into view. It slowed, then surged through the stream bed, spraying water wide and scattering the butterflies before leaping at the rising road beyond. Pandalis and John scrambled further from the road into proper cover before the next two jeeps roared by, scattering the butterflies again.

"Bastards," John yelled after them. "I had him." He sat up and flicked his camera onto 'Play', staring at the blurred images on his screen. He cursed again when he saw he had it on 'Manual Focus' and savagely flicked it round to 'Automatic Focus' again. He ran back to the stream and scanned the mudbanks and the surrounding vegetation but the Emperor had left.

"It was the Emperor." John swung round and stared wide-eyed at the old man. "It was a male *Teinopalpus imperialis*, Emperor of bloody India, but I can't prove it. All I've got are a few blurred images that could be anything. Those bastards scared him away."

"They did not do so deliberately, John Stevenson. They were merely doing their job, which no doubt they need to support their families and put food on the table for their children. Is your butterfly picture more important than a child?"

John stared at Pandalis for a few moments more, and then frowned. He exhaled noisily and ran the fingers of one hand through his blond hair. "No, of course not. I'm sorry, Pandalis. I got a bit carried away there."

"Your Emperor was here last week when you first saw him and here again today. I think it is possible he will be back tomorrow. We must just wait for him."

"And have him scared away again? It's not much use if he only turns up around the same time as the jeeps."

John spent the rest of the day wandering the sides of the roads where flowers grew or hovering near the soak in the hope that the Emperor would return. Once he wandered off along the course of the stream, pushing through the undergrowth, following the water as it meandered down the hill. He found two other mudbanks but one of them was heavily shaded and the other evidently did not have the right minerals though it was bathed in sunlight. Neither place was frequented by butterflies.

That night, John used the last of his supplies, augmented by a couple more ripe mangoes supplied by Pandalis. When he had finished, and rinsed his hands and face again, he leaned back against the rough bark of a sal tree and looked at the old man across the small camp fire.

"You said you knew Jim Corbett, Pandalis. Where and when was that?"

Pandalis looked back across the flickering flames, his eyes in shadow, his face expressionless. "In Naini Tal, nineteen-thirty."

"Jesus." John calculated quickly. "That's over seventy years ago. How old are you, Pandalis."

"How old do you think I am?"

"Well, as I said before, you look about sixty but you're as strong as I am. You'd have to at least been ten

571

years old to know Corbett so I'd say eighty-five, ninety maybe. Then you said you knew other Englishmen before him, so you'd have to be a hundred. How is that possible?"

Pandalis nodded and smiled. "I do not know how old I am exactly, John. I never had a birth certificate."

"Your parents never told you?"

"I never knew my parents."

"I'm sorry," John said awkwardly. He fell silent for a few minutes. Somewhere in the night a tiger called, a coughing roar that brought John to his feet.

"He is a long way away," Pandalis reassured him. "Near the reservoir."

John resumed his seat and his silence. Then, "My grandma was in Naini Tal at around that time. She told me she saw one of the Hindu gods there."

"Really? Which one?"

"She didn't say. Just that it took the form of a wolf and was present at the time her sister's fever broke. The servants said it was a sign from the gods that she would live. And she did, she recovered immediately."

"What is your grandmother's name?"

"Haye. Maud Haye. She was my father's mother."

Pandalis smiled broadly. "I knew this little girl. I am glad that she grew up to have a son and a grandson. How is she? Is she in Australia?"

"She died last year. I'm sorry."

A sigh, deep and ragged. "I am sorry for your loss, John."

"How did you know her?"

572

"How did any young English girl know an Indian man in those days? I performed a service for her. You could say I was a servant."

"What did you do?"

"Her sister was sick. She was looking for the gods of India. I told her how to find them. If, as you say, a wolf helped her, maybe she found the gods after all."

Pandalis turned over and went to sleep soon after, but John stayed awake, thinking about his grandmother and her stories. Something niggled at the back of his mind but he just could not quite grasp it. It had something to do with the old man's name. He had heard it before somewhere. Still mulling over the problem, he fell asleep.

The next day, John's last in the park unless he could find more food, dawned cloudy and cool and for a long time, until the sun at last rose above the bank of cloud to the east, there were no butterflies along the stream or road. John fretted, pacing up and down, scanning the sky, and would not relax even when the sun finally broke through to cast its bright heat on the stream banks. Butterflies gathered and by midday, the situation seemed back to normal.

The Emperor arrived just before one in the afternoon, flapping unhurriedly out of the forest and gliding down to the ground. It was up again within seconds and disappeared into the canopy, followed by a frustrated cry from John. Twenty minutes later it returned, settled on the mud just long enough for John to position it in the viewfinder before flitting off along the stream course. He snapped a hurried shot but missed it entirely. The

573

butterfly came again at half past one and at two, staying for a few seconds, never settling down to drink.

"It's not going to work," John cried. "It's shy now and won't settle." As he said it, the Emperor sailed in again, touching down for a few seconds before lifting off. But this time, instead of flying off, it circled, then hovered and landed. "Yes! This time." John checked his camera quickly and edged closer, stepping slowly and carefully, avoiding sudden movements. The Emperor flicked its wings open and ran a few inches. John froze, holding his breath as the butterfly extended its proboscis and probed at the muddy ground. As it started drinking he eased forward again, moving sideways so his shadow would not startle it.

Softly, but gaining strength every second, the growl of jeep motors jerked John's head around. "Oh God, no," he groaned. "Not now."

"Concentrate on your business, John Stevenson. Leave this to me." Pandalis leapt up and ran off down the hill road toward the roar of the approaching jeeps.

John stared after him for a few moments before turning back to the butterfly. "It's now or never," he muttered, raising his camera. He leaned closer and found his quarry in the viewfinder, zoomed in a little, went to 'Autofocus' and clicked. "Got you, you beauty." As if in response, the Emperor opened his wings and John snapped another.

Behind him, the roar of the jeeps suddenly died and a chorus of shouts broke out. John shut out the noise and advanced another short pace, snapping off another three shots. The sound of running feet in the dirt road came from behind, startling him and his movements made the butterfly roll back its proboscis. John thumbed the dial to 'Video' and as the insect opened its wings to take off, pressed the button.

"Have you finished?" Pandalis asked as he ran up. "I could not hold them for long. They will be here in a few minutes."

John panned the camera as the Emperor flew into the canopy before facing the old man with a big grin. "I've finished. Let's go." They both dashed for cover. Later, after the jeeps had passed, John asked Pandalis how he had delayed them.

"I dropped a small tree across the road." He did not elaborate on how, nor did John press him for details, for he was starting to remember something his grandmother had told him, something disturbing.

Pandalis said nothing when John started hurrying to pack up. The young man made the excuse that he had run out of food and should try to get out of the park as quickly as possible. He tried to say goodbye to the old Pahari, but Pandalis would have none of it, insisting on accompanying him to the park boundaries.

"It is not safe to be wandering this forest alone, John. Besides, I can help you avoid the patrols."

John freewheeled back down the road, pushing the pace, but as fast as he dared go, the old man easily kept pace, loping alongside in silence. He became more and more uneasy as they went, for his grandmother's fantasy was fast becoming reality. At the bottom of the hill, Pandalis indicated the route they should take through the sal forest, but John shook his head, pointing down the road toward the Maidavan.

"They will have gone by now. It would be faster."

"If you go by the road you will have to pass through the long grass meadows. There are tigers, John. That is why the tourists come through there on elephant-back."

"I'll chance it." He rode off before Pandalis could argue further. When he looked round after a hundred metres, the old man was running just behind him, not even appearing to be out of breath. John felt the hairs on his arm prickle.

The Maidavan was deserted and John did not stop, cycling past onto the road that led into the grasslands and the Mandal River.

"Wait, John Stevenson." The steel in the old man's voice made John wince and despite his growing fear, he pulled up and turned in the saddle to face Pandalis. "I promised I would tell you the secret of my long life, before we parted."

"Th ... that's alright. You don't need to tell me."

"Are you afraid of me, John?" Pandalis asked softly.

"N ... no, of course not. I ..." John swallowed and faced the old Pahari. "My grandmother told me the name of the man who guided her in Naini Tal. She said his name was Pandalis, and she said he was an old man. Tell me how you could already be old seventy years ago."

"I am not as other men."

"My grandmother told me she thought you were a god – one of the Hindu gods."

Pandalis smiled. "What is a god?"

"I don't know and I don't care what you are. Please just let me go, I have done you no harm."

"And I do not wish you any harm either, John Stevenson."

"Then ... then I ... goodbye." John pushed off and stood on the pedals of his bicycle, driving hard. His initial wobbling course straightened quickly and he sped off down the rutted dirt track between tall stands of elephant grass.

Pandalis yelled after him, his voice strident with urgency. "Do not cycle through tiger country, John. Please ... behind you!"

John heard the old man's voice and he glanced back over his shoulder. A streak of red paralleled him in the long grass and he jerked round in the saddle, wobbling violently. Unseen by him, Pandalis suddenly disappeared, but John's attention was gripped by the apparition in the grass. He felt terror seize his heart as a tiger burst out of the grass almost alongside him, closing fast.

The next moment, without a conscious warning, John threw himself from the bicycle which continued wobbling on its way. He hit the ground hard and rolled, ending up on his knees as the tiger sprang over him. A stunning blow from a paw hit his left shoulder and knocked him sprawling, and he caught a glimpse of the tiger crashing into the bicycle. The beast roared with rage and surprise and, ignoring the fallen man, bounded off into the grass.

John staggered to his feet and looked down at his blood-spattered tee-shirt. The material was ripped and stained around the left shoulder and he could see two parallel clawmarks stretching from the point of his shoulder to close to his neck. "Oh shit," he mumbled, as a wave of pain washed over him.

Sit down, John.

577

"What? Pandalis, is that you? Where are you?" He looked around, almost falling as a feeling of faintness plucked at his mind. "Why did the tiger attack? I thought the tigers here were safe."

No tiger is safe, but generally they will not attack man. A man on a bicycle is unfamiliar though. He travels faster than a man can run, so he is not a man but a prey animal. Never ride a bicycle in tiger country.

"If ... if you say so. I'm not ... not sure I could ..."

Sit down, John, before you fall.

"Eh, okay, whatever you say." John's legs collapsed under him and he lay back staring up at wisps of cloud in the blue afternoon sky. He drifted out of consciousness, and after a time, for the sun now hung in the eastern sky; he awoke and sat up, looking about him. Squatting a few paces away was the old Pahari man, an enigmatic smile on his face.

John felt his left shoulder through his ripped shirt and felt two narrow scars, already almost healed. "How did you do that, Pandalis? And why?"

"The why is easy, John Stevenson. I did it for the sake of a young girl I once knew. Your grandmother, Maud Haye. As to how, well, examine your memory for yours is mine and mine, yours."

John frowned then opened his eyes wide as memories that were not his came flooding in. "You ... you're a demon, a Rakshasa ... or are you a god now? Shit, you're old ... five, six thousand years at least. Oh my god, you did that?" The young man looked as if he was going to be sick, then the feeling passed as new memories crashed over him. The horror was still there in his face but overlain now by curiosity and satisfaction. "And who is

578

Bala, and Isha? Parvati … oh, I see." He sat still for over an hour, running swiftly through the years of memories. Once, he smiled softly. "Hi, Grandma Maud," he muttered, before falling silent again. "Why have you done this to me?" he said at last.

"I'm not sure, except I wanted to tell someone. I have led a long and lonely existence, John Stevenson. I thought … maybe … you would write it all down."

John shook his head in wonder. "There is enough here for a hundred books."

"Then select stories you like."

"Nobody would believe me."

"Does it matter? Write it as the first of your novels; under another name if you wish. I am making you this gift of my life, John Stevenson. Use it as you see fit."

"How does the story end?"

"However you want it to, John. Make something up or end it right here." Pandalis stood and started walking away.

"Wait. This will be just a dream if you leave now. How will I know you really exist and are not just my imagination? Let me take your picture."

Pandalis considered for a moment before nodding, waiting while John took his camera out and set it up. He posed, a broad smile on his face, and then bowed. "Namaste, John." Turning, he walked into the long grass and was swallowed up within a few paces.

John played back the last picture but where Pandalis had stood smiling against a backdrop of tall brown grass, was a picture of a fuzzy blue flame suspended in midair. The young Australian laughed and put his camera away, then picked up the slightly bent bicycle and started out along the path that led out of Jim Corbett National Park. Already his mind was working on the threads of a story about one of the Rakshasa of India.

Epilogue

I felt both drained and full to bursting after I left John Stevenson. I had never done anything like that before, nor had I even contemplated the possibility. I still had all my own memories but now I had his as well. This should not have filled my mind as I had experienced over five thousand years of existence with rich experiences and colorful memories, while the young man had only a moment of life to draw on, a mere twenty-three years. Then I saw the reason and felt a profound shock. John Stevenson's memories went back much further than his own lifetime. This man had lived before, experienced hundreds of lives over the ages, through an existence besides which I was still an infant.

But how could this be? A man's memories are a function of the physical brain, myriad synaptic connections between billions of neurons. And this physical brain was only twenty-three years old – how could it possibly contain memories older than this?

I laughed out loud when I made the connection. I am not physical, yet I have memories. What stores my memories, my thoughts? My 'body' is energy, a flame of being that men sometimes see as a blue light. I drew on one of John's recent memories and found a term with which to label myself – a force field. Is that an accurate description? I do not know, I do not have the knowledge, but it will do to draw an analogy at least. Gods and demons are energy beings that can, when they choose, clothe themselves in a physical body. Now it seems that man is not too different. He too is energy, but clothes himself – or is clothed, I have not yet worked out whether it is imposed on him or if he does it of his own volition – in a body countless times. He reincarnates, each lifetime another step toward – what? Nirvana? Was the Buddha right?

My mind is in ferment and I must take myself somewhere I will not be disturbed. I shed the form of Pandalis and streak, a barely visible flame, for the high slopes of my old retreat, Nanda Devi. The mountain and its surrounding slopes and meadows are protected now and few people venture there. I can be alone to confront my findings.

I sample the lives of the man who is now John Stevenson and feel what it was like to be him – or her, for he has been a woman too. I see distant lands, hills and plains, foreign peoples and languages, different races and cultures. I am man, woman and child; king, priest and peasant; Christian, Moslem and Jew. I have lived in palaces and hovels. I have feasted and starved, experienced hot and cold, pleasure and agony. I have died in numberless ways, sometimes dreadfully, other times peacefully. I withdraw from the memories of this man I know as John, wondering how any human can exist, tossed in the maelstrom of past existence; and I realize that he is ignorant of his past for he relies on his physical brain for memories, not the energy field, and past lives live on in the energy.

The being that I am was a demon, then a god, and now I know what it is to be man. I tremble, for I feel as if a great revelation, a Noble Truth, hovers on the brink of my understanding. I reform the body of old Pandalis, for now I am closer to him than I have ever been before, though he has never had separate existence. I sit on the cold rock of Nanda Devi's breast and sink my head in my hands, for the first time in my long existence wondering where I go from here. What have I done to myself?

"I think he is ready."

The voice was male; strong, warm and conversational; yet as I looked around in surprise, I saw no-one on the icy slopes that could have spoken.

"I agree," spoke a second voice.

"Who is there?" I called out.

"Perhaps," said a third. "I am not totally convinced he has given up his old ways."

A rich laugh. "You are too hard on him, Lord Krishna," said the first voice again. "Let us show ourselves and we shall see who is right."

A movement caught my eye as the air above the icy ridge rippled as if on a hot summer's day. Three figures formed, wavering and insubstantial at first, firming into the bodies of three men, richly clothed and handsome. With a sinking feeling I recognized the one in the middle. He stood tall, of a dusky complexion, with piercing dark eyes beneath wavy long black hair, and a flowing mustache. Rich garments adorned him in glowing colors and though he was no taller than me, his presence was as of a giant. When last I had seen him he had pursued me from the Khandava Forest to the hills of the Himalayas. If he had caught me, he would have killed me, and for all I knew, he would attempt it again. He was the Lord Krishna, the eighth avatar of Vishnu himself.

The men who stood on either side of Krishna were no less imposing of body or raiment, though their aspect were less fearsome. The one on the right was a tall, handsome, bearded man with a gentle, knowing smile,

583

and a nimbus of holy light played around his head and upper body. His limbs were clad in yellow silk and he held an *amrta-kalasha*, or nectar pot in his right hand. The other man was smaller in stature, and younger, clean-shaven, though his head-locks cascaded in a black wave over his shoulders. His garments were blue silk and he held the trident of Shiva. A snow leopard sat by his feet, its yellow eyes fixed on me.

I stood and made a mudra respectfully. "Namaste, Lord Krishna. And greetings to your companions."

Krishna stood without making a response for a few moments, and then raised his right hand in the *Abhaya* mudra, signifying protection, peace, benevolence, and dispelling of fear. "These are my companions Dhanvantari, physician to the gods," he gestured at the tall, bearded man, "And Pashupati, Lord of Animals."

"My lords," I said, making a mudra of respect once more. "You honor me by your presence."

"You see?" Pashupati said with a smile. "I told you he would not fear us."

"Is that true, Rakshasa?" Krishna stared at me, his piercing eyes boring past the physical shell that was Pandalis to my inner flame. "Are you not afraid of me? I once sought to destroy you."

"My lord, when you pursued me, you had every right to slay me for I was a man-killer, a demon. But I have not killed to feed my flame for over five hundred years. I have vowed never to do so again."

"Interesting," Dhanvantari mused. "A vow is made before a god. Which god did you choose?"

"I vowed in the name of no god, but rather on my own life."

584

"And you have killed no man since taking this vow?" Pashupati asked.

"I have fed off no man, though I have killed when the need arose."

"What need?" Dusky-skinned Krishna asked.

"When the foreign invaders under Bin Tughluq entered Uttarakhand, I killed them, possessing dead bodies, but since then I have tried to guide and to heal. I have led men to their deaths but never innocent ones, and only to help the greater number. In the last hundred years I have tried not to interfere except where a wrong was being committed, nor have I healed unless I have been asked."

"When someone prayed to you, in other words."

I smiled at lord Krishna's words but said nothing.

"The Bliss-Giving Goddess, on whose holy mountain we stand, says you brought an Englishman to her, possessing his body." The snow leopard at Pashupati's feet stirred at his master's tone, growling deep within its chest. "After he died, you buried his body in her high meadow. Was that not interference when no wrong was committed?"

"He was a brave man and one who loved the high mountains. Though he was a Christian, yet he almost believed, so I helped his shattered body to attain his life's dream – that of seeing Nanda Devi." I smiled, remembering. Turning my head, I looked down the long valley that fell away beneath the great ridge we stood upon to where I knew the tiny cairn still stood, and saluted his memory. "He saw the Goddess as he died. I would say that She accepted his presence, so who was I to deny it?"

585

"Nanda Devi accepted him into her presence," Dhanvantari murmured. "She has told us this."

"Tell us of the English girl," Krishna said. "You misrepresented yourself to her, did you not? She thought she was praying to these two gods you see before you."

Despite the god's serious demeanor, I laughed. "Should I have told her I was a demon instead? That would really have inspired confidence."

"What made you choose me?" Dhanvantari asked quietly.

"And me?" Pashupati added.

"I found I could heal, so if I was going to pass myself off as a god, who better to choose than the physician of the gods? And I have always liked animals, often prefering their presence to that of men." I looked at each god in turn, opening myself to them. "My lords, you know that I have always led men to believe it was you bringing these benefits, answering their prayers."

"In the case of the English girl," Krishna asked. "How did you answer her prayers?"

"Her sister was possessed by a demon. I drove him out and when he would not stay out, I killed him."

"Have you had many dealings with other demons?"

"No, my lord Pashupati," I replied. "Only one stands out in my mind, the one who called herself Kali to mislead men into killing in her name."

"The anger of Kali was great when she found out," Krishna said. "She hunted that demon down and destroyed her." The god's serious demeanor softened somewhat and he almost smiled. "She was grateful to another demon that helped stamp out that vicious brood."

"Indeed? I have not seen another god since you chased me, lord Krishna. I have sometimes felt the presence of something, but nothing I could definitely define as divine. I thought the gods had left."

"So you decided to take our place, setting yourself up as a god?"

"I cannot deny it, my lords."

The three deities stood silently before me for a long time. The earth spun beneath our feet, the sun, moon and stars wheeling through the vaulted heavens. Seasons came and went and years drifted like snowflakes. I felt their eyes, their minds, shredding away my physical guise and testing the very flame of my being.

"Why?" Krishna asked at length.

"Why did you set yourself up as a god?" Dhanvantari enquired.

"What made you think you could be more than a demon?" Pashupati demanded.

"The Buddha," I said simply.

"Explain."

"I sat at the feet of a Buddhist monk and learned of the eight-fold path whereby mankind can attain to Nirvana, to oneness with the godhead."

"That is a path for men," Krishna stated. "Why should it interest you?"

"Why should it not?" I asked with some asperity. "I did not ask to be a demon. I found myself in existence with a hunger for the blood of men and a fear of the gods. I did not make myself this way." I turned away and calmed myself as best I could. I was nearly sure that Krishna was here to kill me at last, having searched for me down the millennia, and I was almost content that he

587

should do so. I would not beg for mercy or even defend myself, but I would at least try and make the gods see the injustice of their system.

When I had gathered my equanimity again, I turned back to face my three judges. "Sonaka taught me that there is more to life than seeking pleasure. He spoke to me of right thought, right speech, right intention and right action. Through these things a man might attain perfection after many lifetimes. I only have one lifetime and I started from the worst place possible, but I have tried."

"So you left the feet of the Buddhist monk and became a saint?" Krishna asked, a hint of sarcasm in his voice.

"Of course not. If it was that easy a man would achieve Nirvana within a lifetime or two. It took me many years to stop feeding on men, more until I stopped killing, but I did it. Then I tried to make up for my past actions by helping people, saving lives." I smiled briefly, wryly. "Perhaps I have saved a few over the years."

"Do you know how many men, women and children you have fed on?" Dhanvantari asked gently.

I shook my head. "Thousands. Tens of thousands."

"You were created as a demon," Pashupati pointed out. "A demon is expected to kill. It is fear of demons that leads men to seek out the gods. But it is almost unheard of for a demon to change its behavior. That is what brought you to our notice."

"How many have you fed on since the Buddhist?" Krishna asked. I started to shake my head but he held up a hand to stop me. "Your memory is complete – search it. We will trust your count."

I did, and it took me awhile, but the gods waited patiently. At last I looked up. "Three hundred and forty-seven," I said. "I have counted in innocent men I killed but did not feed on. I feel myself accountable for them too." I straightened my back (Pandalis' of course) and met Krishna's implacable gaze. "I am aware of my actions. Do as you see fit."

"Count again, demon," Pashupati said with a smile. "But this time count how many lives you have saved directly."

"I cannot tell. With a death one can see the end, but a life … how can I tell whether it was my action alone that saved him?"

"We can," Dhanvantari said. "By our count, three hundred and forty-seven, the last being the young man on the bicycle."

"The tallies are balanced, demon. Since your encounter with the Buddhist you have wrought no lasting harm."

"The ones who died by my hand might disagree with you," I said.

"Not even them." Krishna looked deep into my eyes and for the first time I saw the love and compassion that dwelt there. "You forget that men are reborn. Every single one of the ones you killed has been born again into this world."

"So what does all this mean? Have you come to rid the world of one more demon?"

"Yes," Krishna said bluntly.

Pashupati and Dhanvantari nodded.

"I will not contest you," I said wearily. "I will run from the gods no more."

Dhanvantari held out the *amrta-kalasha*, or nectar pot. "Drink."

I looked at it suspiciously. "You will poison me? Is this how demons die?"

The bearded god looked shocked. "The pot holds only nectar and no-one drinks of the nectar save the gods."

"Then why do you offer ..." I stared dumb-founded at the three gods.

Pashupati grinned, looking more like a boy than a god. The snow leopard at his feet rubbed up against his legs, making a sound that strongly resembled purring. "Do you not want the godhead?"

"I ... I have achieved Nirvana?"

Krishna shook his head, though he was smiling too. "Nirvana is for men. You have striven successfully to shed your demon origins and embrace divinity. Accept now the godhead and drink of the nectar."

I reached out and took the pot from Dhanvantari's hand. I swirled the liquid in the vessel, the heavy golden liquid rising up the sides of the container, releasing a scent that is indescribable. I would identify it if I could but I had never smelled its like before. I raised the pot to my lips and took a sip, holding the oily liquid in my mouth for a few moments before swallowing. The nectar was ice cold as it slid down my throat but molten metal in my belly. The fumes of its passing invaded my head, clearing away every doubt and uncertainty. My perception exploded and I saw myself standing on the peak of Nanda Devi with the world spread out beneath me. Men crawled like a plague upon the earth, some

590

believing, others not, the sum of their thoughts and desires humming like a swarm of bees.

I looked up from this chaos. "Is this what it is to be a god? How can you stand it?"

Pashupati soared around me as I stood on the mountain peak. His feline companion had vanished. "You will learn control." He laughed. "You are a very young god, remember."

Krishna, back down on the ridge, pointed and cut one tiny voice out of the surging babble of humanity. "Listen to this one." I concentrated.

"I offer my humble obeisances again and again unto the great Lord Krishna, who is beyond the illusion of Maya and from whom that illusion comes."

"He is a priest in one of my temples," Krishna explained. "Try this one." He cut out another voice.

"Now I lay me down to sleep, I beg the Lord my soul to keep. If I should die before I wake, I beg the Lord my soul to take."

"That is a child in America who is praying to his god Jesus."

"And I can hear them all?" I asked, wonder and horror churning my mind.

"If you choose, but why eavesdrop on the business of other gods. Learn which prayers have your signature and listen to them."

"How will I recognize them? Do any humans pray to me? None of them know I have … have become a god."

Dhanvantari smiled. "There is one. Listen." The signature of a prayer addressed to my mind popped into my consciousness, so I listened.

591

"Dammit Pandalis, why the hell did you ever put this burden on me? I spend all my time writing now … no, sorry, I don't mean that but … I need some assistance and your memories aren't helping."

"Who is that?" I asked, knowing the answer as I spoke. "John Stevenson." I looked at the three gods – while I spoke I had moved to the ridge again – but I asked my question of the dusky one. "Do I have to answer every prayer? At the moment there is just one, but if I become known, there may be thousands."

"That is up to you," Krishna said. "Millions pray to me every day, but my purpose is not to be a crutch. Men must find their own way to salvation. I only step in where I see fit. You may do as you please, though."

"What name will you choose as a god?" Pashupati asked.

"And what will be your realm?" Dhanvantari added.

I smiled. "My single worshiper calls me Pandalis. It seems I have a name already. As for my business, well, medicine and animals are all I know."

"Those occupations are taken," Krishna said, indicating his fellow gods. "You must choose something different. What interests you?"

I thought hard. Many things had interested me down the ages, but nothing that I could consider a passion. I would have to find something new. "I don't know."

"There is one thing," Krishna said softly.

"Something important," Pashupati added.

"Something that is more attuned to your special abilities," Dhanvantari said.

"I have special abilities?" I asked.

"One that relates to what you were," Lord Krishna replied. "You may not have come across many demons, but they are all around us. The gods destroy them when they can but we all have other duties. I ask you to become a specialist destroyer of demons."

I stared at Lord Krishna, my mind in turmoil. "You want me to destroy my own kind?"

"They were once your own kind," Lord Pashupati corrected. "But no more. You have risen above them."

"You have drunk from *amrta-kalasha*. You are one of the gods now," Lord Dhanvantari added.

"You know what it is to be a demon, and what it is that demons do," Lord Krishna said. "Would you, knowing this, allow a demon to live?"

"No, but I changed. Might not another demon seek goodness?"

"In all the long ages of the world, there has only been one demon who became a god. You, Lord Pandalis. It is not likely to happen again." When I hesitated, Krishna added, "Evaluate them. If you find one spark of goodness you may spare them, if that is your wish."

I considered this at length, letting the world turn beneath me. I thought of my past, of the Kali-demon, of the jackal-demon of Naini Tal, and of the harm done by these evil beings. I nodded my acceptance. "I will become a destroyer of demons."

Krishna clapped his hands, the sound reverberating through the air and crashing off mountain sides, precipitating small avalanches. The air around Nanda Devi thickened and burst into life as rank upon rank of gods appeared, standing on the open air. Some I recognized – Nanda Devi herself, Agni, Kali, Ganesh,

Shiva, Brahma, Vishnu – but most were just faces flickering in the nimbus of their godly aspects.

"I present to you Pandalis, Destroyer of Demons," Krishna cried out.

As the gods applauded, I raised my hands and drawing on the energy that flowed within me – awoken by the sacred nectar. I took up my own godly aspect and demonstrated my power. Lightning flashed in the pale blue sky around the peak. Snow, shaken from the rocky sides of the great mountain by the concussion of my gestures, thundered down into the valleys. Again and again I gestured, reveling in my strength and power, until even I tired of my display. I found myself alone on the ridge once more, save for my three fellow gods.

"What will you do first?" asked Pashupati.

"I would answer the prayer of my first worshiper, John Stevenson," I replied. "But I do not know how to find him."

"Follow his prayer," Krishna said. "It will lead you to him."

I rose into the thin air, the body of the old Pahari tribesman falling away to reveal the golden glow that was my flame, and I rode the path of a man's prayer over land and sea to take up my first duty as a god. No longer was I one of the Raksha, I had become Pandalis, Destroyer of Demons, and the newest god in the great Hindu Pantheon.

The End

www.ingramcontent.com/pod-product-compliance
Lightning Source LLC
Chambersburg PA
CBHW011359010726
47495CB00009B/2697